GET
WHAT'S
COMING

Also by Sam Reaves

BURY IT DEEP
FEAR WILL DO IT
A LONG COLD FALL

GET WHAT'S COMING

Sam Reaves

G. P. PUTNAM'S SONS
NEW YORK

G. P. Putnam's Sons
Publishers Since 1838
200 Madison Avenue
New York, NY 10016

Library of Congress Cataloging-in-Publication Data

Reaves, Sam, date.
Get what's coming / Sam Reaves.
p.   cm.
ISBN 0-399-14018-2
1. MacLeish, Cooper (Fictitious character)—Fiction.
2. Chauffeurs—Illinois—Chicago—Fiction.   3. Chicago (Ill.)—
Fiction.   I. Title.
PS3568.E2694G47   1995   94-33195   CIP
813'.54—dc20

Printed in the United States of America
1   2   3   4   5   6   7   8   9   10

Notable among those who assisted
the author in writing this book
are Tim Rasmussen and Ray Espinoza.
The author's views on Prohibition
are his own and should not be
attributed to anyone else.

1

THE NIGHT SEAN McTeague realized that a million dollars in cash was his for the taking, the temperature was still eighty-eight degrees at eleven o'clock. Half the city was out at the lake, whole Mexican families clumped together on the grass, stirring feebly, looking out over the still, dark water into nothing and waiting for a breeze. Ten different strains of music from tape players near and far hung in the air, first one now the other coming tinnily to the fore, the headache beat of somebody's woofers underlying it all. Somewhere a woman screamed, then dissolved in laughter.

"Summer in this town, man," Rolando was saying, sitting on the hood of the old Duster and looking away down the shore to the remote celestial lights of the Loop. "Like livin' in the shower. Never get cool, never get dry."

McTeague studied the embers at the end of his cigarette and thought about how to get Rolando talking about the money again. The feeling in his gut had faded but his heart was still going a bit faster than normal and for fear of seeming too excited, he concentrated on the tip of his cigarette, seeing individual slivers of tobacco glowing like logs in a Christmas fire.

Only once before had Sean McTeague ever had a similar feeling, when Sandrine Lucchesi had called to tell him her husband had left. The second she said it he'd had that cold trickle in the entrails, that weak-kneed certainty of desire about to be fulfilled. Without looking away from the cigarette he said, "What about her old man?"

"What about him?" Rolando took a swig from the bottle and passed it over. McTeague took it and held it loosely at his side. He put the cigarette in his mouth, took a long deep final drag, and then flicked the butt like a meteor out over the rocks toward the water. Somebody in the dark down there below yelled "Hey" but McTeague ignored it. He held the smoke in as long as he could and then sent it out in a rush.

"What's a man like that gonna do when he finds out you're screwing his woman?"

"The man ain't gonna find out."

"You hope he ain't. That kind of confidence has gotten a lot of men in trouble."

"Hey. I got it covered. She don't even call unless she's sure he's gone for the night."

"How's she know?"

"She knows. He's got other places he stays. Other women, too. That's what gets to her. That's why she started callin' me."

"She just called you up out of the blue and said come up and ball me?"

"Not the first time, no. First I just ran into her, in this deli there on Thorndale, hadn't seen her in a long time. Not since the South Side. First it was just hey how you been, our life story, what you been doin' all this time, all that shit. Second time I see her, she says, 'Why don't you come on up to my place, 'cause Dexter's not gonna be back tonight.' I figured she oughta know. Now, she calls me up, I come on over."

McTeague passed a hand over his forehead and rubbed the sheen of sweat on his fingertips with his thumb. "And she just told you about the money, just like that."

"No, man. I found it." Rolando looked over his shoulder, the look of a guilty man, and lowered his voice. "I was lookin' in closets and shit, just pokin' around, and I found it. I thought she was gonna have a heart attack."

"And she asked you back after that?"

"The lady's lonely, man. The sumbitch won't hardly let her out. She's goin' crazy up there and I'm her only friend. Gimme that bottle if you're just gonna hold it."

McTeague passed it back and watched Rolando swig from it, watched the man who had just opened a door and showed him a million dollars. He was already thinking about risks and strategies. "I'd step real careful with the lady if I were you," he said.

Rolando sighed gently at the end of his drink and twisted to hold the bottle up toward a distant streetlight, squinting to see how much vodka was left. "Hey, I hear him comin' in, I'm out the back door. I figure it's the money he's worried about, more than her. Long as I don't touch the money, I'm all right."

The feeling washed through Sean McTeague's gut again; it was all right there suddenly, the man, the plan, the whole thing, handed to him on a plate by dumbass Rolando Brown. "Gimme the bottle," he said.

"Go ahead and kill it," said Rolando.

McTeague killed it, looking out past the end of the bottle as he tilted it up, up past the distant twinkling skyline, past the pallid slice of moon, all the way up to the one bright star he could see above. The vodka ran into his belly and seeped slowly downward, settling things a bit. McTeague hefted the empty bottle a couple of times and then took two quick steps away from the car and flung the bottle with all his might out into the dark.

"Don't kill nobody," said Rolando.

McTeague was listening for the splash. "Don't worry about it," he said.

◆

That was the night they threw Cooper in the lake. It took five of them, and it took them ten minutes to get him across a hundred feet of beach to the edge of the water. Boyle and Emilio did most of the work, with Cooper fighting the whole way. There were lots of people out, sharing a bottle or a joint or just a patch of sand under the stars, and they heard the laughter mixed with the growls and were not alarmed.

In the end, Boyle's two hundred and fifty pounds tipped the scale, and Cooper splashed facedown into the dark water three feet from shore. The others stood panting, ankle-deep in the lake, too tired to cheer. A feeble wave lifted Cooper and let him down again.

"Jesus, he's not moving," said Nolan.

"He's faking, I know him," said Moreland.

"You sure?" said Pappas.

"Shit," said Boyle, and splashed out to Cooper's motionless form. He hooked him under the arms and pulled, and then there was a sudden thrashing and Boyle disappeared with a gigantic splash. Cooper rose from the lake and staggered out, gasping for breath as Boyle floundered in the shallows, swearing.

"I told you," yelled Moreland, fleeing.

Back in Nolan's place overlooking the park, Cooper dripped water on as many items of furniture as he possibly could while the others pretended not to be able to find his wallet. Boyle toweled off and produced more beer, and Nolan shoved in a CD. They wound up out on the balcony again, feet up on the rail, listening to Little Feat and talking about women, their voices a murmur in the dark.

"Lisa, the lady behind the bar over at Burk's on Saturdays? My dream lover. I sit there drooling in my beer watching her sometimes."

"In those jeans she wears? Damn."

"You're outta luck, Chuck. There's a great big dude in a Land Rover comes to take her home at the end of the night."

"I've seen him. Hey, accidents can happen."

"Me, I like the lady runs the café there on Sheridan, right over here, you know? That redhead?"

"Hate to tell you, she's a dyke, man."

"The hell she is."

"The hell she ain't. Susan knows her. She told me."

"Man, that's not fair."

"Well, we can dream. Me, I like that Mexican girl that works at the gyros place over on Morse."

"Watch it."

"Shit, Emilio. I didn't just mention your wife or anything, did I?"

"No, but she's young, man. You a pervert or something?"

"Hey, she's gotta be sixteen. And she's got those deep dark eyes. I'm a sucker for those kind of eyes."

"What's with you and Susan, anyway? You still together?"

"Nah. We're doing the just friends thing for a while."

"For a while? Does that mean I'm free to make my move?"

"What, you? With Susan?"

"Hey, I've liked Susan a long time, man. We go back a ways."

"And I never suspected. Well, hell, go for it. You'll find out."

"I'm not going to ask what."

"Nah, Susan's all right. Nice lady. Just not my type."

"Well, while you two are negotiating over Susan, I'll take her friend, the one that was at Dooley's party, what's her name?"

"Jeannette something."

"Yeah. Now that's a nice-looking lady."

"With a rich boyfriend."

"No shit."

"Commodities trader."

"They always gravitate to money, don't they?"

"So what is it that explains Nolan's success?"

"What success?"

"Come on, Ed. I see you with a different woman every week."

"Well, hey, I don't know. I just sit there picking the olive out of my martini with my tongue and they won't let me alone."

Cooper sat listening, smiling occasionally but saying nothing, working on a beer and trying to get comfortable in wet denim. When the conversation flagged Moreland said, "So, MacLeish, you're really going to do this, huh?"

Cooper took a drink of beer. He let the silence drag on until he could feel them starting to worry. "So it seems," he said.

Before he left they made him take his presents, the mail-order Spanish Fly and the bag of fifty party balloons they had re-labeled *Trojan Economy Pack*. "I'm not sure they'll fit me," Cooper said.

"Sorry, that's as small as they come," said Moreland.

Cooper tossed the presents in a trash can outside and walked down Sheridan Road carrying his shoes, leaving faint wet footprints on the warm concrete. Traffic was still heavy and there were people out on the sidewalks, heading home from the beach or making the rounds of the bars. The neighborhood looked benign tonight, almost friendly: elderly Russians lumbering in packs, sleek black kids moving at a panther's lope, Mexicans in cowboy hats, the white middle class in ugly shorts. Summer in Chicago, Cooper's favorite time. He left Sheridan before he got to Devon and made his way south through the quieter residential streets, not thinking much about anything, feeling good.

He saw Diana and Rachel sitting on the front steps of the six-flat, Rachel smoking a cigarette, Diana looking good, long smooth legs sticking out of the shorts and the auburn hair falling freely about her face. She took in the wet clothes and said, "How was your bachelor party?"

"Strenuous."

"Oh?"

"Things got a little wild when they couldn't come up with enough to pay the stripper."

She believed him for a second but no more, knowing his looks, and she reassured Rachel with a wry sidelong glance. "That's lake water coming out of your ears, I presume?" she said.

"Yup. I'm going upstairs to wash off the slime. See you, Rachel."

From the shower he heard Diana come in, and he thought she was going to do a Psycho on him when he heard her slip into the bathroom. Instead there were rustling noises and when the curtain was gently moved aside it was to reveal Diana as naked as he was, long-legged, trim and golden. She was splendid and the access of desire that hit Cooper was almost painful. "Did you get the slime off?" she said.

"I think so."

She stepped in to join him and they embraced, the just-warm water running over their shoulders and trying to seep down between their bodies. After a long kiss, hands sliding luxuriously over warm wet flesh, she drew back and said, "So. We're really going to do this, are we?"

"So it seems, " said Cooper.

2

McTEAGUE CHECKED THREE places, growing irritated with the heat and the traffic, before he found Rolando. The bar was in an up-for-grabs block of Broadway not too far south of Devon, a hole in the wall with a hand-painted sign outside showing palm trees over a bright blue sea. McTeague could hear the music before he pushed open the door.

It was air-conditioned and the reggae hit him in the face along with the cool air. It was dark inside and the light from the front window didn't reach very far. What McTeague couldn't see he could guess at from the pungent smell. There was a short bar and high stools along the walls, grouped around small shelf tables. McTeague had been in there before but there were no welcoming looks, just blinking white eyes under dreadlocks in the gloom at the back of the room.

Rolando hailed him over the thump-a-thump of the music from the end of the bar. He had a cigarette and a beer going but not much else, apparently; he was alone. McTeague took a stool next to him and clapped him on the shoulder.

"Busy day?"

"I ain't got nothin'," said Rolando. "Try Stoner."

"I don't want anything today. Nothing but your time."

"Hey, my time's valuable, man."

"I can tell."

Rolando laughed in his sleepy way, looking goofy in his baby dreadlocks, and McTeague's heart started to beat faster again. "What's up?" said Rolando.

McTeague waited until he had ordered and paid for a beer from the impressive shower of real dreadlocks that emerged from the darkness. When he was set up he turned to Rolando and said, "Let's talk about the money."

"What money?"

"The money up there in your girlfriend's place."

It took Rolando a while to think of what McTeague was talking about; when the light of understanding entered his eyes he leaned back away from the bar and said, "Uh-uh. No way, man."

McTeague smiled. "Aren't you tired of being poor yet?"

"I ain't tired of bein' alive. That's what counts." McTeague could barely hear him over the music.

"Rolando, tell me again how much money you saw in that suitcase."

"Forget that shit, man. You don't know Dexter."

"Tell me. Just tell me how much you saw."

"I don't know how much. I didn't fuckin' count it."

"You gave me an estimate last night. Tell me again. I want to hear the number. How much did you say it looked like in there?"

Rolando stared straight ahead, into the mirror behind the bar. His arms were folded tight. "You crazy, man." He gave the baby dreadlocks a little shake.

"You said a million, didn't you? Say that for me. A million dollars. Say it."

"Was just a guess."

"I trust your guess. You've seen big wads of cash before. How big was the suitcase?"

"You don't fuck with people like that. They big time. Big time mean."

"A million may be low. Was it a full-sized suitcase, one of these monsters old ladies take to Florida?"

"Don't even think about it."

"Was it packed real tight or lying around loose?"

"I'm outta here, you don't stop this shit."

"You said you saw mainly hundreds. You know what that means. We're talking big money. I'd say your guess was at the low end. I've heard of Dexter. I know the scale he operates on."

"The scale he operates on is, you fuck with his operation, you gone. Like that. You just a memory, Jack."

"A million dollars, man. Sitting in a suitcase in a broad's apartment. A broad who has you up for tea and cookies."

"Uh-uh."

"That's half a million apiece, Rolando. You know what you can do with half a million dollars?"

"Nothin', if you're dead."

McTeague leaned close, to be sure he was heard over the music. "With half a million dollars, man, you are out of here. You said you were tired of the North Side, right? Except you couldn't go back to the South Side? Shit man, with half a million bucks you can find a whole new side. You can buy a condo on Montego Bay if you want. You can visit Africa, look for your roots."

"You ain't been listening to me."

"You can send your little girl to a good school, man. You can set her and her mama up in a nice place."

"Fuck it, I'm gone. You don't wanna live no more, that's your problem."

"Rolando, you've already taken the risk. You've already walked into that place. You're not scared to go up there and jump in bed with her, are you?"

Rolando was silent, still looking into the mirror, and McTeague knew he had done it.

"You've taken the big step. You're up there where you're not supposed to be. Has anything gone wrong?"

"It's different, man. I ain't touched the money. I fuck her, she's still there for him, he don't know a thing. I take the money, it's gone, he knows it, then I'm gone."

"He won't know it's you."

"What the hell you mean, he won't know? How's he not gonna know? Anything happens to the money, she'll tell him anything he wants to hear to save her own ass."

"You haven't heard my plan."

"You got a plan, huh?"

"You bet."

"Whatever it is, it ain't gonna work. For one thing, the money ain't there no more."

"Ah. Now you're talking. Tell me about the money."

"He don't keep no million in there for more than a couple days at a time."

"How often does the pot get that big?"

Rolando took a good hard look at his last chance to say no. His eyes flicked to McTeague's big white eyes. "Every couple months, she says."

"Every couple of months."

"More or less. You know how it goes. When enough of it piles up, he's gotta do something with it."

McTeague watched Rolando in the mirror for a few seconds. "And he just leaves it there with her? He trusts her that much?"

"She's scared of him. He knows that."

"Not too scared to let you in, though."

"Hey, like I said, she gets lonely."

"So let me get this straight. He collects it all and stashes it at her place, and then runs off and leaves it."

"Dexter don't hang around nowhere very long. The man never sleeps in the same place two nights in a row. Sometimes he's up there, sometimes not. When it's time to move it, he packs it up and moves it. She don't know where it goes. All she knows is, it starts to build up, he won't let her go out, then a day or two later he comes by with some people and takes it away."

"What do you mean he won't let her go out?"

"He says she's better than an alarm, somebody being in there to scare away burglars and shit."

"He expects her to guard it? What's he do, give her a piece?"

"Naw, man. It's just if he ain't there he tells her to stick around. He don't expect no trouble there 'cause nobody knows about her. See, she's clean, no record or nothin' so he figures it's safe. And it's a long way from his territory, see? Dexter's at the point now, they watch him good. They watch his people. They see his people hangin' around a place, they know something goin' on there. So now he doin' it different, sneakin' it up to her place, no guards around to attract attention, long way from home. He just tells her to make sure she don't leave it alone."

McTeague turned slowly to face Rolando. "So what you're saying is, any time she calls you, it's because she's tired of being up there by herself."

"Right."

"And she's up there by herself because he's ordered her to stay with the money."

"Uh-huh."

"So any time she calls you up, it means there's a million dollars in the closet."

The music ended and in the sudden quiet Rolando looked stunned, the cigarette smoldering down toward his fingers, staring wide-eyed into the mirror. A bus went by outside with a muffled roar. In the quiet Rolando said, just above a whisper, "Yeah, I guess that's what it means."

The next song kicked in with a nasty chucka-chucka-thump and McTeague leaned closer to Rolando. "You want to hear my plan now?"

A few seconds went by and Rolando finally looked at McTeague. "Think about something," he said.

"What's that?"

"Whatever we pull, Dexter's gonna take it out on Chessandra. Got to. And I don't know if I can do that to her."

McTeague nodded, sagely, sympathetically. "I understand what you're saying," he said. "Now think about something for me."

"What?"

"There's a hell of a lot of women in the world, Rolando."

Chucka-chucka-thump, said the stereo.

◆

The Suit was introduced by Snodgrass, who had put on his own suit jacket for the occasion. The Suit was tall and chiseled and expensively groomed, like every Suit that ever purred into a mike before a Congressional committee, and his black hair was just starting to go nicely gray around the ears. He listened to Snodgrass's introduction with a modest smile, hands casually in the trouser pockets of the dark blue suit, and when Snodgrass had finished he looked over the roomful of skeptical men and a few women in varying attitudes and styles of dress and cleared his throat manfully.

"I want to thank you all for letting me interrupt your working day. I know there's a party going on out there on the streets, and I know you're anxious to get out there and crash it."

The pleasantry was greeted by a polite stir that might have been laughter. In a corner, J.D. Jasper leaned closer to Toni Conte and breathed, "I'm anxious to crash the next party on the street where this guy lives." Toni smiled and looked at a chipped fingernail.

"The reason I'm here," the Suit was saying, "is, among other things, to let you know that back in Washington you have a director who is fighting tooth and nail for you. For you and for the mission that this agency was created for." He paused and looked importantly around the room, carefully making eye contact with five people before continuing. "I know there is a lot of talk, a lot of apprehension about changes, about new directions and new priorities and new ideas in Washington. I have heard the complaints, and I have heard the fears that people are weakening in Washington while you're out here in the trenches. Well, I'm here to tell you that for all the wrangling, and you know there is always wrangling in Washington, there will be no compromising the mission of this agency." It was an applause line, but the Suit knew better than to expect applause from this crowd, so he merely paused and swept the room with his firm gaze again.

"Not for at least two weeks," breathed Jasper.

"You are in a war," said the Suit, "on the front lines. And to fight a war you need support. You need support from headquarters, and you need the support of the people. And I'm here to assure you that you have both. The people of this country have had enough. I have never seen such a groundswell of support for our efforts, your efforts . . ."

"Thank you," breathed Jasper.

". . . as I have seen in the past six months of traveling around this country. The American people know who the good guys and the bad guys are."

"Maybe they can clue you in," breathed Jasper, loudly enough this time to turn heads.

"And we are winning," the Suit said. "For all the wrangling, we are winning the individual battles in this war."

"We?" said Jasper.

"Nationwide we're seizing more kilos of cocaine than we did last year. Arrests of Class One and Two violators are holding steady. With mandatory sentencing we're putting them away in big numbers. We're having an impact. You know that better than I do; I just want to emphasize that other people are aware of the fantastic, dedicated job you're doing. Now I'll let you get to work. I'll leave you with this thought: They are on the run."

"I guess we can go home, then," said Jasper, audibly, as the room came to life, agents standing or merely turning back to their work.

Toni smiled. "Personally I found that very inspirational. I like to know someone in Washington cares."

"I'd like to know someone in Washington knows we're out here."

"Maybe this man will tell them. Look, he's shaking hands all around. Now's your chance to ask him for artillery and air support."

"Now's my chance to puke on his suit. Come on, let's pry Snodgrass away from him and try and get some decent backup out of him for this thing on Vincennes."

The Suit was working his way toward the door, shaking hands, emanating concern, murmuring support, flashing the smile. His eyes lit on Toni, flicked to Jasper, and returned to Toni.

Snodgrass was playing host. "This is Special Agent Jasper, and this is Special Agent Conte. J.D. here's been in Chicago five years, taken a lot of people down. The man's a legend."

"Only in my own mind. Listen, I gotta talk to you about this thing."

"Sure, hang on a second. Toni here has just joined us from Fort Lauderdale. And I understand she was a bit of a legend herself down there."

Toni shot a look at Snodgrass, but he seemed to be playing it straight. She shook hands with the Suit, who swelled a couple of chest sizes and got a bit taller. "I can see why," he said.

Toni just blinked; there was absolutely no intelligent response to a remark like that.

Jasper saved her. "She specialized in removing condoms full of cocaine from Colombian mules. They called her the Proctologist." The Suit looked blank.

"Somebody's got to do it," Toni said, deadpan.

◆

Cooper had to maneuver through traffic like a skipper taking a tanker into the Hong Kong roads, yell back at a cop or two and outwit a limo driver angling for the same spot, but he had the Mercedes 500SEL waiting at the curb, air conditioning cranked up, when Regis Swanson emerged from the north door of City Hall at just past four in the afternoon. Swanson looked unruffled as always, coming across the sidewalk with his hands in the pockets of a lightweight silk suit that was the same color as his neat gray hair and fairly shimmered in the heat. Cooper sat behind the wheel and waited for Swanson to slip into the back; the big man had shaken his head and smiled when on his first day Cooper had gotten out and come around to open the door for him. "I hired you to drive, not open doors," he'd said.

Another thing he hadn't hired Cooper for was small talk; sometimes there was a greeting but today he just got in, slammed the door and said, "Get me out of this town." Cooper put the Mercedes in gear and eased away from the curb. He had the homeward route plotted out; at this time of day the best bet was south, to slip onto Lower Wacker and sneak out of the Loop via Emerald City.

Cooper waited to make his report until he was cruising beneath the city in the eerie green light and he had scoped out the situation in the back seat. Sometimes there was a rustling of papers and no interruptions were welcome. Other times the man would be on the phone, murmuring secrets of the very wealthy just too low for Cooper to hear. A dead silence like this might mean anything: he was deep in thought, dozing, or still pissed off at whatever had happened inside City Hall. "I talked to Jaeger," Cooper ventured as he emerged into the glare on Lake Shore Drive.

"Ah," said Swanson. "And what's his excuse?"

"He says the city's making problems again. He suggested the local alderman might be feeling a bit slighted."

"I had somebody from the fifth floor talk to that alderman last week. Jaeger just needs a kick in the butt. How's the place look?"

"Nice new windows in there, stickers still on them. Just waiting for a bunch of kids with a few bricks."

Over the hum of the car Cooper heard what might have been a sigh. "I tell you, you're just asking for trouble trying to do a good deed in this town. They got people living under bridges and people stacked up in Cabrini-Green, and they're doing everything they can to block this project."

"Jaeger says that pastor was in the papers, accusing you of profiteering."

"Of course I'm profiteering. That's what I do. Thirty-six rehabbed units added to the housing stock in that shit-hole neighborhood is sheer accident, of course."

"I'm not going to argue with you," said Cooper.

After a moment of uncertainty Swanson laughed. "You better not. People who argue with me wind up working for someone else."

Cooper swept past Oak Street Beach, littered with bathers limp in the heat, and scouted the lanes ahead. He wasn't worried; Swanson was easy to work for. If you had the car at point A when he wanted it at point A, the man never complained. Sometimes it took all Cooper's skill and experience to get it there, but that just made it interesting. The little extra jobs were interesting too, the errands, the scouting expeditions, the discreet messages delivered. Cooper was learning a few things about big-time real estate. The work came in spurts; there were days when Cooper wasn't out of the car long enough to get lunch and others when he could dock the battleship for hours at a time and catch up on his reading. He had to get up at six in the morning to get the man into the city, but that wasn't too hard in the summer and it was a very rare evening or weekend when he was asked to drive. The pay was good and Cooper was doing something he liked.

Cooper fought traffic all the way but got Swanson out of the city and up the North Shore to his redoubt on the lake by five. The house was entirely hidden from the road, on a bluff above the lake at the end of a lane that snaked up through a screen of trees. The drive swept majestically by an impressive entrance but Cooper always went on past to drop Swanson at a side door and, after checking instructions for the following day, took the Mercedes around back to park it in one of the five stalls of the old converted stables. Normally then he would switch to the old white '68 Mustang he had rescued and rehabilitated, which had spent the day tucked out of sight at the end of the garage, and drive back into the city.

Today, however, Swanson paused with his hand on the door and said, "You didn't have that wedding ring last week, did you?"

Cooper shook his head. "Nope. I got married on Saturday."

"Well, well. I suppose congratulations are in order?"

"I guess so. So far so good."

Swanson opened the door and said, "Come up on the terrace after you put the car away. I'll stand you a drink."

Cooper walked up onto the wide brick terrace at the back of the house a bit uncertainly; in the weeks he had worked for Regis Swanson, a careful and comfortable distance had been maintained. Swanson had not yet appeared, so Cooper sat on a white-painted Adirondack chair and waited, looking out through a gap in the trees at a distant sailboat gliding over the bright blue lake. The terrace was in the shade of the house and the heat was abating. After a minute Swanson came through sliding glass doors, in shirt sleeves. "Beer?" he said.

"Fine."

Swanson relayed the order to someone inside and sat on a chair to Cooper's left. "There's your million-dollar view," he said. "Some trees and a patch of lake. Less lake than you can see from any park in the city."

"Less noise, too. And fewer people."

"There is that," said Swanson. "Money buys solitude, if you like that kind of thing."

Cooper shrugged. "It can buy you plenty of company too, I'd imagine."

Swanson smiled. "It can. It buys options, let's say."

"That's what it's all about, isn't it?"

"I don't know what it's all about. Maybe you can tell me."

"Me?"

"I'm reliably informed that you're a philosopher of sorts."

"Who told you that?"

Swanson smiled. "I don't hire people without checking them out first."

Cooper shook his head. "I just like to read the occasional improving book."

"That's what my sources say. They also say you're honest. And after my last driver, that was the best recommendation you could have had."

Cooper smiled. "I checked you out too, you know."

"Oh?"

"Sure. I was once warned to watch out for real estate people. I wasn't going to work for a crook."

"I passed, did I?"

"I was told you were extremely sharp but always within the law. The word honest was actually used by one of my informants. Of course, the word ruthless was also used."

Swanson's smile started uncertainly but wound up with perfect assurance. "I am ruthless, if you mean I do what's necessary to get the job done. Within the law, of course. You don't have to play dirty if you have good lawyers and good . . . social skills. But you do have to be ruthless."

"Where's the line?"

"What line?"

"Between ruthless and dirty."

"Dirty is what gets you indicted. Ruthless means you don't worry too much about being called names, or for that matter the livelihoods of your competitors. You don't let yourself be intimidated by bureaucrats, union toughs or what are euphemistically called community organizers. You just plan sound projects and get them completed. When a football coach takes that attitude, he's competitive. When a businessman does it, he's ruthless."

"Fair enough."

"You must not have been too worried about my reputation. You took the job."

"I guess I was curious. I've never worked for a tycoon."

Swanson grinned. "I like that word. You don't hear it too much anymore."

A middle-aged Hispanic woman in a black dress and a white apron came out through the glass doors bearing a tray with two bottles of beer and two frosted glasses. She served them and then retreated. The beer was a German brand Cooper had never seen before and the bottle was ice-cold to the touch and sweating.

"To your marriage," said Swanson, lifting his glass. They drank and he said, "Your first?"

"First and I trust only."

"Good luck with it. May you do better than I. Tell me about your wife."

Cooper looked out over the lake, aware of Swanson's reputation as a rake and faintly jealous. "She grew up in Puerto Rico but she's lived in the States most of her life. She speaks three languages perfectly and she just quit waitressing to go back to school at U. of C. in comparative literature. She's published several translations of modern Spanish poetry and she's got her eye on an obscure series of Latin American novels she says she can get an American publisher for that will make her name as a translator. She's a lot smarter than I am."

"Somehow I doubt that. I drink her health. To . . .?"

"Diana."

"To Diana." They both drank and then looked around at the sound of the glass doors opening again. The man who came out onto the terrace was in his early twenties. He was tall and broad-shouldered and moved in a way that brought the word "nonchalance" to mind. He had light brown hair combed straight back and wetted or oiled, and he had, unmistakably, Regis Swanson's long handsome face, though with dark eyes. He looked at Cooper for a second or two while closing the door behind him, nodding to acknowledge his presence, and then ambled over to the third chair on the terrace and sank onto it. "Greetings," said Swanson.

"Hey," said the young man. "Good day at the office?"

"Fair."

"Grease a lot of palms? Get those widows and orphans out on the street?" The delivery was deadpan, the dark eyes fixed on Swanson.

"Better out on the street than in front of the bulldozers," said Swanson. He turned to Cooper, smiling. "This is my son, Nate," he said. "And this is what passes for wit between us. Nate, this is Cooper, Chesty's successor. We're celebrating his marriage. Grab yourself a beer and join us."

Nate Swanson looked at Cooper again, blankly. He said, "He's letting the help marry now?" A quick wicked smile followed.

"Only if I pledge him my firstborn."

"Just your firstborn? He's getting soft." The two Swansons traded a look. "Well," said Nate, turning back to Cooper, "don't ask him for pointers, whatever you do."

"We've already been through that, thanks," said Swanson.

Nate gave him another vague look and said, "Where are the keys to the Jag?"

"What do you want the keys to the Jag for?"

"What do you think I want them for? To scratch my initials in the paint? I want to drive the damn thing."

"What's wrong with your car?"

"It's in the shop. Clutch went out."

Swanson shook his head and set his glass on the arm of the chair. "Not surprising, the way you drive it."

"There's nothing wrong with the way I drive it. Clutches go out sometimes. Can I take the Jag or not?"

"Where are you taking it?"

"The club, for Christ's sake. Where do you think?"

"You're going to park it on the street in that neighborhood till four in the morning?"

"There's nothing wrong with that neighborhood. It'll be in the alley in back, anyway."

Swanson sighed faintly. "OK. Try and bring it back in one piece."

"Hey, have I ever messed up one of your cars before?"

"I remember a certain Oldsmobile that didn't make it back from the wars."

Nate was smiling. "Where are the damn keys?"

Swanson hesitated for a beat and said, "Third drawer down on the left in my desk in the study."

"Thanks." Nate rose and made for the house. "Good luck with the marriage," he said to Cooper in passing. "The old man knows a good divorce lawyer or two if you need one."

"I'll keep that in mind."

When the door was closed again Swanson said, "Full of the social graces, isn't he?"

Cooper shrugged. "The man has a sense of humor."

Swanson grunted. "'Man' is a little generous for him." He frowned out over the lake. "Young Nate is the product of my first marriage. An immature and disastrous liaison produced immature and disastrous offspring."

After a brief silence Cooper said, "I didn't know he lived with you."

"He doesn't. He's camping with me now because the girlfriend he'd been living with very sensibly kicked him out."

"What's he do?"

Swanson smiled grimly out at the lake. "He runs a nightclub. A rock and roll nightclub."

"I used to tend bar in a nightclub. I don't miss it."

"Well, he's lasted two months already, which is a record of sorts. Every day he goes off to work is a victory. Even if he's losing money."

"It's his place?"

"Mine, really. I own the real estate, but the club's his venture. If he goes bust, he owes me. I wanted to see if having a stake would make a difference. Nate doesn't have a sterling record in the world of productive economic activity."

"Well, he's young, right?"

"What he is is a quitter. No patience, no vision, no commitment. He's failed at everything." Swanson paused for an instant with his mouth open. "I've offered him a shot at the business. Several times. But he's got to start with the grunt work, and he never sticks it for more than a month or two. He didn't finish college, didn't finish night-school accounting, didn't finish three or four trainee programs. I guess he's just a spoiled rich kid."

Cooper studied the label of his beer. "I'm not sure where my sympathies lie here. I was a disappointment to my old man, too."

Swanson seemed to study him for a moment. "What did he want you to be?"

"I think he was hoping for something genteel and highly educated. Running off to enlist pretty well took care of that."

"I don't think Nate ever considered running off to enlist. That would have taken too much initiative."

"How old is he?"

"Twenty-four."

"Hell, he's got plenty of time. He's a baby."

"When I was twenty-four I already owned two buildings."

"You knew what you wanted. Some people do."

Swanson smiled. "Shouldn't you be a little more . . . what's the word I want? Sycophantic or something?"

Cooper gave him an innocent look. "I thought I was off duty."

"I hope I don't regret hiring you," said Swanson, still smiling.

"So do I," said Cooper.

3

REGIS SWANSON SAT in shirt-sleeved splendor at his desk high above Michigan Avenue. Behind him a window framed a view of a magnificent half-mile or so stretching back to the river and the Loop beyond. The river was a metallic green ribbon under the beating sun. Cooper closed the folder and tossed it back on the broad teak desktop.

"Take it with you," said Swanson. "Give it to him. I've got the originals."

Cooper picked up the folder again. "OK. He's not likely to get homicidal or anything, is he?"

Swanson smiled a cool, amused smile. "Maybe."

"I see."

"But then that's why I hired you. To keep me insulated from the sordid realities of the real estate business. To deal with people like Michael Ghislieri."

Cooper stood up. "Fine. If I'm not back by sundown, send the cavalry."

Cooper went looking for Michael Ghislieri at the headquarters of the union he headed, in a square, dull, utilitarian building on Washington west of the Loop. Cooper went through the big glass doors and into a marble-floored lobby that gave onto a short hallway leading toward the rear of the building. There was a reception desk opposite the door but there was nobody in sight. Cooper went down the hallway.

The second door on the right was open and through it Cooper saw an office with three desks. Two of them were unoccupied but at the third, under a window, two men were reading newspapers with their feet up on the desk. They looked at Cooper in the doorway and one of them returned his greeting and said, "What can I do for you?"

"Is Michael Ghislieri around?"

The two men lowered their papers and stared at him, their feet still up on the desk. One of them was bald with a curved nose that opened in enormous nostrils. He looked at the folder in Cooper's hand and said, "Who wants to see him?"

"Regis Swanson."

"You're not Regis Swanson," said the other man, who had gray hair and thick black eyebrows.

"No, but I'm the next best thing," said Cooper. "I'm his faithful Indian companion Tonto."

The bald man snickered and said, "If Regis Swanson wants to talk to Mike, he can call him on the phone."

Cooper nodded and looked thoughtful for a second. Then he left the doorway and went on down the hall. In the office behind him he heard chairs scraping and feet hitting the floor. He opened the next door on the right and saw an empty office. He tried the door across from it and saw a young woman typing.

"Michael Ghislieri?" he said.

"Last door on the right," said the woman, fingers suspended over the keys.

By the time Cooper reached the last door on the right the two men from the office had almost caught up with him. "Don't open that door," the bald man said.

Cooper opened it and saw a fat man with three chins sitting behind a desk with a bronzed pipe wrench on it. The man had a telephone to his ear and he looked at Cooper, surprised. Cooper said, "You Michael Ghislieri?"

Behind Cooper the bald man said, "Sorry, Mike. He just barged in." Cooper moved further into the office, a step ahead of a hand reaching for his shoulder.

Ghislieri murmured something into the phone and hung up. "Who the hell are you?" he said.

Cooper wrestled a chair in front of the desk and sat down. He slapped the folder on the desk. "I'm the messenger boy. You listening?"

"Swanson sent him," said the bald man.

"Shut up," said Ghislieri. He looked at Cooper. "I'm listening." Ghislieri was fat and soft-looking, but his eyes were hard. They were dark brown and heavy-lidded, and they didn't blink.

"Fine. Here's the message. The Madison Place project proceeds, starting tomorrow, and gets completed on schedule. You send your people back to work, abandon your attempts to set a world record for featherbedding, and nobody has any more unpleasantness. You refuse, and the contents of this folder goes to the U.S. Attorney's office. Tomorrow."

Ghislieri's jaw muscles flexed a little, sending little ripples through the three chins. His eyes held Cooper's for a few seconds and then went to the folder. He reached for it and opened it and leafed slowly through the contents. After a silent minute or so he closed it and looked at Cooper again. "This is bullshit."

"You don't sound real confident. What that is is the result of some patient work by a very good private detective."

Ghislieri shot a quick unpleasant look at his associates standing behind Cooper. He pushed the folder back across the desk, slowly, and said, "You look like a working man. How much is that son of a bitch paying you to take his side against labor?"

"I'm not sure what your union provides could be called labor," said Cooper. "There's unions and then there are unions. There are legitimate grievances, and then there's what you're doing to this project. I've looked at that file and I've seen what kind of outfit you're running. Unions like yours give labor a bad smell."

Ghislieri's lips firmed and the point of his chin sank farther into the rolls of fat. "I'm just following the law."

"No, you're not. Swanson's in compliance with all the relevant statutes on this project, as his attorneys will be happy to show in court. And I have to say, having looked in that file, you've got a lot of gall talking about the law. Now, can I assure my boss that work will proceed tomorrow?"

"This is blackmail, is what this is."

"No. This is business. What you're doing at Madison Place is blackmail. But we'll be happy to let the court decide if you want to take the long way around. Only thing is, you might be in jail by the time the case comes up."

The stare-down lasted for maybe five seconds. Finally Ghislieri said, "I'll give your boss a call." His eyes went to the men behind Cooper and he said, "Escort this gentleman to the sidewalk. I don't give a damn whether he lands on his feet."

Cooper had been ready for something along those lines; when he heard movement behind him he leaned forward and plucked the wrench from the desk. He stood up, swinging around quickly, and saw the two men bracketing him, a step and a swipe away.

He fixed on the bald man, hefting the wrench a bit, at waist level. "You lay a hand on me, I'll plant this in your skull," he said.

They weren't really prepared for hardball, he saw. The bald man's chest came out an inch or two, but he moved no further. The other man was in his fifties and didn't look eager; he was past the age. Cooper sidestepped the bald man and said, "I'm going to walk out that door and you're not going to bother me. Let's not ruin a nice summer day." They let Cooper walk out of the office. When he was out in the hall he dropped the wrench on the floor with a clank. He walked all the way up to the front door, listening for steps but not letting himself turn around, and nobody came after him.

In the car, going back east, Cooper shook his head, grinned, and started to whistle. Lunchtime, he thought. I could get to like this job.

◆

The bar was in the South Loop, in the middle of a block of grimy brick façades that had survived the creeping gentrification to the south. There was an Old Style sign hanging above the door and a big front window filled with neon. Across the street rose the sheer blank face of the Metropolitan Correctional Center. Inside it was cool and dark and moderately crowded. The chromed legs of barstools shone in the light from the window and the aroma of old beer and cigarettes lay heavy on the air. Outside it was bright, hot and busy as the Loop emptied in the late afternoon.

Jasper lit Toni's cigarette and then one of his own. He put the lighter on the bar and said, "OK, your turn. How the hell did you get into this racket?"

"What's a nice girl like me doing in a job like this?" Toni blew smoke high and away.

"If you were a nice girl you wouldn't be in a job like this." Jasper grinned, the moustache curling, the blond hair receding from a high forehead, the pale blue eyes intent.

"But I am. I'm a nice Italian Catholic girl who wanted to be a nun, just like all nice Italian Catholic girls. For a week or two, anyway."

"So what happened?"

"I joined the Marines instead."

Jasper stared, then shook his head and smoked. "Man, the world's changing. So you were a leatherneck, huh? A fightin' gyrene."

"A jarhead, yeah." Toni enjoyed giving the cool smile, enjoyed seeing men look at her warily.

"What'd you do? They don't actually let you fight, do they?"

"I was a supply officer. No, don't worry, they won't let us fight."

"Hey, I didn't mean it that way."

"But I did the Officer Candidate Course and Basic School, same as the men. I can fire an M16, the fifty cal, the M60, the Mark 19, even an AK 47. You want somebody to shoot up the landscape for you, I can do it."

"I don't doubt it. I'm not calling your macho into question."

"Go ahead. I'm not very macho." She gave him the smile again.

Jasper took a long pull on the cigarette, watching her. She looked like a hawk, he thought, with her black shaggy hair, dark eyes, Roman nose and that slightly predatory mouth. "No. And I bet macho doesn't impress you too much."

"Not after all the old gunnies I've had to face down just to do my job."

Jasper shook his head again. "So why this?"

Toni shrugged. "It was something to do. We used to run into DEA trainees there at Quantico, and I thought of them when I was deciding what to do when I got out of the Corps. I guess I hadn't had enough excitement."

"Had enough now?"

"Getting there."

Through the smoke, Jasper said, "What happened down there in Lauderdale?"

Toni was still for a moment, not looking at him, tapping ash off her cigarette into the solid glass ashtray on the bar. "I was made, that's all."

"That'll do it. Anybody get hurt?"

She looked up at him. "Just some feelings. You know how it is."

"Sure. I had a guy once, told me he'd never had a friend like me, all that shit. Son of a bitch cried when I busted him. Not angry, just cried. Couldn't believe I'd busted him."

"Yeah. Well, you know how it is, then. There were some hard feelings and news got around and it was decided my usefulness down there had come to an end."

"You brought a rep with you. They say you took a lot of people down."

Toni drew on the cigarette and smiled. "Some of my best friends."

◆

Cooper put draw on the cue ball to knock the last stripe into the corner pocket; he had to have it come back a little to set up the shot on the eight ball, sitting near Emilio's last pocket on the other side of the table. The stripe dropped, the cue ball spun back and settled primly, a little short of perfect but playable, and Emilio said, "Don't get cocky now."

"Never." Cooper took three seconds to line it up, leaning over the table, and stroked with that long smooth confident motion that was beyond thought. The eight ball hit the rail and came home to Cooper's pocket like a child running straight to mama.

"Man, you are hot tonight," said Emilio, leaning on his cue like Zapata with his rifle. "I thought you said you was rusty."

"I am. I haven't played in three weeks."

"Marriage, man. Your life will never be the same."

Cooper grinned. "It's not the marriage. It's the getting up at six in the morning. Working for a living is doing bad things to my life."

"S'what they all say, man. That's what I said, too. But it's the wife, believe me. Once they got you, it's fuckin' over. It's like psychological, man. Can't beat it. I gotta ask Elena for permission to go to the can."

"Shut up and find a couple of quarters. You ready for another one?" Cooper scooped his empty bottle from a table, took Emilio's and headed for the bar. Lisa was working tonight, and as always Cooper flirted a little. "I'll trade you these empties for a couple of full ones, OK?"

"Throw in three-fifty and you got a deal." Lisa had been young and stunning when Cooper had begun drinking at Burk's; now she was moving into the middle thirties with a ripe womanly appeal, a knowing serenity and the same killer smile. Cooper watched her move as she went to get two more beers, long brown hair cascading to her shoulder blades, waist widening to painfully sweet curves.

How long has it been since I looked at Diana like this? Cooper wondered suddenly.

He lost the next game to Emilio and had to give up the table because other names were chalked on the board. He watched Emilio toy with a newcomer until he finished the beer and then left.

What's different now? he asked himself, ambling south along the high embankment of the El tracks in the slowly easing heat. Just in the last week, since that ceremony? You burn through the real passion, the new, urgent, rather-fuck-than-eat part of it in a few months, and then it settles down; hell, that phase is six years behind Diana and me. You settle in, get comfortable, start to really love her maybe; the lovemaking tails off to a once-a-week thing, sometimes less, but it's always there. It's just less urgent. I was happy with that.

I was happy with that; I could look at Lisa and go home to Diana and there was never a problem with that before. What's different, now that I've got this piece of gold wrapped around my finger?

Diana was in bed when he came in, only the hall light on. The temperature was about a hundred degrees in the hallway and Cooper could hear the fan humming in the bedroom. Jesus, he thought. Break down and buy an air conditioner. He used the toilet, brushed his teeth, went and stood at the front window for a minute or two. Go to sleep, one voice said. Wake her up and make love to her, said another. Just to prove a point, he thought.

She stirred when he opened the door, whispered a sleepy hi. Cooper took off his clothes slowly. He peeled back the sheet and she was naked; he could just make out her trim tawny form, dark against the white of the sheet. He knew dispassionately that she was a beautiful woman, a head-turner; he saw the way other men looked at her. He lay beside her, put his arms around her, ran his hands over the warm, smooth, slightly damp skin of her back. Familiar, comfortable. Her arm flopped over him, she kissed him at the base of his throat, a very slight tensing of the lips. The fan hummed, the tone changing cyclically, hypnotically.

With relief he realized she was asleep again. The relief angered him and he told himself to wake her up, but he gave up when he realized that it was not really Diana he wanted tonight; it was Lisa.

◆

"You got the easy part," said McTeague. "I'll even try and let you get your rocks off before it starts."

"Shit," said Rolando. He hadn't said much else since McTeague had climbed into his car.

"Just for Christ's sake remember to leave the door open."

"I got a question." Rolando was cruising north on Broadway through the failing light, steering with one hand on the wheel and his elbow out the window, but looking stiff and nervous all the same.

"Shoot."

"How come you the one to go in and get it? Wouldn't it be better for me to grab it on the way out?"

"Uh-uh. Think about it. The whole point is so she doesn't know you're involved, right? You gotta look innocent. She has to hear the pounding on the door, see you high-tail it out the back. She hears you rooting around in the closet or anything, she knows right away. The last impression she's gonna have is you pounding down those stairs, running for your life."

Rolando shook his head once. He didn't look happy. After a minute he said, "I wanna tell you a story, man."

McTeague looked away, out the window. "Go ahead."

"Couple years ago, out on the West Side. Friend of mine, guy named Spider. He had a bright idea one day, kind of like your idea."

"Hm," said McTeague.

"He knew where the money man lived. He knew where he parked his car and shit. And he knew when he had a lot on him. So he waited for him one day. Waited till he parked the car out back of his place and was gettin' out. And he shot the motherfucker and took what he had on him."

Rolando paused. They were waiting at a red light, at Bryn Mawr. "So?" said McTeague, knowing the punchline already.

"So he kept his head down for a while, right? Nobody saw him for a long time. Like a year maybe. Nobody knew where he went. But everybody knew what he done. Everybody knew in like three days who shot the guy and took off with the money. Three days, and they was saying look out, when they catch up with Spider gonna be some bad shit. And then everybody forgot about it, till one day Spider turns up."

"Yeah?"

"He turned up in about six pieces, man. They had cut off his head, cut off his dick, spread the motherfucker all over the room. And that was a year later, man. Motherfuckers like that are patient, man. They got long, long memories and they don't let nobody get away with nothin'."

McTeague looked out the window. "So Spider was stupid. He talked. That's the only way they could have known, if he went around bragging or something. Keep your mouth shut and you won't have any problems."

"I don't know, man. You know what the best part is?"

"What?"

"They said Spider got about five thousand dollars off the guy. Five thousand. Now, if they gonna do that for five thousand bucks, what are they gonna do if we get a million?"

"Not a damn thing, 'cause we will be long gone."

"I'm tellin' you, man."

"You got your bag packed, like I told you?"

"Shit." Rolando flapped his free hand in a half-hearted gesture.

"You didn't?"

"I don't need no bag."

"But you're still ready to fly, right? OK, cool. You take the suitcase, that'll be your luggage. You can buy yourself all the clothes you need at the other end. I jump in the car, we go straight to O'Hare. We count it and split it up in the car and you go hop on the first flight out."

"I don't know, man. Where am I gonna go?"

"Anyplace. You can be anywhere in the country in four hours. You'll be in the Beverly Hilton before Dexter knows it's missing."

Rolando waited a while, weaving through traffic, before saying, "I don't know, man."

"The hell you don't know. You wouldn't have called me if you weren't going to go through with it."

"I feel bad about Chessandra. I couldn't hardly talk to her on the phone tonight."

"If Chessandra knows what's good for her, she'll split. Chessandra will do all right. You can send her a ticket from Montego Bay. Just whatever the hell you do, act like it was any other night."

The silence lasted all the way to Thorndale. When Rolando put on his turn signal, McTeague knew it was happening. They left Broadway behind and went east, under the El tracks and into the Winthrop-Kenmore Corridor.

The Corridor was a long strip of disputed territory squeezed between the old quiet middle-class neighborhoods west of the El tracks and the condos on Sheridan Road. There was a mixture of old houses and six-flats and gimcrack fifties-era apartment boxes, inhabited by a mixture of blacks, Hispanics, miscellaneous Third-Worlders, stranded retirees and grimly determined gentrifiers. The Corridor was an up-and-down type of neighborhood; it was the best place many of its residents had ever lived, but at the same time it seemed to keep the officers of the Twentieth and Twenty-fourth police districts fairly busy.

Tonight people were out: hanging in groups on the corner, sitting on the front steps, going noplace in particular in the slowly easing heat. Rolando crossed Winthrop and pulled over in the shadows where the big trees overhung the street.

"So we really gonna do this, huh?"

"Looks like it, partner. You ready? You relaxed? You feel like you can go up there and show her a good time like always?"

"I'll be all right. What about you? What if you can't find it?"

"If the place looks anything like the way you drew it, I'll find it. If I don't, I get the fuck out of there and nobody's the wiser."

"What if your plan don't work?"

"It'll work. I scouted it. What the hell you think I been doing the last few nights? The man downstairs goes out every night. The lady stays in there with the kids. She'll be there, he won't. She'll take the bait."

"What if tonight's different? What if she don't take the bait? What if she can't read?"

"Well, I guess you just have yourself a nice evening with Chessandra then. Can you handle that?"

Rolando shook his head and smiled for the first time. "Shit."

"Like the song says, man, all you gotta do is act naturally. Wine and dine her and then run like hell when the commotion starts. Leave the car where you can get it in a hurry and bring it back fast. The whole thing oughta take less than two minutes."

"One more thing."

"What?"

Rolando stared at him through the dark for a second or two and said, "You wouldn't run on me now, would you?"

McTeague blinked at him. "How could I? By the time I come back out, you're sitting there in the alley in the car."

Rolando looked at him for a few seconds longer, just looking, and McTeague thought for a moment that even now he might lose him. But finally Rolando said quietly, "All right, man. Let's go do it."

◆

LuAnn heard the bedroom door creak open and set the bottle of Jim Beam back on the counter with a clunk. She raced back into the hall in time to see Jimmy peering out of the dark bedroom, wide eyes beneath the shock of blond hair. The door slammed shut. LuAnn halted at the door and screamed, blood pressure rising, "You open this door again, you little bastard, I'll skin you alive. Now get back in that bed!" From within the room there was a scuffling sound and then a thin wail rose. LuAnn clenched her teeth, balling a fist, eyes squeezed shut. "You happy now?" she screamed. "You woke up your sister! Well, you can stay in there and listen to her!" For a moment LuAnn rocked on her heels, close to infanticide, then remembered the bourbon sitting on the counter in the kitchen, a beacon of solace and hope, and stalked away.

She poured a stiff one over ice, lit a Camel and went to open the back door. She caught sight of her reflection in the glass as she approached, stringy blond hair and too much fat swelling the old white T-shirt. She looked away; LuAnn never looked in a mirror unless she had to. She pulled open the door and put her face to the screen, but it wasn't any cooler outside. She took a deep drink of the bourbon and waited for her heart to stop pounding.

Behind her she could hear the TV on, way up in the living room, but she was tired of looking at TV; she'd done nothing but look at TV all day. What she wanted was to get out, get away, go someplace. LuAnn was tired of walls. She wanted to talk to people, grown-up people, white, colored, whatever; she'd talk to a Mexican if she had to. She wanted to have somebody say something nice to her for a change. With bitterness she thought of Fred, sitting on a barstool in the tavern over on Broadway, in the air conditioning, pissing the night away with his friends. She heard her daughter's distant wail rising above the drone of the TV and closed her eyes for a moment. Let her cry, she thought. That's one thing she'll have to get used to in this life.

With a deep sharp pang LuAnn had a sudden vision of home, the green rocky hills of eastern Kentucky. For a moment she wanted nothing more than to go home, back to Mama, back to the old frame house at the end of the draw, to sit out on the porch and watch the sun sink over the ridge on a summer evening again. The vision sustained her for a moment, till she remembered all the reasons why she had followed Fred north, and she felt the walls closing in again.

When the doorbell rang LuAnn's heart leapt; she went briskly up the hall hoping this was salvation: a neighbor, Melanie maybe, somebody to talk to, anybody. Not just another mistake, another hustler, another goofball, she prayed.

With a sinking heart she saw the note on the floor just inside the door: nothing but a note, more harassment from the hostile world. She stooped to pick it up; it was written in pencil in capital letters on a piece of kid's school paper. LuAnn read it once, then twice, her heart picking up and her blood pressure soaring, shock spreading slowly through her along with the kick from the bourbon. She read it a third time and the glass of bourbon crashed to the floor; LuAnn was not really conscious of what she was doing now. The note fluttered to the floor as she scrabbled at the locks on the door, starting to swear. As LuAnn charged the stairs out in the hall, screaming now, the note lay soaking up bourbon, still legible: *IF YOU GO UPSTAIRS RIGHT NOW YOU WILL CATCH YOUR MAN SCREWING THAT NIGGER BITCH.*

◆

"What's the matter with you, baby? You a thousand miles away tonight." Chessandra put her hand on Rolando's cheek and turned his face to hers. He resisted a little but not much, closing his eyes briefly and then opening them with focus on her.

"I'm OK. I'm just tired tonight. Had me one of them days." Chessandra's hand lingered on his cheek for a moment, her face close to his, and Rolando looked into her clear, dark eyes and had the closest thing to a pang of conscience he was capable of. She was dressed for him tonight, in a sleeveless red T-shirt that hugged her breasts and short pants that left a lot of long brown leg uncovered. Her hair was straightened and styled, cut to the nape of her neck, framing her round pleasant face. She was a fine-looking woman tonight, and Rolando was totally incapable of responding as a man should to a fine-looking woman on a hot summer night.

She kissed him, exploring and teasing, and Rolando spilled a little beer on his lap. "Lemme set this thing down," he said, pulling away.

"Now you talkin'."

Rolando couldn't look at her; he took as much time as a human being could to set a can of beer down on a coffee table, then leaned back with an exaggerated sigh.

"What's the matter?" said Chessandra, in a sterner tone.

Rolando looked at her and blinked a few times. "I don't know. I guess I'm wondering how you can be so sure he ain't comin' in tonight."

"I told you." Chessandra ran a knuckle along his jawline, leaning close. "He was here last night. Tonight he's out on the West Side. He won't be back till tomorrow. He always tells me."

"And he ain't never fooled you? Just to check up on you?"

"He calls. He calls all the time, tryin' to catch me. God help me if I'm in the bathroom or something, he's like, 'Where you been?' But no, he ain't never come back on a night he wasn't supposed to."

Rolando shook his head, looking around the room. "OK. I hope you right."

"Baby." Chessandra pulled his face to her. "Forget about Dexter. I do the worrying about Dexter around here. Right now it's you and me up here."

Rolando had his arm around her and was trying hard to act natural when the rapid footsteps sounded out in the stairwell and the screaming and pounding started. They both sat upright like somebody had wired the couch and just looked at each other as the words came through the drumbeat on the hall door, female rage and fury.

"Open this fucking door, you bitch! Freddy, come out of there before I break in there and tear your balls off! You bastard!"

Rolando was off the couch without a word, standing for just a moment looking at Chessandra and wanting to say something, but then just hauling ass out, down the hall toward the kitchen, hearing her call his name, running like a motherfucker to get far enough away so he couldn't hear her anymore.

◆

When Chessandra finally got the door shut again, the fat woman pounding away down the stairs to go around and catch her man sneaking out the back, she leaned on it and closed her eyes, feeling sick and feeling her heart trying to come out the front of her chest. "Crazy bitch," she said. She felt like crying from humiliation and the ebbing stress, but she fought it down, thinking maybe Rolando was hanging around out back somewhere, waiting to see which way things went. She hurried to the kitchen and was surprised to find it dark. She wondered for a second, then turned on the light, blinked at the open back door and went out onto the porch. She stood panting at the rail, looking down into the empty alley, and then called softly, "Rolando!"

No answer came, and while she was standing there Chessandra got a very bad feeling suddenly. She went back into the apartment, closed and locked the back door with trembling hands, and headed for the bedroom thinking, "Oh no no no. No please, Jesus."

At the sight of the open closet, the spilled-out shoes and the enormous, gaping, irreparable gap where the suitcase had been, Chessandra sank to her knees and the sobs welled up, this time far beyond her control. "Oh, God. Sweet Jesus. Oh, mama," she sobbed. She cried into her hands for a minute or so, head on the floor, because she knew her life was over.

It took another minute for her to get some control back, and then she stopped thinking about Dexter and started thinking about how she could find Rolando and what she could do to him. She quickly abandoned that line of thought, realizing that sheer survival was going to be the main priority.

Places to run, people to hide with. She stood up and thought about packing what she could, and then started crying again, because she liked it here and she had hoped there wouldn't be any more moves for a while. After a few seconds she made herself stop crying and move for the closet to find something to put a few things in. The enormity of the disaster hit her and for a fleeting moment she thought about lying, thinking of a really good story for Dexter and taking her chances.

She knew Dexter, and she didn't waste much time on that option. It was moving day again, and Chessandra's heart fell a hundred miles as she thought of all she was losing, the hard time that was starting, the chance it might really be all over. Halfway through her frantic packing she had to stop and just cry some more, because once again, one more time, Chessandra realized she'd come into this life to be a victim.

◆

"I don't fuckin' believe it," said Rolando. "You look inside?"

"It's there. You are a rich motherfucker, man." McTeague was struggling with the suitcase resting awkwardly on his knees, forcing his head back.

"I don't fuckin' believe it." Rolando sounded like a zombie and he was driving like one, careening from the alley out onto the street, tires squealing as he headed east.

"Slow down, man. The last thing we need is to get stopped."

"She see you?"

"She was too busy at the front door, screaming at the other lady."

"I don't fuckin' believe it."

"Look, talk to me. How we doing it? You're not up for the airport thing, fine. Take me back to my car. We'll count it there and divvy it up and then not see each other for a while, OK?"

"Yeah, OK, man. Where's your car?"

"In the park district lot at the lake, just north of Foster. Go down Sheridan. And take it easy for Christ's sake."

McTeague managed to get the seat shifted back and the suitcase down between his legs on the floor, wedged under the dashboard. Rolando was still driving too fast but at least he seemed in control. McTeague was surprised to find that he was calm, clicking on all cylinders and thinking ahead. "Put on the air conditioning, will you?" he said, rolling up the window.

They didn't speak again until Rolando rolled through the viaduct under Lake Shore Drive and entered the park. "Too many people around," said Rolando. "We can't count it in the car. Somebody'll see it."

"Let's just look. If it's too crowded we'll think of something else. I'm in the far lot there, next to the lake."

Rolando pulled in next to McTeague's blue Trans Am. There were picnickers on the grass a couple of hundred feet in front of them and other cars wheeling slowly through the lot. "Not here, man," said Rolando. "Take a long time to count money, and this ain't the place to do it. You want a table and everything."

"Maybe," said McTeague. "Let's think for a second." He reached down between his legs and shifted the suitcase a little.

"My place. I'll bring you back here afterwards."

"Shit," said McTeague. "Look at that." He pointed with his chin, out the window to Rolando's left. Rolando was nervous still, and he snapped his head left to look. McTeague brought up the little snub-nosed .38 he had pulled out of his sock and put it under Rolando's ear before anybody had time for second thoughts. Rolando stiffened and started to turn back in the instant before McTeague shot him, but with the muzzle lodged beneath his ear and pointed upward, there was nowhere to go. McTeague squeezed and bad things happened to Rolando with a slightly muffled bang.

McTeague remembered botched mob hits and thought about shooting him again, but the sight of Rolando's head settling against the window in a halo of spattered blood told him it wasn't necessary. "Sorry, partner," he said. Moving fast, he put the gun in a plastic grocery bag he pulled out of his hip pocket, opened the door and struggled out from under the suitcase, trying not to hurry, trying not to look around. The picnickers weren't looking at him and he figured if they hadn't heard, nobody had. He hauled the suitcase out, the grocery bag swinging from his wrist, and took it to the rear of his car. He put it in the trunk, slammed it shut, got behind the wheel with the gun on the seat beside him, and left.

The gun went into the lake off the rocks north of Belmont Harbor, and by midnight McTeague was in the shower, the suitcase sitting on the bathroom floor where he could see it, washing flecks of Rolando's blood off his hands and arms and then hanging onto the side of the shower stall because the shakes had finally hit him, bad.

4

McTEAGUE WOKE UP before it was fully light, not past five in the morning, and the urgency was enough to bring him right out of bed. He'd rolled around on the sheet for a long time seeing Rolando staring at him. He was a long way from rested, but there were things to do. He sat on the edge of the bed for a moment, looking out into the gray uneasy morning, feeling like hell and suddenly every bit as afraid as Rolando had wanted him to be.

He had to look under the bed and see the suitcase lying there, just to touch base, and then he was moving in a fever, tugging on some clothes, going into the bathroom to splash cold water in his face. He left the suitcase under the bed and went out.

He drove west on Montrose, away from the sun. The city looked tired and sullen and hostile in the growing light. The vision of Rolando that had kept McTeague awake had faded a little, but he kept hearing Rolando saying, "They don't let nobody get away with nothin'." McTeague wheeled into an Amoco station and parked by the pay phone. He sat in the car for a few seconds, thinking about phrasing, then told himself it was a simple damn phone call and got out to make it. He'd known about the phone number for a long time and wondered what kind of asshole would ever actually call it; now he knew one kind. He punched it in and listened to the ring, thinking that this was the frosting, the very best part of his plan.

◆

Cooper knew next to nothing about the construction industry; to his eye the building site was a hole in the ground with enormous pipes lying around and massive concrete pylons starting to take shape, rusting steel reinforcing rods sticking up out of them. What workers he could see were moving with great economy and deliberation in the morning heat, some of them shirtless.

Swanson reappeared, looking foolish in a yellow hard hat above his cream-colored suit, exchanged a last few words with the stocky foreman, relinquished the hard hat and came back to the car, smoothing his hair. He was smiling. "Busy as bees," he said. "Everybody here that's supposed to be here."

Rolling past the construction company's trailer toward the street, Cooper maneuvered carefully around a group of hard hats who watched the Mercedes go by with sullen hostile looks. "I think if I hadn't stayed with the car we might have had a couple of flat tires," he said. "Nobody offered me any coffee."

"I hope your feelings weren't hurt."

"A little. But I'll get over it."

Swanson chuckled softly in the back seat. "You know what Ghislieri said when he called me?"

"What?"

"He said, 'Next time send somebody with some manners.'"

"I'll work on it," said Cooper.

◆

The second Dexter let himself into the apartment something hit him; it was too quiet, maybe. He called Chessandra's name once and then closed the door, leaving it unlocked. He listened for a couple of seconds and then pulled the Glock out of his waistband and started walking very slowly down the hall.

He went into the bedroom and saw drawers open, and he had a very bad feeling about things. The closet door was closed and Dexter tore it open without worrying too much about somebody jumping out at him; he knew what had happened.

He called her bitch and every other bad name he could think of for a woman, standing there looking at the space where the suitcase had been, and then he fell silent and put the gun back in his belt. He turned his back to the closet, clamped his hands over his face and rubbed hard, and tried to think for a moment.

He took his hands away from his face and left the room. He stormed around the apartment, looking in every room, kicking furniture out of the way, knocking over a lamp, jerking out drawers. He went through the bathroom and kitchen quickly, having pretty much given up, just going through the motions. Gone, she was gone, long gone.

Think about it now, he told himself, standing in the kitchen. Look. Next to the phone he found a piece of paper with three phone numbers on it, stuck to the wall with a thumbtack. One of the numbers was for a pizza place, one was his beeper number, the dumb bitch ignoring what he said about security, and the third was written under the letter *R*. He grabbed the paper and stuffed it in his pants pocket. He made sure she was gone, and then he stood in the living room looking out at the green leaves drooping in the morning heat and trying to remember everything Chessandra had told him about herself. "Motherfucker," he breathed, thinking what day it was and what kind of people he had to deal with.

When he thought he knew where to start looking he left the apartment, the task very clear in his mind: find Chessandra before they found him.

◆

"Never heard of it," said Snodgrass. He was groomed, professional and tightly wound, and Jasper suspected him of aspiring to Suithood.

"It's on Clark Street," said Jasper. "Up the street from Wrigley Field. It's a rock club."

Snodgrass stared at him. "Your kind of place, huh?"

"I was there once. The crowd was a bit young for me. And it's loud. I mean really loud."

"Business or pleasure?" said Snodgrass.

"I was on a date. Not a very successful one."

"Had to bust your date, huh?" said Toni.

Jasper smiled. "I didn't see much to attract my professional interest. But then I was trying hard not to look." He shook his head. "We could bust every nightclub in this city, every night. If we had the time and money."

"So anyway," said Snodgrass. "You heard of this guy?"

"No," said Jasper. "But the name Dexter D. got my attention."

"Who took the call?"

"Frank. About eight this morning. Brought it right to me when I got in."

"What'd the guy say, exactly?"

Jasper shoved a sheet of paper across the table. "Frank said he talked fast but made sure he got the details. Started off by giving him two names, Nate Swanson and the Blue Angel. Gave him time to write them down and everything. And then he said, more or less verbatim according to Frank, 'Swanson was doing some bragging last night and showed a friend of mine a million dollars in cash. Had it lying on the fucking bed,' or something to that effect. Apparently the friend asked him where it came from and Swanson said he got it from Dexter D. Repeated that. 'From Dexter D.' Frank said he tried to get more but the guy didn't want to chat."

There was a silence while Snodgrass looked at the notes. "OK," he said, and laid the paper on the table. "If this is legit, this is not a very smart individual we're talking about."

"This is one dumb fucking doper."

"It's one doper that should choose his friends more carefully, for sure," said Toni.

Snodgrass nodded. "Probably the usual, this is somebody he screwed on a deal, getting even. Or the guy screwed his girlfriend or something. Who knows?"

"Or," said Jasper, "our snitch was screwing the girlfriend. Frank said he never mentioned the sex of the friend. But the friend was in a bedroom with Nate Swanson last night. And today this guy knows everything Swanson said. Maybe it's girlfriends Swanson has trouble choosing."

"So what's it worth?" said Toni.

"It names names," said Jasper. "I hear Dexter D.'s name, I'm interested."

"Of course, if I wanted to take some guy's girlfriend, framing him would be one way to get him out of the way," said Toni.

Jasper shrugged. "Shit, it's as much to go on as anything that comes over that wire."

"There's that," said Toni.

◆

Dexter sat in the Mercedes, listening to NWA on the tape player and trying to work up an attitude of his own. Out the windshield he could see a ribbon of light, the vast sweep of the airport framed by the concrete decks of the parking garage. Once in a while he looked left to where Mau-Mau and Antone were waiting in Antone's car down the way. It looked to him as if Mau-Mau had dropped off to sleep.

When the footsteps came briskly over the concrete, Dexter tried to follow the man's progress in the mirror, but was startled nonetheless when the passenger door was torn open and the man slid onto the seat. It was the same man as always, the same black hair and pale complexion, the same black wrap-around sunglasses, the same powerful jaw working on the gum.

"Morning," said the man.

"Morning," said Dexter, looking away from the sunglasses.

"United today," said the man. "Flying the friendly skies. I only got about twenty minutes, so let's move. I hope you got me one with wheels this time. I don't have time to fuck with baggage carts."

"There's a problem," said Dexter.

There was total silence for a few seconds. Looking out the windshield at the far-off runways, Dexter could feel the man in the black sunglasses watching him, a chill settling.

"What the fuck are you talking about?" said the man.

"I had a little problem this time. I need a day or two."

This time Dexter could hear the jaws working the gum, fast and hard. He looked at the man, who still had his hand on the door handle. "You don't have a day or two," said the man.

"And you don't have no money," said Dexter. "If you wanna get it, you gotta wait a day or two."

As Dexter expected, the man looked around, out the windows and over his shoulder. Dexter saw him mark Antone and Mau-Mau; he didn't even bother to look for the support he knew the man would have. "Dexter," the man said, "you're disappointing me."

"It ain't my fault. There was a mix-up."

"How in the hell can you have a mix-up over that much money?"

"Shit happens," said Dexter.

The squish-squish of the gum filled the silence. "I'm gonna have to call L.A. about this."

Dexter shrugged. "There's phones in the terminal."

"I don't think you're taking me seriously somehow. You think you're selling magazine subscriptions? You got a daddy gonna make it up out of his pocket if you don't come up with it?"

"Tomorrow," said Dexter. "I'm good for it. You know that."

"All I know is, I'm supposed to get on a United flight in fifteen minutes with one million dollars. That's all I know."

"Go call LA. Just leave me a number where I can get in touch with you."

"Tell you what, Dexter," the man said, opening the door. "Don't call us. We'll call you."

◆

Cooper drew up smoothly at the canopied entrance to the Chicago Club on Van Buren and was gratified to see Swanson just emerging onto the sidewalk. Swanson made for the car without breaking stride or looking at Cooper, as if the car being there for him were in the natural order of things. "One-eighty East Scott Street," he said.

"You got it," said Cooper, heading for Michigan Avenue.

"You know where it is," said Swanson. "I'm impressed."

"East of State and north of Division. High-rent district." He made the turn. "I was a cab driver for a long time."

"I've gotten in cabs where the driver didn't know where City Hall was. I had a guy once, I'm not making this up. He was fresh off the boat, the Middle East somewhere, I told him to take me to Midway Airport. He nods, off we go. We head out the Kennedy, toward O'Hare. I tap him on the shoulder, say 'Midway, Midway,' he keeps nodding. I start yelling when we get up to about Division, he pulls off the expressway and starts waving his hands, screaming 'You say Midway! You say Midway Airport!' Five minutes later I figure out he thought I wanted him to take me halfway to the airport. True story."

Cooper laughed. "A lot of the foreign guys are good drivers. They learn fast. But yeah, there's a weakness in the system if they can walk in on their first day in the country and get a cab. I mean, fly me over to Cairo or someplace like that, ask me to drive somebody to the Pyramids, I'm going to waste a little gas before I get there."

"You'd learn faster than some of these guys, though, I bet."

"Learn fast or go broke. That's the thing about driving a cab. Rewards and punishments are very directly tied to competence."

"You regard that as a positive feature, I take it."

Cooper shrugged. "Sure."

"Then I think we're going to get along."

Swanson was silent for the rest of the trip up into the quiet streets tucked into the angle between Lake Shore Drive and the south end of Lincoln Park. Just making conversation, Cooper said, "Funny neighborhood around here. When I was driving a cab, it seemed like every time I went through here, I got flagged down by little old ladies. Little old rich widows, the lousiest tippers on earth. I used to hate that."

As Cooper negotiated the turn into one-way Scott Street from the east, Swanson said, "You're off for the day now. See you at the office tomorrow at ten." Cooper opened his mouth to ask a question but shut it again. He eased over in front of the address and heard Swanson chuckle softly behind him. "You're right about the neighborhood. There are a lot of rich widows around here. I'm having dinner with one, as a matter of fact."

Cooper found nothing to say.

Swanson opened the door. "She may be a lousy tipper. But she has other virtues. I can testify to that."

"Have a wonderful evening," said Cooper.

"Thanks," said Swanson. "I plan to."

◆

"He's hiding out in style," said Turk. "You gotta have money to live around here." He took the car around a gentle curve, admiring the expensively tended lawns sweeping up to discreetly shielded houses on either side, with the sere brown mountains rising behind.

Ferocious Dick grunted. Turk had learned to read his grunts; this one was the Grunt of Class Envy. Ferocious Dick stared out the window, squinting a little into the sun. He looked, as always, vaguely mistrustful.

"Hey, Ferocious. This is the American Dream. You could wind up in a house like this someday." This time Ferocious Dick laughed, a low rasping sound that caused him to spread his lips and reveal crooked teeth while still looking out the window. He looks like a beaner Ernest Borgnine, thought Turk, glancing sideways. "I mean it, man. A few more years, you put away some more money, you can score one of these houses along here, live like a king. This is heaven, amigo."

Turk wasn't sure what the next grunt meant, but it was time to slow and look for the house anyway. The street curved back toward the distant ocean and a driveway took off to the right and wound up a slight rise. The address was nowhere to be seen but Turk recognized the house from the description and general location: a low rambling stucco palace set back from the street and shaded by trees. He turned into the driveway and rolled gently up to a massive double front door in fake Spanish style with a wrought-iron knocker. Wrought-iron grilles covered the windows and window boxes held flowers in riotous colors. He switched off the ignition.

"Go around the back," he said quietly, already gearing up. Ferocious Dick grunted his "Yes Boss" grunt and got out. Turk got out and closed the door quietly, looking for faces in front windows. He cast one glance at Ferocious Dick scuttling around the side of the house looking like an ape in a sport jacket, and then he mounted the terrace.

There was a doorbell, so evidently the knocker was just for show. Turk pressed the doorbell and then checked his reflection in the tall narrow window to the right of the door. He made sure the tie was straight, the hair still winched tightly back in the ponytail, no hairs out of place. Turk had once been told he was vain and had taken offense; he just liked to look good, especially for business.

The door was opened by a middle-aged woman in a gray uniform dress. She looked up at Turk a little warily and said, "Yes?"

"I'm here to see Mr. Tertzagian, please." He gave her his best Pepsodent smile, hands in the pockets of his white deck pants, rocking easily on his heels.

She looked surprised and a little confused for maybe two seconds, and then she pulled the door all the way open and stepped out of the way. "Come in," she said. "I'm no sure he can talk with you." She had a fairly heavy Spanish accent. She took him into a long tiled hallway that stretched to the back of the house, with a glimpse of green lawn through French windows. Two large leather suitcases with a suit carrier draped over them stood in the hallway. A stairway went up in a broad sweep to the left. "Wait here, please," the maid said, and went up the stairs.

Turk waited, listening hard and watching out the distant French windows. Somewhere in the back he heard a door open and close quietly. Upstairs he could hear the maid's voice and a low indecipherable reply.

When the maid came back downstairs she said, "He will be right down," carefully, as if it were a memorized line, and then she went down the hall and disappeared through an archway to the left. Turk waited, still listening hard. He looked at the suitcases and shook his head.

A man in a flowered shirt, predominantly red, came down the stairs. He was short and swarthy and did not look healthy. He had not shaved that day. He looked at Turk with a touch of belligerence. Turk smiled at him and said, "Mr. Tertzagian?"

"And you are?" When the man reached the bottom of the stairs, he stopped and put his hands on his hips. Turk looked him up and down, a little man with no chest and a pot belly.

Turk nodded at the suitcases. "Leaving town?"

The man stared at him. "Yes, I am. I'm very busy packing as a matter of fact, and I would appreciate it if you would state your business."

Turk smiled. "Oscar says hi."

The man's mouth came open and his eyes widened, just a little. His hands stayed right where they were. Turk could almost hear him thinking, stunned and then recovering a little, his mind concentrated wonderfully. "Oscar," the man said.

"He didn't want you to leave without saying good-bye."

The man's hands came up. "One phone call. Give me one phone call and I can make everything straight with Oscar." He was flailing and they both knew it; Turk just shook his head.

"Too late. Oscar doesn't want to hear anything you have to say." Turk took his left hand out of the trouser pocket and moved the tail of his jacket aside, just a little.

"It's not too late." Now the voice was starting to go. The knees weren't looking too steady either, and Turk decided to hurry it along, before the man tried to run or something and things got messy. He took his other hand out of his pocket and drew the Taurus from the holster under his left arm.

"Who told you?" The eyes were wide now and the words came out in a bleat.

"Your girlfriend," said Turk, grinning. "You sure know how to pick 'em."

"No. Janet?" Shock and indignation made him drop his hands a little, and Turk shot him while he was still thinking about Janet. He shot him three times, a nice little group right where the heart would be, aiming one-handed like Dirty Harry. The range was only eight feet or so, and the shots kicked the man back to the foot of the stairs, where he fell hard against the marble steps and gasped once with his eyes squeezed shut, his hands not doing much of anything. Turk watched him for a second or two and then holstered the gun and went down the hall.

He found the maid in the kitchen, with Ferocious Dick holding her up by the wrists. Her face was gray and she was sagging at the knees and she started crying when she saw Turk come into the kitchen. Ferocious Dick looked Turk in the eye.

Turk looked back and said, "Your call, partner, but she can identify us." The woman turned her face to Ferocious Dick's and started speaking Spanish at him, having trouble getting the words out. Turk couldn't understand a thing and he watched Ferocious Dick's face as he looked down at her, pulling gently against the tug of her arms as she swayed. Ferocious Dick could have been watching TV for all Turk could read there. Ferocious Dick gave him another quick look and shifted his grip, taking one of the woman's elbows in his big rough hand and pulling her upright. He said something to her in Spanish and Turk realized why the son of a bitch so seldom talked; his voice had been nearly destroyed by whatever had left the scar on his throat. Ferocious Dick's voice sounded like a mean dog on a bad day.

The woman's face firmed a bit and she got steady on her feet; she looked at Turk again and there was hope in her eyes. Ferocious Dick gave her a little shove toward the back door and she didn't look back. She took off for the door, her shoes going tap-tap-tap on the tiles. Ferocious Dick gave her three steps and then shot her in the back of the head, a beautiful snap shot on a quick draw. She pitched forward and crashed against the frame of the open back door, sliding to the floor with her head resting awkwardly against the wall, neck at an uncomfortable-looking angle. Turk shook his head in admiration. "You're a menace to society, Ferocious," he said. Ferocious Dick just grunted and put away the gun.

They stopped at a convenience store in Malibu that had a pay phone outside. Ferocious Dick waited in the car while Turk used the phone. When he came back to the car he said, "You're going to have enough money for that house before you know it. Oscar's having a bad week, and we've got more business."

Ferocious Dick grunted his question grunt and Turk smiled and said, "In Chicago."

5

DEXTER SAT IN the Mercedes and watched the rats. They had come creeping out of hiding within a minute or two of his turning off the engine, to resume their frenetic, wary foraging through the litter along the base of the abandoned factory, keeping to the shade. Dexter started counting them and gave up at ten, unsure whether he was counting the same ones twice. Then he started looking for an unbroken window in the five-story facade of the factory. He couldn't find one; every damn window had been punched out, a couple of hundred of them. From time to time he checked his mirrors or craned over his shoulder, still uneasy about being watched even though he'd checked the place out, used it before, and knew nobody could see this patch of dead ground between the old factory and the vast railroad yards south of Roosevelt Road unless they hiked or drove in past the *No Trespassing* signs.

Dexter had taken to watching the rats again when he heard the car; he watched it come down the gravel track in his rear view mirror, recognizing Antone's bright red Dodge Viper. He sat in the car and watched as the Viper came to a stop and four people got out: Antone, Spiky, Mau-Mau and Chessandra. Mau-Mau had Chessandra by the arm, hauling her out of the car and dragging her forward over the rough ground, keeping her from falling when she stumbled over the chunks of concrete and pieces of old iron. Chessandra's face looked as if she were dead already.

Dexter pressed a button and the window went down, letting in a breath of hot wet air. The quartet arranged itself in a semi-circle at the driver's side of the Mercedes, Spiky and Mau-Mau bracketing Chessandra. Antone said, "Special delivery. This the bitch you ordered?"

Dexter looked at Chessandra. When he made eye contact her eyes came a little bit alive for the first time, but she didn't say anything. Dexter asked Antone, "Any trouble finding her?"

"Not after we found her mama. Thought we was goin' have some trouble with her, till Spiky took the baby and held it out the window." Dexter looked at Spiky and saw his mean yellow face split by a wide grin. "Never seen a woman talk so fast."

Dexter nodded and looked back at Chessandra. Her eyes were wide, and he could see her chest heaving under the bright red T-shirt. "Well, how about it?" he said.

It took her a few seconds to get her breath, and then she said, "It wasn't my fault. He done tricked me."

"Who done tricked you?"

"Rolando. He musta had the whole thing planned out, just to get the moncy."

"Who the fuck is Rolando?"

"Just a friend of mine." Chessandra looked a little stronger now, getting her voice back.

"A friend, huh?"

"I thought he was a friend. Dexter, I'm sorry, it was a bad mistake."

"You was havin' a little fun, huh? You was lettin' him up there to get some, huh?"

"No. He was just a friend, somebody I knew from back on the South Side. We would just run into each other, around the neighborhood."

"So how the fuck did he find out about the money?" She didn't answer. "How the fuck he get up there to take it?" Chessandra sagged, closing her eyes briefly. "You let him up there, didn't you? You told him about the money, huh?"

"It was a mistake, Dexter. I swear to God. It was a bad, bad mistake and I'm sorry for it. I never meant for nothin' to happen." Her voice was fading and the tears were coming.

"Tell me about him," said Dexter.

Chessandra wiped tears away with the back of a hand. "His name's Rolando Brown. He lives on Winthrop someplace, I don't know where. He got a sister lives on Kenmore, not too far from me. Her name's Brown too, LaKeesha Brown. Dexter, please. I didn't mean no harm." She was crying full out now, sagging a bit. Spiky and Mau-Mau jerked her upright.

Dexter reached for the ignition and started the engine. He looked at Antone.

"That all?" said Antone.

"That's all," said Dexter. "I don't want to see this bitch no more, don't want to hear nothin' about her." He pressed the button and the window eased up. He put the Mercedes in gear and turned on the air conditioning. He could barely hear Chessandra's cries as he headed up the gravel track.

◆

Cooper waited at the wheel of the Mercedes, watching. In front of the very tony Chestnut Street restaurant, Regis Swanson stood, modeling a natty gray pinstripe suit and emanating a smooth and practiced bonhomie. The trio of middle-aged men who stood with him were swaying ever so slightly with the effects of the long lunch and seemed very pleased with life on earth. Swanson dispensed heartfelt smiles, a companionable clap on the shoulder, and three firm manly handshakes. Then he took his leave with infinite reluctance and made for the car, laughing over his shoulder at a final exquisite joke. His three companions began a crestfallen shuffling, left to shift for themselves in the post-lunch world.

"Get me out of sight fast, so I can turn off the charm," said Swanson as Cooper started the engine. He gave a final wave out the window as the Mercedes pulled away from the curb.

"Your face getting tired, is it?" said Cooper.

Swanson laughed. "It's damn hard work. Even over a fifty-dollar lunch."

"I bet. Who were these guys?"

"These guys were from Teacher's Annuity."

"Funny, they look a little too prosperous to be teachers."

"Don't they? No, these are the people who play with the teachers' money."

Cooper turned onto Michigan Avenue. "They're financing a building?"

"It might take another lunch or two, but they'll finance it, yes."

"Huh. What ever happened to banks?"

"Banks? Oh, I still go to the bank for construction loans. But if you want to put up a big building, you've got to get the big institutional investors in on it. Aetna, Westinghouse Credit, Teacher's Annuity, people like that. They've got the money and they're in it for the long haul, which is what you need."

"So you've got a big one in the works, huh?"

"I've always got a big one in the works."

Cooper drove for a while and then said, "Can I ask a possibly indiscreet question? As part of my education?"

"If you don't mind a possibly evasive answer."

"How much of this town do you own?"

Swanson's laugh was sudden and hearty and sounded genuine. "Not as much as I'd like to," he said. He waited until Cooper had negotiated a pick-and-roll between two buses and said, "Seriously. There are maybe fifty important developers in Chicago. I'm one of them. I've been successful, no complaints. I've put up six major buildings in the downtown area in addition to lesser things. But there's a lot of major buildings in this town. Besides, I don't own too many buildings outright. Things have changed. Nowadays a developer sets up joint ventures with people like Teacher's. They get most of the equity, we take a fee—some percentage of construction costs plus management fees. We might have a bit of a stake, ten or twenty percent, which is still pretty nice to have, but that's a far cry from owning the town. Nobody owns this town."

Cooper grunted, watching the traffic. "That's reassuring, I guess. You're not worried about the real estate glut, I take it?"

"Glut's a relative term. Things are slowing down, some people are overextended, yes. But we're a hell of a lot better off than, say, Houston. Chicago's got the kind of broad-based economy where there's always something going on, something moving, somebody needing something. All you have to do is keep your ear to the ground and figure out what it is. And I'm pretty good at that, finding that market niche."

Cooper accelerated smoothly down the long slope of Michigan Avenue, heading south from the river. He shook his head. "I chew nails over buying a used car. How does it feel to commit millions to a project?"

It took Swanson a moment to answer. "You were in the Airborne, I understand."

"That's right."

"Then you know how it feels. It feels like jumping out of an airplane."

Cooper mused, jockeying over a lane to avoid getting stuck behind a delivery truck. "I can see how you might enjoy the sensation. But only if you're damn sure of the parachute."

"Never failed me yet," said Swanson.

◆

"Red fucking handed," said Patrick McCone bitterly. "They had the girl's jewelry in the car with them and a .38 that had just been fired." McCone was fiftyish and gray, sagging from the fatigue of twenty years of police work, most of it on the West Side. He was dressed as all tactical unit officers dress, like an ordinary working-class guy on his way to the plant or the shop, except for the revolver at his waist. He had circles under his eyes that gave him a haunted look.

"But no girl," said Detective Jeremy Williams, who was young, black and angry.

"Not yet. But they'll tell us. We got 'em just sitting in there thinking now, trying hard not to say anything to each other. They'll tell us where she is and who pulled the trigger."

Williams shook his head and reached for his coffee. "How'd you track 'em?"

"Somebody called it in. A sister, mother maybe. Apparently they'd gone looking for the girl at her mother's place, forced her to tell 'em where she was. The lady on the phone was damn near incoherent, but somebody had gotten Antone's license number. And we know Antone. Boy, do we know Antone."

"Antone that works for Dexter D.?"

"That's the one. We've been wanting Antone's hide for a long time. No I-bond bullshit this time. I don't care how full the fucking jail is, he's a keeper this time. I just wish we'd found 'em half an hour sooner. I don't think we missed it by much. Thirty minutes, man. I'd give a lot for those thirty minutes." McCone was seeing something a long way off through a cinder block wall.

Williams grunted. "Who was the girl?"

McCone shook his head, tight-lipped. "Black girl from up on the North Side, nobody we ever heard of. God knows what Dexter's into up there."

"Maybe it was just these guys, having fun."

"No. You gotta know Dexter's behind it. Those three stooges in there don't just pull shit like this on their own. This was business.

We're looking for Dexter right now, and we're going to have a heart to heart with him this time, I can tell you."

Williams shook his head. "I gotta roll." He slapped McCone on the arm. "Good work, Pops."

McCone drank more coffee, from sheer muscular reflex. The coffee tasted like fuel oil. He stared out over the squad room, vacantly. "Not good enough, man. One half-hour sooner, that's all it woulda took. Thirty short minutes."

◆

Jasper sank onto his chair. "What'd they come up with?"

Toni handed him the papers.

"It checks out, like our friend on the phone said. A guy named Nate Swanson is indeed the owner of a place called the Blue Angel, up on Clark Street."

"They run him?"

"One misdemeanor possession eight years ago. He was just a kid. He's twenty-four now."

"He's twenty-four years old and he owns a nightclub?" Jasper looked up from the papers. "That just piques my curiosity all to hell."

"Yeah, mine too."

"How long has he owned it?"

"About two months."

Jasper smiled. "I like this guy."

"He has that certain something, doesn't he?"

"He's beautiful." Jasper stared out across the office, tapping a finger on the desk. "I want this guy."

The phone on Jasper's desk rang. He picked it up and said his name. He listened for a while, said "Yeah" a couple of times, and then smiled and said, "Speak of the devil." He listened and said, "You want me to go over there?" He got an answer, said OK and hung up. "Check this out," he said to Toni, his hand still resting on the phone. "The cops out on the West Side pulled in Dexter D. this afternoon."

"What for? Don't tell me they have a case."

"No, some people of his pulled some shit today and they're trying to find out what's going on. A cop named Ryan over at Harrison District called Snodgrass to let him know, since they've been working with the task force out there."

"Are they inviting us to sit in?"

"Snodgrass says they promised us a good seat and some popcorn."

◆

Cooper dropped Swanson at the Blue Angel and then had to earn his pay; the club was just up the street from Wrigley Field and the game was just about over. There were cops everywhere and they were determined to keep him moving. Circling the block was a twenty-minute proposition and when Cooper fought his way back around to the marqueed entrance of the old theater, Swanson was standing there with Nate, jostled by a procession of sunburned fat people in Cub caps. Swanson looked impatient; Nate looked relaxed and nicely turned out in a Hawaiian shirt with lurid sunsets on dark blue oceans. He grinned at Cooper as his father climbed into the car and then went back inside the club.

"Sorry," said Cooper. "Ball game."

"Could have timed the visit a little better, I guess," said Swanson, settling onto the back seat. "Who won?"

"The bad guys. Three runs in the top of the ninth."

"These people don't look that unhappy."

Cooper smiled. "You see ninety losses year after year, you learn to take it philosophically."

Swanson was silent while Cooper maneuvered back into the creeping traffic. When they were finally moving east on Irving toward the Drive, Swanson said, "Have you ever heard of a band called Final Solution?"

"Don't think so. What, a rock band?"

"Yeah. Nate's big triumph. He's signed them to play at the club next month. Apparently they're some hotshot East Coast outfit. He showed me their album. The first song is called 'Public Enema Number One.'"

Cooper shook his head and said, "Different generation."

"I suppose. Nate says he'll be in the black with two more months like the last one."

"There's money there. A guy I used to work for in Los Angeles had made a pile of cash as a rock impresario before he got into movies."

"Wonderful. When he makes a million I can brag about my son the impresario. You know, the man who brought the Final Solution to Chicago."

"It has a real ring to it, doesn't it?"

"I guess he's a big boy. You launch them out there and have to watch them swim. I just hope he's right about the prospects, because

I don't want him to fail. He fails at this, I don't know what'll happen to him. I've told him I'm not going to bail him out, and it'll be rough if I have to stick to my guns."

"He'll land on his feet."

"Maybe. When they're little you worry because they're vulnerable. When they're big you worry because you're vulnerable, to all the stunts they pull. It's not family honor exactly, it's . . . it's personal. You like to think you've done a good job. Like putting up a good sound working building. Except buildings don't have minds of their own."

"Yeah, well, that's what lets you off the hook. When you get right down to it, he's going to do what he wants."

After a moment Swanson said, "He always has."

◆

"He's just sitting in there thinking," said Francis Ryan, jerking a thumb toward the closed interrogation room. "As far as he's capable of it, anyway." Ryan was a wise and fierce old cop who carried white hair on a big square head, twenty pounds too much around his middle and an attitude a mile wide. Jasper was on easy terms with him, but Toni had had to work a little to maintain position; the look Ryan had given her when she walked in with Jasper said he still wasn't sure women belonged in a squad room.

"What's he got to say for himself?" said Jasper.

"He's doing his Sergeant Schultz thing. He knows nothing. Those three apes were off on their own, he never heard of the girl, he was just minding his own business, you know. Dexter's a bewildered innocent. He does that real well."

"What about the three apes?"

"They're not going to last much longer. Antone's about ready to kill the other two. We'll leave them in there a while longer, let the pot stew a little more. We'll have a confession by midnight. If we're real lucky one of them might implicate Dexter, but I'm not holding my breath. He's pretty good at inspiring loyalty."

Jasper smiled a grim smile and said, "I don't suppose there's any chance it was just those three having fun or something."

"No. Dexter sent 'em. They looked all over Stateway Gardens to find the girl's mother, then went after the girl. This was a hit, and Dexter ordered it. You got any idea why?"

Jasper looked at Toni, who blinked back for a while. Jasper looked abstracted for a few seconds and then said, "Not right off the top of my head. But I can think of a few questions I'd love to ask him. If you can work them in."

"I think maybe we can make a little room," said Ryan, smiling.

◆

The room smelled, maybe permanently, of cigarette ashes and sweat; under the fluorescent light Dexter's skin was a dark and unhealthy gray. When Ryan came back into the room, Dexter was slouching on the chair, a big muscular fat man with a flattop, a stylized *D* shaved on the sides of his head, three gold earrings in his left ear. He looked bored.

Ryan went to the desk along the wall, and slid onto it, legs dangling, facing Dexter. He set down a mug of coffee on the desk at his side. A young and belligerent-looking detective came in after him and sat on a chair in the corner behind Dexter. He had a ballpoint pen in his hand and he began clicking the tip in and out, in and out. It made a fair amount of noise in the quiet room. Ryan looked at Dexter and shook his head.

"I've been thinking about it, Dexter," he said. "And I guess it makes sense, everything you said." Dexter stared back at him with contempt. Ryan sighed extravagantly and said, "It was just boys having fun. Yeah, I can understand that. Just kids having a good time. Doesn't surprise me a bit. Not even the fact that they looked all over for this one lady, forced her to tell them where her daughter was, went to grab the daughter and then took her someplace and killed her. Like you said, maybe they were just particular. Makes perfect sense to me now."

Dexter gave no sign that he was sentient. After a few seconds he blinked.

Ryan's look hardened. "Come on, Dexter. These guys have to get your permission to go take a shit."

Dexter closed his eyes and exhaled heavily through his nose, subsiding lower on the chair.

"Tell me one thing," said Ryan. "Why was the daughter hiding? Her mother says Chessandra made her promise not to tell anyone she was back on the South Side. Who was she hiding from?"

The silence stretched on, the faint clicking of the pen just audible, until Dexter said, "How the fuck should I know?"

Ryan assumed a look of genuine puzzled curiosity. "She complain about your bad breath or something? You finally get tired of her, is that it?"

Dexter looked at his watch and shook his head. "I never heard of her, never laid eyes on her. You wastin' my time and yours. You got the wrong man."

"You're the wrong man, huh?" Ryan sighed, picked up the coffee mug, and took a drink. He sat looking into the mug, frowning like a man who has just found a cockroach the hard way. "OK, I believe you, Dexter. I believe everything you say. I believe everything you've told me all through the years. I believe your reputation out here is a case of mistaken identity. I believe we've spent thousands of man-hours tracking the wrong guy. I believe that everything everybody between Roosevelt Road and North Avenue tells me about you is all horseshit. I believe you're just an unemployed carpenter like you say, and I believe that unemployed carpenters can afford a car like the one you drive. I believe all that, Dexter, because you have an honest face. But I'll tell you one thing I don't believe." Ryan looked up from the mug, fixing Dexter with a pair of pale blue eyes. "I don't believe you'll let the federal government put you in prison for narcotics trafficking and let Nate Swanson go on walking around outside."

There was a single frozen instant in which Ryan knew he had gotten Dexter's attention. The detective felt it and stopped clicking the pen. Dexter closed his eyes, slowly, and then re-opened them. "Who?" he said.

"Your pal Nate Swanson. The guy who's been showing off the million dollars he got from you."

There was a long silence. Dexter blinked several times while Ryan watched him. Finally Dexter said, "Never heard of him."

Ryan shook his head. "Man, this coffee was bad when it was hot, and being cold doesn't improve it. I'm gonna go look for some more."

Out in the office, Ryan said, "He knows him. He jumped like I stuck him with a knife."

Jasper nodded. "Leave the knife in for a while?"

"Yeah. Let him think a little, think about who we have and what we know. Something will give. When he calls for his lawyer, it means we've got his ass."

Jasper looked at Toni and smiled. "And the rest of him with it."

◆

"The old man was here this afternoon," said Nate.

"Your father?" said Liz, poking through the sweet and sour pork with her chopsticks.

"Yeah." Nate took a pull on his beer. "He's afraid he's going to lose his money."

"Is there any danger of that?"

"Nah. We'll be making money hand over fist soon." Nate shoveled more rice out of the carton onto his plate and flashed a smile across the old battered desk. Liz had big dark eyes and close-cropped brown hair; even with a smear of translucent sauce on her lower lip she was beautiful.

"You're the confident type, aren't you?" Liz wiped at her lip with a long graceful finger. "I noticed that right away."

Nate was still grinning. "Who was that guy you were with, anyway?"

"Just somebody to go to a party with. I'm sure he found his own way home."

Nate looked across the desk at Liz and felt that thrill; he loved the early stages of a new fling, the hunger, the haste. Nothing like a quick replacement after a rough break-up.

"So what'd your father think of the place?" Liz said.

Nate frowned at his plate. "All he could talk about was the improvements that need to be made. He said he'd never have let the place open."

"Sounds like a dad kind of thing to say."

"He's an old bastard."

"You don't get along, huh?"

"We get along OK, on a day-to-day basis. He's just an old bastard." Nate stared out the filthy window of the office at the brick fronts across Clark Street, bathed in the westering light. "He doesn't approve of me. I'm a fuckup."

"He approved of you enough to set you up with this place."

"He's daring me to fuck it up, see?"

"Come on. That much money on a dare?"

"He can afford to lose it. But he's not going to. I'm going to build the best music club in the city and then I'm going to rub that old bastard's nose in it."

"Make him proud of you, huh?"

Nate shrugged. "I don't give a damn whether he's proud or not. All he understands is money. I'm going to make a lot of it, just to see the look on his face. Shock him, that's all I want."

"Bullshit." Liz was smiling.

Nate chewed for a while, watching her across the desk. "Know what I really want from my old man?"

"What?"

Nate looked at her for a second or two, maybe reconsidering. Quietly he said, "Someday I want to make him cry, the way he made me cry when he left my mother. I don't care how I do it—shame, envy, I'll even take a generous rush of pride if he's got it in him. But someday I want to see that old bastard cry."

◆

Dexter had Cleotis drop him at the house on Keeler, figuring it was least likely to have cops sitting outside the door. He had been silent all the way from the station, thinking hard of ways to save his business and maybe his life. Katzenbaum the lawyer had brushed something from the lapel of his suit and told him, "They got nothing on you, not a fucking thing," but Dexter had not found him totally reassuring. Katzenbaum had then gone off to an expensive dinner, while Dexter had had to call Cleotis to get home.

Dexter let himself into the apartment and then re-did the six locks on the door. He wanted to shower and change clothes, he wanted something to eat, he wanted to sleep, and he couldn't decide what order he wanted them in. It wasn't until all the locks were done up and he was heading down the hall that Dexter wondered why the apartment was cool; it was still eighty degrees outside and there hadn't been anybody here to turn on the air conditioning. When he walked into the living room Dexter froze and just stared at the man in the armchair.

"They let you go, huh?" said the man. He sat there by the window in the late evening light like he owned the place, hands clasped on his belly, legs crossed on the ottoman. He was a good-looking white man in a light gray sports jacket over a black T-shirt, beige pants and white deck shoes. His hair was pulled back tight in a ponytail.

"What the fuck?" said Dexter.

"Hey, that's my line," the man said. "What the fuck." He spread his hands in a gesture of appeal.

Dexter stared for maybe five more seconds and then said, "OK. You from L.A., right?"

"Good guess, Dexter. You're sharp today. I hope the cops were polite, a man of your stature and all?"

Dexter moved carefully over to the couch. He could feel thin ice cracking beneath his feet. How in the hell you find this place?" he said, sinking onto the couch.

The man in the armchair clasped his hands again. "Don't forget, you work for us." Dexter just stared. "And your lawyer works for us, too."

Dexter nodded, stupidly, starting to feel walls closing in. "Uh-huh." He was thinking, one guy? If there's just one guy there's a chance.

"So, Dexter." The man smiled, a bright friendly grin. "We were wondering about this million dollars. The people in L.A. take that kind of thing very seriously." The grin faded.

Dexter pointed a big meaty finger at him. "I was ripped off. I was set up and sold out. By that bitch."

The man shook his head. "Man, if I had a nickel for every time I've heard that one. That's what all this was about today?"

"Yeah. But she didn't have the money anyway. She just set me up."

"Now that's unreal, man. I mean, we're talking about a fairly considerable sum here, aren't we, Dexter?"

"Listen to me. She set me up, with a dude she was cheatin' on me with, name of Rolando Brown. Except he don't have it either, 'cause he'd dead, I found out. Somebody shot him, probably his partner, who's gotta have the money. Got to. And I know who he is."

The man in the armchair blinked. "I'm listening."

Dexter wiped sweat from his upper lip, aware he was talking for his life. "OK, now you ain't gonna believe it, but the cops give me the name, when they was questioning me."

"What do you mean?

"I mean they give me the name. They go on and on about Antone and them, but I'm saying nothin', I don't know shit, they was just off on their own, and the cops see they ain't gettin' nothin' that way. So the dude goes out of the room for a while, leaves me sittin'. Then he comes back and suddenly he's axin' me about this dude I never heard of. You know how they work. They don't never ask a question they don't already know the answer to."

"Yeah, I know how they work."

"So he says he can't believe I'm gonna let the Feds put me in prison and let this motherfucker go on walkin' around outside. And he says the man been talkin' about a million dollars he got from me." Dexter paused, but the man with the ponytail just looked at him. "And I'm still sayin' nothin', except now I know this is the man that ripped me off. Got to be. What musta happened is, the motherfucker set me up with this Rolando, shot him for his share, and then somebody else dropped a dime on his ass. Now the cops after him, too. But we got time, 'cause they don't do nothin' in a hurry."

The man in the armchair blinked at him for a while. "This man got a name?"

"Nate Swanson."

The room was silent for a moment. Dexter was starting to think maybe he'd talked fast enough and smart enough. The man in the armchair said the name slowly, distinctly: "Nate Swanson."

"See how it worked?" said Dexter. "Him and Rolando got to Chessandra, and she let 'em get at the money. Then this Swanson shot Rolando, and then somebody else, maybe another partner, didn't like his cut and picked up the phone on Swanson."

"So, who is this Swanson? Ever heard of him?"

"No. But he owns a nightclub. Katzenbaum heard of him."

"What's the name of the club?"

"I don't know. But it's on the North Side, Katzenbaum thought. Can't be too hard to find out. We talking about a few telephone calls."

The man in the armchair sighed and shook his head. He ran a hand back over his smoothed-down hair. "Pretty good detective work, Dexter. So, what do you suggest?"

Dexter stared; he couldn't believe the man was asking him for his opinion. After a couple of seconds he said, "I suggest we go find the motherfucker."

"I'm glad you said 'we,' Dexter. I really am. 'Cause I'm afraid the folks in L.A. are gonna insist that I keep you on a pretty tight leash."

"That's cool, that's cool. You the boss."

The man in the armchair nodded. "That's the spirit."

Dexter felt a little easier suddenly, thinking he had a chance. "Listen. Lemme go piss, 'cause I'm about to bust wide open. After that I'm ready to go."

The man shrugged. "So go piss."

"Be right back." Dexter hauled himself up off the couch and left the room. He went down the hall toward the back. Instead of turning left into the bathroom, he turned right into the bedroom and walked quickly, not bothering to tiptoe, to an armoire that stood against the far wall. He reached up on top of the armoire and brought down a TEC-9 with a magazine in place. He put his hand on the bolt handle, ready to rack it, but decided to wait until the last second so as not to give it away by the sound. He made for the door.

He swung out into the hall and stopped with a jolt at the sight of an ugly dark little man that looked like a bulldog. He had come out of nowhere, the kitchen or the bathroom maybe, and was pointing a revolver the size of a howitzer at Dexter's chest. Dexter twitched the muzzle of the gun upward but stopped, knowing he didn't have time. The little dark man had absolutely no expression on his face.

Dexter froze, thought for a second and said, "Hey, let's talk."

The man with the ponytail moved into the hall, standing in the golden evening light from the living room, hands in his pockets. "Too late to talk, Dexter."

Dexter whipped the TEC-9 upward but never even got the round chambered; as he lay on the floor with his ears ringing and his chest hurting, hurting bad, so bad, the last thing he saw was the little ugly man leaning down for the coup de grace. "Mama," said Dexter, feebly.

6

"OK," SAID JASPER. We've gotten a good start on this guy. You know who this kid is?"

"Who?" said Toni, a bit bleary-eyed but coming to life under the reviving influence of coffee. She, Jasper, Snodgrass and four other agents were ranged around the table.

"This is the son of Regis Swanson."

"Who?"

"Regis Swanson is a big-time real estate developer here in town. The man who put up the Michigan Tower, a bunch of other buildings. We're talking about a very wealthy background here." Jasper paused. "A fucking rich kid, in other words. The kid has one misdemeanor possession bust, nothing else on his record. One thing to do is track down acquaintances, friends. Girlfriends, ex-girlfriends especially. Always a prime source." Jasper looked around the table; a couple of heads nodded.

"The big thing right now, of course, is to look at the money situation. The son's on all the licenses for the club but the building belongs to his father."

There was a silence. "Which maybe means nothing," said Snodgrass.

"Maybe," said Jasper. "But if the family's mixed up in it, fur is going to fly."

Snodgrass shrugged. "It's something to look for. If there's something there, it could be the son's own thing."

"Hey. A rock music club? If I wanted to run a whole bunch of cash through the washer, I can't think of a better place to do it. And a really rich daddy would make things a whole lot easier. At the very least there's got to be some willful blindness there. If Dad owns the fucking building, hey."

"We'll see. Right now we're looking at this as an extension of the task force work on Dexter D. and the Disciples."

"Fine." Jasper's look lingered for a moment on Snodgrass, impassive at the end of the table. "Now. Mike, you get the financial stuff, the bank stuff, TRW, all that, 'cause you have the soul of an accountant." Jasper paused for the puffs of laughter. "For now we'll go with administrative subpoenas. Toni and I'll take care of that today. Phone records, MUDDs and tolls, Jack, I thought I'd put you on that to start because I know how much you love it."

"Thanks a bunch."

"My pleasure. As for the surveillance, I want to get a schedule worked up before we leave here." Jasper looked around the table with a wicked glint in his eye. "I don't know about you, but I'm looking forward to this one. I don't get to mix with high society much."

From the end of the table Snodgrass said, "I don't need to remind you that this all rests on an anonymous tip, do I?"

Jasper looked at him and said, "I've been doing this for fifteen years, Doug."

"So you know how it goes."

"Oh yeah," said Jasper. "I know how it goes."

◆

McTeague parked the car by a hydrant; he was past worrying about things like that. He walked down the block to the courtyard building at the corner. Three stories of dark red brick rose in a U shape around a strip of grass with tired-looking flowers in the middle. Blocking the way to this Eden was a massive brick and concrete gatehouse, a strange conceit on a block of solid and seviceable apartment complexes. It sheltered an iron gate and a speaker above a row of pushbuttons with black plastic labels beside them. McTeague looked at the gate for a moment and thought that leaning down to yell into a speaker was a poor approach.

He went back down the block to the driveway of the equally imposing apartment building next door and turned into it. At the back of the building was a row of garages. A chain-link fence separated the driveway from the back steps of the apartments in the courtyard building. McTeague didn't bother to look around; he just went for the fence. He got over it without too much difficulty and dropped onto the walk on the other side. He made for the back steps of her apartment.

She lived on the third floor, and it was a long way up in the heat.

McTeague paused on the landing to pant a little and wipe sweat from his hairline. He saw that the back door of her place was open, only the screen hooked shut for security. He leaned on the bell.

She came into the kitchen tentatively, wondering. When she saw him she stopped and folded her arms. "Hi," he said.

"Well," she said, standing hipshot. "Look who's back." She was dressed in a cool white cotton dress that crawled over her hip and dived straight for the floor but ran out just below her knee, showing a long smooth shin. McTeague could see her breasts pushed together by her folded arms, just the beginning of the swelling showing above the low neckline of the dress. Her hair was the color of honey, shoulder length but hooked behind her ears, very slightly matted with sweat at the temples. The fierce eyes looked out from under the straight dark brows, the lower lip swelled just a little too perfectly for a man's peace of mind. Seeing her again McTeague had the same stir in the gut he'd felt when Rolando had told him about the money.

"I heard you were unattached," he said.

She was looking at him from just the other side of the screen, two feet away. Her arms rose and fell just perceptibly with her breathing. "I thought you'd dropped off the edge of the earth."

McTeague smiled. "I been busy. Can I come in?"

Her look was cool. "What if I told you I had a friend here?"

"I'd want to meet her."

She shook her head, giving up. She flicked the hook out of the eye and turned her back on him, padding on bare feet back through the kitchen. McTeague came in and followed her through the dining room and up the long hall to the living room, watching her haunches work under the thin cotton.

She was heading for the balcony when McTeague put a hand on her arm, stopping her. She half turned and watched as he drew the little white box out of his shirt pocket. "I brought you something," he said. She kept the cool distant look on her face as she took the box and lifted the lid. She looked at what lay inside and her eyes flicked back to his. "It's from Egypt," he said. "It's solid gold."

She looked skeptical, but she seemed to heft the box, feeling its weight. When she looked back at him she looked less skeptical; she looked alert. She replaced the lid. "I'm not for sale," she said.

"That's a gift," said McTeague. "If you don't want it, you can give it to one of your poor relations."

There was a fan going in the front window, stirring the heavy air.

It was the only sound. She looked into McTeague's eyes for a few seconds. "This wasn't necessary. I just want you to know that," she said. McTeague reached up slowly and put his hand on the back of her neck, fingers buried in the honey-blond hair. He pulled her face toward his and caught that perfect lip gently between his upper teeth and lower lip, then put his tongue out to meet hers, just for a moment.

"You're flying first class from now on," he said, and kissed her again, finding her hip with his free hand.

She drew back enough to say, "When do we leave?"

"Now," said McTeague. The box dropped to the floor.

◆

"Hey, check it out. You like baseball, Ferocious?" Turk braked to a stop at the wave of a cop's hand. The street swarmed with pedestrians and lines were forming at the gates of the ball park that loomed above the intersection. Turk pointed at the big red sign on the facade of the ball park. "That's where the Cubs play. Worst team in the history of baseball."

Ferocious Dick grunted, looking at the sign.

"They play baseball down there where you're from?" said Turk. Ferocious Dick gave his "yes" grunt. "I played Little League when I was a kid," said Turk. "My stepfather forced me to. First game, I got picked off first with the old hidden ball trick. My old man screamed at me all the way home. Next day, I waited for the kid who did it, the first baseman, you know? And I beat the shit out of him, I mean stomped him. They kicked me out of the league. My old man screamed at me again, but at least I didn't have to play baseball anymore."

When the cop waved them on, Turk went on north up Clark Street. "Look at all these damn people. OK, we gotta be getting close. There it is, look. Got a big marquee and everything. There we go, the Blue Angel, look at that." The traffic was slow enough that they got a good look at it as they cruised past, the old yellow brickwork with the chipped stone decoration, the sagging marquee with *FRI SAT FUNKY MONKEYS* spelled out in caps. "Good-sized place," said Turk.

He was silent all the way up to Irving, where he turned left, went half a block or so and turned into the parking lot of a Burger King. He pulled into a slot facing the street and put the car in park. "Lunchtime," he said.

When they were back in the car and well into the meal, napkins and greasy paper spread all over the seat, Turk said, "We got a busy afternoon ahead of us. Make a few phone calls, lie a little. Do a little scouting. You like rock music?"

Ferocious Dick grunted.

"Well, if we can swing it right, you won't have to actually hear any." Turk fed three french fries into his mouth. "I mean," he said with his mouth full, "why pay a cover charge if we don't have to?"

◆

Cooper dropped Swanson at the side door of the big house and took the Mercedes on around to the back. It was nearly five o'clock and the heat was easing a little, the sun starting to decline. Through the trees Cooper could see sails, brilliant white on deep blue, far out on the lake. Cooper was tired, his shirt was sticking to his back, and Diana would be waiting at home, another novelty of this uncommonly hot summer.

Since Cooper had gotten out of the cab and Diana fled waitressing, they had exchanged their lie-abed mornings for more conventional evenings together. Cooper still missed his mornings, but there was something to be said for these long unhurried slides into night, sitting out on the open back porch of the apartment with ice clicking gently against the side of a glass, walking slowly along the beach with the breeze starting to pick up and the water lapping at bare feet, falling asleep in Diana's arms in front of the TV in the early innings of a ball game from the West Coast. Cooper had decided he could live like this, at least until fall.

First, however, there was the twenty-minute drive back into the city. Cooper parked the Mercedes in the middle stall of the garage, closed the door and headed for the old Mustang tucked out of sight around the end of the garage.

He wasn't going to get the Mustang out without help; somebody had parked a snappy little Honda CRX directly behind it, blocking it in. Cooper turned back toward the house and was halfway to the terrace when the sliding glass doors opened and Nate Swanson came out, followed by a vision of big dark eyes and long bare legs. The young woman had hair cut like a boy's, but she was unmistakably female in a form-hugging T-shirt and khaki shorts that flared just below her hips. Nate caught sight of Cooper and gave him a nod and a grin, and he and the girl skipped down the steps off the terrace, heading for the garage.

"That Honda wouldn't belong to one of you, would it?" said Cooper, cocking a thumb over his shoulder.

The young woman noticed him for the first time, stopped in her tracks and blinked, and said, "Oh, shit. I'm sorry." She came trotting across the gravel, trying to unzip her purse. "I didn't think anybody . . . I guess I just didn't think. I'm sorry." The smile she gave Cooper made him incline toward forgiveness.

Nate stood with him and watched as she backed the car out of the way. "What is it with women?" said Nate. "I got in a fight once because a girlfriend blocked a guy in. He had to be an asshole about it, and I wound up with a busted lip."

Cooper shrugged. "It happens."

"Still married?" said Nate by way of small talk.

"Hanging in there." Cooper nodded at the young woman behind the wheel and said, "She decided to take you back, huh?"

Nate's grin widened and he said, "Nah, this is a new one. Ain't she sweet?"

"That's a pretty girl," said Cooper.

The pretty girl had rolled down the window. "You want me to drive?" she called to Nate.

"No, I want to take the Jag. I got an image to uphold, know what I mean?" He took his leave of Cooper with a slap on the arm. "Just like the old man. Gotta go in style."

"Take care," said Cooper. The girl trotted past with another apology and Cooper smiled at her. He had the Mustang in gear before the Jag was out of the garage, but as he rolled past the front entrance of the house, the Jag overtook him with a squeal of tires and a honk before disappearing down the long tree-lined drive toward the road.

"He's a spoiled rich kid, all right," Cooper said to Diana an hour later, feet up on the porch rail. "But at least he's friendly. And he seems to have some energy. You get the feeling he could amount to something if somebody pushed him a bit. What he needs is a little adversity in his life."

Diana smiled her crooked smile, swirling ice cubes in a tall glass. "It's always fun to prescribe adversity for someone else, isn't it?"

"Hey," said Cooper. "As Friedrich Nietzsche said, or maybe it was Ray Nitschke, I forget—if it doesn't kill you, it makes you strong."

"It's the first part that's tricky, though, isn't it?"

"Sometimes," said Cooper with a survivor's smile. "Sometimes."

◆

"Looks like the ball game's over," Turk said. "Must have been a late game. It's after six. Pretty good timing, though. Lots of people around, everybody had to park in the next county, just like us. Try

and look like a ball fan. How about them fuckin' Cubbies, huh?"
Ferocious Dick grunted. To Turk he sounded peeved; perhaps his
feet hurt. The closest parking place Turk had found was on South-
port, five blocks west. They reached Clark Street and turned left,
falling in with the post-game trek to distant cars. A block south, the
old ball park was still disgorging people. Traffic crawled up Clark,
blue-shirted cops waving and snarling.

When they reached the Blue Angel, Turk ambled over to the big
glass doors without hesitation and pulled on the handle, which didn't
give. He put his face close to the glass and shaded his eyes, looking
inside. "Gotta be a doorbell or something. The man's expecting us."
He pounded on the glass with the heel of his hand, then turned to
scan the passing crowd with a benevolent smile on his face. Ferocious Dick stood at his side, watching sullenly. "They got a show
tonight, but these places get rolling late," said Turk. "I'm hoping
he'll be alone in there." He pounded on the door again, grabbed the
handle and rattled it. In a few seconds a man appeared and pushed
open the door.

He was tall and dressed in black jeans and a black T-shirt; his long
stringy hair and beard were black. He carried a ring of keys at his
belt. "Yeah?" he said.

"Mr. Swanson's expecting us," said Turk. "I called earlier. I manage a band. I got a tape for him to listen to."

The man in black stood aside, holding the door. "Your name
Tertzagian?"

"That's me. This is Mr. Lopez, my assistant." Turk and Ferocious
Dick followed the man to the back of the lobby, where a flight of
steps on either hand led up to a landing decorated with peeling gilt.

The man led them up the right-hand staircase. On the landing, paus-
ing in the door to the ballroom, he pointed up a second flight. "Up in
the hallway, go down to the end, the door on the right," he said.

"Thanks. Mind if we have a quick look in the room?" said Turk.

The man in black shrugged. "Be my guest." He held the door for
them.

The lights were on; the cavernous old ballroom was empty. A bar
had been built into the wall on the right. Up on the stage, framed by
the ornate decoration of the baroque twenties, were stacks of black
amplifiers and speakers and a rank of microphones. "Who's playing
tonight?" said Turk.

"Numb Nuts," said the man over his shoulder, heading for the
stage.

"Never heard of 'em," said Turk. "Thanks for the look." He drifted back toward the door, meeting Ferocious Dick's eyes for a second or two. Ferocious Dick nodded once.

Turk went on up the stairs and into the hallway, where he stood listening for a moment. He heard nothing. He went down the hall to the end and opened the door on the right without hesitation.

Inside was a shabby little office with a dirty window overlooking the street. There was a desk, a filing cabinet, a couch and two straight chairs. A man sat behind the desk with a tabloid-sized newspaper spread out on the desktop in front of him. On the couch lay a young woman with the best-looking legs Turk had seen all week, eating an apple and reading a paperback book. Both people looked up at Turk in surprise.

"Nate Swanson?" said Turk, his hand on the knob, flashing a smile.

"Yeah. You must be Mr. Tertzagian."

"The one and only. Nice of you to see me. I know you're a busy man." Turk closed the door behind him.

"Not particularly." Swanson stood up smiling and extended a hand across the desk. "Slack time right now, just waiting for nightfall. You know how the business goes."

"I know." Turk was looking at the beauty on the couch, who had swung her legs to the floor.

"This is Liz Webster, my ah, associate."

Turk smiled at her. "Don't get up. Just go right on with what you're doing. I'll just sit here and admire the view."

There was a second's pause and then Swanson said, waving at one of the chairs, "So, you're from L.A."

"Yep. And I got a band that's ready for the big breakout. We're getting a tour together that'll really put 'em on the map." Turk slouched on the chair, turned toward the couch, an arm hooked over the back.

"What's the band?"

"The Swede Killers. Taking L.A. by storm, let me tell you."

"The Swede Killers?" Swanson said carefully. "I thought I knew most of the L.A. bands. Never heard of the Swede Killers, though."

"You will," said Turk. "You will."

Somewhere in the building below there was a loud bang. Everybody in the office looked blank for a second. Swanson and the girl exchanged a look. "That sounded like a gunshot," said Swanson. He looked at Turk.

"By God, I think it was," said Turk.

7

WHEN COOPER CAME up the long drive in the relative cool of the early morning, the sun splintering through the trees into his eyes, he had to brake suddenly because the area in front of the house was filled with cars. There were three, and Cooper didn't recognize any of them. He took the Mustang carefully around to the rear.

A driveway filled with strange cars at six-fifty-four in the morning is not an entirely reassuring sign, and Cooper hesitated a moment after locking the Mustang. His instructions were to have the Mercedes waiting at the side entrance at seven o'clock, however, and he figured he would be told in due time if there was any change in plans.

He got the car out of the garage, pulled up at the entrance, and rang the bell as usual. He stood on the steps with his back to the door, listening to birds in the greenery, not thinking about much of anything in the last few seconds before his workday began.

When the door opened it wasn't Swanson who stood there; instead it was Felicidad, the Mexican cook. Cooper had never seen her answer the door and to him she looked at first glance like a frightened woman. To his surprise, she stood aside and said, "Come in, please."

He followed her through the sprawling house to Swanson's study; the door was open and she motioned Cooper in. Swanson sat at the desk, slumped in the swivel chair, chin resting on his right fist. He was wearing a green polo shirt and he looked ten years older than he had the day before. On the couch to the right was a short squat man in a rumpled white shirt with no tie who needed a shave. He was leaning forward with his elbows on his knees.

"Morning," said Swanson, his voice empty.

Cooper nodded, took in the scene and said, "What happened?"

Swanson closed his eyes and passed a hand over his face. "Nate's dead."

The man on the couch was looking at Swanson intently, not moving. Swanson opened his eyes and looked at Cooper. Cooper said, "I'm sorry." Swanson nodded, just perceptibly, and fixed his eyes somewhere far away. After two or three seconds Cooper walked to the armchair to the left of the desk and sat down. "How?" he said.

There was silence until the man on the couch said, "He was murdered. At the club. Somebody killed him, his girlfriend and a janitor."

Cooper took a deep breath. "Jesus." He waited for inspiration but none came. He had begun to wonder why he was there when Swanson swiveled in the chair with a faint squeak and looked him in the eye.

"Maybe it's you," said Swanson. "You were around the last time somebody in my family got killed, weren't you?"

Cooper went cold looking into Swanson's pale blue eyes. He took it for a moment and then stood up, already tracing his path to the outside door.

"I'm sorry," said Swanson. "It's been a hell of a night." The hand was passing over his face again. Cooper paused.

The man on the couch got up. He was bald, bullet-headed and getting heavy in his middle age. He came toward Cooper with his hands in his pockets, casting a concerned look at Swanson. "We had police here half the night. We had to go, ah . . . make the identification, we had phone calls to make, people to talk to. We didn't get any sleep. I'm Buzz Hayden, by the way." He held out his hand and Cooper shook it. The hand was plump and strong.

"I'm sorry," said Swanson again, recovering. He sounded and looked exhausted.

"You should go to bed," said Hayden.

"You think I could sleep?" Swanson's face was as empty as his voice.

"At least lie down. Get some rest." Cooper watched Hayden looking at Swanson and didn't need to be told that here were two best friends.

"No," said Swanson. "I need to keep moving or I'll lose it. Keep moving till I drop." He turned to Cooper. "That's your job today. Catch me when I drop."

Cooper nodded. "OK."

Swanson said to Hayden, "Tell him what happened. I can't."

Hayden scowled at him and said, "You want us to go somewhere else?"

"Just tell him."

Hayden turned to Cooper with a look of deep distaste. "It happened early in the evening sometime. Just before people started showing up to open the place, apparently. A bartender found the janitor and called the cops, the cops found . . . Nate and the girl, up in the office." Hayden paused with his mouth open, the look of disgust deepening. He closed his mouth and swallowed hard.

"What was it, robbery?" said Cooper.

"They don't know. There was a safe but it was intact and the bartender said Nate had cleared it the day before, taken receipts to the bank. They don't know anything at this point."

"They'd been shot," said Swanson, looking at something about a thousand yards beyond the wall of the study, somewhere out over the lake. "Somebody shot my boy."

A painful silence was interrupted by Felicidad's appearance in the doorway, bearing a tray with a pot of coffee and cups and saucers. She still looked frightened. She set the tray on the desk and Swanson thanked her in a quiet voice. When she had gone Swanson occupied himself in serving them coffee, with a grave look on his face. He poured three cups and shoved two of them toward the edge of the desk. Hayden wandered over and took one and after a few seconds Cooper took the other, because it seemed to be expected. "He shouldn't have gone for the gun," said Swanson.

Hayden stared at Swanson for a moment and then turned to Cooper and said in a tight toneless voice, "They found Nate with a gun in his hand. There was a desk drawer open and it looks like Nate pulled out the gun and got shot for it. The girl was killed with one shot to the head." Hayden looked at Swanson, hung his head, and went back to the couch.

Swanson took a sip of coffee. "The police wanted to know why Nate would have a gun."

Hayden scowled across at Cooper. "They don't have the faintest idea what they're doing. Not a clue. All they wanted to know was what enemies Nate had. Hell, Nate was the best-natured kid in the world. He didn't have any enemies."

"Just me," said Swanson, head starting to sag. "Just me."

◆

"We're looking at a pretty high mortality rate all of a sudden here," said Snodgrass.

"I don't know whether to laugh or cry," said Jasper. "I mean, it's hard to root against somebody shooting Dexter D., but on the other hand, I hate to lose that cocksucker just when we were in a position to get something out of him."

"Swanson, too," said Snodgrass. "Somebody's cleaning house."

"What we're seeing here is shit flying off the blades of the fan," said Jasper. "This isn't normal."

Toni nodded. "Swanson was all over the news last night. They were speculating robbery."

"It was no robbery," said Jasper. "I talked to the dick who got the case. He said whatever the shooters wanted wasn't there. They were after something Swanson wouldn't give them."

"You know what I want to know?" said Snodgrass.

Jasper's look hardened. "Yeah, I know. How can a guy we have under surveillance get killed right under our noses?"

"Well?"

"Because of the fucking Cub game. They couldn't park anywhere and there were hundreds of people on the street. With all the people going past somebody just sneaked in and then out again. I had a talk with them, don't worry."

"OK. Any thoughts?"

There was a pause and then Jasper said, "Let's put it together. Swanson has money he says he got from Dexter. Dexter has the girl killed, then Dexter gets killed, now Swanson. I get the impression this isn't business as usual."

"No," said Snodgrass. "I get the impression somebody made a mistake."

"Somebody fucked up royal. What I see here is something working its way up the food chain. The girl, Dexter, Swanson. Punishment is getting dealt out here, starting with the lowest and working up."

"So what went wrong?"

"What usually goes wrong? Somebody talked or somebody got ripped off."

The two men looked at one another for a few seconds and Snodgrass said, "Swanson?"

"Good place to start," said Jasper. "Look for the guy walking away with the cash."

Snodgrass nodded, looking past Jasper. "So where is it?"

"Somewhere inside Swanson Enterprises, maybe."

"You still like the family firm theory, huh?"

"I love it. It's perfect."

Snodgrass sighed. "I don't want to think about that until we're damn sure the money's not still in a suitcase under a bed somewhere. Or in the club, under the floorboards."

"Maybe under a bed at Swanson's house. The kid was living with his father."

"We don't have near enough for a search. Not near enough. The club, that's different. CPD found about a gram of cocaine in one of the dressing rooms. We're getting a team in there to take the place apart this afternoon."

"Man, I hope they secured that place," said Jasper. "I don't want anybody doing any housecleaning."

There was a pause and then Toni said, "There's one guy we're forgetting about."

"Who's that?" said Snodgrass.

"The guy who phoned in the tip. Who's he?"

Jasper shrugged. "Who knows? He'll show up sooner or later."

"If things go the way they usually do," said Snodgrass, "he'll come out in the wash."

◆

McTeague scanned the name tags slipped into the little plastic slots above the bells. The building was infallibly placed on the socioeconomic scale by the handwritten tags and the names on them: *Abdelrahman* in capital letters that suggested that the writer had acquired the Roman alphabet late in life, *Salinas, Kim, Zupcic, Patel, Khan* in a variety of scrawls, and one strip of paper with the neatly typewritten inscription *Flannery/Berger.* McTeague pressed the bell under it.

He stood with his ear close to the speaker but nothing came out of it; instead the door buzzer went and McTeague scrambled to open the door. He rode an ancient and feeble elevator to the fifth floor. The long hallway smelled of insecticide and stretched a hundred and fifty feet to a window that had no sunlight falling on it. McTeague found the door he wanted and knocked.

The door opened until stopped by a chain and in the gap McTeague saw an older woman with orange hair, eyebrows laboriously penciled in, and a face that had given in to gravity long since. She wore a terrycloth bathrobe and she looked at McTeague with careful neutrality. In the apartment McTeague could hear Oprah on TV bullying somebody. "Yes?" said the woman.

"I'm looking for Harold Berger," said McTeague.

She was silent, looking him up and down, for a few seconds and then she said, "Who are you with?"

"I'm not with anybody," said McTeague. "Not the FBI, not the police, not the IRS or the Treasury. I'm an old friend and I want to do him a favor."

"You're too young to be an old friend of Harold's."

McTeague smiled. "He used to give me bubblegum when I was a kid."

The lady looked at him for another long moment and said, "Try the coffee shop, down at the corner." She was already shutting the door.

The coffee shop had old-fashioned swiveling stools at a counter and booths going back on both sides. In the rear of the place was a large booth that filled a corner. The table was littered with breakfast remains. There were four elderly men in the booth; something in the way they looked at McTeague as he came down the aisle told him they had known he was coming. He stopped at the table and scanned the faces, four hard-bitten old men's faces, looking for a memory.

"I'm looking for Harold Berger," he said. The men looked at one another blankly.

"What makes you think he's here?" one of the men said.

"The way you guys are acting," said McTeague. He turned toward the hallway that led to the phone and the restrooms. At the far end he could see another old man, small and stooped in a rumpled suit, just visible in the shadows. McTeague smiled.

There was silence in the booth as the little man came up the hall into the light, peering at McTeague. The man had some gray hair left, a toothbrush moustache and bifocals perched on an oversized nose. He stood before McTeague with his hands in his pockets, looking like a man who can't quite put his finger on something, and said, "I know you."

"You used to," said McTeague. "But it's been a while."

"Sean," said the man, light dawning. "I'll be god-damned." He stuck out his hand and McTeague shook it.

"She makes a pretty good early warning system," said McTeague, inclining his head roughly in the direction of the apartment building.

"She knows what's good for her," said Harold Berger. "Sit down, sit down." He waved at the booth, where the old men were looking a little less blank.

"Thanks, but I was hoping I could talk you into a walk in the park."

Harold Berger stared for a moment, narrowed his eyes, and said, "Just to catch up on old times, huh?"

"Just to pass the time of day," said McTeague.

The old men in the booth were looking blank again, checking watches, peering into coffee cups. Berger made a noise that might have been either skeptical or bemused and said, "Sure."

It was farther to the park than McTeague had thought; by the time they were in sight of the lake, flat and brassy under the sun, Berger was laboring a bit. "Slow down, boy. I'm not what I was when your mom was bringing you around to the office." They sat on a bench facing east and the old man watched with a hollow exhausted look as joggers and cyclists drifted by. McTeague sat patiently, watching with him. They were in the shade and the heat wasn't too bad.

"So," Berger said after a couple of minutes. "You didn't haul me out here to talk about your mom, did you?"

"No," said McTeague, nervous now, about to tell. "I brought you out here to talk about money."

The old man started to laugh, a long slow drawn-out sound like a car engine trying to turn over on a winter morning. "Money," he said finally. "Go to the library, you want to know about money. I'll give you a reading list."

"The library won't help me. I need expertise. I need experience. I need discretion."

"Uh-uh," Berger said. He tugged at his limp blue tie and cleared his throat with a distressing rattle. "No siree. I'm finished. I'm a poor old retired accountant who just wants to die in his own bed. Twenty months in a federal prison killed my spirit of adventure dead."

McTeague said nothing. He sat with the old man and watched. The lake sparkled, an overweight man held in by Spandex labored by, the hum of traffic rose from the Drive behind them. Sparrows hopped aimlessly at the border of the bike path and a very slight hint of a breeze moved against their faces. "I have a million dollars in cash," said McTeague.

Another minute went by before McTeague looked at the old man. Berger was looking down at his feet in their scuffed brown wingtips. "I didn't hear that," he said softly.

McTeague smiled. "OK. You didn't hear it. We can go back now. I'll walk you back to your penthouse suite up there."

Berger sighed. "You're just like your old lady," he said.

"That's what I'm told."

McTeague waited him out again; he knew every second the old man stayed on the bench was a second in his favor. There was a big white boat out on the lake, a long immaculate cabin cruiser, heading north. "Everything's different now," Berger said. "Everything's harder."

"I didn't say it would be easy. I said I had a million dollars in cash."

The old man hitched up one trouser leg, shifting on the bench. "That's a hell of a lot of cash. I hope it's in a safe place."

"There's no safe place for that much cash. That's why I came to you."

"You came to me because of a reputation that's twenty years old. I'm nearly dead, boy. Find somebody else."

"You're not dead yet. And your part of it could make your last decade or so pretty comfortable."

Under his breath Berger said something that sounded like "Oy." He fished a handkerchief out of his breast pocket, took off his glasses and dabbed at his forehead and eyes. "You had to find me, didn't you? You had to come and tempt me like this, huh?"

"You're the best, Harold. And better yet, you're out of circulation. Nobody's watching you these days."

"You're right about that." Berger put his glasses back on. "And that makes things harder. I don't have the contacts anymore. It's all contacts."

"I know. And those contacts are why I can't go to the usual people. Certain people get wind of the fact I'm moving that much money, I'm in a little bit of trouble."

"I see." Harold Berger looked out over the lake and nodded a few times. "I think I see your problem."

McTeague was following the white boat on its passage north, squinting a little. "So. Now that you've heard all about it, I guess I can walk you home again. It's been nice talking to you."

The sigh that came out of Harold Berger this time was long and wistful. He watched a trim young woman lope by, blond ponytail bobbing. He might have been sighing for her, but McTeague didn't think so. After half a minute or so Berger said, "I don't think I've ever seen that much money in one place, not even in the old days."

"It's quite a sight," said McTeague. "It kind of takes your breath away. A sight like that could take a few years off your age."

"Maybe it could at that," said Berger at last, and McTeague smiled.

"It can be arranged," he said.

◆

"Well, it ain't London," said Turk. "But I guess we're getting our money's worth. A big black skyscraper and a river the color of snot. That's something to write home about, all right." Ferocious Dick grunted. The red double-decker bus swayed a little as it lurched over the Michigan Avenue bridge. Ahead of Turk and Ferocious Dick, a handful of other tourists sat motionless, looking

down from their vantage point with all the interest of sunstroke
victims. "Get a load of that," said Turk, pointing at a long-haired
redhead in shorts and T-shirt making her way along the sidewalk.
"She oughta have to carry a license, walking around looking like
that." Turk craned to track her as the bus pushed on, losing her in
the crowd. "My, my."

Ferocious Dick growled something, closed his eyes and rubbed
them vigorously with both hands. "OK, let's talk tactics," said Turk,
settling back onto the seat and looking at the backs of the nearest
people, six seats ahead. "You don't like the way it went, I'm listening for better ideas. The only thing that went wrong was, the guy had
more guts than most. I've used the Russian Roulette thing before,
never had it fail. Usually you put the gun to the girlfriend's head, the
kid, whatever, you don't even have to squeeze the trigger once. They
can't wait to talk. This guy showed a little backbone and you had to
shoot him, that's all."

Ahead they could see the long down slope of Michigan Avenue
stretching north. "It might have worked anyway. You just shot him
too many times."

Ferocious Dick shrugged and made noises in his throat.

"Anyway," said Turk. "You saw the paper. They told us everything
we need to know, right there, except the actual address for the father.
Sounds like he's loaded. That's where the money will be. And I'll
tell you something." Ferocious Dick grunted. "There's nothing I like
better than getting to know rich people. My, my. Look at that little
blonde in the short, short skirt."

◆

"It's creepy," said Sherry, looking out the fourteenth-floor window
at the silent sunlit parade on Michigan Avenue below. "I mean, he
was just in here the other day. It's like, he can't be dead."

Across the office Mrs. Keller was sifting papers aimlessly; Sherry
looked to her for a response but got none. This made Sherry feel
foolish; with Mrs. Keller presiding over the office, she spent much of
her time feeling foolish and inferior. She went back to her desk and
sat down, but there was nothing to do. The noise of shuffling papers
stopped and she looked at Mrs. Keller again. The older woman had
one hand to her face, eyes closed. Sherry stared, aghast, until Mrs.
Keller took her hand away and looked up.

"It's awful," said Mrs. Keller in a quiet voice. "Just awful."

Mrs. Keller had worked for Regis Swanson for fifteen years and enjoyed his confidence in a way that Sherry could never imagine herself attaining. Sherry sat meekly, waiting for more.

"I saw that boy grow up," said Mrs. Keller, something glinting in the corner of her eyes. She went back to sifting the papers on her desktop.

Sherry looked down at her nails. When the phone rang she picked it up with dispatch. "Swanson Enterprises," she said brightly.

"Yeah," said a man's voice. "Tele-Blossoms here, I'm trying to track down an address, for a Regis Swanson? I got a floral wreath to deliver, and the address is something in Glencoe, but I can't read it, and back at the office they can't find who took the order, and they told me to call you."

"Uh . . . Can you hold?" Sherry punched a button and looked at Mrs. Keller for guidance. "It's some florist. They want to know Mr. Swanson's address so they can deliver some flowers."

Mrs. Keller's brow clouded for a moment. "Pretty quick off the mark, aren't they?" She shook her head and sighed. "All right," she said, "give them the address."

◆

"He's asleep," said Buzz Hayden, emerging from the house to join Cooper on the flagstoned front terrace. "Finally." Hayden had found time somehow to shave, change clothes and maybe rest a little, and he looked alert, energetic and angry. The heat was starting to ease and he took in a lungful of air as if it had been in short supply inside. He blew it out and said, "Everything secure here?"

Cooper shrugged. "There was another reporter. I gave him a non-statement and made a few noises and left."

Hayden gave a whiff of disgust. "Vampires. Reporters love blood. And tears. Blood and tears make their mouths water."

"And the lady who came in the Olds there. I let her in."

"Yeah, that's fine, that's an old friend of the family. She's in there with Sally now."

"How's she doing? I wasn't sure she was quite aware of her surroundings when I picked her up at O'Hare."

"She's just sitting there crying quietly in a dark corner of the living room. Nate was her only child." The two men stood watching the shadows lengthen for a moment. Hayden said, "That damn cop was here again. Going on and on about Nate, the drug bust and stuff." He shook his head. "That was years ago. And Nate never ran with that bunch again. But the cops are looking for something easy. They want an enemies list, something they can sink their teeth into."

"They have to start with the obvious, I guess."

"What's obvious here is it was a robbery gone bad. Some coked-up asshole thought they had money up there, got mad when they didn't. You read the papers? You know what kind of deranged animals there are walking around the city these days?"

"I know," said Cooper.

Hayden exhaled loudly, a man at odds with the world around him. "They'll keep at it for a while, maybe get the guy, some dopehead kid probably, and he'll get a twenty-year sentence and do six or eight. Makes me sick to my stomach."

Cooper said nothing; there was nothing to say. After a minute Hayden said, "I think you can take off now, actually. There'll be people here tonight, we got some friends and neighbors coming in. And Regis isn't going anywhere. I think we got things under control."

"I'll stay if I'm needed. I don't punch a clock."

"Nah, take off. Maybe be here as usual tomorrow." Cooper nodded and Hayden went back inside. Cooper wandered down the steps to the drive and was heading for the back when the sound of a car climbing the drive came up through the trees. He waited and saw a blue Chevy Cavalier come wheeling up into sight, slow as it came onto the level space in front of the house, ease past the three cars already parked there, and stop at the steps. Cooper walked toward it as a man emerged from the passenger side.

Music business, thought Cooper. The man wore light brown hair in a short neat ponytail, with a sport jacket over a pale green shirt buttoned to the neck without a tie. He was tall and his long square-jawed face combined the clean lines of a sportswear model and the hard, slightly wasted look of a man who treats stress with chemicals. He nodded at Cooper and said, "Is this Regis Swanson's place?"

"That's right." Cooper glanced at the man behind the wheel of the car and got an impression: short, squat, dark. "What can I do for you?"

The man with the ponytail stood with his hands in his trouser pockets, looking gravely at Cooper. He opened his mouth to speak but hesitated. "I was a friend of his son's," he said finally. "I heard about the, uh, the tragedy this afternoon. I was hoping to speak to Mr. Swanson. Just to give my condolences, you know? Nate and I were pretty tight." He finished with a tight-lipped look of repressed emotion, sorrow manfully borne.

Cooper had lived in L.A., many years before, and something about the way the lines were delivered brought back Hollywood. "Mr. Swanson's asleep," he said. "He's had a rough day."

"I can imagine. He must be pretty devastated." The man looked meaningfully at the front door, lips parted on the brink of speech again. "I wonder if I could just step in and wait for a while. He's not likely to be down for the night yet, is he?"

Cooper frowned slightly. "Probably not. But I couldn't say when he'll be up. If you'll leave your name I'll see that he gets it. I'm sure he'll appreciate your coming."

This guy's not used to hearing no, thought Cooper as the man's stance hardened just a little. He looked at Cooper the way people look at the hired help. "I've come a long way to see him," the man said. Cooper met the stare; after a couple of seconds the expression softened and the man said, "I'd appreciate it if I could just step in for a moment." He nodded at the line of cars in the drive. "It doesn't look like I'd be the only visitor. If I could leave a note, maybe use the phone to make a quick call while I'm at it, I'd be grateful. Can you do that?"

Cooper looked into the very slightly bleary hazel eyes a moment longer and then shrugged. "What's your name?"

"Pete Best."

The name rang a faint bell with Cooper but he couldn't think why. "Hang on a second." He went up the steps to the door, which Hayden had left unlocked to facilitate the frequent comings and goings, and went inside, closing it behind him. He found Hayden in Swanson's study, standing at the desk talking on the phone. When Hayden hung up Cooper said, "There's a friend of Nate's out there who says he's come to deliver condolences. Somebody named Pete Best. He wants to come in and wait."

Hayden frowned and came away from the desk. "Terrific. They come out of the woodwork at a time like this, don't they?"

They went up the cool tiled hall to the front door and Cooper pulled it open to reveal the man in the ponytail standing there with his back to them, looking at the trees. He turned around and stuck out his hand to Hayden. "Pete Best," he said.

Hayden gave his name and squeezed the hand. Cooper eased past them and went toward the steps. "I'm sorry if I'm intruding," the man in the ponytail said. "I just wanted to speak to Mr. Swanson. I was a good friend of his son's."

Cooper heard Hayden ask him in and begin explanations as their voices faded behind the closing door. Cooper was left staring at the blue Cavalier: the man behind the wheel had disappeared. Cooper blinked at the empty car for a moment and then swept the area; the little dark man was not in sight.

Cooper came down off the porch and started following the drive that led to the back. He rounded the corner, walked under the porte cochere, and came in sight of the stables without finding anybody. At the rear of the house he saw the short man standing on the terrace, forehead against the glass door, peering into the house.

"Can I help you?" Cooper called, walking briskly toward the terrace. The little dark man turned and stood motionless, waiting for Cooper to join him. He wore a dark sports jacket and khaki pants. He had a face like a pit bull, very dark-complexioned, with a crooked tooth just peeking out between the lips. He looked blankly at Cooper.

"It's a private house, friend," said Cooper, striding up onto the terrace. "Wait with the car."

The little dark man smiled, revealing more crooked teeth, and made a pantomime gesture of drinking from a cup. He growled a few unintelligible syllables and jerked a thumb at the glass doors.

Cooper stood in front of him. "OK, you want a drink, I'll bring it to you. Wait with the car."

For a moment Cooper thought the man hadn't understood. He stood perfectly still, looking at Cooper very intently, before relaxing perceptibly, casting a last glance through the glass and moving away from the house.

Cooper led him back to the front, not attempting any small talk. He wasn't sure what language that was he'd heard. He watched the little man open the door of the car and get in, told him he'd bring a glass of water and went in the front door. He closed it behind him, stood still for a moment looking at the locks and flicked the bolt shut.

He went down the hall into the vast airy living room with the arched window overlooking the lake. He saw the man in the ponytail standing in quiet conversation with Hayden. Nate's mother and the woman who had come in the Olds sat nearby, watching. The man in the ponytail caught Cooper's eye as he went through the room, giving him a quick sharp look. Cooper went on down the back hallway to the kitchen.

Felicidad was nowhere to be seen, so Cooper hunted in cabinets until he found a glass and filled it at the sink. He made his way along another hall to the sliding glass doors that gave onto the terrace. He tugged on the handle, just making sure the doors were locked.

When he came out the front door with the glass of water, the little dark man was sitting behind the wheel. Cooper went to the driver's side of the car and handed him the glass through the window. The man drank half the glass, staring straight ahead through the windshield, and then handed it back to Cooper. He said "Thank you" in a deep growl that hinted at an injured throat and a thick accent, probably Spanish.

"Any time," said Cooper. He emptied the glass with a sweep of his hand, sending a spray of water glinting out through the evening light onto the asphalt. "Who's your friend in there?" he said.

The dark man at the wheel of the car looked at him for a couple of seconds and shrugged. He growled something, only a few syllables, that was absolutely unintelligible to Cooper. Cooper stared back, said, "Yeah," and went to set the glass on the front steps.

The door opened and the man in the ponytail came out, ushered by Hayden. "Thanks for coming," said Hayden tonelessly, his hand on the doorknob.

The man said nothing, striding past Cooper with a glance, trotting down the steps with his hands in his pockets. He went to the car and got in. The little dark man started the engine and drove away carefully, turning to head down the drive. Cooper and Hayden watched them go.

"You meet the nicest people in show business," said Hayden as the car disappeared.

Cooper nodded. "I thought he had that look about him."

"He said he managed a band. Which might explain why he was here pretending to be bereaved."

"Pretending?"

Hayden was scowling into the sinking sun. "He made all the right noises, but I got a distinct impression he was here for something else."

"He did have kind of a purposeful way about him, didn't he?"

"You noticed. Yeah, I got the feeling this was maybe somebody Nate owed money to, something like that."

Cooper thought about the little dark man and the glass of water. He was on the point of saying something when Hayden turned on his heel and went back inside. Cooper walked slowly around the side of the house to the back, wishing for no good reason that he had thought to look at the license plate of the Chevrolet.

◆

"The name Pete Best mean anything to you?" Cooper said, look-ing past treetops and apartment roofs at the deepening indigo over the lake. He had his feet up on the rail, a tall glass full of gin and tonic in his hand. Beside him Diana sat cross-legged in the old bat-tered armchair they had relegated to the back porch. Their clasped hands rested on the arm of the chair.

Diana mused, frowning at him. "Pete Best. Wait a second. Wasn't that the fifth Beatle, the guy who Ringo replaced?"

Cooper tipped his glass to her. "Brilliant. I figured you'd know."

"One of those facts you have rattling around in the brain. How come?"

"I met a guy today who introduced himself as Pete Best." Cooper took a long slow drink.

Diana shrugged. "There could be more than one, I guess. Who was this?"

"He called at Swanson's house. Said he was a friend of Nate's." Cooper paused; don't tell her, he thought. Don't get her worrying.

For a time there was only the murmur of distant traffic. "Cooper," she said finally. "How long are we going to take this?"

"Take what?" he said, though he knew what she meant.

"Living in a town where murder doesn't even make the front page. Worrying about murder more than people in most places worry about getting rained on. How long are we going to put up with that?"

Cooper shrugged. "Don't get carried away. We're not in a high-risk group. We're white, middle-class, mature and legally employed."

"That's that third drink talking. You were shook when you came home."

Cooper stared into his glass. "Sure I was shook. Any time some-one you know gets killed, it's going to sour things for a while. But let's try and keep perspective."

"My perspective is, I see murder on the news every day. Every single day, Cooper. I'm not sure I want to live in a place like that anymore."

Cooper watched bubbles rise and pop. "Where are we going to go?"

"I don't know. Someplace where murder is still an event."

"Yeah, that would be nice." Cooper drank and set the glass on the floor. "What we have here is an epidemic produced by two spectacu-larly successful federal programs—the Great Society and the War on Drugs. One Democratic initiative and one Republican, just to make sure everyone gets credit. One of them institutionalized poverty and the other one offered the poor a fast way out, if they were ruthless enough. Presto, Prohibition all over again, except there's more money in dope. Add to that a relentless campaign to relieve people of responsibility for their actions and you've got our current body count. A feat of social engineering to be proud of."

"You're getting sententious on me. I don't want the soapbox tonight, I want comfort."

Cooper looked at her, dark-eyed and sad in the twilight. "I'm not sure I have any to offer."

"Let's get away." The words hung in the air for a while.

"This is a bad day to spring this on me," Cooper said. "Things will look better in the morning."

"Maybe, maybe not. Let's get away just for a while. Just a vacation. A real honeymoon, for example. The Drake was nice, but a weekend in a fancy hotel room isn't really a honeymoon."

"I just started the damn job. He won't owe me vacation time till next year."

"I know, I know. Maybe you can take a week unpaid or something. I was talking to Darcy on the phone the other day, out in Vancouver? She says it's beautiful up there. We could get away into the woods, go camping or something. You'd like that, wouldn't you?"

"I had all the camping out I could stand in the army. And I'm sure Darcy's nice and all, but staying with your friend isn't my idea of a honeymoon."

"Don't be a pain. Out in the woods it would just be us. Look, if you don't want to camp, we'll find a lodge or something. Lie by a fireplace, fish in a lake. Get away, Cooper. Just get away from this . . . horror, that's all I'm saying. This city's a bad place."

Cooper sat and held hands with her as it got darker, sorting out feelings. "This city's our home. It's been pretty good to us. Are you going to let the assholes spoil it for you?"

"They already have," said Diana.

8

"OK, WHO THE fuck is this?" said Jasper, pulling the report toward him. "A Chevrolet Cavalier. Rented from Budget out at O'Hare on Tuesday by a T. J. Rooney of Houston, Texas, turned in Wednesday.

And on Tuesday evening Mr. Rooney paid a visit to the home of Regis Swanson, along with all these other people."

"All of whom are solid citizen types, friends of Swanson's. The sort of people you'd expect to show up after a death in the family." Toni sat back with her legs crossed, tapping a pencil on the arm of the chair.

"Uh-huh. Except for the guy in the Mustang, right?"

"Right. And he appears to be the chauffeur. You can see him driving the Mercedes in the video."

"OK, so who is Mr. T. J. Rooney and why is he calling on Regis Swanson?" Jasper shoved the papers away.

"We're checking on the Visa card he used to rent the car. The clerk at the rental agency does not remember Mr. Rooney, unfortunately. It was a busy day, she says."

"Mm. The video shows two people in the car. Useless for ID, though."

"Except you can see what looks like a ponytail on this one."

"Great. I'll run that on the computer. Known narcotics offenders with ponytails."

After a moment Toni said, "Well, there's still the funeral."

Jasper smiled. "Yeah, there's a cheerful thought. Nothing I like better than a nice family funeral."

◆

"I'm sorry, I'm having a little trouble understanding your friend." The middle-aged, battle-hardened waitress glared at Turk.

Turk looked up from his menu. "He said he wants a fried egg to go on his french fries."

"A fried egg? On his french fries?"

"It's something they do down there where he's from. Can you do that? Just fry up an egg and throw it on the fries? Over easy, he likes it."

The waitress shook her head, a jaded woman finding something even she hadn't seen yet, and scribbled on the pad. "I guess they can do that. Where's he from?" She pointed at Ferocious Dick with the pen.

"I don't know. South of the border somewhere." Turk gave his order and the waitress went away with the menus, giving Ferocious Dick a final alarmed look. Turk watched her go, morosely. Ferocious Dick was staring out the window onto Adams Street, where the sun beat down on a sidewalk full of tourists shambling out of the Art Institute into the light. They sat in silence until the food came and then ate in silence. With his mouth full of yolk-soaked fries Ferocious Dick growled something and waggled his right hand.

"Too many people," said Turk, shaking his head. "In too many places. A big house like that, it had the potential to get real messy." Ferocious Dick's jaws worked on the fries, the steady crunch audible over the hubbub of the restaurant. "No, we're going to have to work on getting Mr. Regis Swanson by himself someplace. For the kind of interview we need to have with the man, you don't want to be interrupted."

Ferocious Dick sucked back half his glass of water, speared three fries on his fork and swirled them in the bright yellow pool on his plate. Turk averted his eyes. "I'll tell you what else we need to do. We need to research the man a little bit. I mean, his son's out of the picture, so we need some other leverage. Other kids, a wife or a girlfriend maybe. There's always the house. A little creative arson can go a long way. Whatever. We blew the quick fix with the kid, now we need to do some homework. So it might take a few days. I talked with Oscar. He didn't sound particularly impatient. With him it's not the money. He's fucking swimming in money. It's the principle, he says. He wants people to know they can't fuck with him. All he said was make sure somebody gets the message. Course, we don't get the money, we don't get our cut. So I'm prepared to give it a while."

Ferocious Dick swallowed with the little grimace he always showed, as if his throat still hurt. He was looking out the front window, his eyes focused far away. He grunted.

"I know, I know." Turk pushed the rest of his Reuben sandwich away. "It's a drag. It means another night in that fucking motel. Maybe a new one to be safe. Switching cars again. More restaurants, and me explaining your food habits. I swear I'm getting to be like fucking Sonny Petruzzi. I ever tell you about Sonny Petruzzi?" Ferocious Dick looked briefly at Turk before jabbing at the french fries again. "Sonny Petruzzi was a guy I knew in the joint, the most pathetic weenie I ever saw. He would do anything I asked him to do for me, in exchange for me keeping people off him. Trying, anyway. Poor fucker used to be drummer in some band, then got busted for selling, I don't know, two grams of blow to an undercover guy. Threw him in with all us hard cases, got his wicked ass off the street. Guy was born to be raped. Anyway, he used to sit next to me and tell me all about touring the country with this piece of shit band whose name I can't even remember, all the big acts they opened for. Stories about Jimmy Page's girlfriend shoving him into a wall, Grace Slick throwing up, shit like that. I mean, stories that would keep you on the edge of your seat. And I heard 'em all a dozen times. But then Sonny would give me this like, wise old man look and say, 'But you know, it's not all glamour on the road.'"

Ferocious Dick was looking at his empty plate. He wiped his mouth with a paper napkin and then looked at Turk and grunted softly.

Turk just blinked at him for a few seconds. "Having a conversation with you is like playing tennis with a blind man, you know that?'"

◆

Cooper fished out his suit for the funeral, the one Diana had persuaded him to buy for the wedding. "Twice in a month," he said, knotting the tie with the early light streaming into the bedroom. "Who'd a thunk it?"

"You look good," said Diana from the bed, auburn hair splayed on a white pillow. "You look like a man of substance." She smiled, and Cooper hoped the sunlight had restored her spirits.

He donned the jacket and shot his cuffs. "In this get-up, I could talk a banker into a loan. I could talk a cop out of a ticket."

"You could talk me into just about anything in that get-up."

"I'll be back," said Cooper. "Don't go away."

◆

Cooper drove the Mercedes from the discreet high-end funeral home to the distant cemetery, with Swanson and his long-estranged ex-wife staking out opposite corners in the back. Nate's mother had stopped crying but looked as if mere motion took great effort. She was a slight pale woman with colorless hair and a fatigued, withdrawn look. Swanson stared into the distance with a face of granite.

If there was more sobbing at the graveside, Cooper didn't hear it, since he was standing by the Mercedes at a respectful distance, at the head of a file of expensive cars parked just off an asphalt track that wound through the trees. There were two other chauffeurs waiting out the proceedings; Cooper nodded at them but made no attempt to join their quiet parley.

He was watching the trees. He was sure the man in the ponytail would not have the name Pete Best on his driver's license. Under the circumstances he thought it would be a good idea to watch, just to make sure nothing disturbed the fragile dignity of a funeral happening fifty years or so before it ought to.

When the long white sedan pulled up at the crest of a low hill two hundred yards away, Cooper watched for a while without moving. He could see two people in the car but no distinguishing features, and the car was just sitting there. Finally it had sat there long enough for Cooper to move slowly to the door of the Mercedes and get in. He sat behind the wheel considering, and then started the engine and eased as softly as he could onto the road, hoping the ceremony at the grave had a while to run yet. He steered smoothly away from the site, drawing a couple of looks from the fringes of the small crowd.

The track went a long way through trees and over gentle rises, curving out of sight of the grave and the white sedan but leading inexorably back to the main gate. When Cooper knew he was out of sight of the funeral party he stepped on it a bit and took the curves as fast as safety and decorum permitted. At the main gate he swung back along the way he had driven in previously, looking for the turnoff that would bring him up behind the white sedan.

It was an Olds Ninety-Eight, pulled off on the left-hand shoulder, and there were two people in it, but they were not the ones Cooper was looking for. He eased to a halt in the middle of the road, level with the Olds, and the face he saw looking at him from the passenger side of the car was a woman's.

She was middle to late twenties, with black shaggy hair, aquiline features, black-marble eyes and a deep vertical cleft between eyebrows that were frowning at him. Across the seat from her, behind the wheel, was a man with blond hair retreating from a high forehead and a ragged moustache. Cooper got out of the car. The window on the woman's side was open and Cooper stepped to it and leaned on the door.

"You with the Swanson party?" he said.

"No," she said. "You with the highway patrol?"

"I'm with the Swanson party, and I was just kind of wondering what you're doing up here in the bushes, watching the fun from a distance. I thought maybe you were too shy to join the rest of the family."

The man behind the wheel spoke. "We're looking for my mother's grave. You mind?" Cooper stared the man down for a second or two; he had the eyes of a bar fighter.

"Must be a pretty small grave," Cooper said, nodding at the camera with the foot-long lens that lay on the seat between them.

"That's for my wildflower studies. Now take a hike. We'd like to be alone with our grief."

Cooper smiled, first at the man and then at the woman. "I'll go tell Mr. Swanson to try and give you a good profile, how's that?"

"That's just fine, big guy, you do that." The man gave him a lazy thumbs-up sign but the look in his eyes stayed near freezing. Cooper exchanged a brief look with the woman, who was looking at him with amused interest.

"I'll tell you something, too," Cooper said to the man. "You get any closer than this, you'll be picking pieces of expensive photographic equipment up off the asphalt."

There was a second's pause and the man said, "Oh, dear. I think I'm gonna piss my pants."

"You won't be the first reporter to do that when things get rough." Cooper straightened up and walked to the front of the Olds. He took a good look at the license plate, reading it out loud. He went back to the Mercedes and got in. "Don't forget to take the lens cap off," he said, putting the Mercedes in gear.

He coasted back to the head of the line of cars. The ceremony at the grave was breaking up. Cooper waited in the car, adjusting the side mirror so he could watch the Olds. As the mourners drifted back to their cars, the Olds rolled away through the trees.

◆

The post-funeral gathering convened in the living room of Swanson's house. There was nothing of release in the atmosphere, only dumb relief at having completed the civilized forms. There were coffee and tea and places to sit, and the half-dozen guests, all intimates, tended to fall silent, their eyes drawn to the big arched window that gave onto the lake, a remote vivid blue.

Cooper had been excused from sentry duty at the front but told to stick around. He made his way to the kitchen and asked Felicidad if there was a phone he could use. She pointed him to a wall phone tucked away in a pantry and he dialed a number that started with seven-four-four. A policeman answered at the other end and Cooper asked for Lieutenant Valenti. There was a short wait and somebody said, "Yeah."

"It's MacLeish."

"Jesus. Don't tell me. Whatever it is, I got enough to do already."

"Relax. Just called to say hey. I saw you on TV a month or two ago."

"When we got the guy with the crossbow? Hey, we get lucky once in a while."

"You looked good. You made me feel safe, sitting there watching you."

A low chuckle came over the line. "What the hell do you want?"

"I want you to run a license number for me, if you have a spare moment."

"Christ. The last time I ran a number for you, the guy got shot."

"Don't talk to me about it. I didn't shoot him."

"So you say. The time before that, you got shot."

"Well, I guess that makes it your turn this time."

"That's what worries me. I told you no more favors, didn't I?"

"You did. I'm hoping enough time's gone by that you're not pissed off anymore."

"I'm not pissed off anymore, but I'm older and wiser."

"Me too. But I still get bothered by strangers now and again."

"I never met anybody who got bothered by strangers as much as you do. Who's bugging you now?"

"I was at a funeral today. And somebody was watching it."

"You lost me. Funeral's public, ain't it?"

"So why did they need a telephoto lens?"

"Hm. Whose funeral? Anybody I know?"

"I don't think so," said Cooper, carefully. "A kid who drove too fast."

Valenti made a noise, a distant rumble at the other end of the wire. "Is there a story here I should hear?"

"The story is the kid's dead and somebody's watching the funeral. I'd like to know why."

"Friend of yours?"

"I work for the kid's father."

Cooper's hopes rose as the seconds ticked past. Finally Valenti said, "You know, MacLeish, with you my better judgment gives way to curiosity every time. I just can't wait to see what kind of shit you're going to pull next. What's the number?"

Cooper told him the license number of the Olds, gave the number of the phone he was speaking from, and hung up. He was sitting at the kitchen table with a cup of coffee and a day-old *Tribune* when Felicidad came in with an empty teapot and said, "The police is here again." Cooper's eyebrows rose and he went back to the paper.

The next he heard of it was when Buzz Hayden wandered back to the kitchen with his hands stuffed into his pockets and a scowl on his face. "They're at it again. Two of 'em. Big dumb cops from the city, poking at Regis with sticks, trying to get him to say Nate was a gangster and had it coming. It kind of broke up the party, not that it was much of a party. I think I need a drink, and I don't say that very often." He waved Felicidad aside and found the liquor himself, pouring himself a fairly long scotch and wandering away again.

Cooper finished the paper and went outside to stand on the terrace. The lake was a deeper blue and the light was shading to gold as the sun declined. He sat in the Adirondack chair and thought about two men in a Chevrolet Cavalier and a man and a woman in an Olds Ninety-Eight. Felicidad found him there some time later.

"Telephone for you."

Cooper followed her in and took the phone. "Where the hell are you?" said Valenti at the other end.

"At work, more or less."

"So who's your boss?"

Cooper leaned on the wall. "Found something interesting, huh?"

"Not really. The car belongs to an auto leasing outfit."

"I see. What's the name of the company?"

"Why? You gonna go poking in the bushes again?"

"I might. You got any objection?"

"Hell, try your luck. They might tell you who leased it, but I doubt it. Now who you working for?"

"Man, you're curious all of a sudden." Cooper stared at his feet for a few seconds. "I think I'm starting to get a clue here. Let me take a wild guess."

"Do I have to listen?"

"My wild guess would be that the people in the Olds belong to some kind of law-enforcement agency."

Three or four seconds went by. "You waiting for me to say something? I told you who the car's registered to. They could have leased it to just about anybody. Now how about my question?"

Cooper looked over his shoulder into the empty kitchen. "I'm working for Regis Swanson."

"Hah," said Valenti. "I see. A kid who drove too fast, huh?"

"Yeah. Hey, thanks for your time. I appreciate it."

"MacLeish, just sit and watch the parade this time, huh?"

"You bet," said Cooper. "I'm just trying to earn an honest dollar."

Cooper was staring out the kitchen window when Hayden stuck his head in the door.

"Regis wants you in the study."

When Cooper got to the study he found Swanson standing at the desk, still in his funeral suit, scraping papers into a black leather attaché case. "You're working overtime tonight," he said to Cooper. "I haven't been to the office in two days and I just don't believe Connie when she says everything's under control. Normally I'd drive myself but I won't vouch for my condition around midnight." He snapped the case shut. "If you want to call your wife or something you can use the phone here."

Cooper shrugged. "I'll call her from downtown. Meet you at the side door?"

Out on the road heading south against the grain of the evening traffic, Cooper felt things building up in the back seat. Just inside Chicago, Swanson spoke for the first time. "You think cops do it on purpose?"

When he had decided that the question was more than rhetorical, Cooper said, "Do what?"

"Come and talk to people when they're most vulnerable."

Cooper downshifted to take a bend in the road. "I'd say that was pretty good technique."

"Yeah." Swanson was silent for half a minute and then said. "These two gorillas this afternoon kept harping on Nate's supposed drug dealing. I said I thought I would know if he was. You think I would?"

Cooper drove for a few seconds and said, "Not if he was any good."

After an icy silence Swanson said, "No, I suppose not. He got busted once when he was a kid for having less than a gram of co- caine. I told him then I'd take him in myself if he ever touched the stuff again. Nate broke a few promises in his day, but I don't think he broke that one. I think he was clean."

Cooper steered around a slowing bus. "He wouldn't have to be on it to sell it."

"Oh, thanks. That's just what I want to hear right now."

"All I can tell you is that somebody with a big telephoto lens was at the funeral today."

It had much the effect Cooper had thought it would; Swanson was dumbfounded for a block or two before saying distinctly, "What?"

"I got the license number of a car that was hanging around at the cemetery, and I had a friend run it for me. It was a leased car, nice and anonymous. That's all I can tell you."

After that Swanson was silent until they were on the Drive. "Char- lene would know," he said suddenly.

"Who?"

"Nate's old girlfriend. The one who kicked him out. She'd know if Nate was into something like that."

"Probably."

"Maybe that's why she kicked him out. I thought it was because he was a slob and a deadbeat."

"Call her, if it'll make you feel better."

"I already told the cops to go talk to her." There was a long pause. "Maybe they're right. Maybe he deserved to get killed." Swanson sounded detached, deflated after his burst of energy.

Cooper waited a few seconds and said, "Why would he deserve it?"

"If he was pushing drugs? Wouldn't you say he deserved it?"

Cooper switched lanes and settled into a groove. "I'd say the only crime that deserves murder is murder. But then I'm funny that way. I don't think it's any of the government's business how I drug myself. I happen to favor alcohol, which they say is OK. I'm not sure how they make those fine distinctions. I've seen a lot more reckless fucked-up behavior from drunks than I ever have from people on coke or acid."

"What are you saying?"

"I'm saying personally, I wouldn't want to own a bar, but I'm damn glad there are people that do, 'cause I like to drink. So I wouldn't judge Nate too harshly unless he was selling to school kids or something. And he didn't strike me as the type."

Swanson was silent for a mile or so. The skyline of the Loop was drawing closer, the western facets reflecting gold; over the lake the sky was a vivid turquoise. "That's a noble attempt to make me feel better, but I'm not sure I'm buying it. Whatever the rights and wrongs are, drugs are illegal, and I can't condone selling them."

"I can't either. I'm saying there are worse crimes, that's all. You sell drugs to somebody, it's a voluntary transaction. Nobody's getting hit on the head or shot or raped."

"Maybe."

"I will say one thing."

"What's that?"

"It's one hell of a dirty business. There is no Better Business Bureau with drugs. It's a damn good way to make enemies, and if he was selling, that's where I'd look for them."

The silence in the back seat deepened. Cooper got off the Drive and went south down Michigan, crowded and cheerful-looking in the slowly easing heat. Swanson had put up some state-of-the-art skyscrapers, but he maintained his offices in a venerable fifteen-story building on Michigan north of the river, a survivor of the opulent twenties with either Biblical or mythological scenes—Cooper had never quite figured out which—in bas relief on the façade. Cooper dropped Swanson at the front entrance and asked him when he wanted to be picked up. "Call me in an hour," Swanson said.

Cooper made a back-tracking detour of several blocks to get to the self-park lot just behind Swanson's building. He left the Mercedes there and walked slowly up Rush Street in his suit to a restaurant which had a canopied sidewalk terrace with white plastic tables and chairs. Cooper sat at a vacant table at the end of the terrace and ordered a beer. There was another restaurant across the street but nothing else on the block except parking garages and the back entrance to the Marriott Hotel. Cooper sat and sipped his beer and fiddled with his tie and watched.

He had made no attempt to watch until he had gotten off the Drive; going up Michigan he had quickly lost track of the three cars that had followed him off. But the maneuvers he had made to get the Mercedes to the parking lot had required a blue Toyota to exert itself a little to keep up. He didn't expect to see the car again, but he was interested to see who might join him on the terrace.

Cooper didn't know much about surveillance, but he figured any kind of cop would be better here in the city than in the broad vistas of the cemetery. For ten minutes he watched people come and go, seeing pretty much what he expected to see: nobody obvious. Cooper figured if they were any good at all he just wasn't going to be sure. He finished his beer, paid and left. He had time to kill and to amuse himself he went looking for the blue car; he didn't find it. He crossed Michigan and went into a cheap Chinese place, where he called Diana to tell her he'd be late and then ordered dinner. He ate slowly, watching the street. When he finished eating he called Swanson.

Swanson sounded relieved. "Come get me. I can't concentrate on a damn thing up here."

"I'll be in front in five minutes."

Swanson was waiting, looking uncharacteristically slack, when Cooper slid over to the curb. Swanson had been staring at something high over the lake and he looked a little startled when the car stopped in front of him. He climbed in without a word.

"Where to?"

"I want to go see Charlene."

"OK. Where does she live?"

"Someplace on Irving. Give me the phone." Cooper passed him the car phone and marked time while Swanson riffled the pages of a pocket address book and then punched in a number. There was no answer and Swanson passed the phone back to him. "She must be at work. Let's try her there. She's a hostess or something at Ivor's, on Lincoln Avenue."

Cooper jogged west and then headed north, watching the mirrors. As he crossed Chicago Avenue on La Salle street, he thought he saw the blue Toyota. By the time he got into third gear on Lincoln Avenue, it wasn't there anymore.

Ivor's was a fashionable three-and-a-half-star beanery sporting a maroon awning in the first block north of Fullerton. "Wait for us," said Swanson. "I'm going to see if I can get her to step out for a moment." Cooper slid to the curb, wondering about the chutzpah of a man who presumed he could descend on a woman in the middle of her working day and get her to step outside for a moment. Swanson disappeared inside the restaurant and Cooper looked for the blue Toyota in the mirror.

It took a few minutes, but when Swanson came out of the restaurant, it was with a woman in tow. She had reddish-blond hair, a turquoise jacket and a black skirt, black stockings, and a look of deep suspicion on her face. Swanson opened the door for her and she slid onto the back seat. "Take us around the block a couple of times," said Swanson, getting in with her. Cooper slipped into gear.

"I can't be gone more than five minutes, and that's asking a lot," the woman said in a tight voice. She paused in scooting across the seat, long enough for Cooper to get a good look at her in the mirror. It was a dark-eyed, clear-skinned, full-mouthed face, framed by the hair and set off by a flash of gold at the earlobes and another, a little less discreet, nestled in the hollow of the throat. What he saw didn't look like a stylistic match for the Nate he had known.

"I squared it with your boss," said Swanson. "Five minutes ought to be enough anyway."

Cooper eased into traffic and tried hard not to look as if he were listening. He heard her draw a deep breath. "Mr. Swanson, I'm very sorry about Nate. I should have called or something. But I don't see what we have to talk about."

"I wanted to ask you a question," Swanson said softly.

There was a silence and then she said, "You and everybody else."

"Who else? The police?"

"God. All kinds of police. The local variety and the government kind, the drug people."

"Ah. Maybe that answers my question, then," said Swanson.

"You want to know all about Nate's drug deals, right?"

After a second or two Swanson said tightly, "Right."

"Well, there weren't any. Not while I was around."

Cooper eased to a stop at a red light, flicked on his turn signal and waited.

"He wasn't selling drugs," said Swanson, just audible above the hum of the car.

"Not when we were together. I'll tell you what I told the cops. If he was dealing, it was something he got into after we split up."

"You would know, right?"

"Of course I'd know. You can't live with somebody who does that and not know. For one thing, he'd have had more money. He wouldn't have been broke all the time."

Swanson digested that, perhaps considering the very slight acid note, and said, "Did he ever use drugs?"

Cooper made his turn in the midst of another pause. As he headed north, Charlene went on slowly. "Mr. Swanson, don't get the wrong idea, but if you mean did he ever, like at parties, smoke a joint or maybe even do a line, well, yes. But if you mean did he have a problem with it, he absolutely did not."

Swanson shifted on the seat. "Did he have any . . . friends, acquaintances, contacts who had problems, or sold the stuff, or anything like that? I'm sorry if I'm starting to sound like the police. But I'm groping for some reassurance here."

Surer now, the initiated talking to the hopeless *naïf,* she said, "Nate knew a lot of people. He knew a lot of musicians, and what they say about musicians is pretty much true. But there was nobody he hung around with, like, regularly who was a real obvious, I don't know, dope dealer or junkie or anything. Mostly they were just . . . I don't know, I'm sorry."

"What? What were you going to say?"

Cooper drove, eyes on the street. "Mostly they were just spoiled rich kids like him," said Charlene.

This silence lasted the rest of the way around the block, down Halsted and back to Lincoln. "I'm sorry," said Charlene in a thick voice, finally.

"That's all right. I pretty much knew the score." Swanson's voice was dry, parched. Outside the car, somebody honked, somebody yelled, people milled.

Louder, Charelene said, "But he wasn't dealing. No way."

"Fine."

"I'm sorry. I'm sorry it didn't work out. I just couldn't . . . He was your son and you loved him and all, but . . ."

"But what?"

"Maybe he just needed to grow up a little. He needed . . ."

Cooper turned up Lincoln again, waiting for the end of the sentence, which never came. He pulled over in front of the restaurant. There was a murmur in the back seat and no movement for a time. Gently, Cooper reached for the mirror and adjusted it so he could watch Charlene composing herself. When the golden head came up Cooper saw a dark-eyed face, expensively decorated, with something icy about it. Her eyes met his briefly in the mirror and flicked away. Swanson had the door open and she slid across the seat again, exchanged an inaudible murmur with Swanson on the sidewalk, and stepped briskly back to the door of the restaurant. Five seconds later Swanson got back in the car and slammed the door. "Home," he said.

Cooper drove, back east toward the lake. "You hear all that?" said Swanson after a while.

"I heard."

"Maybe we should put that on the headstone. 'He needed to grow up a little.' There's an epitaph for you."

Bitter, thought Cooper. That's the word for that tone of voice. "How old is she?" he said, just to say something.

"I don't know. I think she's a couple of years older than Nate. Maybe that was the problem."

"That's a good one. A twenty-six-year-old telling a twenty-four-year-old to grow up."

"You can knock it off. You've already earned your salary today."

Cooper pushed through the traffic gently, in no hurry. "So. You believe her?"

Cooper had given up on getting an answer when Swanson finally said, "I did. Until you asked me the question in that tone of voice."

"Hell, I believed her. But then I'm a sucker for a pretty face. If you want to be hard-headed about it, you've got to ask yourself if she could be a damn good liar. If he was dealing and she knew about it, she'd keep quiet."

"Well, what was I going to do, hold her feet to the fire? I asked her a question, she answered."

"If she lied to the cops, they'll smoke her out. Cops take nothing at face value. But here's another possibility."

"What's that?"

"Nate wasn't dealing, but he was running money through the club. Maybe he had a deal going with somebody he knew, to do their laundry in exchange for a cut or something. How closely did you monitor the books?"

"Me? Not very closely. Nate had a guy who did the books on a day-to-day basis. But Stan kept a pretty close eye on things. I think he would have noticed something screwy."

"Maybe you should ask him."

"OK, I'll ask him. But I think I've had enough for now. Just get me home."

Cooper gave it a little gas. "Can I make a suggestion?" he said.

"What?"

"Don't go home tonight."

After a silence Swanson said, "Why not?"

"I don't like the attention you're getting. We've got people watching us again."

Swanson said nothing for a while. "Are you sure?"

"Ninety-nine percent. I spotted one of them but they've probably replaced him by now. If it's the cops or somebody, they're going to be real careful after the cemetery today. But it's not the cops that worry me."

"What the hell are you talking about?"

"There are other fish in the water. While you were asleep the other day two guys showed up wanting to talk to you. They were a bit too pushy for my tastes. They claimed to be in the music business. They sure as hell weren't cops. I keep waiting for them to pop up again."

"Why didn't you tell me about it before?"

"They didn't worry me a whole lot until I found out somebody thought Nate was a dealer. Now they worry me."

"I see. So what am I supposed to do?"

"Sleep somewhere unexpected tonight." That brought no response. Cooper said, "Who's out at the house?"

"Tonight? Nobody. Sally wouldn't stay there."

"How about the help?"

"They'll be gone."

"So you don't want to go home to a big empty house, right? You got a place in the city?"

Swanson was silent for a few seconds. He said. "I could stay at the club, but that wouldn't be any better than the big empty house." Cooper was wondering whether it would be impudent to bring up the rich widow friend when Swanson said, "Buzz'll put me up. I'll give him a call."

"Where's he live?" said Cooper.

"Kenilworth. You don't think this is a little melodramatic?"

"I sure as hell hope so." Cooper gave it some gas. "Watch out the back, see if you can pick out the tail."

Cooper drove; he could hear Swanson shifting on the seat. "There's a whole line of cars behind us."

"I never said it would be easy."

After a minute Swanson said, "Why me?"

Cooper considered. "The Mount Everest effect, I guess."

"Huh?"

"You're big, and you're there."

◆

The moon rode above the lake, flitting behind trees as Cooper drove. Traffic was moderate but he made no attempt to sort out the headlights in the mirror. He coasted down into the ravine toward Swanson's drive and put on his turn signal. It was a hairpin turn and normally Cooper enjoyed taking it fast and smooth, but tonight he crept into the drive watching at the limit of his lights.

Cooper had just about decided that if the man in the ponytail and his wandering friend were going to pop up again, it would be here. After dropping Swanson, Cooper had thought about just how far his duties extended, and he decided they extended at least as far as a look. Just a look, for broken windows or stray Chevy Cavaliers or whatever. Just a cruise up the drive, put the Mercedes away if things looked OK, take the Mustang home.

His headlights swept over hedges and the big front door. The big sprawling house looked empty; there was light showing from behind curtains on the ground floor but it looked like an afterthought. Cooper rolled slowly past the front of the house, looking. In second gear, just crawling, he followed the drive around the corner and went through the porte cochere at the side, the lights falling on the converted stables now, everything looking normal. He pressed the button on the garage door opener and the middle door went up. Inside the stall he saw only what he usually saw, the back wall with shelves and clutter. He eased in, punched the button again, doused the lights, turned off the ignition. The door creaked and thumped and the garage went dark and silent. Cooper got out of the car.

Outside, the moon hung fat and sassy and orange above the trees. Cooper eased the door shut behind him and listened. All he heard was summer, the faint stirring of the breeze through the leaves, the crickets, the gentle wash of the lake somewhere behind him.

He walked slowly toward the Mustang, his stiff wedding shoes going clop-clop on the asphalt. The moonlight showed him the terrace at the back of the house, the lawn beyond, the tangle of trees and brush to his left, where a path led through a thicket to a flight of steps down to the beach.

There was something white under the trees, just off the path to the beach, he thought. Cooper paused with his key in the lock of the Mustang, trying to make it out. It was in the deep shadow and he could only see shapes: two low white shapes close together. He got in the car, started it and turned on the headlights, and instead of backing straight toward the terrace as he normally would, he backed in a curve to the left, to bring the headlights sweeping over the underbrush to bear on the two white objects.

Somebody had moved two Adirondack chairs from the terrace. They sat just off the path where there was no brush, out of place and positioned to give a view of the house and the stables. Cooper stared, trying to remember; he had walked out the back door, across the terrace, to get the Mercedes when he had taken Swanson into the city. All three chairs had been there; he remembered stepping around them. Cooper put the Mustang in first gear and turned the wheel, creeping forward to the edge of the asphalt and playing the headlights over the thicket that hid the lake. All he saw was bushes.

When something moved, it was fifty feet from the chairs, just a quick phantom shifting of pattern in the dark at the edge of his vision. Cooper brought the lights to bear and saw tree trunks, big enough to hide a man.

Cooper did a little damage to Regis Swanson's professionally tended lawn in clawing back onto the asphalt. He went back around the corner of the house, made the tires squeal a little to miss one post of the porte cochere, and then he was away down the drive.

The two town cops he found drinking milkshakes in their squad car parked at the red-brick commuter railroad station took it calmly but seemed decently concerned; trespassing in a wealthy North Shore suburb was something they took seriously. Cooper followed them up the drive in the Mustang, got out and showed them the chairs under the trees, the marks he had made on the grass. They poked around a bit with their flashlights but there was nothing to find. Cooper stuck close to them and debated whether to tell them about Pete Best, the forgotten Beatle.

9

"YOU SEE THESE?" Jasper shoved the surveillance reports across the table to Toni. "This guy is interesting. The chauffeur."

"The guy that flushed us." Toni stirred her coffee with one hand and sifted the papers with the other.

"Hey. He didn't flush us. He thinks we're reporters. He's proud of himself because he spotted the car and drove up behind us. Big fucking deal."

Toni shrugged. "So what's interesting about him?"

"First of all, the tough guy stuff. The guy thinks he's in a Mafia movie. Then last night, look at this. After he drops Swanson at the place in Kenilworth, he goes back to the ranch, stays about two minutes, comes tearing out and comes back fifteen minutes later with the cops. I called up there just now and talked to the chief. Turns out the guy thought he saw some trespassers on the property. The cops didn't find a thing."

Toni blinked at him. "So?"

"So I think the guy's acting a little nervous. I think he's acting like a man with something to fear. Or like his boss has something to fear."

Toni set down the spoon. "Do dopers call the cops when somebody trespasses on their property?"

"If they've got a respectable facade to maintain. Regis Swanson isn't some dipshit punk. If we're right, he never touched any drugs, never got his hands dirty. He just does the laundry."

Toni shrugged. "So what next?"

"Next we find out what kind of agenda this MacLeish character has. I've got a feeling this is the guy that does the dirty work."

◆

"Nothing but a guess," said Cooper. "But it's an educated guess. I mean, this guess has a Ph.D. It was those two bozos, and they were sitting there in the dark waiting for you."

Regis Swanson frowned down the length of a pencil at his desktop. He said "hm" or something like it and set down the pencil. He looked at Cooper and said, "What did you tell the cops?"

"I didn't go into the whole thing with them. But the police on Nate's case have got to hear it."

Swanson arranged the pencil exactly parallel with the edge of the blotter with small careful fingertip pushes. "You think these guys know something about that?"

"I think they're in it somehow. They bother me."

Swanson stared at him. "We'd better tell the detectives then, I guess."

"They leave you a number?"

Swanson nodded. He looked as if focusing were hard for him this morning. "Somewhere," he said.

"Give it to me. Did you talk to your accountant?"

"Yes. Stan says everything was kosher at the club. He would have known if Nate was running some kind of fiddle. The amounts he deposited were about what you'd expect given the capacity of the place, the cover, the liquor they sold, all that kind of thing. Stan says he paid pretty close attention because that kind of place can be trouble, what with people skimming and all. He says there's no way Nate could have been doing anything major without something funny showing up. And there was nothing."

Cooper waited, looking for signs of life in Swanson's eyes. He said, "OK. Don't sit here all morning. Don't do anything predictable. Get a little melodramatic, watch your step."

Swanson frowned at Cooper and then swiveled to frown away out the window up Michigan Avenue. "Mount Everest again?"

"I don't know," said Cooper. "With these guys, I get the feeling it's personal."

◆

"As you're probably aware," said Harold Berger, "there are a number of ways to go." The old man took a careful sip of the Chivas Regal that McTeague had poured over four ice cubes in a tumbler for him and leaned over the table. His eyes were wide behind the lenses of the horn-rimmed glasses. "The main problem, of course, is the initial step. What you have right now is nice, anonymous bills. Cash is good to have—it's portable and convertible, instant gratification. You'll want to keep some of it, because you'll need it. The only problem with it is, it's easy to lose, and unlike rabbits it doesn't multiply. Sitting in a suitcase, it's not real wealth."

McTeague nodded. He sat with his crossed forearms on the table, looking intently at Berger. The storefront was cool and dim because of the covered-over front window; the big box fan McTeague had stationed in the open back door kept a feeble current of air moving through the cramped kitchen where they sat.

Berger grasped his glasses delicately between thumb and index to settle them more firmly on his nose. "If you want real wealth you need to have nice safe accounts that no cop or federal agent is going to sniff out and seize. And the hardest part of that change is the first step. Once you've got a piece of paper that says you're worth so many dollars, you can shift those dollars all over the world so fast they'll never catch up. But the first step is the hardest."

"What do you recommend?" McTeague said.

Berger drank, pursed his lips and sighed. "Well, the G delights in putting obstacles in our path. The main obstacle is currency transaction reports. Any time any person does anything with cash that amounts to ten thousand dollars or more, it has to be reported. If you go the legal route, open checking accounts or get cashier's checks or whatever, you have to do it in batches of under ten thousand. Well under, because anything near ten thousand makes bankers suspicious nowadays. Now divide a million by ten thousand and think about how many cashier's checks we're talking about. That's why drug dealers employ smurfs. They hire these peons to do the menial labor, go around to a bunch of banks and change bills into cashier's checks. You don't want to go that way."

"No. I don't know anybody I trust that much."

"You got it."

"So what do I do?"

"Well, a lot of people just plow it into luxury items. But that has drawbacks as well. You still have to worry about CTR's. If you walk in and plunk down thirty thousand in cash for that Porsche, the dealer's got to report it. You can try and work out some creative financing scheme so you never give the guy more than ten thousand at a shot, but auto dealers are getting careful about that kind of thing. Too many of them have gotten busted for it." The old man took a drink and paused with the glass halfway back to the table. "There's always the occasional flyer on stolen property, but the problem with stolen property is that it's stolen. You can never really stop looking over your shoulder."

"No. The idea is to launder it, not make it dirtier."

"That's it, that's the point. Anyway, cash transactions have their limitations. That's the way a lot of small-timers go, just buying stuff off the shelf, selling off or trading what they don't want to actually keep. If you're careful you can work your way through a few grand like that, but for major wealth it's just not an efficient way to launder money. Get yourself a few luxuries, by all means, but don't try and move the whole sum that way."

"OK, what's next?"

"The bank accounts, same thing. Open a few accounts here and there, well under ten, just for folding money. But the same applies. It's small-time. It's inefficient. It takes too much effort to get your wealth into the form you want it in, namely a small number of secure accounts, preferably without your name on them."

McTeague nodded and shoved the bottle of scotch toward the old man, who nodded and poured another finger or so into the glass. "Offshore banks," said McTeague.

"Offshore banks." Berger settled his glasses and frowned in concentration. "The main problem is just getting it there, of course. We're still not past that first step. What do you do, physically, with several pounds of currency, when airports are full of inquisitive customs officials?"

"I see."

"And quite apart from increasing international political pressure on the higher-flying type of financial institution, there's the dilemma that the kind of outfit that will give you the most advantageous deal and ask the fewest questions and so forth is also the most likely to do a BCCI on you and leave you holding a bunch of worthless paper. You have to be careful. Another problem, just from your point of view, is that those are the channels that are most likely to be familiar to the people you're trying to avoid, if I've understood your exposition of the problem correctly."

"Mm." McTeague toyed with his glass while the old man took a long swallow. "So what do you recommend?"

Berger looked at the glass in his hand with something approaching reverence. "What I recommend," he said, "is the perfect marriage."

"Say what?"

"You need to find the perfect partner. Someone who has property of the type and in the form that you want, and needs to liquidate it in such a way that he can avoid capital gains taxes and a paper trail and all of that. Somebody with a cash flow problem, or a mobility problem or something of that nature."

McTeague raised his glass to his lips. "And here's where you come in, right?"

Harold Berger smiled. "That's how I earn my ten percent. By finding you that perfect match. Hopefully several of them."

McTeague smiled. "Polygamy's allowed, is it?"

"Well, it's just like real marriage. One partner's probably not going to give you everything you need."

◆

Heading west on Belmont, Cooper went with a hunch and swung south at Clark, looking for parking. He stashed the Mercedes in the lot of a grocery store and hiked back up Clark to the preciously Bohemian coffee house nestled between a futon shop and a Thai restaurant. The place was decorated in black, with small round tables, much-thumbed books on shelves along one wall, and oversized portraits of leftish literary lions brooding over it all. There was a counter in back with the usual imported Italian espresso machine and piles of muffins going stale under plastic covers. There were two customers at widely separated tables and one young man reading a newspaper on a high stool behind the counter.

"Jesus Christ, what happened to your head?" Cooper said.

Dominic looked up from the paper and gave Cooper a cold stare. He shook his head, folded the paper carefully and laid it on the counter. "If you lived on this planet, you'd recognize a fade when you saw one," he said. "This is what we humans call style."

Cooper looked at the kid, the sides of his head shaved, the dome thatched with thick brown hair. "I was afraid for a second you'd taken vows or something."

Dominic smiled, just barely, and shook his head. "Hey. Sticks and stones. I'm beyond the mockery of small-minded people."

He's a grown-up, thought Cooper. The long mournful face had been shaved that morning and the voice had rounded into an adult fullness. And by God, thought Cooper, he's starting to look like me. "Can I get a cup of coffee here? Just coffee? I don't want a latte or a mocha or a double express cappucino foamer with a twist. Just a cup of coffee."

"You're a cultural illiterate. Colombian or Sumatran?"

"Surprise me. How's school?"

Dominic shrugged, pouring the coffee. "It's not all it's cracked up to be."

"I was afraid of that. Got a minute to talk?"

Dominic cast an eye at the two immobile customers and said, "Till we get a rush here, which ought to be sometime in September. What's up?"

"Just need some gossip." Cooper tossed money on the counter and doctored his coffee. He stirred it, taking his time, thinking how much better he got along with his son since he had abandoned all claims to a paternity that had never been more than biological. In a quieter tone he said, "You still go dancing at that place up by the ballpark, the Blue Angel?"

Dominic leaned on the counter. A small device that resembled a wind chime dangled from his left earlobe. "Where those people got blown away the other night, you mean?"

"Yeah."

"Sometimes. Man, was that a blow to the chest. I was like sick when I heard about it. I knew the guy."

"The owner?"

"Yeah. Nate Swanson."

"You knew him real well?" Cooper laid down the spoon.

"No, not real well. I'd like met him and stuff. I have friends who knew him. The guy had really upgraded the place, you know? They were getting some good fucking bands in, man. What a waste."

"Yeah. That's one way to put it."

"I mean, that's not what I mean. You know what I mean. Bummed me right out."

"So what's the theory? What do his friends say? Who killed them?"

"Who knows? Some asshole looking to rob the place." Dominic shook his head, gazing out the big front window at the sunlit street.

Cooper took a sip of coffee. "I hear about something like that, I think drugs."

Dominic gave him a look, lips tight with disgust. "You would."

"You wouldn't?"

"Nah, man. Why?"

"A nightclub owner? Talk about a great place to deal."

"Ah, bullshit. He'd be stupid to deal out of the club. Too public." Dominic was barely audible, eyes flicking to the customers. "Anyway, I'd know. Everybody that deals around here, on my socioeconomic level anyway, I can tell you. Word gets around."

"Maybe he was more careful than most."

"Shit, you can imagine anything you want. And I can't prove a negative. All I'm saying is, I never heard anything about that and I think I would. What's the deal, anyway?"

"His old man's my boss."

Dominic gave him a long look. "Drag. That's gotta be tough."

"It's tough. He wants to know why it happened. The cops say drugs."

Dominic flicked a crumb off the counter. "What's drugs? Somebody might have done a little Ecstasy in the john, but they weren't selling crack or anything. What the fuck do cops know, anyway?"

"I might ask you the same thing."

Dominic cocked his head to one side, giving it an honest look. "Enough to say Nate Swanson wasn't one of the names that came up when people talked about who could get what where. And the Blue Angel wasn't one of the places. I think they were pretty clean. But then, there's a lot of people dealing. He could have been Pablo Escobar's right-hand man for all I know."

"But no rep."

"Not that I know of." Dominic gave Cooper a blank look. "I hope that makes his old man feel better."

"It might," said Cooper. "Just a little bit."

◆

Cooper pushed on out Belmont to Western. He'd been to Area Six before; he found his way to the second-floor squad room without difficulty and asked the sergeant at the operations desk for Detective Reichardt or Detective Benitez. It was Reichardt he had spoken to on the phone, but it was Benitez who looked up at the sergeant's call and came up the row of desks to shake his hand.

Cooper had dealt with dicks of all ages, hues and ancestries, and he had learned that there was nothing typical except the careful contained movement and the look that went up one side and down the other and had you tentatively graded before it got back to your eyes. Benitez was dressed in a lightweight tan suit with the jacket open to show a flat stomach and a hint of revolver at the hip. He had broad shoulders and thighs that strained the material of the trousers; he was under six feet, and along with the name his close-cropped black hair, neat moustache and very dark eyes said Puerto Rico from across the room. To Cooper he looked like a ballplayer, probably an infielder, but with some pop in his bat. "Good of you to come in," he said, shaking Cooper's hand.

They went back to the desk and Cooper told him about the night before and about Pete Best. Benitez listened without moving, hardly blinking, a professional listener. "But they didn't find anything," he said when Cooper had finished.

"No. But they didn't go down on the beach. I think that's where the two guys came from. I think they parked somewhere in town, hiked out to the lake, slipped through somebody's property and came along the shore to Swanson's place."

"Why do you think that?"

"Because that's the way I would have done it."

Benitez just looked at him for a moment. "And why are you sure it was the same two guys who showed up before?"

"Because they didn't act like mourners. They acted like guys who wanted something. And they didn't get it."

"What do you think they wanted?"

"I don't know. Probably the same thing they wanted from Swanson's son."

"You think these are the guys that killed him?"

"It's a hypothesis."

Benitez let a few seconds go by, watching Cooper. Then he shrugged, just a small movement of his head. "So what did they want from the son?"

"I don't know. What does anybody kill for?"

"You tell me."

"You want me to guess, money will always be at the top of the list. Then there's information control. Maybe revenge. I don't think it was a crime of passion."

Benitez smiled. "You know what the kid did for a living?"

"He was a music promoter, I'm told."

"Apparently." The detective blinked a few times, perhaps framing another question, perhaps waiting for one.

Cooper shifted a little on the chair. "Can I ask you a question?"

"Shoot."

"Why do you think he was dealing drugs?"

"Who says we do?"

"Regis Swanson. I'm asking because the consensus among those who knew him seems to be he wasn't. And I think that kind of thing's hard to hide."

"Not if you're any good."

"OK, I'll grant that. It's just that I've known people who dealt drugs, and it wasn't much of a secret. Word gets around. Here it was a secret. I'm just wondering how you knew."

"Don't worry, we got it on the best possible authority."

Cooper nodded slowly. "OK, I guess I can't argue with that."

Benitez showed a very thin smile. "How long have you worked for his father?"

"About two months."

"And you're what, a chauffeur?"

"Mainly. I run errands now and then. Deliver messages, check out things he doesn't have time to check, stuff like that."

"Where were you when the kid got shot?"

"If he was killed when you say he was, I was probably sitting on my back porch with a drink in my hand."

"I didn't say when he was killed."

"It was in the news."

Benitez nodded slowly. "You got somebody can back you up, I'm sure."

"You want a phone number? I think she's home now."

"In a minute." The detective reached for a folder. "Can you give me a description of these two guys?"

"I can paint you a picture if you have enough time. I've been seeing these two in my sleep."

◆

Cooper made sure to be early at the door of the Chicago Club so as not to make Swanson stand exposed at the curb. When Swanson came out into the sunlight, he looked right and left with the air of a man bemused by his surroundings. He got in the car and slammed the door; Cooper waited for orders but got none. After a few seconds he looked. Swanson was staring out the window at nothing, chin on his hand. "Where to?" said Cooper.

Swanson came to and looked at him blankly; his mouth opened and stayed open but nothing came out. Finally he said, "Fifty South La Salle. Buzz's office."

Cooper put it in gear. "The cops get back to you?"

A few more seconds passed before Swanson said, "No. Not yet. I imagine they're fairly busy."

"They never have a slow day." Cooper eased onto Michigan. "Do you see a black Cutlass Ciera back there?"

Cooper had never heard Regis Swanson cuss seriously and was surprised at the pithy Anglo-Saxon syllable that came over the seat. "They can follow me to the god-damn toilet if they want," he added.

"They probably have it bugged," said Cooper.

"Thanks, that's very helpful."

"Sorry. Bad joke, bad timing."

"I'm under federal investigation," said Swanson abruptly.

"What?"

"I said I'm under federal investigation. They're after me."

Cooper sneaked through an intersection at the tail end of the yellow. "Who are we talking about?"

"The Drug Enforcement Administration. They searched the club yesterday and found something, I don't know what. And I am, of course, the owner. Now they've subpoenaed my bank records. I didn't think they could do that. It's supposed to be a secret. I wouldn't know a thing about it except Joe Hollins collared me just now and filled me in. He heard it from some of the Teachers' people. Somebody slipped them a word to the wise. That's why Peterson canceled on me this morning. Light dawns."

Cooper digested this. "But you can prove you had nothing to do with whatever Nate was up to, right? Your money's got the best pedigree in town."

"Maybe so. But the problem is, even if I'm totally absolved, it's already killed the Teachers' deal."

"You mean because they wouldn't want to commit a whole bunch of money to a deal with a man who might be thrown in jail?"

"Not even that. A man who might have all his property confiscated at any moment. See, the government can seize my property if they think it came from drugs."

"The club, maybe. But why would this kill the other deal?"

"Would you put money into a venture with somebody under federal investigation?"

"I see."

"If the news gets out, I'm dead in this town. I mean I'm wiped out."

"They can't seize everything you own. They're not going to find a judge whose imagination stretches that far."

"They don't have to. That's not the point. Look, I'm at the point where I need Teachers' or somebody like them to step in on the Madison Place project. Chemical Bank wants its construction loan off the books. If Teachers' backs out, they could foreclose on me, and I've put other properties up as collateral. I've got other loans to pay, too."

"Ouch. Dominoes, you mean."

"That's what I mean. This couldn't have hit me at a worse time. I need Teachers' bad right now."

Cooper made a turn, negotiating the angry traffic of the Loop. "Maybe your lawyer can call off the dogs yet. The Feds are the Feds, but they still have rules to follow. I think."

◆

Cooper was not privy to the deliberations of Regis Swanson and his lawyer. Instead he sat in the Mercedes in a parking spot under the El tracks on Wells and thought. Traffic went by and he made a few idle attempts to spot vagrants in the mirror, but mostly he thought.

After a half hour Swanson called him on the car phone and told him to come pick him up.

The man waiting in front of 50 South La Salle looked angry. He glowered across two lanes of traffic as Cooper fought to the curb. Swanson tore open the door of the Mercedes and said, "Take me home."

Cooper worked back into traffic, waiting.

Swanson settled himself on the back seat and just sat for a while before he spoke. "They found something, some kind of dope, in a dressing room at the club. Probably left there by the Final Solution or somebody like that. They haven't seized the club, but apparently they're in full hue and cry. Buzz says to seize they'll have to prove either that it was purchased with proceeds from drug trafficking, which it clearly wasn't, or that it was used to facilitate drug trafficking. That's what they're thinking, apparently. Hence the subpoenas and all the rest."

"What next?"

"Buzz is going to talk to the DEA. He says we lay the records open, cooperate fully, and then, in his colorful phrasing, tear a new asshole in somebody over there. Buzz is a formidable opponent when he gets worked up."

"I can imagine."

"He says I've got nothing to worry about. Of course, the damage has already been done."

"Nothing irreparable, I hope."

"We'll see. All I want now is to go home and stare at the ceiling for a while."

"I don't think that's real wise," Cooper said.

"Don't give me a song and dance. Get me home."

Cooper turned east and waited until he stopped at a red light. "Call it a song and dance if you want. It's still a bad idea to go home."

"I'm not paying you to baby-sit. I'm paying you to drive."

"Listen to me. Somebody shot your son. The DEA is probably not the only one that thinks your son was just half the business. Now if I'm the guy that shot Nate, and I shot him because I don't like the way you do business, what's my next logical step?"

Swanson had not found an answer by the time the light changed. Cooper went through the intersection and pulled over at the first clear stretch of curb he found. He put the Mercedes in neutral and twisted to look over the seat. Swanson was hunkered down in the corner, looking fierce. "My next step is to find you and shoot you, too," said Cooper. "And so far, you're making it easy for me."

Swanson glared at him. He said, "I'm not scared."

"Then your judgment is clouded. That's the charitable explanation." He let Swanson stare at him and then said, "Now. Having the Feds on our tail doesn't worry me. They're not going to shoot you. They might, in a pinch, even stop somebody from shooting you. But I wouldn't count on it. They might not be close enough, or interested enough. They didn't keep those two from camping out in your back yard last night."

"How do you know that wasn't the DEA?"

"It didn't look professional enough to me. And it didn't look like they were there just to watch. They were there to get the jump on somebody. And they'll be back. There, your office, anyplace they think you're likely to show up. So it's time to find a place to hide. Got any ideas?"

Swanson looked out the window and said, "Keep driving."

Cooper had taken Swanson all the way up to Erie before Swanson spoke again. "How long do I have to hide?"

"I don't know. Till they get the people who killed Nate, probably."

"How am I supposed to get any work done?"

"Worry about your safety. The work will take care of itself. I can do a lot of the running around for you."

"I could stay at the club, I guess."

"No good. Everybody knows you're a member. I'd stay away from Hayden and your lady friend, too."

"You mean really drop out of sight, huh?"

"I mean find a bunker, keep your head down, yeah."

Dead silence followed for a block or two, and finally Swanson said, "OK, I'm sure there's a vacant unit or two somewhere in my vast empire. I'd have to make some phone calls."

Cooper handed him the car phone. "You find the place, I'll get you there."

◆

Turk came out of the Harold Washington Public Library and blinked in the sunshine. Libraries were not a congenial environment for Turk, and he wanted two things rather badly: something alcoholic to drink and something female and compliant to take back to the frowsy Ramada Inn southwest of the Loop where he and Ferocious Dick had shifted their base of operations. The alcohol would be easy, but Turk knew that the quest for pussy would distract him fatally from the execution of his duty, so he grimaced and mustered his resolve. He crossed Van Buren to the little corner park that benevolent city planners had planted in the shadows of the South Loop.

When he caught sight of his partner he had to stop and put his hands on his hips. Ferocious Dick was perched on a low stone wall that encircled a patch of grass, and instead of slouching sullenly, staring at nothing, as Turk had expected, he was leaning toward a female next to him and waving one hand with a jerky emphatic motion. The female was a rough match for him, Hispanic and past the bloom of youth with a dark complexion and a low center of gravity. She wore lots of makeup and a pink dress and held her short legs demurely together, hands clasped on an enormous white purse on her lap. She was looking into Ferocious Dick's eyes as if he were Julio Iglesias in mid-croon and smiling in a slightly dazed fashion.

Turk shook his head and walked toward them. He could hear Ferocious Dick's low rumbling growl as he approached; amazingly, the woman seemed to understand it and was nodding. Ferocious Dick didn't see Turk coming and started when he sat beside him and clapped him on the shoulder. The woman looked at him with alarm.

"I hate to break things up, amigo," said Turk, and smiled at the woman. She smiled back, uncertainly. Ferocious Dick looked at him murderously. "Business," said Turk.

Ferocious Dick scowled at him for a second or two and then turned to the woman. He growled and rumbled, cocking a thumb at Turk, and her face went quickly through several changes, winding up at polite blankness as she rose. She extended her hand to Ferocious Dick and Turk in turn. Turk beamed at her and waved as she walked away.

Ferocious Dick slouched, staring sullenly at nothing. "Believe me, she's not your type," said Turk. "Besides, we've got work to do. I know more about Regis Swanson than his own mother does now."

Ferocious Dick grunted once.

Turk shifted on the wall, getting comfortable. "I found a whole feature article about the guy, in a magazine, along with a dozen or so mentions in the paper over the last year or two. Hell of a man, our Regis. Money, power, you name it, he's got it."

Ferocious Dick grunted and applied himself to the unwrapping of a stick of gum.

Turk smiled at a pair of teen-aged girls with big hair who came past. "Only problem is, he hasn't been too successful in his personal life. Divorced his first wife, the second wife got herself shot or something. Only had the one kid. Tragedy seems to stalk the man, the paper said. Regis Swanson carries on in the face of personal disasters. So what does that leave us with, you ask?" Turk watched Ferocious Dick chew, amazed again at the power of the jaws. "I'll tell you. Twice in the last month or so ol' Regis got himself in the gossip columns along with a lady named Zina Manning, a very nice-looking piece of work indeed if you can trust those newspaper photos. One of these society ladies, the kind that goes to charity balls and stuff. Well, rumors are flying, amigo. Regis and Zina are hot, let me tell you. The columnists all say so."

Ferocious Dick rolled the gum wrapper into a little ball and shot it out onto the path, where it rolled to a stop. He grunted.

"I'll tell you something else that kind of surprised me," said Turk. He raised his face to squint up at the massive facade of the library. "Zina Manning's in the phone book."

◆

"Northpoint Towers," said Swanson, handing the phone over the seat to Cooper. "There's a unit there we sold to an old family friend before he moved to Switzerland to be closer to his money. It's fully furnished and I don't think the old bastard would mind my camping there for a while. I can pick up a key from Orloff."

Cooper replaced the phone. "OK. We may have piqued the Feds' interest a little, but that shouldn't matter too much."

"What do you mean?"

"There are systems that can monitor cellular phone frequencies. I wouldn't bet against the DEA having one."

There was a shocked silence in the back seat. "They can't do that, can they?"

"You didn't think they could get your bank records."

"So they know where I'm going."

"Maybe. Like I say, they're not the ones to worry about."

After another silence Swanson said, "And how do you know the ones to worry about aren't following us, too?"

"I don't think they're that good. But even if they are, they won't be in a couple of minutes."

"Why not?"

"You're jumping out as soon as I get around that bus. There's a subway entrance just past the bus stop. I won't even stop rolling. Just make sure to slam the door. They won't see you because of the bus. Get yourself to Northpoint. Pick up a toothbrush, shaving stuff, whatever you need on the way."

"What are you going to do?"

"I'll figure that out as soon as I get around the corner."

10

EMILIO HAD AN elderly Buick up on the lift and was staring up at the springs, thumbs hooked in the pockets of his overalls and shaking his head.

"Can you save her, doctor?" said Cooper, coming into the garage.

Emilio grinned through his beard. "For a couple hundred bucks I can get her limping again. What's up, man?"

"What you got back in the alley there these days? I need some wheels."

"Don't tell me the Mustang broke down."

"Nah, the Mustang's fine. I need something anonymous for a few days, that's all."

Emilio stared and then laughed. "Don't tell me."

"OK, I won't."

"You in trouble again? You got the law on you?"

"Man, you got the wrong idea about me. I'm a straight-shootin' hombre."

"All I know is, when I ain't bailing you out of jail, I'm lending you cars they can't trace to you."

"It's for my job this time. The boss wants to avoid attention for a while."

Emilio shook his head and headed for the office. "I got a nice Mercury Marquis I just picked up last week. Runs great."

"Sounds good."

Holding out the keys, Emilio said, "I want you to explain to me sometime what it is you do for a living."

"Let me get back to you on that, OK?" said Cooper. "It might be kind of in flux right now."

◆

"Wow," said Cooper, coming in the door past Swanson. "It's not exactly a hole in the ground, is it?" He moved past Swanson toward the slightly convex line of floor-to-ceiling windows opposite the foyer that showed a distant slash of blue lake behind the foreground clutter of high buildings. He laid a garment bag over the back of a chair and set a Pullman bag on a mahogany cocktail table that seemed to be the only thing between the cream-colored contemporary sofa and a twenty-five-story drop.

"Be careful of the finish," said Swanson. "The owner of this place stops in about once every two years, but he notices things like scratches."

Cooper moved the bag to the floor and turned to look at his boss. Swanson was in shirtsleeves, his blue oxford looking forlorn without a tie. He was shaved and combed and yet somehow still managed to give an impression of dishevelment, perhaps because of the way his eyes moved haphazardly around the room, as if looking for a lost object.

"So what happened last night after you dropped me?" he said.

"Nothing. I drove back to your place, left the Mercedes and picked up this stuff from Felicidad, drove my car home. This morning I got us something a little less conspicuous to drive. I got your little flip phone from the house to use in it. I can run over to the office now and pick up whatever you need from there."

Swanson nodded. "I'll call Connie, have her get the stuff ready for you. I'd like to get over there myself sometime today, though."

"Why? You've got a telephone here and property managers, accountants and a chief financial officer over there. If they couldn't keep the ship running you wouldn't have hired them. So far your empire is holding together."

Swanson smiled grimly as he walked to the Pullman bag, picked it up and looked inside without much interest. "Maybe." He snapped the bag shut and set it down again. "I've been talking to creditors this morning."

Cooper waited. "And?"

"And the sun might be setting on my little empire. People are calling in the debts." Swanson frowned at him for a moment before losing focus and wandering toward the window.

"Afraid they'll lose it all to the government?"

"I guess so. Even though Buzz is saying this morning the DEA doesn't have a case, nothing at all. But all a creditor needs to hear is just a hint that they're looking at me. Just a hint. See, that's the beauty of these forfeiture laws. They don't need a case. They can just take it. It's a very powerful tool against organized crime, I'm told."

"I'm sure it is." Cooper came to join Swanson at the window, hands in his pockets, looking out toward the lake. "How badly is this going to hurt you?"

Swanson shrugged. "It won't kill me. But I'm going to have to scramble to appease these people. I'm in decent shape but you're always working with some debt in this business. Let's just say that even in the best-case scenario I'm not going to be as rich a week from now. Worst case, I might have to go to work for a living again." Swanson made a little whuffing noise that might have been a laugh. "Maybe that's what I need, a little wake-up call. In any event, I'll need to be over at First National for a meeting at one. Can you get me there intact?"

"I can give it a shot," said Cooper.

◆

Snodgrass looked peeved, whether with the way things had turned out or the way Jasper was taking it, Toni couldn't be sure. "He pledged total cooperation. They're laying the records wide open. We're meeting with Hayden and the bankers this afternoon." He paused for a beat. "That doesn't sound like a guilty reaction to me."

"Of course it doesn't," said Jasper. "You think the man's a fool? He's not going to have the dirty money on the books. That's what buying the club was all about."

"We're getting the club finances sorted out. They're pretty simple and so far it doesn't look as if there's anything shady there. If Swanson's handling drug money in any quantity, it'll show up. Borland will find it. He's an expert."

"They'll show you what they want to show you. They won't show you the real books."

"Look, Borland's been at this a while. He knows what to look for, he knows what to look at. He knows what legitimate books look like and he knows what a great big hole in the books looks like. If Swanson's people try and feed him some kind of bullshit, he'll know."

"What I want to know is who tipped him."

"Has to be somebody from the bank."

"Find out who and prosecute the son of a bitch."

"We'll try. Trouble is, people like Swanson never have a shortage of friends."

"Yeah. That's why you have to work extra hard on them."

"Right now, the man's cooperating. If there's anything funny, Borland will find it."

"Terrific. I say keep the surveillance on anyway."

Snodgrass laid his pencil on the table. "We need the people elsewhere. We've got half a dozen things going at once here. Where am I going to put the people, on a guy we know is moving ten kilos a week, or a guy we've got nothing on but an anonymous tip about his son and who's doing everything we ask him to?"

"Did you see the report from yesterday?"

"I saw it."

"They pulled some shit to shake us. Swanson never went home last night. He's gone into hiding. That, I'd call a guilty reaction."

"You lost him. Forget it. It's on hold for the moment. You've got plenty of other work to do."

"We didn't lose him. He shook us. There's a difference."

"Look, right now Borland's doing all we're going to do on Regis Swanson. You two, I've got other plans for."

Jasper shook his head. "You're gonna let him off the hook."

"J.D., there's so many fish out there, we'll have another one on the hook by lunchtime. I'm putting you back on Stu's task force."

Half an hour later, sitting in a battered Chevy van in a West Side garage with the engine idling, Jasper chewed on a nail and said, "Here it comes again. The fix, the cover-up, the influential friends. Fucking Snodgrass, getting ready to buckle again. I bet he's getting phone calls from everywhere. City Hall, Washington probably. Swanson's got a lot of fucking friends, like he said."

Toni had been waiting for the sequel. "Maybe. Forget it, J.D. We got work to do."

"Tell me something."

"What?" she said, carefully fastening her seat belt.

"If the whole thing with Swanson is bullshit, what happened to the million dollars?"

Toni considered. "You mean the million dollars Nate Swanson supposedly got from Dexter."

"There's no god-damn supposing about it. If there was no million dollars, how come Dexter, the girlfriend and Nate all got killed? This is not a fictional million dollars. This is a million dollars that killed three people. Hell, more than three, you add 'em up. I'm inclined to take that kind of money seriously."

"One of Nate's low-life friends has it. He had a whole network apart from his father. It'll turn up."

Jasper gunned the engine, just for practice. "I'm telling you, papa has it. You've been in this business long enough to have hunches. All right, the man's clean enough to show us his books. Maybe he hasn't been involved, till now. But the way he and that chauffeur of his are acting, I'll be damned if I believe he's clean now. That fucking chauffeur's getting on my nerves."

Toni stared out the windshield at the subterranean gloom of the garage. "Well, what are you going to do about it? We're just grunts. We've got our orders."

Jasper put the car in gear. "You ever heard of unpaid overtime?"

"What, you're going to maintain full surveillance on this guy all by yourself, just in your spare time?"

Jasper grinned, gunning it up the ramp to daylight. "There's more than one way to skin a cat. And I won't be all by myself."

"Oh yeah?"

"Yeah. You and me, baby, we're gonna bag us a big one."

◆

Zina Manning settled the reading glasses on her fine straight nose and opened the manila envelope. The prospectus slid out onto the leather-lined top of the Regency pedestal desk and she began to read with a critical eye, making an occasional note on a sheet of watermarked stationery with a gold-plated ballpoint pen. Occasionally she raised her eyes to look pensively out the bow window at the lake beyond. The air conditioning breathed just audibly in the background.

When the telephone rang, Zina pushed away from the desk and strode across the blue Isfahan carpet to answer it. She swung her blond hair away from her ear with a graceful toss of the head and put the receiver to it. "Yes?"

"Ms. Manning? George at the desk."

"Yes, George."

"There's a gentleman here by the name of David Hertz to see you."

"David Hertz?"

"That's right, ma'am. And another gentleman."

Zina was speechless for a moment, wondering why the director of CAUSE, the Chicago AIDS Union for Social Empowerment, would show up on her doorstep unannounced, but her ingrained sense of service, or perhaps merely her reflexive politeness, caused her to say, "Send him up, please."

She bustled about trying to tidy an already impeccably tidy room while the elevator climbed eighteen floors. When the doorbell chimed gently she remembered to stuff her reading glasses back in the desk drawer before she walked gracefully down the hall to the door and opened it.

"Good morning, ma'am. We're sorry to barge in on you like this, but we hope you'll understand." By the time the big man finished the sentence, he was past Zina and halfway down the hall. She hardly noticed the second man because she was fixed on the first, a handsome big-boned man with a strong-jawed face and light brown hair in a ponytail. The door was gently disengaged from her fingers and she looked to see the second man closing it swiftly but silently, a smaller, darker, rather nasty-looking man. He smiled at her as the latch clicked, showing crooked teeth.

"It's good of you to ask us in," said the first man, already looking into the living room. "I know how valuable your time is, and we won't take much of it. Mr. Hertz speaks very highly of you. What a lovely place this is." He was heading for the windows, hands in the pockets of his white duck trousers.

When Zina found her tongue it was with a rush of indignation. "You're not David Hertz," she said.

"No. I'm sorry if there was some confusion down there. I think the fellow at the desk garbled things a bit. I asked him to say Mr. Hertz sent us. I'm Joe Friday. This is my associate Mr. Dick."

Zina found herself in the middle of her living room, head swiveling from the tall good-looking man to the little squat dark man in the doorway to the hall, bewildered. "How do you do?" she managed finally, warily.

"Fine, thank you, now that we're here. It was touch and go for a while. I'm afraid we lied to you." He smiled, showing fine white teeth.

Zina felt herself flushing, and she put her hands on her hips and firmed her lips. "Who are you and what do you want?"

"Your cooperation," the man said smoothly. "That's all."

"I'm a very agreeable person. All you had to do is ask. I don't appreciate being lied to."

"Nobody does. May I?" He stuck out a hand at the japanned parcel-gilt sofa.

"No, as a matter of fact. You may not. State your business. I must say, whatever it is, I'll make sure David Hertz hears about this." Zina cast a glance at the short dark man, who hadn't moved.

"Don't bother. I picked his name out of the paper. Maybe you should sit down."

Zina glared for a moment longer and then whirled and stalked toward the phone. The short man was there before her, just standing in her way so that she would have to go around him or shove him aside. A look into the blunt hard face discouraged her from trying. "Who are you?" she said, turning back to the tall man, alarm just starting to vie with indignation.

"I told you who we are. Now listen and I'll tell you what we want."

Zina Manning had faced down importunate suitors, impecunious relations, drunken husbands, meddlesome reporters, desperate fund-raisers, megalomaniac lawyers and even an incompetent rapist. She drew herself up to her full five feet seven inches and said, "You have ten seconds."

"Should be enough. We need to talk to your boyfriend."

Zina glowered. "I do not have a boyfriend. I'm forty-four years old and I do not dally with boys anymore."

"OK, what do you call him? Your gigolo? We need to talk to Regis Swanson."

Zina looked from one man to the other and back, contemptuously, though privately she was contending with a growing sense of apprehension. "If you have something to say to Regis you're free to contact him yourselves. I can't imagine what you're doing here."

"Mr. Swanson is not in the office and will not be available for several days. That's verbatim, from his receptionist. And he's not answering calls at home."

"Well, there you have it, then."

"But you can reach him."

"What on earth makes you think that?"

The man with the ponytail sighed as he sank onto the sofa. He crossed one leg over the other and clasped his hands in his lap. "Zina, baby. We're men on a mission and we're in a hurry. We don't have time for bullshit. If you wanted to keep your thing with Regis out of the papers, I'm sure you could have, but you didn't. Now I want you to call him and get him over here, and I want you to make it sound good."

Zina stood with arms akimbo and glared at him with her heart racing, trying to think. Finally she said, exerting a good deal of control over her voice, "Regis is in mourning. His son was killed the other day. I have talked with him once, by telephone, since it happened. We are friends, but we are not so intimate that I can share this difficult time with him. We agreed that he will be in touch, but he did not say when. And he did not leave any secret unlisted phone numbers. I'm afraid I can't help you."

The man with the ponytail assumed a regretful but resolute expression. He looked around the room, starting with the damask curtains, skimming over the George III giltwood mirror, lingering for a moment on the genuine Bonington above the Hepplewhite satinwood-inlaid sideboard, and coming to rest finally on the magnificent Imari vase on the occasional table by the door. He looked at the small dark nasty man and nodded once toward the vase.

The small man stepped over to the table with a total lack of expression and, as Zina raised her hands, dumb with horror, plucked the vase off it with both hands, the lid plunking onto the rug, and in a swift vicious swipe shattered it against the frame of the doorway into the hall. The crash died away into the clatter of fragments on the uncarpeted hall floor.

Zina swayed on trembling legs and put a hand to her lips to repress what was trying to force its way out. She kept the hand there, the room settling into silence, until she felt able to speak. "That was worth ten thousand dollars," she said quietly before she choked.

"And cheap at the price," said the man in the armchair. "Now. They gotta know you at Swanson's office. You're gonna call them and have them put you through to him. You're gonna tell him you need him and you're gonna get him over here. There will be no bullshit, no code words, no cleverness. Mr. Dick here will dial the number for you. If you feel brave and decide to shout help into the phone, the police will find a million dollars worth of smashed antiques on the floor when they get here. If you do what we're asking you to do, there won't be any more breakage. I might even be able to get my boss to pay for the vase."

In her turmoil Zina remembered what her mother, a survivor of two rough marriages, had told her in a rare moment of loquaciousness, long ago: "Honey, if it gets down to a shoving match a man is going to beat you every time, because men have the weight advantage. But that makes them complacent, and you can beat a man the way a rattlesnake beats a grizzly—you just sit there and watch and wait for his mind to wander." Zina took a deep breath and said, "All right. I presume your colleague knows the number?"

The man on the sofa smiled. "I made him write it down."

◆

Toni saw it coming; looking out the window of the van onto West Side wasteland two blocks north of the Eisenhower Expressway, weeds growing where houses once stood, she watched the old black lady come laboring up the sidewalk on swollen legs that looked like sausages in their laddered stockings; she saw the two teen-aged males in knee-length baggy hip-hop shorts come sauntering up behind her, watching but not watching, slowly catching up.

"J.D.," she said. Jasper came to life and scuttled along the floor of the van to the window beside her. "I think we're about to see a mugging."

Jasper watched for a moment and said, "Looks like it." The two kids were just about in striking range; the lady had heard them and stopped, turning suspiciously, holding the purse closer to her and leaning shakily on the cane. Toni reached for the door handle.

"What the fuck are you doing?" Jasper stopped her with a hand on her wrist.

"They're gonna . . ." She stopped and watched it happen, as one boy ripped the purse from the old lady's grip while the other put her on the ground with a hard shove. The lady's thin wail was audible in the van. "Shit," said Toni.

"None of our business," said Jasper. As they watched, the kid with the purse took off running toward the van. The second kid lingered long enough to snap the old lady's head back with a casual kick before following his partner. The lead punk, purse dangling, was coming up the block at a leisurely lope, grinning.

"We can wrap 'em up," said Toni, shooting a look at Jasper.

"Stay put. What we do is, we call it in to the cops."

"Dammit, J.D."

"We jump out of this van, we blow ourselves sky high. A month's work down the tubes. What the fuck's the matter with you?"

The two boys ran past the van, within arm's reach, laughing. Toni could hear the old woman crying now, could see her on hands and knees trying to rise or perhaps just staying put for a while. She could see the drops of blood, bright red, dripping one by one onto the concrete. The sound of footsteps faded. A man came out of a storefront and bent over the old lady, not touching her.

"Call it in," said Toni, frozen.

"I will. Come on, Toni. You know what we're here for."

Toni watched another man join the first. He looked around warily, as if afraid someone were watching. The old lady was sobbing, great racking sobs, still on her hands and knees. The first man straightened up, said something to the second, shrugged. "Yeah," said Toni. "I know what we're here for. We're here to watch a couple dozen people go in that house across the way and make a purchase. When we see enough of them, maybe we'll arrest somebody for giving them what they want. That'll put a stop to that shit, all right."

Jasper stared at her for a long time; Toni could feel his gaze on her as she went on watching the old woman, struggling to her feet now with the half-hearted help of the two men. "You need a vacation or something," Jasper said.

"Or something," said Toni.

◆

"May I go to the bathroom?" Zina was grateful that her voice sounded normal.

The man with the ponytail looked up from the copy of *Financial Privacy* he had found on a foray into the nether reaches of the apartment. "Sure. Just as soon as Mr. Dick here checks it out." He looked at the little dark man, who had settled into immobility on the Sheraton chair in the corner. "Go make sure there's nothing in there she can make mischief with, will you? No guns, no knives, no attack dogs?" The little man grunted softly and left the room, heading down the hall.

The man with the ponytail smiled at Zina. "Just a precaution. I hope you won't take it personally." He laid the magazine aside. "I have to say, that was masterful on the phone. And I'm sorry about the vase, I really am. Like I say, I'd be willing to bet my boss will spring for a replacement."

"It's irreplaceable," said Zina quietly, with venom.

"Restitution, then. He's a reasonable man. See, Zina, I guess you could say stunts like breaking the vase are just kind of a cost of business with us. We had to make you see how important it is to us to talk to Swanson, you know? Nobody likes the rough stuff. And since you're cooperating just as nicely as we could ask, I'm going to do everything in my power to see that my employer comes up with restitution for the vase. I promise you that."

Zina looked into the handsome square-jawed face with its hard corrupt eyes and had to clench her jaws to fight the nausea. "Spare me," she said.

She fled his look then, looking away out the bow window toward the lake, until the other man came back. "OK," he said, in a deep broken growl, hanging back in the hall.

"Go ahead," said the man with the ponytail. "Don't worry, I won't let Dick hover. But listen. One thing, OK? Don't try and just hide in there and hope we'll go away. When you hear furniture breaking, you'll know it's time to come out."

Zina rose with great dignity and marched out of the room and down the hall, past the nasty dark man and toward the bathroom at the rear. Her apartment looked strange to her, as if viewed for the first time or perhaps in a dream. She went into the bathroom at the end of the hall, closed and bolted the door, and looked in the mirror.

She saw a strange woman there, a woman not unattractive despite the lack of makeup and the advance of years, a woman once beautiful and perhaps still, a classic face with classic blue eyes and blond hair needing just a touch of restoration, but right now a strange face, an unfamiliar one, a frightened one. Zina closed her eyes for a moment, hoping it would all go away, all prove to be a restless dawn dream.

When she opened her eyes, she looked in the cabinet immediately and began shifting objects, looking for something, anything. A weapon, a ruse, an inspiration. Hairspray, nail clippers, a Lady Remington. For a moment Zina wished she had kept Reed's old .45, one of the first objects she had gotten rid of after his death.

She gave up after a minute or two and composed herself. She heard her mother's voice again and sat on the closed toilet, thinking of the rattlesnake in the Lincoln Park Zoo, motionless behind glass.

◆

Cooper set two bags of staple foods and supplies on the counter in a totally virgin kitchen and brought Swanson up to date. Swanson was looking a bit more focused and he had put on his jacket and tie. He listened and said, "Fine. I'll deal with all that after I get done at the bank. Right now you need to get me to Scott Street in ten minutes."

"Your rich widow?"

Swanson nodded. "We're having lunch."

Cooper looked at his watch. "That might be cutting it close for the bank."

"That's OK. I might need her at the bank. She's offered to help."

"What, with money?"

Swanson's look told Cooper he was getting a bit presumptuous, but he nodded. "When I say rich widow, I mean rich. You know who Reed Manning was?"

Cooper thought for a second. "Manning Foods? That Manning?"

Swanson smiled. "That Manning. The TV dinner tycoon. 'Cordon Bleu in Your Freezer,' remember?"

"I remember."

Swanson snapped the briefcase shut. "Well, I'm hoping ol' Reed won't mind helping to keep me out of the freezer this time."

◆

Zina sat on the sofa with her arms folded, looking out the bow window at the painfully beautiful, terribly remote blue waters of the lake. She was calm now; she had found somewhat to her surprise that even high levels of tension became no more than background if prolonged. She stared out at the lake, hearing seconds tick off the pendulum wall clock in the hall and thinking about death. She found she was rather less inclined to be philosophical about it than she had imagined.

The man with the ponytail came back into the room with a glass of water in his hand. He gave her a look that meant nothing, absolutely nothing, and Zina realized that even at this late date she was still looking at him hopefully, like a dog that can't believe its master is really going to beat it. Zina looked back out at the lake and felt something get harder inside.

The man with the ponytail exchanged a look with the small dark man, still stolidly in place on the chair in the corner, and took another drink. He set the glass down on the sideboard.

"Please don't put that there," said Zina. "If you must set it down, there are coasters in the cabinet in the dining room. You can put the glass on one of those two occasional tables."

The man with the ponytail smiled at her and picked up the glass. He brushed his fingers across the place where it had been. "Relax. No harm done."

"Not yet."

He shook his head, looking amused. "You have any children?"

"Why?"

"I'm just wondering if you give them as much attention as you do the furniture."

Zina gave him a malevolent stare. "Why don't you tell me what's going to happen when Regis gets here?"

"OK. When he calls up, you answer and be natural, just like before. Any tricks, the same goes. Your living room is going to look like a trailer park after a twister. Then your job's over. When he gets up here and knocks on the door, you'll be right here on the couch. I'll let him in and we'll have our little talk. When we're through, we'll leave you two to your lunch."

Zina believed the man in the ponytail about as much as she had believed Reed Manning when he had sworn there was nothing between him and the pert redhead from Dallas. She looked away out past the balcony again, and this time she was thinking of Nate Swanson and of her own cowardice.

"That clear up all your questions?" said the man in the ponytail.

"I think so," said Zina, just as the telephone rang. She took a deep breath and rose from the sofa. At the same time, the little nasty dark man stood up and moved toward the telephone stand. He watched her as their courses converged, head lowered a little, looking like a mean dog tracking her from behind a fence. The man in the ponytail stepped out of her way and made an ushering gesture with his hand. Zina marched straight, eyes on the phone.

She picked up the receiver, swung her hair away from her ear, and said, "Yes?"

"Ms. Manning, Mr. Swanson is here."

Zina could see out the bow window to the distant blue of the lake. She drew breath, thinking how hard and bitter a thing true courage must be, and said, "George, whatever you do, don't let him come up here. Please call the police immediately. Those two men you sent up earlier. . ." The dark little man's hand slammed down on the switch hook.

Zina took the receiver away from her ear and replaced it on the cradle, just missing his hand as it was withdrawn. She looked at the man with the ponytail. "Get out of my house," she said.

He looked back with a perfect absence of expression. "God-damn it," he said.

Zina was surprised to find that she felt no panic. She remembered the incompetent rapist and had time for the thought that it was most likely going to cost her a great deal more, by any reckoning, to survive this. Her eyes dropped to the table at her side and slowly, sadly, she reached for the Worcester pear-shaped bottle that stood there, her favorite, exquisite in blue and white. She folded it to her breast and looked up again.

The man with the ponytail was looking at the nasty little dark man. "Blow her fucking head off," he said.

What followed was reflex. The dark man had the revolver halfway out of his jacket when Zina cracked the bottle over his mouth, shattering approximately one thousand dollars' worth of antique pottery and perhaps a couple of crooked teeth.

Zina bolted for the hall. Out of the corner of her eye she could see the other man coming; in passing she caught the edge of the six-leaf painted chinoiserie Dutch screen and tugged, hurling it into his path. She heard something crack as he hit it but she was beyond worrying about the furniture; she could see the bathroom at the end of the hall. She had thought far enough ahead to know that she would never have time to get out the front door and there was no place to run out in the hallway anyway; but the bathroom had a stout door and a heavy bolt.

The bathroom, however, was thirty feet away.

◆

Cooper had an hour and he wanted lunch, but he was also curious. He doubted that anybody was following him today, but precautions were cheap. After he dropped Swanson at the dark green awning that stretched to the curb from 180 Scott Street, he sat there for a minute, watching the mirror. A black LeMans with a woman at the wheel came around the corner and went past him, going all the way up to State and turning south. A blue Sentra flashed across the mirror, going south. Cooper put the car in gear and went up to the corner, turning north.

The neighborhood had old solid houses cheek by jowl with towering high-rises, narrow streets, carefully tended gardens, and ivy climbing on old brick. The lamp posts bore signs saying *No Cruising*. Cooper thought if there was ever a spot to shake a tail, this was it. He went up a block, made a right and pulled over halfway down the block next to a small, shaded park, waiting for something familiar to appear in the mirror. When nothing did in half a minute or so, he went on to the corner, turned south, and rolled slowly down toward Scott and the completion of the circuit.

When the two jokers came out of the alley behind 180 Scott, the man with the ponytail and the one who looked like a pit bull, Cooper stepped on the brake out of pure dumb surprise. They came up the block from the mouth of the alley toward him, and for a moment he thought they were coming to get him. He had started to twist the wheel to peel out when he realized they weren't looking at him at all. The tall one was striding with purpose, a scowl on his face, and the short one was holding a handkerchief to his mouth, almost trotting to keep up. Cooper could see blood on the handkerchief.

He eased off the brake and rolled past them at normal cruising speed, getting a look as they came by. By the time he could see them in the mirror, he had sorted out his thoughts and was looking the choices square in the face. "God-damn it," he said.

Impulse number one was to rush in there and see if there was anything left to salvage after the ambush. But if the two jokers were walking away, they'd already done what they'd come for; it was too late. Priority one was to keep them from getting away. Cooper saw the two figures in the mirror disappear around the corner, going west.

He gave it another two seconds' thought and accelerated, swinging right and blowing past the entrance to 180. He went up to the next corner and went right, then eased off the accelerator, going up the block slowly enough to give them time to come into sight.

They never did. By the time Cooper reached Goethe Street nobody was in sight except old women walking dogs and young women walking children. Cooper crawled across the intersection, looking every which way, and didn't see them. He stopped and looked over his shoulder, scanning the park. He reversed across the intersection, looking again, and swore. They had vanished, vaporized.

Or they had been parked just around the corner, and had pulled out, heading east, while Cooper was coming up the block. They could have turned north or south, and they were gone.

It was cold sweat time, and Cooper had bad visions of what was going on back at 180 Scott Street. He tore down Goethe at a speed that drew hostile looks from the mothers in the park, rounded the block and pulled up at the dark green awning just as a squad car came down the block against the one-way signs from State Street, Mars lights flashing. Cooper got out of the car and had time to think that they sure as hell got there fast in a rich neighborhood before Regis Swanson, looking distraught, burst out of the doorway onto the sidewalk, much to Cooper's relief.

11

"THEY FOUND HER in the bathroom," said Swanson, a fierce cold light in his eyes. He was pale and rigid, standing in the fluorescent glare of the emergency room. "Bleeding in the bathtub. She managed to get the bathroom door bolted and climb in the tub, but they shot her through the door. They tried to kick it down but they couldn't and so they split."

"I saw them," said Cooper. "I tried to follow but I lost them."

"I can't believe they shot her."

"She'll make it, right?"

"That's what they're telling me. But she lost a lot of blood. I can't believe they shot her."

"They shot your son, too."

Swanson looked at him then. "The same guys."

"I'd bet on it. But the one they really want is you."

Swanson looked at him for a long moment without blinking. "Why?"

"Simple," said Cooper. "You've got something they want."

"What, for God's sake?"

Cooper shrugged. "What do you have a lot of? My guess would be money."

◆

"This is so chic. It's very contemporary. It's stylish and very sexy. It's very you." The hairdresser was a carefully painted and scented blond woman, forty trying hard to look thirty, and Turk thought her delight at his new haircut was a little excessive. In the mirror they looked like an old married couple stiffly posed for a portrait. Turk turned his head from side to side, looking at the shaved sides and back, the bangs sweeping artfully into his eyes.

"It's very me, huh? You sure it isn't a little too Halston or something?"

"Oh no," the hairdresser said, uncertainly. "I think it's perfect for you."

"Well, it's different."

"Believe me, this is your look," she said, rallying. "To be quite honest I don't think the ponytail suited you. The ponytail look for men is out."

"Damn," said Turk, climbing out of the chair. "Nobody told me."

Out in the heat, Turk walked down Wabash Avenue under the rattling El tracks until he came to a discount eyewear store. He looked in through the window to make sure it was busy, then went in and wrote "Jim Morrison" on the register. He wandered around a bit, looking over the frames in the wall display. After a couple of minutes he checked the mirror to make sure no one was watching and slipped a pair of heavy black sample frames into his jacket pocket. Then he looked at his watch, made dissatisfied noises, struck his name off the register and left.

He walked down to Harrison and took the bus back to the motel. He went up to the second level and walked along until he came to Ferocious Dick's room. He knocked and waited until the door was opened, then slipped into air-conditioned comfort.

Ferocious Dick's upper lip looked like a blood sausage. The television was on and Ferocious Dick was in his sleeveless undershirt. He looked about as ferocious as a road-killed raccoon. He glared at Turk's new haircut and then shook his head and growled something, heading back to the bed. The bed was rumpled and a pint of Jack Daniels stood on the bedside table along with a bright red Coke can and a glass of ice. "Thanks," said Turk. "I like it too. It's very me, they tell me."

Ferocious Dick settled himself on the bed, both pillows behind his head and his legs crossed at the ankles. Turk pulled the glasses frames out of his pocket and set them on the bedside table next to the bourbon. "From now on you wear these in public," he said. Ferocious Dick picked them up and laughed once, a noise like a clogged drain clearing. He flung them across the room and looked back at the TV. Turk walked to the TV and turned it off. In the silence he walked to the head of the bed and sat in the plastic-upholstered green armchair beside it.

"We have to move again." Ferocious Dick just stared at him. "And we're on a cash basis now. We've run through our credit cards for this trip. That means no more rental cars. The best thing might be to buy something cheap, find some beater on a lot somewhere." Ferocious Dick stirred and Turk said, "I know. It wasn't supposed to take this long." He reached for the bourbon, studied the label, and took a drink from the bottle. "It ain't supposed to be this hard, partner."

Ferocious Dick laughed again.

"I don't know what else can go wrong," said Turk, "but if we run true to form it will. Oscar's getting impatient, and to be real frank with you I am too. I don't know how you could let that woman take you like that." He took another sip of bourbon and put the bottle down.

Ferocious Dick just stared for a moment, and then his hand went under the sheet and came out with the big revolver. He aimed at Turk's head and there was no particular expression on his face. Turk looked at the gun and then into Ferocious Dick's eyes.

"OK, you're pissed off. The fact remains, she took you. Now put that thing away and let's talk sense."

Ferocious Dick gave the muzzle of the gun one little jerk that was as articulate as Ferocious Dick ever got, and slid it back under the covers. He swung his legs to the floor with a faint grunt and reached for the bottle on the bedside table. He mixed some bourbon with the last of the Coke, screwed the cap onto the bottle and took a drink.

Turk watched him, shaking his head just perceptibly. "Got that out of your system? OK, listen. The worst thing we could do now would be to start pressing too hard. Our descriptions are going to be all over town and it's going to be harder than ever to get close to Swanson. The best thing to do is just chill for a while. Find a place to lie low, work out a new approach. Maybe split up for a couple of days. Work on not being who they'll be looking for. You get used to the glasses and I'll get used to the faggot haircut. In a few days, we'll see how the land lies."

Ferocious Dick was looking into his glass. Turk stood up. "I'm checking out," he said. "I think you're OK here for another day or so. Just keep out of sight. I'll find a new place and call you to let you know where I am. Then you move. You got cash?" Ferocious Dick grunted. "OK. Tomorrow, you get a car. Look in the paper or find a used car dealer in the phone book or something. Nothing fancy. Maybe a van, they're always useful. We'll only need it for a couple of days. Now you suck on some ice or something. I'll be in touch." He paused with his hand on the doorknob. Ferocious Dick looked up from the glass and Turk drew on him, bringing the automatic out from under his jacket. Sighting on Ferocious Dick's broad forehead, he said, "And don't ever pull any shit like that on me again. *Comprende,* partner?"

Ferocious Dick grunted into the glass and Turk put away the gun and went out into the heat.

◆

"Leave town," said Cooper. "Tonight. Go someplace far away and exclusive where you can't be traced." He stood at the curved window looking down into the streets; behind him Swanson sat on the edge of the couch, elbows on knees, apparently studying the label of the bottle of Swedish vodka that stood with its cap off next to a glass full of ice.

"I can't leave town," said Swanson. "Not till I get my finances straightened out. I've rescheduled the meeting at the bank for tomorrow morning. If things go well—if—then maybe in a day or two I'll be able to get away."

Cooper turned. "With telephones, faxes, computer networks and all, you still have to physically be here to conduct your business? I don't believe it."

Swanson looked up at him with sudden irritation. "I don't pay you to believe or disbelieve what I say. This kind of thing is all contacts, favors, back-scratching, persuasion. It's got to be face to face. I can't skip out with my fortune going down the drain. I have to be here." He poured vodka into the glass, leaned back on the couch, and drank some.

"OK," said Cooper. "But I can't guarantee you nobody's going to find you. If they had Zina scoped out they could know about any of your usual associates. I'm not going to stand here and tell you I can keep you safe. I'm not a bodyguard."

Swanson looked at him, the glass clutched on his chest, close to his chin. To Cooper he looked scared, finally. Swanson blinked a few times and said, "I called Felicidad with a list of things I want from the house. I'll call her back and add one more. Can you use a .38?"

Cooper gave a whiff of laughter. "I can use anything that has a trigger. But I'm not trained to protect you from professional assassins. What you really need, short of getting out of town, is twenty-four-hour professional bodyguarding, for you and your friends. There are agencies that can provide it. It would cost you an arm and a leg, but it would be worth it."

"Right now I'm not sure I have the money to hire bodyguards."

"They'd probably take a credit card. Look, if it was just you the odds would be on our side. But it's not just you. You're vulnerable as long as there are people you care about, and that's the tack they're taking so far. That method's tried and true."

Swanson frowned. "I have a lot of friends. I can't afford to protect the whole city."

"You can at least pick out an inner circle, your nearest and dearest, and make sure they're covered."

Swanson stared out the window for a while. "Nearest and dearest," he said. "I'm afraid Nate was about it."

Cooper turned back to the window. "Are we on our own, then?"

"Well, there's the police."

"Yeah, there's them."

"And there's you."

"Yeah," said Cooper. "There's me."

A few seconds went by and Swanson said, "I'll pay you a one-thousand-dollar bonus to keep me safe for one week. I think I can afford that. After that I'll take your advice and go far away. Is that a deal?"

Cooper thought about it, just for a moment. "I've got a wife now."

Swanson looked into his vodka. "OK. You want to leave, that's your prerogative. What do I owe you?"

"I didn't say I was leaving. I'm paid through the end of the month, and I'll be here." Cooper let out a long slow breath. "Look, if you're going to try to carry on a semblance of a normal lifestyle, you're going to need big-time help. Guards in the building, a team in a car, maybe two for moving around. I can't recommend anything less. Sure, you might be OK as long as you're not too predictable. As long as we keep your crib a secret and move carefully, I think they'd have to be lucky to find you. But it makes me damn nervous. If you don't want to go the whole nine yards, the only thing I can tell you is sit tight right here, lie low."

"Till when?"

"Till you're ready to leave town. Do your business on the phone or have your bankers come here."

Swanson tilted his head a little, thinking. "Maybe."

"Who knows where you are? Orloff, me, you. Anybody else?"

"Buzz. That's all."

"OK. You tell Orloff to keep his mouth shut?"

"He knows."

"Fine. If you keep your head down, you're probably OK here. You could probably get by with a couple of guards."

Swanson looked up sharply. "What are they going to do, sleep with me? The building's got good security."

"OK, you're the boss. But I'd get in touch with a decent security firm and see what they say. Hell, I'd put somebody down in the garage, somebody in the hall. I'd put one in your office, too, whether or not you plan to be there. That's an easy target if they want to try something like they did with Zina."

Swanson nodded. "OK, you take care of it. Call somebody."

"All right."

"I'll still need you to run errands, even if I'm not moving. I have a feeling there'll be a lot to do."

"OK."

"And you get the thousand anyway. Call it combat pay." Swanson took another drink and his head lolled back on the couch.

Cooper watched him for a moment. "Thanks. Let me give you one more thing to think about."

Swanson gave him a sidelong look. "What?"

"This started with Nate and so far it seems to revolve around him. It's his enemies the cops want to know about. But given the way things have fallen out, I think maybe it's time we started thinking about yours."

Silence stretched on for a long moment. "What enemies?" said Swanson.

"The ones who got you into this. The ones who would be happy to see you out of the business. I don't know, you tell me."

"But I don't have any enemies."

Cooper shook his head, looking down into the shaded streets.

"Everybody's got enemies. I've got enemies, and I'm nobody." He looked at Swanson. "The name Michael Ghislieri leaps to mind."

Swanson waved it off. "That's business. We had a talk, we understand each other now. He's an adversary, not an enemy."

"Man, that's a fine distinction from where I'm standing. But OK, if not him, somebody else. Maybe enemy is the wrong word. Maybe it's just a rival, somebody who wants a bigger slice of the real estate business. Who's your competition? And how scrupulous are they?"

There was silence for a while. Swanson looked dazed, and Cooper saw suddenly that for all the iron will over the past few days, the heart had been cut out of the man.

"I don't know. I'll have to think about it," said Swanson.

"Do that," said Cooper. "Give me an enemies list. Put it at the top of the agenda today." Cooper made for the door. "I'll leave you to sort things out," he said. "Go easy on the vodka."

"Don't worry about it," said Swanson. "There's only one bottle."

◆

It was still bright and busy outside, still dark and cool inside the bar. This time they were in a booth in the back, Jasper facing the door as always from deep-rooted habit, Toni across from him, confident that if anything bad came in, Jasper would see it.

"You get close to him and we flip the son of a bitch," said Jasper. "He's the key guy. A man like Swanson always has people to do the dirty work for him. Run off reporters, change flat tires, hide suitcases full of money. He's the guy."

"Flip him how?" Toni leaned across the table. "There's no suggestion he's selling anything. I know how to flip dopers. This guy's not a doper."

"He's something. He's not on the level, not working for somebody like Swanson."

"All you have on Swanson is suspicions. They called us off for a good reason, J.D. For all you know the man's as clean as a whistle."

"That million went somewhere. The kid got killed for some reason. I don't think much of drug dealers, Toni, but I'll give 'em one thing. They know how to protect their interests. And if they went after Nate Swanson, it's because Nate Swanson had their million dollars. And if we haven't found it yet, it's because it went into Daddy's money machine somewhere. There's no place else it could have gone. The club? We turned it upside down. The girlfriend's place, too. The girlfriend, the ex-girlfriend, the drinking buddies, we smoked 'em all. All known associates of Nate Swanson check out clean on this. Except one. His father. Who he lived with. Who heads one of the city's biggest financial empires. Where else you gonna look?"

Toni drank beer. She scrabbled a cigarette from the pack on the table and lit it. She leaned back on the bench. "It's not authorized. Snodgrass called it off."

"No. He pulled us off surveillance. That's all. What I'm doing here, Toni, is exercising initiative. You've never followed a hunch? Never done something they didn't spell out for you? Snodgrass never said we couldn't follow our noses. He said the surveillance was off. Meanwhile, there's an investigation going on. Snodgrass will back us up when he sees what we've got."

Toni looked everywhere but at Jasper: at the cigarette, at the TV over the bar, at the beer company advertising mirrors on the rear wall. "We're doing this one on spec, huh?"

"We're doing what we're paid to do. Look, if the hours are getting to you, fine. Go home. I'll work on it myself."

Toni leaned across the scarred black tabletop, stabbing at Jasper with the cigarette between two fingers. "That will be the day, J.D., the day you outwork me. I just like to go by the rules."

"In this business? Toni, open your eyes."

"Don't you pull rank on me, mister. Don't even try. In Fort Lauderdale I saw everything I need to see about this business. I just want to know that it's worth it before I go out on a limb."

"You don't ever know that till you try. Who the fuck promised you guarantees on this job?"

Toni sat back and smoked. She smoked for a minute and listened to the country whine of the jukebox and the rumbling of old men at the bar. "Anyway, how do we approach the guy? He's seen us."

Jasper slumped a little, just easing off, having won. He reached for his beer and drank. "Yeah. And he thinks we're reporters."

"How does that help us? He's not going to talk to reporters any more than he's going to talk to us."

"We spook him."

"What do you mean?"

"I mean we let him know we're there. Just show up, hang in the background. Irritate him. Make him nervous. He sure looked nervous that day at the cemetery."

Toni nodded. "And if his nervousness takes the form of direct confrontation, we've got him."

"That's right. He gets a look at federal charges for impeding an investigation or better yet assaulting a federal officer, and he'll flip."

Toni smoked until the smoke was just smoke in her lungs and then stubbed out the cigarette. "J.D., you got a dirty mind."

Jasper smiled. "I'm just a man in tune with his environment."

12

"HERE'S THE STUFF Felicidad got together." Cooper walked past Swanson and set the gray canvas duffle bag on the rug. Swanson looked fit, tanned and rested this morning, decked out in a sober blue suit.

"Thanks. What's the bodyguard situation?"

"At ten o'clock I'm meeting the head of the security company downstairs. I'll bring him up. He'll custom-tailor the coverage for you. I'd suggest a man in the office on Michigan and up at the house, at least. He'll give you a quote when you talk to him."

Swanson grunted. "Is the gun in there?" he said, nodding at the bag.

"It's there. You know how to use it?"

"I can handle it."

They stared at the bag together for a moment. Cooper said, "Anybody can squeeze off a round. Accuracy is the hard part, but if you do have to use it, marksmanship will probably be the least of your worries. If they get up here, it's going to be a close-range type of situation."

Swanson looked at him. "Are you sure you wouldn't rather have it?"

"I don't plan to be anyplace or do anything where I'll need it. You've got the pros now to worry about the rough stuff."

Swanson nodded, making for the window. "If I get restless, can I step out for lunch or something?"

"See what the security guy says. I think they'd have to be damn lucky to just spot you on the street. My guess is they've been going by obvious landmarks so far—your house, your office, so forth. I don't know how they got on to Zina, but if they had any idea where you were I don't think they'd have bothered with her. But the more people you bring over here, the more you step out for lunch, the greater the chances word gets out where you are."

"I have to go to the hospital. Zina's doing well enough I can see her."

"I wouldn't. Not for a few days. That's an easy guess for them."

Swanson turned from the window, scowling. "I shouldn't have

gone public with Zina. I nearly got her killed because I wanted people to see her on my arm."

"Hell, it's not your fault."

"No," said Swanson, silhouetted against the lake and the sky. "I guess not. None of this is my fault, is it?"

◆

McTeague had a little trouble finding the place because there was no sign, and after he had located it he had even more trouble parking because it was on one of those streets where you had to have a sticker on your car saying you lived there or they towed you. Finally he left the car down on Taylor and walked back up to the little side street that was now the northern frontier of what had been Little Italy. Across from the row of small tidy houses on the south side of the street was nothing: a vast parking lot attached to one of the architecture-school fantasies that gave the university its bleak socialist planned-city look.

Berger had told him about the war between the old neighborhood residents and the university people, the reason there was no sign on the restaurant. When the original Mayor Daley had ripped the heart out of Little Italy to put through the expressway and build the university, the Italians who were left had dug bunkers and sworn eternal enmity. When university people had started bringing their uncertain smiles and bright chatter into the place, the sign had come down and business had been purely word of mouth ever since.

McTeague paused just inside the doorway and met the stares. There was a bar on the left that ran the length of the room with mirrors and sports trophies and crossed American and Italian flags behind it. The stares were coming from a white-haired man with glasses and massive forearms who was behind the bar and three or four members of his peer group sitting at it. McTeague looked past them to the door at the rear. Through it he could see tables and chairs.

"I'm looking for Eugene Pacelli," he said.

The man behind the bar inclined his head. "Back there," he said.

The back room looked like the church basement on bingo night, a very plain room containing long tables covered with white paper bearing baskets of bread. The room was nearly empty; the lunchtime rush had come and gone. In the far left corner three men sat at the end of one of the long tables, smeared plates pushed aside and elbows on the paper, cigarettes going.

McTeague assumed one of them was Eugene Pacelli, probably the one who was watching him as he made his way past the tables, heading for the corner. As he came, the other two men fell silent and the one with his back to McTeague twisted to look. The other two were middle-aged and heavy, with the hostile looks of men used to arguing over everything from a restaurant check to a five-figure bribe. "Mr. Pacelli?" said McTeague, fetching up at the table and looking at the man in the corner.

"That's right. Your name better be McTeague."

McTeague pulled out a chair and sat down next to one of the hostile men, making an even foursome at the end of the long table. "Or what?" he said.

"Or you're in the wrong place." Pacelli's white hair was going on top but was a little long on the sides, giving him a tousled Julius Caesar look. He wore glasses with black rims in an aviator pattern, and the skin was sagging at his throat under a small chin and a mouth with a decided downturn at the corners. He looked like a malevolent turtle.

"You want to see ID?" said McTeague.

Pacelli smiled. "No, but I want to make damn sure this conversation is private."

McTeague nodded. "Go ahead." Pacelli looked at the man sitting across from him. The man shifted on his chair and ran large hands over McTeague's torso, feeling nothing but muscle beneath the thin cotton shirt, as McTeague sat up and raised his arms a little. McTeague looked calmly at Pacelli for the brief seconds it took.

"He's OK," said the man.

"Fine. You want something to eat? A drink?"

"I ate already," said McTeague, settling himself on the chair.

"Have some wine." Pacelli shoved a bottle across the table and raised his voice. "Rita, give us a clean glass here, will you?" Waiting for the glass, he said to McTeague, "I apologize for the reception. But I been stung that way. That's what got me in this fucking trouble."

"Don't worry about it."

Pacelli was silent while a large brisk woman set a clean glass in front of McTeague and gathered up the dirty plates. McTeague poured two inches of red wine into the glass. The three other men sat stonily watching the woman work. When she had left, Pacelli said, "You got something I need, I got something you need."

McTeague took a drink of wine and nodded. "I need a place to live. One that moves would be nice."

"And I need something that's not traceable. Something nobody has a list of numbers for somewhere."

"Nobody's got a list of these numbers. They're fresh off the street."

Pacelli nodded gravely. "Berger tell you the price?"

"Yeah. He said he already did all the bargaining there was going to be."

"That's right. It's a hell of a price. I'm taking a loss on the deal."

McTeague shrugged. "Consider it a fee for the service."

"I think the service is mutual, isn't it? Berger got his fee, I'm sure."

"Tell me what I'm getting," said McTeague.

Pacelli shook his head once. "It's a beauty. You better take damn good care of it, too. You know about boats?"

"I know."

"It's a Regal Commodore 400. Forty feet long, twin 300 horsepower Cummins." McTeague nodded. "I run that beauty all over the lake. It'll sleep six if you want to have a party and it'll take you as far as you want to go. It's a steal at two hundred thousand."

"Where is it?"

"Montrose Harbor. The mooring fees are all paid up through the end of the season. She's at a slip. Everything you need right there."

McTeague nodded. "What about the title?"

"You'll get a title, perfectly legal."

"Not in my real name."

"Any name you want. When does this all happen?"

"As soon as I get a look at the boat."

Pacelli looked across the table at his dining companion. "Now he wants a look at it."

McTeague picked up the glass. "I'd suggest we meet at the boat later this afternoon, this evening maybe, whenever you want. I'll look over the boat and the papers, and you count the money. Then we shake hands, if there are no problems."

"There won't be any problems with the boat or the papers. You make sure there won't be any problem with the money."

McTeague took another drink of wine. "Don't worry. I never saw anybody yet who had a problem with hundred-dollar bills."

◆

Swanson was tight-lipped and frowning when he let Cooper into the apartment. He was in shirtsleeves and his tie was loosened. "Nobody followed you, right?" he said, taking the armful of accordion folders from Cooper.

"I don't think so."

"Connie said they've started getting calls from the papers. That guy from Crain's that did the hatchet job on me last year. Those people get ahold of this, it's all over."

"I don't think I brought anybody with me. Reporters or anybody else."

Swanson dumped the folders on the table and drifted toward the big windows, hands in his pockets. "I just talked with Cliff. Chemical Bank wants their money."

"How serious is that?"

"Pretty damn. I'm going to have to make some tough decisions and I'm going to lose a lot of money."

Cooper wasn't sure of the proper etiquette for consoling millionaires on the disappearance of large amounts of their wealth, so he trailed Swanson at a cautious distance. "You need to call Brooks. He got me on the car phone, making ominous noises about some crisis over at the Erie Building."

"He's irritated because he's not on Connie's list of people she can give this number to."

"I hope it's not a very long list."

"It's not." Swanson sank onto the sofa. "I'll call him. Look, I'd really like to get over to the office. I have to sit down with Cliff to get a handle on things. Can we make a little run over there?"

With a shrug Cooper said, "If you want to, we'll go. And we'll probably make it. But it is a risk. You want to go joy-riding around the city, you should hire another few hundred bucks' worth of protection. You count on me to drive you around, you're doing it on the cheap."

"You said yourself they'd have to be lucky just to spot me on the street. And there's a man at the office, right?"

"Right. Yeah, we'll probably be OK. I'm just trying to get across to you that I'm not a pro at this. Don't put your life in my hands because I might fumble it."

Swanson gave him a long appraising gaze. "For a thousand-dollar bonus you should at least be able to get me to my office."

"It's your thousand bucks," said Cooper, turning to the door. "And it's your life, too."

◆

Freedom, thought Turk. It was like slipping off a ball and chain to get free of that ugly beaner pit bull for an evening, have a chance to combine business and pleasure. He was perched on a high stool with his travel bag at his feet, the Taurus wrapped inside his spare trousers, wearing his light sports jacket over a fresh T-shirt. He drained his beer and considered for a moment before signaling the Mexican bartender. He couldn't afford to get wasted; there was work to do. The noise level was high; beyond the chest-high partition was a large stuccoed dining room with a tile floor, piñatas and plants hanging everywhere, Mexican waiters hustling between tables with overloaded trays.

The lady at the end of the bar was singing again; the guitarist was standing there strumming and grinning at her as if he were really enjoying the experience, decked out in his chintzy mariachi outfit. The lady was swaying a bit on the high stool, making the bartender nervous. She was into the second verse of *"Cuando calienta el sol"* now, putting some soul into it, making eyes at the guitar player, the cigarette in her left hand perilously close to depositing ash in her margarita. She wore a white cotton dress with a Mexican design, bright embroidery around the skirt and collar. She was blonde and no longer young and no longer quite sober. Turk had seen a million like her, in L.A., Cancún, Acapulco.

He caught the bartender's eye and ordered another Dos Equis and a margarita. While he waited he watched the woman sing and started psyching himself, feeling for the old repertoire. His skills were a bit rusty but the instinct was still there; the minute he'd spotted her he'd known the blonde at the end of the bar was his. She showed the right mix of shamelessness and self-deception; this was a desperate woman.

She had finished the song and the guitarist was grinning at her, edging away; she was applauding herself or maybe him and yelling something in sophomore Spanish that the guitarist clearly didn't understand. Her neighbors at the bar were looking at her with polite astonishment.

Turk picked up the drinks and slid off his stool. He walked to where the lady was just turning back to the bar and set the margarita in front of her. She looked at him with blue eyes under the blond bangs, startled, and he gave her his best number-one grin. "That was terrific," he said. "Have one on me."

It took her a moment to get over her surprise and Turk thought it would be easier if he were the dark Latin type, but it wouldn't matter much. "Oh," she said. "Thank you." Now she smiled, the round, slightly flabby, slightly flushed face lighting up. "I love that song."

"Me too," said Turk, warmly. "You've spent some time south of the border, haven't you?"

"Oh, just a little." She set down the cigarette and shifted her stool a little, giving Turk room to slide in beside her. "I've been to Acapulco and Cancún. I just love Mexico."

"I thought so," said Turk. "You have that look."

◆

Diana declined the invitation; she was going to bed early with a Vargas Llosa novel. Cooper was grateful for the way she tacitly conceded Burk's to him as a bachelor refuge. He kissed her and went out into the night. He wanted to forget Regis Swanson and his troubles, forget all about them for a couple of hours. Cooper could work like a horse if he had to, but responsibility for other people's lives was not a part of the job he enjoyed.

Burk's had been getting less crowded over the months and Cooper wondered how the bar was making it. The neighborhood was changing: places had closed, people moved away, and Cooper was afraid Burk's was going next. Tonight Burk himself was behind the long polished bar, staring gloomily at one of the two TV sets high on the wall, watching the Sox sleepwalk through the late innings. Burk was going to fat and had given up shaving. There were six customers in the whole place, a couple of familiar faces and the usual deadbeats. The jukebox was silent but the video games gave out random beeps and manic electronic tunes. It was dark, shabby, and comfortable. Cooper got a beer, put a couple of quarters in the pool table, and started shooting, just knocking the balls around, taking pleasure in the feel of a good easy stroke, calculating angles, watching the balls drop.

Kelly came in and they played some eight-ball, nothing serious, just social pool, something to do between swallows of beer. Kelly was thinking of moving his shop; two stores in his building on the other side of the El tracks had been hit, crude amateur panel-punch jobs.

"It's getting bad, man. Might be time to move west."

Cooper shrugged. "Down where we are, things are pretty tranquil."

"Don't kid yourself. Read the police reports sometime. The neighborhood's going, man."

Cooper nodded, depressed. "Rack 'em up. I'll think about moving tomorrow."

Cooper spotted the woman while waiting for Kelly to line up a complicated shot that was well beyond his talents. She had come in during a mild late-evening rush and sat at the bar, alone, drinking something clear in a tall glass and smoking. She had drawn his eye first just because she was a good-looking woman. When she started to get attention from one of the deadbeats, she moved her drink and cigarettes to the pinball machine, where she stood working the flippers with little spasms that shook her whole body. She had on a big white T-shirt over calf-length purple tights; she was trim and fit-looking with black shaggy hair. It took Cooper a while to remember where he'd seen her before.

He straightened up from the pool table and gave her a shocked look, her back to him at the pinball machine. "What's the matter?" said Kelly.

"Nothing. I just remembered something." Cooper re-sighted the shot and missed it.

He beat Kelly anyway, and by that time there were other names chalked on the board, so Kelly left to slump at the bar. Cooper took on the next player but his heart wasn't in it. He won, sloppily, and then gave up the table. He went to the bar, ordered another beer, and took a good look at the woman at the pinball machine.

She hadn't once looked his way that he was aware of, but Cooper figured there was no such thing as coincidence where law-enforcement agencies were concerned. He leaned on the bar and wondered.

There was one good way to test for coincidence. Cooper left Burk's and went east, under the El viaduct and along the quiet tree-lined street toward the lake. He didn't bother to look behind him; if she was coming with him he'd flush her in the park.

Unless there was a team and they had somebody else coming with him. The guy from the Olds, or somebody different. This guy walking the dog, maybe. Did they lease dogs to the DEA as well as automobiles?

Cooper waited at the light at Sheridan Road, late-night traffic sparse but zooming by in a hurry, and took one casual look back. There she was, white T-shirt coming along the sidewalk on the other side, a hundred yards back.

Cooper shook his head and crossed the street. He took the half-block to the park slowly, giving her plenty of time to keep him in sight in case she got stuck at the light. It was close to eleven and the cops were sweeping through the park chasing people home; Cooper spotted the cruising squad far to the south, the spotlight moving over grass. The cops would thin the crowd but anybody with enough sense to keep his head down could spend the night at the beach, killing a six-pack on a warm patch of sand. Cooper stepped into the shadows under the trees.

He went south toward the Farwell Avenue breakwater, dodging

the squad, steering clear of the deeper shadows. By the time he got to
the pier the crowd was trickling back; on a hot night the cops weren't
going to keep people away. He started down the long concrete pier
toward the light tower at the end. It was darker here with the lights in
the park well behind, and the skyline eight miles south was slightly
fuzzy in the heat.

The light tower sat almost at the end of the pier, blocking the way
except for a two-foot-wide passage around its base to the right. Beyond the tower was a square space railed by cables: land's end and a
good spot for fishing, reflection and the occasional mugging. Cooper
went warily but the two figures that sat at the end, feet dangling over
the water, were not interested in him. He crossed the pier and looked
back along the base of the tower.

There were five or six people along the two-hundred-yard pier, but
only one was moving: the woman in the white T-shirt. Cooper
looked for back-up; he was sure there would be some but he couldn't
pick it out. He drew his head in a bit as she came closer; she was
dawdling, looking south, out for a late-night stroll, asking for trouble. She had turned a couple of heads as she came along the pier.

She disappeared behind the base of the tower and Cooper wondered if she was going to come right out to the end, but after a few
seconds she hadn't shown up. She would be waiting just short of the
tower, trying to eavesdrop maybe, watching the passage where he
had to come out.

Cooper listened to murmurs from the lovers at the end of the
pier and thought. It was obvious as hell and he wondered about
that; he was also pissed off and he'd had three beers and he just
decided to do it. He slipped through the cables and made his way
along the base of the tower outside them, hanging out over the
waves rolling in eight feet below him, hands on the cable and feet
on the edge of the concrete. He took a look when he got to the corner of the tower and there she was, just leaning on the cable on the
other side, head turned in profile, listening. Cooper slipped back
through the cables as quietly as he could, the wash of the water
along the pier covering the noise. Somebody was moving a hundred feet down the pier, the backup now, coming closer. Cooper
ignored him.

She started at the sound of his step behind her and came around
fast, but recovered, watching him intently, as he leaned on the cable
beside her. He said nothing, just trying to make out her face in the
light from distant lamps. She stood rigid, one hand still on the cable.

"If this is a surveillance job, you've got a lot to learn," said Cooper.

In the darkness he couldn't read her reaction. "I didn't come out here to be hassled," she said.

"Then you don't know the neighborhood. But I'm not here to hassle you, either. I'm just wondering why in the hell the DEA thinks I'm worth following around."

She was still for a long moment. "Who the hell do you think you're talking to?"

"Did you really think I'd forget your face?"

After another long pause she said, "OK, you spotted me. But you got it wrong. I work for the *Tribune*."

"The hell you do. That was my first guess, but I think this one's better. You're probably with the Feds because only the Feds can afford to waste time and money the way you are. I'm not dealing drugs, Regis Swanson isn't dealing drugs. You people are so far off base it makes me want to help you."

"You've mistaken me for someone else," she said.

"If I had, you'd be running right now. You don't seem scared and you don't seem surprised. You're either armed or that nervous-looking gentleman down the way there is your partner or maybe both. Is it the same guy who was with you at the cemetery?"

She seemed to relax, just a little. "You're pretty entertaining, mister." She pulled cigarettes from under the tail of the shirt and shook one out of the pack.

"OK, you want me to keep talking, I will. You're on the wrong track with Swanson. I don't know what the kid got himself into, but the father's clean. I'm clean. Whatever Nate was into, his father wasn't part of it."

In the sudden flash from her lighter her hawk's face shone yellow, with black eyes that flicked to his just before the light went out. A soft giggle reached them from the end of the pier. The cigarette glowed. She smoked in silence for a while and then spoke. "Why did you shake us, then? Why the tough-guy act at the cemetery?"

"Because I'm trying to keep my employer alive. There's two guys, probably the same ones who killed Nate, who are after his father now in a big way. Don't you ever talk to the police in this town?"

"Who are the two guys?"

"I don't know. I've seen them, and I could pick them out of a lineup, but I don't know who they are. If this whole thing is drug-related, you may have them on file somewhere. You need to talk to a pair of homicide detectives at Area Six named Benitez and Reichardt."

There was another silence. In the glow from the cigarette Cooper could make out her face, searching his. "I'm afraid homicide is not my business," she said.

"No. I know what your business is."

She caught his tone and after a second she said, "You got a problem with it?"

"Yeah, I got a problem with it. What you do makes thugs into millionaires and private vices into public headaches. What Prohibition did for Al Capone, you're doing for every two-bit gang-banger with a little initiative."

"Shit, I'm not going to stand out here and debate with you."

"Fine. I'm trying to help you, I really am. If you really want to catch drug dealers, take a walk around the neighborhood here. Just about any time. You could keep busy twenty-four hours a day. You could put away everybody who sold a gram today and there'd be as many back on the streets tomorrow."

"We try not to waste time with the small fry."

"OK, go for the big guys. Put Regis Swanson in jail and anyone else you have the remotest suspicion of. Put 'em away, invade Colombia, bomb Peru. Burn the Andes bare. People will find some other way to stew their brains. That's a human constant, and making it a crime just means that along with deadbeats with bad habits you now have psychopaths with ten-figure bank accounts. The drug war's made this country into outlaw heaven—there's never been a better way for assholes to get rich."

"It's nice to know you're on our side."

"I am on your side. Sister, I know all about dead-end wars. I fought one before you were born. And don't get me wrong—I know the fact that the war's a lousy idea doesn't make the other side the good guys. So if the enemy's whoever shot Nate Swanson, count me in."

The cigarette glowed and died away. She shifted, ready to move. "Yeah. Well, it's been real."

Cooper stopped her with a hand on her arm. "Let's make it easy. You can wire me if you want, put a tracer on me, whatever you people can do nowadays. You want an informant, I'll inform. I'll tell you when Regis Swanson goes to the bathroom if you want. After about a day and a half, you'll see you're barking up the wrong tree."

"My, you're an eager beaver."

Cooper laughed softly, sagging back against the wire. "Fine, just do one thing. Tell me how I can get in touch with you. That's all. A phone number."

Back on shore a loudspeaker crackled and the beam of a spotlight came sweeping up the pier. "We're about to get run off of here," said Cooper. "What do you say?"

She was moving away now, saying something too soft for him to hear. He followed her. "Say what?"

Over her shoulder she said, "We'll be in touch."

13

A MUTE AND abstracted Regis Swanson let Cooper into the apartment and pointed him to the sofa by the window before disappearing down the hall. The smell of brewing coffee hung in the air. The sunlight came off the surface of the lake and between the high buildings into Cooper's eyes. He stood just past the sofa looking down at the coffee table. On it were a closed photo album, an open shoebox and a litter of snapshots that had spilled out of the box. In the photographs four or five different Nate Swansons looked up at him, from the pre-teen in a Little League uniform, already with that confident world-beater look, to the toddler perched on the shoulders of a younger and happier Regis Swanson.

Cooper stood and looked at the pictures until Swanson came into the room, groomed and jacketed but just a bit haggard. He saw what Cooper was looking at and became busy with his pockets. "Want some coffee?" he said.

"Had some already, thanks." Cooper moved away from the window. "What's on the agenda today?"

"Pleading. Cajoling. Scheming. Maybe even a little begging. And a trip to the hospital. Zina's out of intensive care, they tell me."

"I don't know if I can recommend that."

"I'm going." He shot Cooper a look that wasn't going to fade.

Cooper shrugged. "OK, we can probably dodge the gunslingers. The reporters might be a little tougher."

"You're a capable man. I'm sure you can figure out how to get us in and out."

"I can try."

"Do that. Before that, though, Cliff and I have to go talk to these damn bankers. Your first assignment is to sneak me into the Chicago Club. I've already talked to the desk guy over there. He'll meet us in the alley." Swanson bent over the coffee table, stuffing handfuls of photographs back in the shoebox. He replaced the lid and set the box on top of the album. "There's not a lot to do in here at night," he said.

Cooper had the car keys out, heading for the door. "Well, let's hope you won't have to be up here much longer."

◆

Crucial moment, crucial moment, thought Turk as he heard the toilet flush. Time to go to work. This morning his adversaries would be hangover and remorse, which he had found took virulent forms in women. He passed a hand over his face, wishing he could just roll over and go back to sleep.

Instead, he was lying on his back, hands clasped behind his head, staring at the ceiling with a faint smile when Kathleen came warily back into the bedroom. She had put on her pink bathrobe, and she looked godawful in the morning light, blond hair going in six directions and the soft doughy face a little red and puffy. Turk turned the smile on her. "Hi, gorgeous," he said.

"Morning," she said, looking startled.

Turk looked her up and down. "Let me see you," he said. "What are you all covered up for?"

"I have to go to work. I have to be there in an hour."

Turk kicked back the covers and swung his legs to the floor. He stood up, buck naked, and walked slowly across the carpet toward her. She watched him come with a look that seemed to be teetering between alarm and anticipation. Turk stood before her and tugged at the belt of the robe. He parted the robe and looked down at her body, thinking there were easier ways of making a living. "My God," he said softly.

Kathleen tried to close the robe but he had his hands on her waist and she gave up. "I really do have to go to work," she said.

Turk kissed her, gently. "So it's over?" he said, looking into slightly bleary blue eyes.

She pulled away. "It doesn't have to be over." She closed and belted the robe, a little regretfully, Turk thought. "Where are you staying?"

"Like I said last night, I'm looking for this old partner of mine." Turk turned and made for his bag, lying under his clothes in the corner. "Dude I used to run a little charter fishing outfit with, down in

Baja. He lost a leg to a great white shark and came back to Chicago, told me to come look him up if I ever needed a job."

"Where does he live?" Kathleen had folded her arms and was standing a little stiffly in the doorway.

"I don't know. All I have is a phone number." He pulled a wad of bills out of his bag and peeled off a hundred. He came and held it out to Kathleen.

"What's that for?" she said with a touch of sharpness.

"Rent, groceries, phone bill. For a day or two. Just until I find my partner. The party doesn't have to end." He smiled at her again, hoping he was reading her right.

He saw her soften, her eyes flicking back and forth between the hundred dollars and him. "I don't need the money," she said, pushing his hand away.

"I always pay my way." He gauged the look in her eyes and folded the bill into his palm. "Tell you what. I'll save this till tonight. And then I'll take you out for a dinner you won't forget, you name the place. French, Italian? Nouvelle cuisine? You name it, we'll find it."

She blinked at that for a while, wondering, remembering things her mother had told her. "You want me to leave, I'll leave," said Turk.

"No." She shook her head, perhaps a bit quickly, and said, "You can stay. Till you find your friend."

Turk lifted her chin with a finger and kissed her lightly on the lips. "You're unbelievable," he breathed.

◆

McTeague liked the way she rode, the wind coming in through the window whipping her hair across her face and wrapping it around her neck; she showed no fear at the way he drove. She put a single steadying hand on the dashboard as the Trans Am slid over a couple of lanes, leaving people with less car and less panache behind. The lake spread out blue and hard under the pale heat-washed sky. "Where are we going?" she said.

"My new home." McTeague drove with a hostile intensity, head forward and eyes to the front or flicking to the mirrors, waiting for someone to do something stupid.

"You moved out of the storefront?" Her hand went to the dashboard again as he braked, slewing toward the Montrose exit from the Drive.

"Not yet," he said. "Soon." In a moment they were passing under the Drive and heading straight east, into the park and toward the lake. They went over a rise, and the harbor spread out on the right, a forest of masts rising above placid water. McTeague went all the way around the harbor, following the road out onto the spit of land that enclosed it. The wind coming in the window was hot. There were old men and other shiftless types fishing in the harbor, leaning on the rails watching their floats. There were boats moored along the concrete wall and others, mostly sailboats, out in the middle of the harbor moored to stardocks. There was a solitary duck out on the water, paddling aimlessly.

McTeague turned off the road into a parking strip that ran along the edge of the harbor. A high chain-link fence barred the way to the water's edge here and a sign said *Private Pier.* McTeague shut off the engine and looked at her, waiting. "This is your new home?" she said.

McTeague smiled. "Come on." They got out and walked to a gate in the fence. McTeague pulled keys from a pocket and unlocked the gate, closing it after they had passed. A long wooden slip jutted out into the harbor, boats moored along either side. McTeague took her halfway down the slip, past sterns bearing names like *Dreadnought* and *Sea Queen II.* He stopped at a boat that was sleek and streamlined, with a blue hull and white superstructure, a canopy over the raised bridge and four small portholes along either side. On the stern was painted the name *Lucrezia.* McTeague hopped aboard and helped her to climb after him.

"Welcome to the ranch," he said.

She raised an eyebrow, perhaps a little unsettled at the gentle movement of the deck beneath her feet. "This is where you get your mail now, huh?"

"The only mail I get is bills. Now, not even them." He stepped to a door under the bridge and fit a key to the lock. The door slid open and he led her inside.

Below it was hot and dark and McTeague worried for a moment about the smell: plastic, oily, aquatic. He went forward through a hatch and opened a skylight. "Once we get going it'll air out real nice." He came back to find her just standing there, looking at the curved settee around the table, the small galley, the bar. McTeague stood stooping just a little under the low ceiling, waiting for some reaction other than that cool, distant smile.

"Where are we going?" she said.

"Out. Away from all this."

"I have a performance tonight."

"We'll come back whenever you say, don't worry."

McTeague took her up to the bridge and showed her the impressive triple-tiered dashboard, talking boat talk that he could see meant nothing to her. He shut up and looked at her, standing there with her arms folded and that smile on her face; for a moment he nearly panicked, looking for signs of boredom and contempt. She looked out past the rank of boats, past the trees on the headland, and said, "Let's go."

McTeague put her in a swivel chair on the bridge while he made the engine roar to life and then crept about the superstructure like a cat, casting off. Finally he took the boat carefully away from the slip and went slowly past the lined-up powerboats and the sailboats at their docks and mooring cans, out between the twin light towers that marked the entrance to the harbor and into cool breezes and sunlight bouncing off water.

The skyline to the south was pure geometry; the parkland above the rocks that lined the shore was a heartbreaking green. McTeague took the boat away from land, easing the throttle higher, bouncing over waves at a comfortable clip. He took a look at her, riding easy here as in the car, head back a little, hair streaming. McTeague had to take a quick deep breath.

They turned south, skirting sailboats and crossing the wakes of smaller craft, and McTeague poured it on a bit, smiling, showing off. The Loop was on their right now, a long way off. McTeague took them away from shore again in a long sweeping curve and they were going due east, toward the wide open spaces of the lake and the Michigan shore somewhere over the horizon. He throttled back and the ride got smoother, the noise less. "Home sweet home," he said.

"I didn't know you knew anything about boats."

"One of my stepfathers had boats and I spent a lot of time on them. Out here on the lake, off the Keys when we went south. Fishing, diving, just running around. I always wanted to live on the water, but I never could. Now I can."

They were silent for a while, just feeling the motion, watching the water fly. McTeague took them back north; she was staring at the distant city. "You planning on leaving?" she said.

McTeague smiled into the wind. "Maybe. Want to come along? I can take this thing down the Mississippi and we can go a long way."

"I don't know. I'm not sure how long I'd enjoy running."

He said nothing for a while, and then: "What makes you think we'd be running?"

She smiled. "You look to me like a man getting ready for a fast getaway."

"Hey, that's freedom. Always having that fast getaway there."

After a moment she said, "It wasn't legal, was it?"

"What wasn't?"

"This deal you made. All this money."

McTeague looked at her, his most distant smile in place. "There's all kinds and shades of legal. Read that list they publish in *Forbes* every year. Every name on that list does essentially what I did." She said nothing, and after a moment McTeague went on. "I'm not asking you to play Bonnie and Clyde. I'm just offering you a chance to enjoy the ride."

She looked ahead over the sparkling water and for a bad moment he thought he'd lost her. "OK," she said. "Take me for a ride."

◆

"I think he's on the level," said Toni, looking out the back window of the van at the distant playground, where a game of basketball was growing lethargic in the heat.

Jasper sat with his legs stretched out across the van, resting on the padded bench opposite. "I thought you two were getting a little close out there last night. What'd he do, stick his tongue in your ear?"

"Seriously. I know how dopers talk. This guy doesn't sound like a doper."

"Come on, Toni."

Toni raised the binoculars and focused on a group of young men standing at the edge of the cracked basketball court. "I've been bull-shitted by experts, J.D. I don't think this was bullshit. I could be wrong, but what you go on in this business are quick judgments, and my quick judgment here is that the guy's not hiding anything. He's on the level."

"He set up an ambush on you out there. I was two seconds away from drawing down on him. He didn't look like a man with nothing to hide."

"He took the bait we set out for him. It was a bad tail job and he saw it. Look, the man offered to wear a wire for us. He flipped himself."

"I know. That's what makes me suspicious. He offered. I don't consider anybody flipped unless I've got one of his balls in each hand. He was working something on you."

Toni lowered the binoculars. "I don't know. It's possible, sure. But think for a second about why we're interested in Swanson in the first place."

"Because his son got himself shot in a dispute over a pile of drug money. In a nightclub his daddy bought for him which is the perfect place to launder a whole bunch of drug money. That's why we're interested."

"But how do we know why Nate Swanson got shot?"

"Because he got shot at the same time as Dexter did. And he had Dexter's money."

"How do we know?"

"The tip. Somebody snitched on him."

"You've never gotten a false tip? Anything you get from one source is suspect, you're always saying."

"His getting killed is proof he had it."

"No, it's proof the killers thought he had it."

"And they would know, that's what I'm saying. They don't need warrants and subpoenas. They go in and kick ass and find out. If they thought Nate Swanson had their money, they had good reason."

"Maybe Dexter told them."

"Fine, Dexter told them. What's the point?"

"Who told Dexter Nate had the money?"

"Hell, I don't know. Nate stole it off Dexter and Dexter found out."

"I'll tell you who told Dexter Nate had his money. We did."

"What?"

"The cops called us when they picked up Dexter. We had just started getting interested in Nate and we had that cop ask Dexter about him. Dexter claimed he'd never heard of him. Maybe he hadn't."

It was very hot in the van. Jasper watched her, his head lolling against the wall. "Horseshit."

"I don't know."

"You're trying to tell me we set Nate Swanson up."

"Without knowing it. That's the pretty part."

Jasper shook his head. "Boy, that's a hell of an imagination you got there, Toni. There's your second career, in Hollywood writing TV movies. Man, I'd make a point of watching that one."

Toni raised the binoculars again. "So prove me wrong."

Behind her Jasper swung his feet to the floor of the van with a thump. "I'll prove you wrong. Provided they let me. Provided the Suits don't call hands off Regis Swanson. Maybe even if they do."

◆

"They smell blood," said Regis Swanson. "The frenzy's starting." He had the look of a hunted man, huddled on the back seat.

Cooper pulled away from the curb. "Well, they missed us this time. They'll have to make something up again."

"The speculation is starting to get a little wild. I guess what Buzz and the police have been giving them is too tame."

"Reporters love misery and disaster, especially if it's novel. People are tired of reading about black kids shooting each other. And they love to see rich people take it on the chin. You're the best thing to happen to the news business in this town in years."

"Splendid. Maybe they'll manage to be there when these two gunmen catch up with me. Should make great video."

"I'm starting to think you're fairly safe, actually."

"Why?"

"You're the man with the money. They need you. They need you to open a safe or pull a suitcase out of a locker. A threat to kill you isn't credible. At least not until they have their money. That's when you have to start to worry. Till then, it's your friends and associates who need to look over their shoulders."

"I'm doing what I can. They've put a man in the office, with Zina at the hospital, over at Buzz's office."

"I guess that's about all we can do. That and keep you out of sight."

Swanson was silent for a block or two. "I can't take another night up there by myself. Buzz and Julie are having me for dinner tonight."

Cooper shook his head. "I think that's a bad idea."

"He's arranged for the police to be there. It should be all right."

"How about the security company? They have somebody up there?"

"At Buzz's house? I don't think so. Just his office. But he said the police chief up there had promised him a squad car."

Cooper checked the mirrors, judged the traffic, and pulled a quick turn without signaling. "OK. What time you want me to pick you up?"

"Say six. Buzz offered to take me but I told him you'd probably say that was poor security."

"You're catching on," said Cooper.

◆

Turk brought the sandwich into the living room, turned on the TV and sat on the couch. He put his feet up on the coffee table, perilously close to a ceramic figure of a Mexican boy leading a burro down the garden path, and leaned back and ate. The news came on and Turk waited to hear about himself and his doings. He listened with professional interest, edged with anxiety, and only a touch of personal pride. The business section of the morning's *Tribune* had carried a brief resumé of the rumors about Regis Swanson's troubles but nothing else about Zina Manning. Turk knew that whatever they had on the news would be only a fraction of what the cops had, but it was information, and information was what he needed. Turk had an uncomfortable feeling he was running out of time and ideas.

There was the usual business, fires and dead children and semis going off bridges, and then after a commercial the luscious dark-eyed female newscaster looked straight into Turk's eyes and started talking about Regis Swanson. Turk stopped chewing to listen, the sandwich halfway from the plate to his mouth. After an intro about Swanson's mysterious withdrawal from the public eye, they cut to the tape and there was a bald-headed middle-aged man with a moustache talking into a bouquet of microphones. "The rumors are false, the innuendo is vicious, and we *will* be vindicated," he said, scowling. The subtitle identified him as Norbert Hayden, Regis Swanson's lawyer.

Turk listened to the whole piece before he resumed eating. He finished the sandwich, watching a story about a city lawyer caught with his hand in the till, without really hearing it. When he finished the sandwich he set the plate on the sofa beside him and said "Norbert Hayden" out loud.

◆

The sun had gone down and the streetlights had come on, feebly. The lights seemed to be largely for ornamentation, dim globes on quaint cast-iron posts, and their light was largely blocked by trees. Cooper sat in the dark on the terrace of Buzz Hayden's house and worried.

The promised police protection had boiled down to a cruising squad car that crept around the circular drive at irregular and steadily lengthening intervals. Cooper had talked to the driver on his first pass, telling him there was real danger and asking what had happened to Buzz Hayden's clout.

"It's a small town," said the cop, a middle-aged man with wire-rimmed glasses and thinning hair. "Get on the phone if anything looks funny. I can be here in five minutes, max."

"Five minutes is a hell of a long time with firearms involved," said Cooper.

The cop shrugged. "We'll be back, don't worry. We got other things to check."

Cooper shook his head remembering, wishing there were a squad car sitting on the drive, wishing Swanson had not accepted the invitation, wishing he were home with Diana. I'm a chump, thought Cooper. I'm the front line in somebody else's war.

He was thinking of the ways two people could approach the house in the dark. Hayden's house was a two-story fake colonial with a broad front, a built-in garage to the left of the door and a long brick-floored terrace stretching along the front of the other wing. On the terrace were a round table and four chairs, all made of white plastic. Cooper rose from his chair, stretched and looked at the windows behind him, with light showing around drawn curtains.

He moved toward the corner of the house, where the terrace ended at a screen of bushes. Cooper stepped off the terrace, around the bushes, and made for the back of the house. A high wooden fence separated Hayden's property from his neighbors. In back of the house was at least a half-acre of land, with a couple of dozen trees just visible in the dark. Cooper made his way through the trees to the back of the yard, where he found another fence. He stood listening: somewhere a television was going and a few blocks to the east he could hear the traffic on Sheridan Road.

He came slowly back toward the house, looking at lights, thinking about Swanson and Hayden and Hayden's wife relaxing behind the curtains, thinking how easy it was in a more or less civil society to do just about anything you damn pleased, provided you were ruthless enough. He completed his circuit, coming around the garage side of the house and onto the blacktop driveway.

The Marquis sat to one side of the drive. Cooper walked to the car, got the key out of his pocket, and opened the trunk. He rooted around until he found the tire iron. He closed the trunk and carried the tire iron back to the terrace. He wasn't sure what good it was going to do him if push came to shove, but it made him feel better, marginally.

He sat down on the plastic chair again and laid the tire iron on the table. The air had cooled off and a breath of wind was making a peaceful sound in the leaves above him. He could hear kids shouting somewhere not too far away, tearing around in somebody's back yard. It's a small town, the cop had said.

They won't find him, Cooper thought. Not here, out in the boonies. They're lying low someplace, back in the city, or maybe they've given up. After the fiasco with Zina Manning they would run, the job blown to hell, maybe in trouble with their bosses. They're not going to storm a lawyer's house in a quiet suburb.

He had just about convinced himself when the man came walking quietly up the drive. Cooper had heard no cars approaching; he froze and watched him, a tall man in a light-colored sports jacket, hands in his pockets. As he came close enough to be illuminated by the light over the porch, Cooper saw the long handsome face, the ponytail gone now, the same easy stride. The man stopped about twenty feet from the porch, scanning the front of the house, intent. Cooper was a stone, a block of ice. He was fairly sure he couldn't be seen but highly conscious of the disparity between a handgun and a tire iron. Now, thought Cooper. Now is the time for a bored cop to make another pass around the driveway.

The tall man looked to his right, past Cooper into the darkness beyond the end of the house, and Cooper remembered the little dark man who had needed a drink of water. Now, he thought. Where the hell are you? Five minutes was not going to do it, even presuming somebody could make it to a phone.

When the tall man stepped toward the front door, every muscle Cooper had wanted him to stay in the chair, stay quiet. It's not even my god-damn fight, he thought bitterly. But he knew he couldn't let that doorbell get rung. "Evening," he said.

The tall man's head snapped toward him. Three or four seconds went by, and then he came slowly toward the terrace. Cooper reached for the tire iron and slipped it quietly off the table and onto his lap. The man stepped up onto the terrace, backlit from the porch, and kept coming until he was standing in front of Cooper, hands in his pockets and rocking on his heels. "Well," he said softly.

"You looked better in the ponytail," said Cooper.

"That look is out, they tell me. I didn't expect to see you here. Does this mean your boss is inside?"

It took Cooper about a second and a half to realize that lying was useless. "That's right."

"I'm in luck, then."

Cooper nodded, stalling for his life. "How about your friend over there in the bushes? Is he just along for the ride?"

The tall man said nothing for a moment, then shrugged and looked to his right. He jerked his head once, and leaves rustled as a dark figure came onto the terrace from the other end. It was only a shape, but the dimensions were familiar. "Have a seat," Cooper said.

"Hey, that's nice of you," said the tall man, "but I think we'll give it a miss. We're on a mission here. No time to waste."

"Slow down a second," said Cooper. The short man had halted just to his left. "We can have a lot of noise and bother, or we can sit here and talk about things in a civilized manner."

There was just enough light for Cooper to see the tall man's eyes flick toward his companion. "OK," he said. "I'm a reasonable man." He pulled out a chair and sat opposite Cooper. The other man went behind Cooper and took the chair on his right. "So what do we have to talk about?"

"We can start with why you're pestering the man."

A soft laugh came across the table in the dark. "You want to talk, it better be serious. My bullshit tolerance levels are getting low."

"Am I going to bullshit somebody who's got me outnumbered and outgunned? Let me tell you how things look to me."

"OK, tell me how things look to you."

"It looks to me like you're trying to make my boss responsible for some quarrel you had with his son."

"No quarrel. Just came to collect some money."

"What money? Swanson doesn't have any money that belongs to you."

"Somebody's got it. His son stole it from us. Who else we supposed to collect from?"

Cooper peered at him through the dark. "How do you know his son stole it?"

"We got that from the very best authority, man."

"Who would that be?"

"The cops. Good enough for you?"

"The cops?"

"That's right. And that money hasn't turned up yet. I'm just making an easy guess about who's got it."

"How much money are we talking about?"

Teeth shone in the darkness as the man smiled. "One million dollars, brother. Cash money, legal tender."

Cooper let out a long slow breath. "So let me get this straight. You get your money and you go away and leave everybody alone?"

"We get our money, we're history."

Cooper believed him about as much as he believed repentant congressmen. "So what we got right now is your basic shakedown," he said.

"That's kind of a rude term for a man in your position to use, but if you want to think of it that way, I guess I can't stop you. The point is, when and how do we get the money?"

"A million bucks is a lot of bucks. Swanson can't just go down to the bank and fill up a paper bag."

"It was all nice and liquid when his son stole it. It's probably still in a paper bag somewhere. Maybe inside the house here."

Cooper saw there wasn't much more stalling he could do. "OK," he said. "Why don't you let me go in and confer with him?"

"Why don't you kiss my ass? I can come up with three better ideas without straining."

"Fine, name one."

"Well, how's this? You take us inside and we tell Swanson and his lawyer which end is up."

Cooper sighed. "You ought to know better than to ask me to do that."

The soft laugh came again. "You're talking like a man with a bargaining position. You forgotten about the outnumbered, outgunned part of it already?"

"You're going to shoot me, huh? Make a lot of noise, get sixteen neighbors on the phone to the cops at the same time?"

"You haven't been keeping up with the technology, have you? If we shoot you, they won't hear it inside the house, much less next door. Now, you can ring the doorbell or I can ring it. It's up to you, man." The chair scraped on the terrace floor as the tall man shoved away from the table.

"Hang on." Cooper stopped him with a raised hand, knowing time was up. "I may not know the technology, but here's an observation on technique. There's at least three people inside there, maybe more. Swanson, the lawyer, the wife, maybe a kid or two, a cook and a maid probably, in this type of neighborhood. That's a lot of people to watch. You fucked up the last hostage situation you got, and there was only one of her. You want to make it clean and quiet, here's what I'd suggest. Take me."

Silence, maybe three seconds of it. "You."

"Me, that's right. I'll come with you, and then it's a matter of making phone calls. I'll be the kind of hostage that can do you some good. I know how to get in touch with Swanson any time, and he'll listen to me. If he's got your money, I'll get him to cough it up. No fuss, no muss, no screaming children. You're a lot better off taking me, because I'm not going to go hysterical on you."

He was thinking about it, that Cooper could see. Cooper sat and let him think, resisting the temptation to reach up and wipe the sweat away from his hairline. Cooper did not like the prospect of walking off to be a hostage, but if he tried to keep them out of the house by force he liked his prospects even less.

"You talked me into it," said the tall man.

Cooper let out a long, slow breath. "OK, lead the way."

Even as the tall man rose, Cooper wasn't sure what decision was about to get made. Going with them had the appeal of confrontation postponed; resisting promised only immediate escalation.

What decided him was the need to do something with the tire iron in his lap. The smaller man was a beat or two behind his partner, maybe because he hadn't quite followed the conversation; he was just pushing away from the table as Cooper started to get up and felt the iron sliding off his lap. He gripped it near the end and the picture was clear all of a sudden: going with them was madness.

He cracked the small dark man across the face with a sharp back-hand stroke of the tire iron. The other man was on his feet already, his hand going inside the jacket, as Cooper kicked free of his chair, wound up and flung the tire iron at his head. It missed but it gave him time; he heaved the table on top of the tall man before he could come out of his duck and charged for the end of the terrace. Somebody was growling like a sick dog and somebody was knocking plastic furniture around.

Cooper crashed through the screen of bushes, arms protecting his face, to fall onto the grass beyond and roll to his feet. There hadn't been any shots yet and Cooper hoped the tall man was enough of a pro that there wouldn't be any, but he wasn't going to bet his life on it. He ran for the darkness behind the house.

He ran until he saw tree trunks coming at him in the dark, and then he slid like Lou Brock going into second. He clipped a tree, rolled and wound up on the ground panting, looking back at the house.

Nobody was coming after him that he could hear; whatever was going on at the front, it was quiet. Cooper hoped they would do the rational thing, concede the round and withdraw, but he also knew that the front of the house was now unguarded and one of them was possibly completely unhurt. He lay there for three more seconds and then was up again, going for the garage side of the house as fast and as quietly as he could across the grass.

He slowed as he came to the front corner of the house. The light showed the empty driveway; he couldn't see much in the direction of the terrace. He heard nothing. In five seconds he had the door of the Marquis open and was leaning on the horn, making enough noise, he hoped, to get a streetful of neighbors pissed off and a cop on the way.

14

THE VODKA BOTTLE was not in evidence when Cooper came into the apartment, but Regis Swanson's appearance suggested what might have become of it. He was unshaven, bleary-eyed and in yesterday's shirt, and he moved as if bipedal locomotion required a certain amount of concentration. "I just got up," he said apologetically, closing the door behind Cooper.

"Go back to bed if you want," said Cooper. "I can mind the store."

Swanson frowned at him. "It shows, huh?"

"It shows, a little. Rough night?"

They moved toward the windows, in step. "It all seemed to come down pretty heavy after I got back here," said Swanson.

Cooper took in the coffee table with its litter of photographs, Swanson's shoes lying under it. "Just remember, the booze can start to come down pretty heavy all by itself if you're not careful."

"Why don't you mind your own damn business?" said Swanson, not quite bringing off an indignant look.

"I'm speaking from experience," said Cooper. "You wake up one day and realize now you've got two problems instead of one. If you're lucky, it's not too late to cut back."

"Let me worry about that," said Swanson, stalking off toward the kitchen.

"It's your life," said Cooper. He looked around the apartment, seeing signs of entropy. He heard crockery rattling. After a minute he went down the hall. Looking into the kitchen he said, "I'm talking to the cops again this morning. After last night there isn't much doubt what's going on. It's just a matter of time before they wrap these two up."

Swanson was looking at a can of coffee as if it were a Chinese puzzle. "Fine," he said. "I don't have any plans today. Today's a waiting day. I sit by the phone and wait and see what kind of life I have left." He set the can on the counter and looked at Cooper, shamefully.

Cooper looked at the man and wondered if there was anything useful he could say. "Do that," he said finally. "Just remember, bankruptcy is not death."

"No," said Swanson, "I know that. Death is what happens to people I love."

"It'll happen to you someday, too," said Cooper. "Don't rush it."

◆

"It's pretty simple," said Cooper. "They want their money, and if they get it they say they'll stop trying to kill Swanson's friends and family. It's a pretty basic sort of approach."

Reichardt and Benitez listened with practiced blankness. Cooper had talked to Reichardt on the phone and set up a time, and both detectives had been waiting for him in the big squad room on the second floor. If Benitez was a second baseman in the prime of his career, Reichardt was an old defensive end, tall and heavy with the muscle going to fat but the slow grace of a fighter still there, hair gray at the temples and high on the forehead.

"How did he find out Swanson was there last night?"

"I don't think he did. I gathered he had come to talk to Hayden and didn't know Swanson was there till he saw me."

"Just got lucky, huh?"

"I guess so. I told Swanson I thought it was a bad idea to go there."

"Did he say why he was there?"

Cooper thought. "Not in so many words. But I assume he was there to do to Hayden what he did to Zina Manning. Put a gun to his head and make him call Swanson. Or maybe just go direct for the money, figuring Hayden had access. I don't know."

"Did he say anything about Zina Manning?"

"No. But it has to be the same two. And they've got to be the ones who did Nate Swanson. Can't you compare ballistics from him and the lady?"

"We did. They weren't shot with the same gun."

"Well, they probably both have the necessary equipment."

Reichardt nodded. "We're working on the guns. Prints, too. We got some off some things they touched in her place."

Cooper smiled. "OK, you're a step ahead of me all the way."

"Why do you think they were willing to negotiate last night?"

"Because I was there, and I was willing. But I wouldn't really call it negotiating. They were willing to take me as security and set up a swap, me for the money."

"Why didn't you go?" said Benitez.

"Would you have gone?"

"I don't know. I'm not sure I would have taken a swipe at them, though."

"Well," said Cooper, "all I can tell you is, it seemed like a good idea at the time."

"Did they show you any weapons last night?" Reichardt said.

"No." Cooper blinked. "Should I have waited?"

Reichardt shrugged. "You're sure it was the same two you saw at Swanson's?"

"Oh, yeah. The guy got rid of the ponytail but the face, the voice, everything else was the same. I could pick him out of a lineup."

Benitez swiveled on his chair. "It was dark, you said. How can you be sure?"

"I saw him in the light from the porch. The ponytail guy, I mean, the tall guy. The other guy, a shape in the dark. But unmistakable, the same guy."

"You see their car?"

"No. They walked at least a block. I didn't hear them drive up."

"Take me through the conversation again," said Reichardt. "Who brought up the son?"

"I did. But then the tall one said, and I think I'm quoting fairly exactly, 'His son stole it from us.' I asked him how he knew and he said he found that out from the police."

"From the police."

"That's what he said. I thought that was real interesting."

Reichardt did not appear to find it so interesting. "Did he elaborate?"

"No. I thought maybe you could."

"He said the police told him? What did he say exactly?"

"As close as I can remember, he said something like he got it from the best possible source—the police. Maybe I should have asked for details but I didn't."

The two detectives exchanged a look of deep professional intimacy. "The best possible source," said Benitez.

"I talked to a DEA agent the other night," said Cooper. "They seem to be convinced my employer was in the drug business with his son. I told them about these two guys and told them to call you. Did they?"

"We keep in touch," said Reichardt.

Cooper nodded. "OK, don't tell me anything you don't want to tell me. But listen for a minute. You and the Feds need to put your heads together. You've got one end of the rope, they have the other. I think somebody's pulling a fast one here."

Reichardt studied a cracked thumbnail. "What do you mean somebody's pulling a fast one?"

"What kind of evidence do you have that Nate Swanson was a dope dealer?" Nobody answered and Cooper went on. "Maybe he wasn't. If the Feds think he was dealing, maybe somebody lied to them. If I were you I'd try to find out who. Because that lie got Nate Swanson killed. Somebody's covering his tracks."

This time the look the two dicks gave each other was almost soulful.

"Am I getting warm?" said Cooper.

Reichardt looked at him with that cop look that reminds you who you're talking to. "Do you have someplace you can go for a couple of weeks?" he said.

Cooper laughed, without humor. "I already thought about that. I've got a feeling they'll be back."

"I'd bet on it," said Benitez.

◆

"That's what really makes the dish," said Turk, "the sauce. You have to take the time to cook up the sauce beforehand. You can't just mix up vegetables with scrambled eggs and call it huevos rancheros." He hoisted a forkful for inspection before putting it in his mouth. Across the table Kathleen was chewing stolidly, uncombed and still in her bathrobe.

"It's good," she said through the mouthful. "Where'd you learn to make it?"

"From a Colombian guy I knew in L.A. Big dish in Colombia." Turk concentrated on his plate so he wouldn't have to look at Kathleen.

"Have you ever been there?" she said.

Turk shook his head. "The Colombians I've known, they don't make me real anxious to go there, most of them."

"What do you mean? Are they drug dealers or something?"

"Aren't they all? Nah, just low-lifes. That's why I left L.A. Too many low-lifes."

"Well, it's not as if we don't have any here." Kathleen set her empty plate on the table. "That was almost good enough to make me forgive you for standing me up last night."

"I didn't stand you up. I called you."

"Just because you called doesn't mean you didn't stand me up."

"I told you. I had to go with this guy. See, my old partner moved and his ex doesn't know where he went, except he hangs out at this place . . ."

"I know. You told me the story."

"So I had to go with the guy, to look for my partner."

"OK, OK. I guess you made up for it later." She was coy for a moment, and Turk had to look down at his plate. "Just tell me one thing."

"What?"

"Why is there blood on your pants in there?"

"There is? Shit, you're kidding."

"No. Above the knee. Three or four big drops."

"Damn that guy. There was this guy, see. It didn't look like that bad a place, but they'd had a fight or something and this guy was standing there at the bar bleeding from the nose. Somebody'd walloped him, I guess. He was really bleeding, and he was like wiping his nose with his finger and shaking it off on the floor, you know?"

"Yuck. Where on earth was this?"

"I don't know. Up north somewhere. This other guy drove. I was like lost. Damn, my good chinos. He must have got me when we were leaving or something. We just like ducked in, looked for my partner and left."

Kathleen looked at him over the rim of the mug, only the blue eyes showing. She said, "So how long are you going to keep looking for this guy?"

Turk shrugged. "A couple of days. Some friend, huh? Calls me and tells me to move to Chicago and when I get here he's disappeared." Kathleen was still giving him a skeptical look, and Turk heaved an inward sigh, gearing up for the labor needed to keep her happy for another day. "You have to work today?"

She nodded. "And I've got to be on time today, after yesterday."

"Christ, can't you call in sick?"

Kathleen seemed to waver and he feared for a moment he had been too convincing. Finally she shook her head. "That wouldn't be honest."

Turk nodded solemnly. "No, I guess it wouldn't." He glanced at the clock over the sink. "Well, there's one advantage to getting up this early."

"What?"

Turk stood up, the towel wrapped around his waist, and went around the table. He stood above her and gently lifted her chin, bending to put his lips close to hers. "There might just be time to find our way back to the bedroom."

"Oh," she said, pretending to grimace, but she didn't struggle at all.

◆

Cooper looked in the phone book for the number of the DEA office downtown. He didn't have a name but he figured somebody would see that the message got to the right person. He asked the woman who answered the phone to put him through to the agent in charge of undercover operations; after some probing and stalling she handed him over to an expressionless male voice.

"The name is MacLeish," Cooper said. He spelled it and gave his home phone number and the one for the cellular phone in the Marquis. "I need to talk to the female agent who followed me out on the Farwell Avenue pier the night before last. Five-six or so, black hair, mid to late twenties. Works with a blond guy with a moustache who's losing his hair. I don't know her name but she'll know me. Have her call me and tell her it's important."

"What is the subject you want to discuss with her?" said the voice.

"My ass," said Cooper. "Specifically, keeping it in one piece."

◆

McTeague and the white-haired man crossed the street from the parking garage to the apartment building, walking slowly in the heat. It was a typically crowded block of a typically crowded Streeterville street east of Michigan, with expensive cars oozing past the awnings of pricey restaurants, and uniformed doormen with their hands clasped behind their backs taking the sun in front of buildings with cool dark entrance halls. McTeague watched everything with the quiet wariness of a man carrying a dozen or so banded stacks of hundred-dollar bills in a blue gym bag. Beside him the white-haired man in the gray suit walked with a slight stoop, looking faintly pained.

The entrance of the building they went into was suitably cool and dim and presided over by a formidable-looking black man in a green uniform. McTeague gave his name and the name of the woman who was expecting them, and after a moment's delay while the doorman used the telephone, they were ushered into an elevator.

McTeague watched the numbers light up in succession above the door of the elevator and took a couple of deep breaths. The white-haired man turned to him. "Harold found this person, did he?"

McTeague nodded. "He may be retired, but still seems to know where the money's hidden."

The white-haired man smiled and shook his head. "Always did."

"He said she drives a hard bargain but rumor has it she's in trouble, which works to our advantage. He also said if she tries to haggle any further, change the terms, gives us any trouble at all, we just walk. She needs me more than I need her."

On the tenth floor they found their way down a carpeted hall to a door with the number they were looking for. McTeague pressed a button and heard a chime inside and waited.

The door was opened by a man who needed an emergency fashion makeover. He had no hair on the top of his head, a surplus of it, matted and gray, around his ears, and a beard that looked as if it could use a stiff comb or maybe a pair of shears. His glasses had been fashionable in the early sixties and hadn't quite made it back. His green T-shirt, bearing a picture of a gun muzzle and the question *Feel lucky punk?* was stretched to the limit by a large, perfectly spherical gut and tucked neatly into black and white checked pants. He looked from McTeague to the white-haired man and said, "Yes?"

"I'm here to see Mrs. Ross," said McTeague.

"She's expecting a Mr. McTeague. Would that be you?"

"It would."

"And you are?" the fat man said, looking at the white-haired man.

"He's my advisor," said McTeague.

The fat man looked at both of them for a moment longer with a touch of hostility and then stood aside. "My mother's in the parlor."

The parlor turned out to be two rooms away, at the end of a trek that rivaled Burton and Speke's. The apartment was sizable, gloomy and perilously littered with heavy angular furniture. Every available square foot of wall space was occupied by framed pictures of what had been called Negroes when the artwork had been executed: caricatures all, with thick lips and white teeth, bare feet and kerchiefed heads, grinning, dancing, singing, picking cotton or plucking a banjo. There were hundreds of pictures. McTeague and his companion exchanged one blank look as they followed their host across a thick dark carpet. Before them, the fat man trailed a faint but unpleasant odor of long-unwashed linen.

He ushered them into the parlor. Here there was sunlight coming in through a window, but no relief from the Negroes. Here there was also statuary: pickaninnies designed to dispense salt and pepper, a full-sized lawn darkie from somebody's yard.

"My mother," announced the fat man. The person sitting on the couch at the end of the room would have fooled McTeague: he would have guessed eunuch before recognizing it as female. She was dressed in trousers and a dark blue shirt; she had short white hair and a round ageless face. She was fatter than her son.

"Forgive me for not getting up," she said in a husky voice. "It's an effort."

"That's OK," said McTeague, sinking carefully onto a chair her son had pointed him to. The white-haired man sat in an armchair to his left.

"You're admiring my collection," said the woman, no doubt notic-
ing McTeague's stunned expression. "It's the largest collection of its
kind in the world." There was no pride in her voice, only a ruthless
matter-of-factness.

"It's a sight," said McTeague with a shake of the head.

"Who's your friend?" the woman said.

"I'm Joseph Ruskin," the white-haired man said, unruffled. "I'm
here at Mr. McTeague's request to examine the property."

"He doesn't trust me, huh?" The woman smiled.

Ruskin shrugged. McTeague said, "Trust but verify."

She barked, or perhaps it was a laugh. "Smartest thing old Ronnie
ever said. Very well. Evelyn, show these gentlemen what they came
to see."

The fat man produced a key from a pocket and went to a sideboard. He unlocked a drawer and pulled out a flat leather case about
six inches wide by a foot long. He opened the case and held it out to
Ruskin. The old man took the case and frowned at the coins ranged
inside. From where he sat McTeague could see gold.

Ruskin pulled a surprisingly large magnifying lens from his jacket
pocket and, holding the case on his lap, examined the dozen or so
coins one by one. He took each one out of its slot, turned it over,
looked at it through the lens and with the naked eye, rubbed it with
his thumb. The process took several minutes but nobody moved.
McTeague tried to watch Ruskin but his eye was fatally drawn by the
ghastly ranks of Negroes on the wall. Traffic noises came up from
the street.

Finally Ruskin looked across at McTeague. "How much were you
offering?"

McTeague pronounced a six-figure number. Ruskin put his head
on one side, sucked in one cheek, nodded slowly. "That's a good
price. All in the MS60 range, I'd say. And as far as I can tell without
going to the trouble of testing specific gravity and so forth, they're
genuine."

The eunuch stirred. "Of course they're genuine. What do you take
me for?"

Ruskin gave her a thoughtful look. "That's only the second uncir-
culated 1796 Quarter Eagle I've ever seen. There are precious few
collections of this quality around, and I thought I knew about all the
ones in this city. When one surfaces like this, genuineness is the first
thing I look at." He closed the case and held it out in McTeague's direction. It was deftly taken from him by the fat man.

"I believe we need to see some money," he said.

McTeague picked up the gym bag and unzipped it. "Who's counting it?" he said.

"I am," said the woman. McTeague rose and went to the couch. He pulled out handfuls of cash and tossed them on the cushion at the woman's side. He pronounced the figure again. Then he went back to the chair. He watched as she carefully counted each stack of bills, riffling through them with practiced fingers.

"All right," she said when she had finished. She nodded at her son, who came over and delivered the case to McTeague.

"Thanks." McTeague zipped the case into his gym bag and stood up. Ruskin did the same. "Pleasure doing business with you," McTeague said, expressionless.

"Likewise." The woman was carefully stacking the bills on her ample lap, absorbed. She did not look up as her son led them out. McTeague held his breath for the last twenty feet.

"Did you park in the garage across the way?" the fat man said at the door.

McTeague turned. "Yes."

"I thought that would be your best choice. Otherwise it's tough to park around here."

McTeague blinked at him. "Yeah. Thanks for the tip."

In the elevator he and Ruskin exchanged another look. "Quite a lively household," said the old man.

"I've seen some strange ones," said McTeague, and failed to finish his thought.

"Odd combination of money and squalor," Ruskin said thoughtfully, a student of humanity.

"The old lady used to own the top three whorehouses on the Near North Side, according to Berger."

"That might explain it," said Ruskin.

McTeague extended his hand. "Thanks for your help."

"Easiest thousand dollars I ever earned." The old man nodded at the gym bag. "Take care of those."

"I plan to," said McTeague.

Out on the sidewalk under the drumming sun he halted and put a hand on Ruskin's arm. "Would you mind a whole lot grabbing a cab or something?"

Ruskin looked surprised. When no explanation came, he nodded, lips pursed. "Certainly," he said. "Tell Harold hello from me."

"You bet." McTeague watched the old man walk slowly away toward Michigan in his elegant gray suit, hands in his pockets, head down. McTeague crossed the street.

He went past the entrance to the parking garage and around the corner, looking into the shadows of the lower level. He saw nobody besides the attendant in his booth, but he didn't expect to see anyone there. His Trans Am was on the second level. He found the stairway exit where he expected to find it, halfway down the block. He opened it and stepped inside. At the bottom of the stairs he paused to unzip the bag. He began to climb slowly up the stairs, his footsteps echoing in the concrete shaft.

He saw the man when he came around the turn of the stairs leading up to the second-level landing. He was waiting at the fire door, holding it open with a foot so he could watch through the crack. He was young and black and dressed in an oversized orange T-shirt and a University of Michigan baseball cap, worn backwards. He was still panting a little, having run up the stairs from a nearby phone just a minute or so ahead of McTeague.

Of course, thought McTeague. Who else would they hire? The kid had been listening as McTeague came up and was watching over his shoulder, waiting to see if McTeague was trouble. When McTeague came into sight he pulled his foot out of the door and went through the motions of changing his mind about what floor he wanted, taking a couple of steps toward the stairs leading up. He made brief eye contact with McTeague.

McTeague kept coming, watching him go up three or four steps. When McTeague had reached the landing he turned and saw the kid standing there looking at him, almost decided. Before he could make a move McTeague reached into the bag and pulled out a Smith and Wesson .357 magnum revolver and pointed it at the kid's chest. "Surprise," he said. The kid's eyes got wide and he froze. "Slow," said McTeague. "That's the key word. You're going to do what I tell you, but real slow. You make me nervous, I'm gonna put a couple of big holes in you. You read me?"

The kid opened his mouth and after a second or two sound came out. "Uh-huh," he said.

"You're gonna lie down on the stairs," said McTeague. "You're gonna turn around and lie face down on the stairs, arms and legs spread. Do it now and do it slow."

The kid did what he said and McTeague dropped the bag and walked up the three steps and felt under the T-shirt at the waistline. He pulled a little .25 automatic out of the waistband of the kid's jeans and went back down to the landing. "This is a fucking popgun, kid," he said.

Looking over his shoulder, the kid said nothing.

McTeague knelt and put the automatic in the gym bag, holding the .357 on the kid. He picked up the bag. "How much they pay you for this?" he said.

After a moment the kid said, "T'fuck you talkin' about?"

"Don't bullshit me. How much did the fat guy offer you?"

Several heartbeats went by. "Five hundred," said the kid.

"What was the deal, you hit me, take the box, bring it up? Or is he gonna meet you somewhere?"

"You a cop?"

"No, I don't have any rules to follow. You getting tired of talking?"

"Uh-uh."

"So what was the deal?"

"I get the box, meet him at the alley door."

"What if you don't show? What's he got on you?"

Another few seconds passed. The kid's eyes were still wide, still fixed on the muzzle of the revolver. "He throw my mama out. She work for him."

McTeague shook his head. "You ever been up in his apartment?"

"Uh-uh."

"Well, right now there's about twenty times that much, more even, up there. In cash. You find a way to get up there, they won't put up much of a fight. And be sure to take a look at the artwork on the walls while you're there." McTeague waited a beat or two. "I don't want to see your black ass again, you hear me?" He was backing through the door.

"I hear you," said the kid, and McTeague was gone.

◆

When the phone rang Cooper had just stepped out of the shower, limp from a three-mile jog up the lakefront and back. Diana knocked at the door of the bathroom and leaned in. "For you," she said. Her expression was odd, watchful. "Female. She said to tell you it was the lady you met out at the lake the other night."

"Ah." Cooper wrapped the towel around his waist with great concentration. "That'll be my DEA agent."

One of Diana's eyebrows rose, just a little. "What happened out at the lake?"

"We had a little talk. I neglected to mention it to you." He walked past her, avoiding her eyes. He went up the hall into the living room and picked up the phone. "Yeah."

"You wanted to talk to me." The voice was familiar.

Cooper sank onto the sofa. It was nearly dark outside, still luminous above the rooftops to the west. Diana's footsteps came softly up the hall. "Yeah, I did." Why the hell did I give her this number? thought Cooper.

"I'm listening," she said.

"OK," said Cooper. Diana was standing in the doorway, arms folded. Cooper could calculate fast when he needed to; he saw there wasn't really any way to dodge it. "I was hoping we could help each other," he said.

"What's the problem?"

Cooper's eyes were locked with Diana's. "The problem is the two gentlemen who visited me last night up at Swanson's lawyer's house. Did the Chicago cops call you?"

"Not that I know of. I just got off fourteen hours of surveillance. What happened last night?"

Cooper took a breath and jumped. "What happened was the two bad guys showed up, looking for my boss. We had a heart-to-heart and they left. But I think they'll be back. They're not real happy with me."

"Why not?"

"I hit one of them with a tire iron."

Diana closed her eyes. The woman at the other end of the line laughed. "So what do you need me for?"

"We need each other," said Cooper. "I need you to stay real close to me with lots of heavily armed people, and you need me as bait."

"Bait?"

"Yeah. I'm the worm on the hook now. I'm the lure you troll slowly across the lake with. These two guys are going to come for me, and I want you to be there. You and your friend with the moustache and any other friends you have who don't have anything better to do. All you have to do is watch me and sooner or later you'll get a shot at a couple of prime assholes."

There was silence on the line. Diana had come to the sofa and sat at the other end, her face in her hands. Cooper looked at her long bare legs and waited for the woman to say something.

"We're not a protection firm. Bodyguarding is not our business," she said at last.

"Hey, lady. I'm offering you a chance to prevent a crime. A real crime. If you're happier sitting around all day watching poor people blow their welfare checks, fine. I just thought you might want to set your sights a little higher. These are big-leaguers. You catch them, you got a line on the money people. And you just might save my worthless ass in the bargain."

There was another silence, and then, "I can't promise you anything."

"I'm not asking for help. I'm offering you help."

"My, that's generous."

"Look, you probably already know where I live. These days I'm driving a brown Mercury Marquis, license number KDL 297. Right now it's parked on Lakewood Avenue just south of Devon. Tomorrow morning I'm going to get in it and drive downtown. You want to follow me, I'll feel better and you might get lucky. Now I have to hang up, because I'm about to have the first real fight of my marriage."

"Wait a second."

"Still here."

There were two seconds of silence. "I can't tell you anything right now. But let me give you my pager number. If you see them again, call me."

"I hope you're fast."

"I told you I couldn't make any promises."

"Fine. Let me get a pencil."

He found one, and she read him the number over the phone. "Good luck," she said.

"I appreciate that," said Cooper, and hung up.

Three seconds went by. Diana looked up and said, "How long have you been lying to me about this?"

"I haven't been lying. I've been editing a little."

"Editing? That's what you call it?"

"I didn't want you to worry."

In the lamplight she looked pale and betrayed, the dark eyes above the high feline cheekbones fixed on him. "For a smart man, you're unbelievably stupid sometimes."

"Thanks."

"You really think I'd rather not know?"

Cooper stood up and adjusted the towel. "I thought you might sleep a little better, yeah. Can I go get dressed?"

Now she was up off the couch, and her voice was rising. "I have to find out my husband's in danger of his life when some FBI spy lady he's been meeting in secret calls up?"

"She's DEA."

"I don't care what she is. Why don't you tell me these things?" Cooper stood his ground as she came.

"You were asleep when I got home."

"I woke up the next day. You don't think that's worth telling?"

"I should have told you. I'm sorry. Look, until last night I really didn't think I was in danger."

"That was twenty-four hours ago. Who the hell do you think I am, Cooper? I'm your wife, for God's sake. You don't think I have any stake in this?"

Blew this one bad, thought Cooper, looking into her face two feet from his. "I'm sorry."

"Are they out there now? Watching the house? We gonna have to move again?"

"I don't think so. I don't think they know who I am."

"Then why the hell you have to ask this lady for protection? Stop lying to me."

"It's a precaution. They don't know who I am, but they might find out. I'm trying to cover all the bases."

She jabbed herself in the chest with a thumb. "Here's a base you can try covering. Me. Your wife, remember? The lady who lives with you."

Cooper opened his mouth to reassure her and thought better of it. "I'm sorry." He stood haplessly looking at her, one hand holding the towel at his waist.

In a moment she eased off a bit, rocking back a little. "How do you do it?"

"Do what?"

"How do you manage to get in the way every time? Every single time."

He shook his head. "This time I'm just standing where the rain falls. None of this is my fault."

She drew herself up. "All right, we're out of here. Tonight. We're leaving, you and me."

"I can't leave."

"Why the hell not?"

"I have a job to do."

"Cooper, your job description doesn't include taking bullets for that son of a bitch."

"He's paying me extra. I have to be here till he's out of the woods."

"You don't have to be here. Call him and resign. Send back the money."

"I can't do that."

"Why not?"

Cooper thought about it, looking into those dark eyes. "I was hired to do a job. I can't quit when it gets rough. I just can't."

She looked at him for a few seconds more, then abruptly closed her eyes. Something gave way, and she spun and took off down the long hallway. "No," she said. "You can't, can you? Not you."

15

JASPER HUNG UP the phone first; with his hand still resting on the receiver he looked across the office at Toni, who was frowning as she hung up her extension. "Don't say it," said Jasper.

"What?"

"Anything. Before you go getting all smug, listen to me."

"Who's feeling smug? All I did was listen to what the man had to say."

"You think this proves you right."

"I think it ought to get our attention, yes."

Jasper got up and came slowly across the office to sit opposite Toni. He leaned his elbows on the desk and said, "Just because a couple of overworked Chicago homicide dicks can't sort out the social life of a rich kid doesn't mean I'm wrong about him."

Toni met his stare. "If Nate Swanson spent the night before the tip was phoned in with a dozen witnesses, all of whom say he never left the club and the only money they saw him handle was receipts from the club, where did the million come in and who did he flash it to?"

"The million came in in the wee hours, after the club closed. He flashed it to his girlfriend. She blew the whistle, to a brother or a back-door lover or somebody they haven't found yet. Or else it was the accomplice, whoever actually stole the money from Dexter. Nate stiffed him or something and he got pissed off and called."

Toni shrugged. "You heard what the man said."

"Yeah, I heard him. And like I say, just because they claim they've traced everybody's movements for the night doesn't mean they really know what happened. The accomplice could have been waiting at the girlfriend's place when she and Nate got there from the club. Or they stopped off someplace on the way. How the fuck can they know what happened that night?"

"You're positing an accomplice there's no evidence for. Somebody Nate Swanson would trust with a million bucks. All his friends have been checked out; they're all accounted for that night."

"You don't pull something like that with a friend, necessarily. You pull it with some shady asshole doper who then gets pissed off about his cut and drops a dime on you. That's what happened."

"Look, the cops have narrowed down when the cash was stolen. And Nate Swanson did not participate in the theft. Too many witnesses say he didn't, there is no time unaccounted for that night. If he masterminded it or something, it had to be somebody he had a relationship with. Who's going to steal a million dollars and faithfully bring it to him except somebody he's tight with? And there's nobody like that in the picture. The tip was a setup to cover someone else's ass."

"Shit, anything's possible if you start exercising your imagination. But I have to go on what I see and how it smells. And it smells to me like the rich kid tried to pull a fast one and got shot for it."

"So trace the suitcase for me. Where is it?"

"Sitting in a closet in Regis Swanson's house. The kid took it there the morning after. I wanted to get a fucking search warrant on day one, but no. You don't do that to people like Regis Swanson. Not even if you're in the middle of a war, declared in Washington by the type of people who have lunch with Regis Swanson. The money's still stitting there, unless the chauffeur's been able to take it someplace and start washing it, thanks to our pulling off the surveillance. Jesus, Toni. What do you need to see?"

Toni shrugged. "Evidence. I can see different scenarios here, that's all."

"You let the fucking guy coo into your ear and you bought it, that's the problem."

"And you got a hard-on for spoiled rich kids, that's your problem. We both have to stay detached and look at the evidence, J.D."

Jasper sagged away from the desk. "Don't lecture me, little girl. Don't tell me about staying detached."

Toni stayed cool; she smiled after a second. "Little girl. I like that. OK, what are the big boys going to do next?"

"Piss the case away down the drain, it looks like."

"Can I make a suggestion?"

Jasper seemed to slack off just a bit, exhaling. "I'm sorry. Talk to me."

"Whether or not the chauffeur's on the level, it makes sense to watch him. Slap the surveillance back on. I think he's right. Sooner or later, the enforcers will want to talk to him again."

"If he's telling the truth."

"You think he's making it up, about the other night? Somebody shot Zina Manning."

"Oh, yeah. The enforcers are real. I just think they've probably already made their deal with Swanson. The other night was smoke."

"Huh?"

"They caught up with Swanson, things got settled. It was just a sideline for Swanson, he pays off the kid's debts out of petty cash, they go away. Only they can't just fade away without explanation. Swanson has to go on being persecuted, until his right-hand man plays hero and chases them off. That's what they staged the other night. Who got a look at the two bad guys besides the chauffeur? Nobody."

"The way he told it to the cops, it didn't sound very conclusive. If he was staging something, he would have made it more convincing."

"Hard to do that without leaving a body. You watch, they won't be back, and before too long everybody will forget all about it."

Toni shook her head. "I think you're working too hard on this one. But there's one way to find out, isn't there?"

"It's too late. When he asks us to watch him, it means we're only going to see what he wants us to see. They've gotten away with it."

"Maybe. But he could be telling the truth about these two assholes. And who are we to turn down a chance to wrap them up?"

Jasper stared at her across the desk, chewing on his moustache. "Here's a rule. Any time you do anything an informant suggests you do, you've lost control."

"Here's another rule," said Toni. "Any time you let an informant get killed, even an iffy one, you've lost an informant."

"Fuck it. How are we going to get Snodgrass to go for it?"

"Play up the L.A. angle. Presumably these people are working for Dexter D.'s connection. And that's somebody we've been wanting for a while."

Jasper stared at her. "OK, little girl. You talked me into it."

◆

Swanson was sporting another day's growth of white beard. Cooper watched him pad across the carpet to the dining table and sit down. There was a coffee cup on a saucer and a bowl of something in front of him. While Swanson resumed his breakfast Cooper walked to the coffee table by the window. The litter of photographs was still there, with one addition. Cooper picked up the revolver and turned to Swanson. "What the fuck is this doing here?"

Swanson made a beckoning motion. "I'll put it away."

"Don't tell me," said Cooper. "I really don't want to hear that you were sitting here thinking about putting this in your mouth."

"I was a little depressed. It doesn't mean anything." Swanson took a drink of coffee and set the cup back on the saucer.

Cooper broke open the cylinder, saw it was loaded, snapped it back. "This is a mistake. Having this thing in here is a bad mistake if you're that depressed. Why don't I take it off your hands?"

"Fine, take it. It's not important." Swanson scraped at the bowl with his spoon.

Cooper hefted the revolver and stuck it in the side pocket of his sport jacket. "You thinking about travel arrangements?"

"I can't leave yet."

"I thought yesterday was the wrap-up."

"Yesterday was just the beginning."

"Let Hayden take care of things. You need to think about saving your skin."

Swanson shoved the bowl away. "I need three more days."

"OK, I'll make plane reservations for Saturday."

"I don't know where I'd go. Maybe I won't have to go anywhere. Maybe they'll catch these two."

"Maybe they won't. You got any relatives you could go stay with?"

Swanson waved him off. "A couple of sisters. We don't talk much."

"A vacation home?"

"What the hell would I do in a condo in Miami Beach that I can't do here?"

"Step outside without ducking, for one thing."

"It would be just like being here. Empty. Except I could look at an ocean instead of a lake."

"You've got to have a friend somewhere who would put you up for a while."

Swanson shook his head. "Not really. Everything I have is here in town. What's left of it."

Cooper shook his head. "You're not safe here."

A silence ensued. Swanson sat with his head in his hands, staring at the rug about six feet beyond the table. "I've lost it," he said finally.

"Lost what?"

"Purpose," he said. "Nothing means a damn thing anymore. Nothing."

Cooper pulled a chair out from the table and sat down. "You're lucky," he said.

Swanson raised his head. "What the hell is that supposed to mean?"

"With you it didn't happen until what, the late fifties? Are you sixty yet? Me, it hit at age nineteen. Maybe twenty, to be a little more precise. I had a purpose as long as I was in Vietnam—make it out of Vietnam. Once I was out, that was when I lost the purpose. But you know what?"

Swanson stared at him for a few seconds, something like interest flickering in the bloodshot eyes. "What?"

"You can get it back again. I promise you. You can get it back again. Just don't do anything too stupid while you're waiting."

Swanson looked back at him with the look of the hopelessly whipped, then looked away out the window. "Terrific. Those are words to live by, all right. Don't do anything too stupid."

"It's better advice than a lot of people get." Cooper pushed away from the table. "Hold the fort. You got people working for you. You may be broke, but you're not dead yet."

"No," said Regis Swanson, looking far away, "not quite yet."

◆

Turk was pouring coffee when Kathleen came into the kitchen, fully dressed, coiffed and made up. He looked up and said, "My, my. You look nice."

"I want you out of here," she said. She stood with her arms folded, tense and staring.

Turk stared back, then set down the coffeepot. "Why?" he said, innocently, injured.

"You're a liar," said Kathleen. She sagged against the doorframe.

"What?"

"You've been lying to me. You're not what you say you are. You're not *who* you say you are."

Turk held the injured look as he sat down slowly at the table. "What makes you say that?"

"I looked in your bag," she said after a brief struggle.

Turk looked down at the tabletop, his expression changing to one of disappointment, then displeasure. "That wasn't very nice," he said.

"I'm sorry if it's not nice. I don't think it's nice to lie to people."

"And just what was it that you saw in there?" said Turk, looking up at her now, calculating already.

Something changed on her face, as if for the first time she realized that she might not have acted wisely. "Your ID's," she said. "All of them."

"And the gun?" said Turk.

She was frightened now, going pale and straightening up, her arms falling to her sides. "Don't hurt me," she said.

Turk raised his hands, palms up. "I'm not going to hurt you. Why the hell would I hurt you? We've had a beautiful little interlude here."

"Look. I won't say anything to anybody. Just please leave." She was backing out of the door as Turk rose.

"Hey, baby. You want me to leave, I'm out of here. I'm just kind of hurt, you know? I mean, I thought we were having a good thing here." He backed her into the living room; she was stumbling against furniture.

"You lied to me. You've been lying all along." Kathleen stepped out of his way, putting the sofa between them.

"Yes, I lied." Turk stopped and faced her, hands on hips, facing the charge manfully, a regretful look on his face. "I told you some fibs. I'm not trying to find my old partner. I'm trying to find the man who killed my brother."

She stared at him, wide-eyed, for at least three seconds before her expression hardened. "I don't believe you," she said.

Turk shook his head sadly. "That's the truth. I have to move undercover because the killer's a very powerful man. I'm close, real close to finding him. And when I do, I'm going to avenge my brother. It's taken me three years to find him. And I don't want to blow it now."

She just stared, totally blank, before saying. "I still want you out of here. I'm sorry. It's just not going to work. I'll give you your money back."

Turk shrugged and moved toward the bedroom. "Keep the money. We had a good time. I'm just sorry you don't believe me." He went into the bedroom and sat on the bed, pulling the bag across the floor toward him. He unzipped it and reached inside and pulled out the automatic to check it, though he was fairly sure she hadn't tampered with anything. He released the catch and slid out the magazine, saw that it was still loaded, slid it back but didn't rack the slide. He looked up to see her in the doorway, wide-eyed and backing away.

"Please," she said, breathless.

"For God's sake, Kathleen." Turk shoved the gun back into the bag. "I'm not going to hurt you." He went into the bathroom and got his toothbrush, stuffed it and one stray shirt into the bag, and moved into the living room. Kathleen was rooted in the middle of the rug. "Hey," said Turk. "I'm out of here. Stop looking at me like I'm fucking Ted Bundy or something." He took his jacket off the back of a chair and put it on, picked up the bag again, and made for the door.

She edged out of his path, standing like a little girl watching a big mean dog walk by. Turk halted in front of her, looked into Kathleen's big blue eyes, and said, "It was good while it lasted. I'm sorry there won't be any trip to Cancún."

"Just go, please," she said, arms folded again, not meeting his gaze.

"OK. *Ciao.*" Turk went on toward the door. After two or three steps he turned, saw her just starting to follow, and whipped around with a right cross. The punch caught her just above and to the right of the mouth and it sounded like an axe hitting a tree trunk. He saw her eyes go unfocused as she fell backwards. She bounced off the sofa and rolled onto her face, not out but not really there, either. Turk dropped the bag and flipped her over on her back and put a knee on her chest and his right hand to her throat. As his grip tightened, her eyes widened for an instant, clear and conscious, but the focus went away again and then it was easy.

◆

Where do you go with time on your hands and a gun in your pocket on a hot summer day? Cooper pushed east toward the lake, watching the mirrors. Ball game, he thought. Let 'em try a hit in front of thirty thousand people, Steve Stone saying, *There seems to be a disturbance of some sort in the right field bleachers, Harry.*

Cooper settled on a place where nobody could get too close without being seen, with clear fields of vision for trailing federal agents. He wound up leaving the car in Lincoln Park near the zoo and walking north along the lake, watching waves tickle the rocks and people neglect their duties. Sky and water were bright and benign, inviting indolence. He paused at intervals to watch boats on the lake and look behind him. He saw nobody in particular. The unfamiliar weight of the revolver in his pocket reminded him occasionally of certain present concerns.

Eventually it was time to sit and think. Cooper sat at the base of a tree, back to the water for security, and tried to get a handle on what was happening to Regis Swanson. His mind wandered frequently.

When a middle-aged man with a shamefaced look sidled by and struck up a peculiarly pointed conversation, Cooper decided it was time to leave.

◆

McTeague could see the car coming, drawing slowly nearer down the long gentle slope between the high, high walls of the alley, blank concrete walls on either side. Above, the sky was gray. He watched the car coming with dread, wishing there was some other way, just about any way, to get out of the alley, but knowing it was miles long in either direction. The car pulled up in front of him and Rolando leaned across the seat to open the passenger door. McTeague stepped back, not wanting to get in, and Rolando smiled, white teeth and whites of his eyes showing in the black face, under the brim of the straw hat. "Jump in, man, it's a long way to Beverly Hills," said Rolando.

"Forget it, man, I'll walk," said McTeague, seeing the Jewel bag on the seat beside Rolando.

"Well shit, you wanna walk, that's your problem," said Rolando. "Just don't forget this." He picked up the Jewel bag and held it out to McTeague.

McTeague knew he had to take it. He went to the door of the car and leaned in far enough to take the bag. It was heavy; it hit the door frame as he was backing out and the revolver inside went clunk, but there was something else in there, too, something squishy that was leaking out through a hole in the bottom of the bag. "What the fuck you put in there?" said McTeague.

"I ain't touched it," said Rolando. "Have a nice walk."

McTeague slammed the door and backed away, holding the bag away from him. He leaned down far enough to see Rolando at the wheel through the window, and then Rolando's hand went to the brim of the hat and McTeague drew a deep breath and tried to yell, because he didn't want to see what was under the hat. The yell wouldn't come and his legs wouldn't move and all he could do was watch as Rolando doffed his hat, the baby dreadlocks coming off with it, and showed him the top of his head, like a big fat watermelon with the end sliced off.

McTeague managed to force a sound out of his throat, and then he was in a different place, light and sound and awareness flooding back as he thrashed. He focused and saw her standing naked and hip-shot at the foot of the bed, backlit against the light coming in from the balcony, and for a moment he couldn't see her face and was afraid again. He was sweating and the sheet was stuck to him.

"Honey," she said, hands going to her hips. "That must have been some dream."

McTeague sagged back on the pillow. He wiped sweat from his face with both hands. "Did I say anything?"

She was silent while she took a robe from the back of a chair, put it on and moved to the side of the bed, tying the sash. "Just something about a body buried under the chrysanthemums. But don't worry. I won't tell."

Seconds passed; McTeague laughed. "Hey. If I ever killed anybody, there wouldn't be a body to find."

"That's good to know," she said. "I guess."

◆

The door was opened by Buzz Hayden, tie loosened and sleeves rolled up, looking sullen and formidable. "Where the hell have you been?" he said.

"Getting a suntan." Cooper moved toward the windows. Evening sunlight shone in a thousand panes of glass outside and the distant lake was the color of blued steel.

"I have to get going and I didn't want to leave him alone."

"Where is he?"

Hayden looked down the hall toward the bedroom. "He seems to have drunk himself to sleep."

"That's out of character, isn't it?"

"Christ. The man's taken enough to drive anybody to drink, wouldn't you say?"

"Hey, I'm all for it." Cooper sank onto the couch.

Hayden had picked up his jacket and was pulling it on, eyeing Cooper. "What'd you do before he hired you?"

"A lot of things. Drove a cab."

Hayden adjusted his tie and stood watching him for a moment. "I never thanked you for the other night, up at my place. I understand you were in some danger."

"Not by choice." Cooper was tired, very tired.

"Regis takes chances on people. He has hunches. A few times he's been wrong, but usually he's right and it pays off. I'm hoping you're one of his better hunches."

"Me too."

Hayden looked out into the clear evening air, hands in his pockets.

"He's a hell of a man. I've known Regis since we both went to Amundsen High School, up on the Northwest Side. His old man worked two jobs, his ma worked, too. They still had time to raise three kids and practically adopt me, too, when my folks split up and I kind of went off the rails. You talk about Protestant work ethic, that family had it. Everything Regis has done, all the money he's made, he built it up from scratch. And he spreads it around, too. He's given more money to more causes in this city than anybody. That's why this all makes me so sick. There are people out there sharpening their knives, getting ready to celebrate because Regis Swanson is being hounded into bankruptcy. People just hate success, you know? It's not even just envy. Some low-life wins a million bucks in the lottery and he's a hero. A guy like Regis builds up a business from scratch, people can't wait to bring him down. It's the actual quality of hard work and success they hate. Makes me sick."

"Let me interrupt you for a second."

"Huh?" Hayden turned from the window.

"You've been talking to the DEA. Why do they say they think Nate was dealing drugs?"

"It's total bullshit. They have no case at all. They're backing right off, but the damage has already been done."

"That's not what I asked you. Why did they think Nate was dealing?"

Hayden blinked. "They said they got a tip."

"That's what I figured. How good a tip?"

"What do you mean?"

"I mean I think Nate was framed."

Hayden just stared at him. "Framed?"

"Yeah. You've been proceeding on the assumption Nate was up to something, right?"

Hayden shrugged. "Who knows? The point was, it had nothing to do with his father."

"Maybe, maybe not. Let's try another hypothesis—Nate wasn't involved in drugs at all. He got killed because somebody ripped off a drug dealer and then got word to the DEA that Nate Swanson did it. That tip was the frame."

Hayden came and perched at the opposite end of the sofa, moving slowly. "How do you know?"

"Just putting together things people tell me. These two assholes want their money. They claim they found out from a cop that Nate stole it. I haven't figured that one out yet. But the cops, I think, got it from the DEA. The DEA isn't talking, but I can make an educated guess. Think about it. If I stole a million dollars from a drug gang, I wouldn't want to look over my shoulder for the rest of my life. If I had a way to throw the blame on somebody else, I'd take it. And what better way to convince the gangsters that Joe Blow did it than to get the Feds interested in Joe Blow and count on word getting back to the gang?"

Time went by. "Jesus Christ," said Hayden.

"Talk to the DEA people again tomorrow. Try to find out, if you can, just what happened when they got the tip. Work on it from that angle."

"They can't do that. They can't ruin a man on the strength of an anonymous tip."

"Let's hope not. Work on it from the other end, too."

Hayden stiffened and shook his head, a brief shudder. "What do you mean?"

"Whoever framed Nate could have picked him because he had something against him. But then he could have picked Nate because he had something against his old man."

Hayden said nothing.

"I asked Swanson for an enemies list, but he wasn't very helpful. I think he believes Nate was a drug dealer, and he can't quite believe he would have any serious enemies."

"He doesn't."

"Maybe not. But I see his life coming down around his ears because of an anonymous tip. I'd like to know who made that tip."

"I see what you mean."

"So I'm asking you. Who are his enemies?"

"Christ, I'd have to think about it. Regis is very well liked."

"Business rivals. Other things. What about people who have taken him to court, for example? You'd take care of that, right?"

"Right."

"Has he ever been sued?"

"Not successfully." The answer was brisk.

"It's the unsuccessful plaintiffs I'd look at. But that's just an example. Maybe it's someone he cut in on at a society ball, I don't know. You're in a position to know who would have it in for him. I'm talking real grudges."

Hayden's gaze drifted away. Outside, the city looked as if it had been spray-painted gold. After a minute Hayden slouched back on the sofa. "You don't think this might be just a little far-fetched?"

"Of course it might be. So's the fact that Regis Swanson has to hide out up here in this million-dollar treehouse."

Hayden nodded. "I'll have to do some thinking."

"Do that. You can get going if you want. I'll hang around until he wakes up, see if he needs anything."

Hayden was reaching for his briefcase. "To tell you the truth, I don't want to leave him alone. Can you stay the night?"

"I'll see. Maybe we can get Felicidad down here again or something."

"He needs help right now. Lots of it."

Cooper walked with him to the door. "I'll see that he makes it through the night. You give me something to work on tomorrow."

Hayden paused. "You make it sound like a personal project."

Cooper shook his head. "Just trying to do a thorough job for the paycheck."

◆

"You're out of your mind," said Diana in the dark. "I'm not leaving without you." Around the edge of the curtain over the open window came distant traffic noise and a feeble stirring of hot air.

"Listen to me," said Cooper. "We're both safer if you go. You understand?"

"We're safer if we both go. That I understand."

"We've been through that already. I can't leave yet. But you can. You have to. The way these guys work, they don't go for the target directly. They go for somebody he values. It's a very effective way of applying pressure. That's why Swanson's probably been in the least danger all along. And that's why with you out of the picture I'm safer."

His thigh touching hers, he could feel her fierce, mute protest. "I won't go alone."

"I'll join you at the beginning of the week. Swanson's business will be wrapped up by then and he'll be on an airplane, too. You just keep the drinks cold and the bed warm for me."

"Some vacation, waiting to get a phone call about my husband being shot."

"It won't happen. There's danger but it's minimal. They don't know who I am, and they'd have to get very lucky to find out. Besides, I'll be nursemaided by the best the federal government has to offer."

"Yeah, I've heard you talk about them. Your admiration for them is unbounded."

"Hey, some things they're good at."

"I won't be able to sleep, I won't be able to eat."

"Darcy will keep your mind off things. Once I get there, we'll rent a car and take off on that honeymoon."

They lay in silence until he felt her shake, heard the hands go to her face. He raised himself on one elbow and watched her cry, just visible in the light creeping in around the curtain. She squeezed words out of a constricted throat. "I can't take this. I didn't marry you for this."

"For better or worse. This is the worse. It'll get better."

When she was calm, she said, "I don't think it will. I think you're the type of man that needs this kind of thing."

Lying in the dark, hearing her breathing somewhere on the far side of the bed, he gave it some honest thought. "What I am is the type of man that needs to see people get what's coming to them."

"We have a justice system for that," she said, softly.

"I'd love to see some kind of justice. The legal kind, the poetic kind, the rough kind, I'm not particular. As long as people don't get away with acting like animals, I'm happy. But I don't see a lot of justice out there these days. I see a whole culture built on excuses. I see people blaming crime on objects and substances instead of people. I see people acting like animals and getting fan mail. So when I get a chance to put my hand in, shove things a little closer to something that looks like justice, I'm going to take it."

Diana's voice hung somewhere in the dark, disembodied and infinitely sad. "It's all bound up together, what I love about you and what you do that hurts me, I know that. I know I can't separate the man who loves justice from the man who loves a good fight."

"That's not fair. I don't go looking . . ."

"Listen to me. I know you well enough to know I have to accept that. Just think about something. Putting your life on the line is putting my happiness on the line. I've been widowed once already, and it wasn't fun."

"I'm not looking for a fight."

"Then quit. What do you owe Regis Swanson?"

That shut him up; Cooper had to lie there and sort that one out. Finally he said, "A decent job for the money he's paid me."

"You can send it back. We're not starving."

"There's more. The man's hurting. Somebody killed his boy. That cuts close. Even though my boy was never really mine, that cuts close."

She sighed, not theatrically but from mere exhaustion. Cooper was angry for a moment, angry because Diana would never reach the cold hard place where his sense of honor lay. By the time the anger was gone, leaving a desolate sadness, she was asleep and he was afraid to touch her for fear of waking her.

16

"I FIGURE WE have about three days," said Turk. "Even with the refrigerator cranked up all the way, I don't want to give it much more than that. And Oscar's finally starting to get pissed off. The man sounded aggravated last night."

Ferocious Dick sat on the couch, looking like Boris Karloff as the Mummy, his face criss-crossed with tape. He growled something and jutted his chin in the direction of the kitchen.

"I know," said Turk. "It's a drag. I almost forgot and opened it up to look for some juice or something this morning. But she's got to stay in there unless you want to try sneaking her out of here in a garbage bag or something. And that's how people get caught."

Ferocious Dick grunted. He was looking around at the furniture and knickknacks, sitting as if he didn't want to get anything dirty.

"Relax," said Turk. "We're out of sight. It's secure and it's anonymous. And you gotta admit it's an improvement over where you've been."

Ferocious Dick shook his head and made a noise like tires on gravel.

"I know, it was a lot of driving, especially with a busted nose. But you gotta know the cops here checked hospitals. We had to get you outside their radius. And now you can tell the folks back home you've seen Kankakee, Illinois." Turk rose and went to the window. They were twelve stories up and he could see the patchwork topography of the near North Side as it straggled out west past Cabrini-Green under a yellow haze. "You need to just lie low for a day or two because you're conspicuous as hell right now. Nobody's going to bother you. There are a few messages on the phone machine but nobody sounds anxious yet. I'll do the scouting and work on the next step. If we don't let too many people see us going in and out of the building we can last three days here easy. And three days is plenty of time."

Ferocious Dick looked at him, black eyes blinking on either side of the bandaged nose. He growled something.

Turk scowled at him. "Say what? Speak up, will you?" Ferocious Dick muttered, articulated syllables emerging, and Turk said, "Ah, yeah. Check the bathroom, I bet she has some aspirin in there."

◆

Buzz Hayden's office was on the eighth floor of a solid and self-important La Salle Street building, up the street from the Board of Trade and the banks. There was a reception area with a few chairs, a small tree in a big tub, some magazines that appeared to be devoted to cigar smoking, and a window above a counter that could be shuttered in case of angry clients. A sturdy-looking man in a brown blazer sat in one of the chairs with a magazine on his lap and gave Cooper a professional eye. Cooper nodded at him and got a response that was just perceptible.

Cooper looked over the counter at a severe young woman who was sitting at a computer, fingers suspended over the keyboard. "May I help you?" she said.

"Mr. Hayden's expecting me. MacLeish."

"Oh yes, Mr. MacLeish. Would you have a seat, please? I'll see if Mr. Hayden's free."

The man from the security company did not look like an extrovert, so Cooper read about the best cigar shop in Amsterdam, hearing doors open and close and distant murmurs. After a couple of minutes the severe young woman came and opened a door beside the counter and ushered him back to Hayden's redoubt.

It was a corner office that had windows to the north and east and a sobering view of City Hall. Hayden sat behind a desk that had been lovingly carved from several mahogany logs sometime in the nineteenth century, when people still knew how to carve lovingly. There was more dark wood paneling the walls, and there was a good deal of polished brass setting it off: lamps, an antique inkstand, even a genuine spittoon.

"How's Regis?" said Hayden, pointing at a chair. He was dressed in a dark gray suit, a no-nonsense white shirt, and a tie of regal purple. His head looked as if it had been waxed and burnished for the interview.

"Hung over and cantankerous. But a little more focused today. He'd agreed to meet Levine and Tompkins at the Chicago Club, so I dropped him there. I think they'll be at it for a while."

"Is that safe?"

"I think so. They've put on a little extra security."

Hayden nodded. "I thought about what you said. I came up with a couple of names. And the more I think about them, the more ridiculous it seems."

"It may be. I'd still like to just kick them around, see what falls out."

Hayden sat with his elbows on the desk, a silver-plated pen revolving slowly in his fingers, giving Cooper a look of distant but wary scrutiny. "Who are you, really?" he said. "I mean, that I should discuss Regis's private affairs with you."

"I'm nobody," said Cooper. "I'm just the chauffeur. I don't know real estate and I don't know the law. But I do have a little experience with homicidal assholes. And I do have an idea right now. Just one, but that's one more than your friend has about what's happening to him. If you don't want to trust me with his secrets, I'll understand. I just thought we might put our heads together and come up with something we might take to the cops."

Hayden waited a long three seconds or so before nodding, but then he put down the pen and clasped his hands. "All right. Regis seems to trust you, so I guess I will, too. There are two people I can think of who might be holding a serious grudge against him. One of them is a highly respectable political figure and the other one is his ex-wife. The surviving one. And I don't think she would engineer the death of her son."

Cooper nodded. "I think we can leave her out. Who's the politician?"

"Perry Koster."

"Huh." Cooper looked out the window at City Hall a block away. "He's respectable all right, I guess."

"He's just about ready for canonization. Mr. Incorruptible, from the U.S. Attorney's office to City Hall to the State House. They loved him here, they loved him in Springfield, so far they seem mildly infatuated in D.C. The media love him, blacks love him, whites love him, even the Republicans don't mind eating lunch with him. I'm as cynical as your average La Salle Street lawyer, but I have trouble imagining Perry Koster cooking up a plot to do in Regis Swanson."

Cooper nodded. "OK, me too. Why the grudge?"

Hayden's mouth tightened just a touch. "Regis had an affair with his wife."

"Ah."

"Koster was most displeased, they say."

"I imagine he would be. How long ago was this?"

"About three years ago. The Kosters have since reconciled. Perry needs her in Washington."

"Huh." Cooper stood up and went to the window. Outside, La Salle Street was in shadow, full of lawyers scurrying to get indoors before the sun climbed high enough to reach street level. Cooper leaned on the window frame and watched them. "You said Swanson had been sued."

He looked over his shoulder to see Hayden frowning. "Not successfully. And not recently. Not for years."

"Would it have to be recent? Some people have long memories."

Hayden reached for the pen again, frowning at the desktop. "You want me to dredge something up from thirty-five years of legal practice? It'd be a guessing game, just fantasy."

"I just thought something might leap out at you. What kinds of things have people sued him for?"

"Petty disputes over design changes, a few nuisance suits from the save-our-slum crowd. Nothing we couldn't settle out of court or get dismissed. Well, with one exception. But that was . . . that was nothing."

"What was nothing?"

"A suit we defended successfully. Thirty-odd years ago."

Cooper looked down at the street again. "That's the only time you took on somebody in a trial and beat them?"

"Yes."

"That might nurture a grudge."

"Come on. That was in . . . Christ, I think it was in nineteen fifty-eight. Getting close to forty years ago."

"What was it?"

"Look, it can't have anything to do with this. It just can't."

Cooper shrugged, wandering away from the window and toward the bookshelves. Beneath the uniform ranks of law books was a shelf with a motley variety of spines showing. "OK, you would know." Cooper stood and read book titles: *Under the Volcano, Finnegan's Wake, The Horse's Mouth.*

"It had nothing to do with business," said Hayden. "The lady was just trying a quick score."

Cooper looked at him. "The lady who brought the suit?"

"Yeah." Hayden was examining the tip of the pen. "It was a paternity suit. We were able to prove Regis wasn't the father. Blood tests, you know. She was a bit of a nut case. Regis had . . . been involved with her briefly. He was young and a bit wild in those days."

"Before he learned to limit himself to senators' wives." Cooper was staring at the books again.

The pen clapped onto the desktop. "Look, I don't appreciate that kind of thing. I don't think you really have anything constructive to offer here, and I'm a busy man."

"What happened to the kid?"

"What kid?"

Cooper turned. "The kid in the paternity suit."

Hayden's look went blank. "How should I know?" Cooper stood and watched him think, watched the eyebrows lower, watched thoughts crystallize.

"What was the lady's name?" he said.

"I don't remember. I'd have to look it up. It was a long time ago."

Cooper meandered back toward the window. "The kid would be in his middle thirties."

Hayden nodded. After a few seconds he said, "You've got a hell of an imagination."

Cooper smiled. "And people still keep surprising me."

◆

"Shave it," said Turk. "We're talking boot camp. I want it all gone."

The octogenarian barber smiled, his eyes misting at the memory of bygone days. "You going into the service?" he said, revving up the clippers.

"No," said Turk. "I'm starting a political party."

"A political party. What would your platform be?" The clippers bit and hair started cascading to the floor.

"Free food, free beer, free love. Restore slavery, exterminate homosexuals."

The barber frowned at the pale skin of the emerging scalp. "Sounds a bit extreme to me," he said, working carefully.

"Hey," said Turk. "I'm a reasonable man. I'd be willing to compromise."

"Yeah?"

"You bet. I might settle for slavery for the queers. After all, we'll need somebody to do the banners for the rallies."

"I don't think you're serious," said the barber, stepping back to admire his handiwork and smiling uncertainly.

"You're sharp today, pops. I gotta hand it to you. The truth is I'm on the run from the law and this is part of my disguise."

The old man giggled, shook his head and turned to set down the clippers. "You're a real comedian, son."

"I got the gift of laughter, they tell me," said Turk, admiring his skull in the mirror.

◆

"I don't want to go back to the apartment," said Swanson. "I want to go home this afternoon."

Cooper switched lanes and shifted gears. "Not yet."

"You're still going to argue with me, huh?"

"As long as you're paying me to keep you alive, yeah."

"OK, take me someplace for lunch. Take me to Lino's."

"I'd stay away from there. I'd stay away from anywhere you're a regular."

"Dammit, I want some lunch."

"I'll take you slumming. There's a million places to get lunch in this town."

"I'm not eating any hamburgers."

"The place I'm thinking of has the best greasy-spoon chef in the city. He makes your basic meat and potatoes into an art form."

"Fine. Just get me some lunch."

Cooper wheeled the Marquis around a corner on a yellow light. "How'd the meeting go?"

"As well as could be expected. We're working out the details of the liquidation."

"You think of where you want to go, come Saturday?"

"No. I've had too much on my mind."

Cooper drove. After a minute he said, "I got a question for you."

"You too, huh?"

"What was the name of the lady who hit you with the paternity suit back in 1958? Hayden couldn't remember."

"What?"

"Hayden told me about it. What was her name?"

"What the hell are you two up to?"

"Just taking wild shots in the dark. You remember her name?"

"Of course I remember her." There was a silence. "How could I forget? Rosie McTeague."

◆

The bank stood on a corner, just up Halsted Street from the half-dozen splashy restaurants that made up Greek Town, a survivor of better times. The West Loop was mainly parking lots now, but the bank was still there, the sign still giving time and temperature to anybody who was interested. Halsted shimmered in the heat.

The driver pulled the Caddy over in a no-parking zone directly in front of the bank and hustled around to open the back door. McTeague looked across the seat at the man with unnaturally black hair. "Wait here," said the man. He got out, moving a bit stiffly in his white linen suit, the briefcase at his side. McTeague and the driver watched him cross the sidewalk and enter the bank.

"Shouldn't be too long," said the driver, getting back in and adjusting the rear view mirror so he could look at McTeague. He was forty or so, balding, with a nose that had taken some shots and eyes that had seen a few things. His neck strained at his collar.

"I've got all day," said McTeague.

"See, he has to do it this way," said the driver. "I know it's a pain in the ass, having to come all the way down here, but he's gotta worry about security, you know?"

"I know."

"He does it this way, any kind of deal. He's gotta see the money, it goes in the trunk, then we come and get the goods. He's got 'em in there in a safety deposit box. You check 'em out, if everything's fine we drop you someplace. You don't like 'em, you take the money out of the trunk and walk home." He laughed, a wheezing sound.

"That's the way I'd do it," said McTeague. He looked east, at the eruption of skyscrapers on the other side of the expressway. He wanted to be out on the lake.

"Smoke?" The driver was holding a pack of Camels over the seat back. McTeague took one. The driver lit his with a genuine Zippo. "How'd you get in touch with Mr. Chronos?"

"Mutual friends."

The driver nodded wisely. "You know enough to keep your mouth shut, right? Shut real tight?"

McTeague looked away from the window and into the eyes in the mirror. "So far, you're the one making all the noise."

After a moment the driver said, "Just trying to be friendly. I'm gonna ask you again. You know enough to keep your mouth shut, right?"

"You think Mr. Chronos would have agreed to do business with me if he hadn't had the right kind of recommendation?" McTeague looked out the window again and smoked.

After that they sat in silence until the man with black hair came out of the bank, a security guard holding the door for him. The driver

jumped out and held the door for him. The man with black hair got in
with a little difficulty and sat holding the briefcase on his lap. Behind
the lenses of the black-rimmed glasses the eyes were small, slightly
moist and very dark. He opened the briefcase and slid out a manila
envelope. "Take a look," he said.

McTeague opened the envelope and slid out the bonds. There was
an engraved border and some florid script along the top. The lines
which informed McTeague that the bonds were payable to the
bearer, however, were written in a very clear and workmanlike type-
face. McTeague checked the amounts on the bonds and looked them
over carefully, looking for things Berger had told him to look for. He
nodded. "Fine."

"Don't lose them," said the man with black hair. "That right there
is just like cash. Except scarcer. Since eighty-three or so there are no
more bearer bonds. These are vintage. Good as gold."

"I know," said McTeague. He slid the bonds back into the envelope. "Except it's a lot more portable."

"Takes up less room in a suitcase."

"That's right," said McTeague. "Pleasure doing business with
you."

"Pleasure's mine. Tell old Harold not to make himself so scarce."

The driver's eyes were on McTeague in the mirror. "Run you back
to the house, pick up your car?"

McTeague looked back at him for a moment, into the very experi-
enced eyes. "No. Drop me downtown. I've got things to do. I'll pick
up the car later."

The driver shrugged. "Suit yourself."

"Can't be too careful with those," said the man with black hair.

"Relax," said McTeague. "It's my problem now."

◆

The third time Cooper called he was informed that Mr. Hayden
had returned; he was patched through without delay. "Things have
been a little crazy," said the lawyer. "I've been shouting at some people over at DEA, and they don't like it one bit."

"Lots of luck. Did you look up that case?"

"I did. Sean Patrick McTeague. Born December 17, 1958."

"Sean Patrick McTeague."

"That's T-E-A-G-U-E, not T-I-G-H-E. I already looked in the
phone book. There are only a couple of McTeagues spelled that way,
and neither of them's a Sean."

"How about a Rose?"

"No Rose either. You talked to Swanson, huh?"

"Yeah. He spoke highly of her."

"He did?"

"He said after all these years he'd forgotten the lawsuit and all he could remember was the way she looked walking into the Pump Room in a tight silk dress."

"That's the problem with Regis. He's sentimental."

"Well, when I told him why I was interested it seemed to put out the fire a little. He did say he hadn't heard anything about her or the kid in all these years, except for one rumor sometime in the sixties that she was shacked up with some Outfit guy."

There was silence over the wire while Hayden digested this. "No," he said. "This is not real, it can't be."

"It's only a hypothesis."

"So what are you going to do?"

Cooper considered, phone to his ear and toothpick at the corner of his mouth. "I guess I'll try to find Sean McTeague."

◆

"I'm on the waiting list," said the big blond man, standing with legs apart like John Wayne at the crest of the ridge, hands on his hips spreading the tails of his brown blazer, not incidentally giving a glimpse of the piece on his hip. "The next class they take down at the Academy, I'm in. Meanwhile, there are worse ways to make a living than pulling sentry duty in an office with two beautiful women." The big blond man grinned, his neat moustache spreading across his face.

Sherry smiled politely. Behind her she could practically hear the middle-aged Mrs. Keller rolling her eyes. "Your job must be fascinating," she said, thinking she had seldom seen a more thoroughly bored human being and wishing he would wander back into the waiting room and leave her alone.

He shrugged. "There are good days and bad days." He scanned the office, eyes narrowed, looking for threats from Mrs. Keller in her corner, from the water cooler, from under the Xerox, from the windows above the street. "A lot of waiting around. You have to stay alert."

"I'm sure." Sherry looked desperately around her desktop for something she could pretend was urgent work. When the phone rang, she snatched it up with relief. "Swanson Enterprises." The security man faded away, still grinning.

"Yeah," said a man at the other end of the line. "I don't know if you can help me. I, um, I was in an accident this morning with a car driven by one of your employees."

"Oh dear," said Sherry. The caller said nothing, so she said, "What happened?"

The voice was uncertain, with a hint of embarrassment. "Well, I was driving behind him on Van Buren there, west of the Loop. And he pulled up kind of suddenly and I rear-ended him. It wasn't too serious, nobody got hurt or anything, but there was a little damage to the front of my car."

"Well, I'm sorry to hear that, sir. But I'm not sure what I can do for you."

"Well, see, the guy said he was in a rush and he couldn't wait around for the cops, so we traded addresses and everything and he took off. Except he gave me a card with the name of your company on it but he didn't leave his name."

Cautiously, Sherry said, "I see."

"And I just talked to my insurance agent, and he said he's got to have the name of the guy that was driving the car to process the thing."

"Well," said Sherry, "I suppose we can talk to our driver and have him contact your insurance company."

"Well see, my guy says he can't even start to process it until he's got a name and address for both drivers. So I'm hoping you can give me those. Guy in his forties, moustache, brown hair, driving a big Mercedes."

"Um, can you hold for a moment, please?"

Sherry punched a button on the phone and looked across the office at Mrs. Keller. "There's a man here who says he hit Mr. Swanson's car, and the chauffeur gave him our card but didn't leave his name. He says he needs the name for the insurance report."

Mrs. Keller stared across the office at Sherry over the top of her reading glasses. "Didn't the police take care of it?"

"The gentleman says Mr. Swanson's driver wouldn't wait. He just gave him the card and left."

Mrs. Keller gave Sherry a terrifying look of deity pestered by mortals and then sighed. "Of all things." She laid down her pen. "That's all he needs? Just the name?"

"And address, he says."

"And it was Mr. Swanson's chauffeur? What's his name, with the moustache?"

"Sounds like it. In the Mercedes."

Mrs. Keller gave in and opened a drawer. "What is that man's name?" she said, rummaging. She pulled out an index card. "Here we go. Cooper MacLeish."

Sherry put the phone receiver to her ear, finger poised over the button. "How do you spell that?"

◆

Things were changing around the neighborhood; one of Valenti's long-time haunts on Morse Avenue was gone, burned out and replaced by a discount clothing store; another on Clark Street had metamorphosed overnight into a video store. Having been informed at the station that the lieutenant was probably having dinner somewhere, Cooper wasn't sure where to look. He took a chance driving down Broadway to Thorndale, where a longtime cop hangout had been remodeled beyond all recognition but not, Cooper hoped, beyond the tastes of a hungry policeman.

Valenti was alone in a booth in the now-garish back room, in the white uniform shirt and splendid loneliness of the watch commander. His hair was a little grayer and his torso a little broader, lending physical substance to the weight of his authority. He had a *Sun-Times* spread out at his elbow and a stuffed pepper laid wide open on his plate. "I hope this is a concidence," he said with his mouth full when he looked up to see Cooper coming.

"Five minutes of your time," said Cooper, sliding into the booth.

Valenti chewed, watching Cooper with a look of amused skepticism. "You still got the Feds on your tail?"

Cooper blinked at him. "You knew, huh?"

"Course I knew. I got curious when the auto agency clammed up about who they'd leased that Olds to. Couple phone calls, it became clear."

"But you couldn't tell me."

"Fuck, no. And let your boss know he was under investigation?" Valenti took a sip of coffee. "He's had a rough week, hasn't he?"

"And it ain't over yet. That's why I'm hoping you can help."

"Christ," said the cop softly. "What do you want now?"

"I want you to run a guy for me this time. A name. I can give you full name and date of birth."

"Talk to the dicks who have the case."

"This is a long shot, a hunch. I figure they're too busy to listen."

"And I'm a man of leisure, huh?"

A waitress was holding a menu out to Cooper. He waved it off and said, "I'll tell you the story. I think you'll enjoy it."

Valenti shook his head. "You got till I finish dinner."

"That ought to do it," said Cooper.

◆

"He's talking to a cop," said Toni, closing the door of the van as she settled onto the passenger seat. The bright lights of Broadway shone half a block ahead; here on the side street it was dark.

"So what?" Jasper was behind the wheel, keys in the ignition.

"So maybe nothing. I'm just wondering, all the cop friends this guy has, can he possibly be what you say he is."

"OK, he's a saint. He's a Boy Scout. He's the All-American boy. He's still in the middle of it. Till I know what happened to that million bucks, he's number one on my list."

Toni shrugged. "I was thinking."

"That's a good sign."

"Just supposing that Nate Swanson was a poor chump who got set up."

"Not that again."

"Just supposing. All we had was the tip when we asked Dexter about him, remember?"

"The tip and the nightclub connection. Remember?"

"OK. Just supposing Swanson wasn't connected with Dexter, though. A gram of cocaine lying around in a dressing room doesn't sound like a major dealer to me. It sounds like a rock guitarist with no brain left."

"Jesus."

"Humor me. How would you go about finding out who phoned in the tip?"

"Stand on the corner of State and Madison and go eenie-meenie-mynie-moe."

"Seriously. I don't think we've thought enough about that tip. Who phoned it in?"

"I told you."

"No, you didn't. You made some people up. People there's no evidence for."

Jasper stared glumly through the windshield. "You know what you're asking me to believe?"

"Yeah. I know. It sucks, doesn't it? Now who phoned in that tip? He's got to be a blip on the screen, somewhere."

Jasper let out a long breath. "I don't know. All I know is, this guy is where the action is right now. Whatever action's left."

"That seems to be the consensus," said Toni.

◆

Cooper got lucky and found a parking space within fifty feet of his apartment door. He switched off the ignition and tried to decide what to do with the revolver locked in the glove compartment. Leaving it in the car was irresponsible; taking it inside would scare the hell out of Diana. He sat in the car and weighed possibilities: somebody hitting him between here and the door, somebody swiping the Marquis. The fear of domestic strife decided him and he got out of the car without the gun.

He was almost home when the car doors swung open just ahead of him, first the passenger side, then the street side. The interior light showed two men climbing out. Cooper didn't recognize them; they were large, sturdy and apparently focused on him. The doors slammed and one of them was crossing the grass strip to the sidewalk in front of him, the other coming up the line of parked cars out in the street. Cooper stopped. The man in front of him was carrying an aluminum baseball bat loosely at his side, the fat end bouncing lightly against his leg as he walked.

By the time Cooper had registered what was happening, the man in the street was behind him, ready to cut off his retreat. Cooper stood still, wondering where all his neighbors were and remembering the revolver, hopelessly distant.

"You MacLeish?" said the man on the sidewalk ten feet in front of him.

"Nope. You got the wrong guy."

"Bullshit," said a voice behind him.

"Where you been? We were getting worried," said the man in front. He looked like every bouncer in every Division Street bar Cooper had ever been in, muscle going to fat and a neatly trimmed moustache. He brought the bat up in front of him, two-handed.

"What the fuck do you want?" said Cooper, in the throes of a major adrenaline rush.

"We have a little message for you," said the man with the bat. "From Michael Ghislieri."

Cooper stared at him for a moment and then laughed, just put his head back and laughed. "You guys have any idea how irrelevant you are?" he said, just before he broke for the street, because the footsteps behind him were getting too close.

There was a car there but Cooper dived onto the hood just ahead of a swipe from the bat that dented the side with an ugly booming crash. Hands were grabbing at his legs and he twisted and planted a foot in the man's face, driving him back but clearing the way for his partner to wind up with the bat again. Cooper rolled toward the street with everything he had and felt the head of the bat just miss his before slamming onto the hood as he tumbled into the street. He was up and running before he had quite sorted out the sensations.

Suddenly things were happening everywhere: doors were flying open and feet were pounding. Somebody was shouting. A van came around the corner in front of Cooper, tires squealing, and skidded to a halt, rocking on its shocks. A man jumped out the side door with a gun in his hand. Cooper cut to the curb and looked back to see the Neanderthal with the bat in the middle of the street, looking like a deer caught in the headlights; two men were converging on him with pieces drawn. His partner was taking off down the sidewalk but as Cooper watched he was headed off at the pass by men who had come out of the van. He put on the brakes and put his hands high. "Drop it!" somebody was yelling out in the street, and the aluminum bat clanked onto the pavement.

Cooper watched as what seemed like a full platoon came out of nowhere and had the two Neanderthals plucked and trussed in about five seconds flat. He had started to laugh, sagging against a car, when the blond man with the ragged moustache came over and said, "You all right?"

"I'm having the time of my life," said Cooper.

The blond man peered at him. "Why don't you sit down or something?"

"You got the wrong guys."

"What?"

"You got the wrong guys. These guys have nothing to do with it."

The blond man grabbed him by the shirtfront. "You better start talking, and it fucking better make sense," he said.

"It'll make just as much sense as the rest of my life does right now," said Cooper.

◆

"What are they mad about?" said Diana in a hushed tone, with a fierce grip on Cooper's arm. Car doors were slamming.

"They're not very happy with me," said Cooper. The van was pulling away, an agent shooting Cooper a last malevolent glance out the window. The neighbors were drifting back inside, trailing awed looks at Cooper. "They think I've been freeloading on their valuable services." He disengaged himself gently from her grasp and walked into the street. He picked up the aluminum baseball bat and came back to the sidewalk, looking. When he found his man he walked toward him slowly, flipping the bat handle-to-barrel and back again. The larger Neanderthal emerged from the entranceway of the building next door.

"Let's make a deal," said Cooper, holding the bat out handle first. "You get in the car and get the fuck out of my life, and I won't call Michael Ghislieri and tell him what a couple of turkeys you are."

The Neanderthal was still a little dazed, and he took the bat meekly. Cooper turned his back on him and walked away.

Upstairs, Diana had made something wonderful; the smell of fowl cooking in wine came up the long hallway. "I don't know what shape dinner's in," she said. "I just dropped everything when I heard the shouting." She bustled down the hall to the kitchen. When Cooper joined her she was busy at the stove, a tear tracking silently down her cheek.

"Hey," said Cooper. "It worked. My plan worked like a charm."

She covered the pan and turned to him. "I think it'll be edible." She wiped the tear away with her fingers.

Cooper folded her into his arms. "I could live off the smell alone."

"My plane leaves at eleven-ten tomorrow," she said.

"I'll run you out to O'Hare. I don't think Swanson will need me in the morning." He held her, just held her, until she stopped trembling.

They ate at the dining room table, mostly in silence. The chicken fell apart under the knife. They polished off the wine and watched the light fade. "This wasn't the end of it, was it?" said Diana.

"No. This was just comic relief. But it proved they can protect me."

"If they decide you're worth it."

"They won't quit now," Cooper said, not believing it. He could still hear the blond man saying, *Here on out, you're on your own, asshole.* He reached across the table and stroked Diana's cheek, wondering if he would ever be able to take the sadness out of those dark eyes.

The telephone rang. Diana was closer to the sideboard and she picked it up, listened, said yes and handed it to Cooper across the table.

"I'm gonna make you a happy man," said Valenti.

Cooper watched Diana rise and start gathering the plates. "Bingo?"

"Bingo. Sean Patrick McTeague. One criminal damage to property, one misdemeanor possession."

"Possession. Of what?"

"A controlled substance. That's all I can tell you."

"Would he be in jail?"

"Not in this state. The possession arrest was in 1986. He's not exactly a career criminal judging from this. Just a generic deadbeat, probably."

"Who's had some contact with the drug trade."

"I can't feed your hunches any more than this."

"You got a last known address or something?"

"Now why in the hell would you want that?"

"Just habit. I have an inquiring mind."

"Skip it. Take it to the dicks on the Swanson case if you think it's significant."

"All right. Thanks for your time."

"No problem. Just promise me one thing."

"What's that?"

"Don't make me sorry."

"I won't." Cooper rose and hung up the phone. Diana stood in the doorway to the kitchen, waiting. She looked serene, or at least resigned.

"That was Valenti," said Cooper. "Just working on a hunch of mine."

She leaned on the doorframe. "He approves of what you're doing, does he? You've got some adult supervision on this?"

Cooper laughed. "It's under control."

"That's comforting," she said, disappearing into the kitchen.

17

THE WEATHER BROKE. In the night the hot air grew heavy and still, and lightning flashed in silence far out over the lake. When the rain came it came with thunder; Cooper and Diana awoke and held each other while the windows rattled and then subsided under the patter of the raindrops. In the morning the sky was a clean hard blue and the temperature barely at seventy, a cool steady breeze coming down the lake from Canada.

Cooper spoke with Swanson on the phone; he and Hayden were huddling at the apartment and there was a climactic meeting at the Chicago Club at two o'clock. If Cooper could have him there on time he could have the morning free. Cooper and Diana ate a silent breakfast in the dining room, sunlight making the sanded floor glow. Diana was collected, taciturn. She had packed a carry-all and a garment bag.

At the gate they embraced, in silence, and Cooper brushed a strand of auburn hair from her eyes. "Three days," he said. Diana nodded, mute, and pulled away after a final kiss. Cooper stood at the window and watched until the plane was towed away from the gate.

On the expressway he looked in the mirror and wondered. He left another message at Area Six for Reichardt and Benitez: call him. Then he went to find Boyle. He'd heard Boyle had an office now, but he figured the first place to check was the café on Sheridan Road. Boyle was at his accustomed spot in the window, with the newspapers and the half-drunk coffee. He looked like an irritable walrus with the two hundred and fifty pounds and the ponytail and moustache and the surly expression.

"How's business?" said Cooper, sitting across from him.

"Business is fine. There's never a shortage of deadbeats."

"Why aren't you out pounding on doors?"

"Hey. There's no rush. By the time a creditor comes to me, he's waited so long for his money another day or two won't matter."

"You got room in your busy schedule to do a job for me?"

Boyle turned over a page of the newspaper, frowned at it, and looked up at Cooper. "You talking about a favor? Or a job?"

"Make it a job. I think I can get my employer to pay for it. I don't know how hard it's going to be."

"The harder the better, if he's paying. What's shaking?"

"I need somebody found."

"You try the phone book?"

"Yeah. That's why I'm talking to you."

Boyle shrugged. "What is it, a debt?"

"No. Just history. I'd like to know if the guy's still around, that's all."

Boyle looked into the coffee cup but didn't drink. "That's all?"

"Get me a current address. What do you do, go to the utility companies?"

"We have our little ways."

"Find the guy, give me a call. A quick afternoon's work for you."

"Maybe. Sometimes it's a month's work."

"Give it a shot. Send me a bill, you'll get paid."

Boyle scowled at him and the big moustache twitched. "You got anything more than a name?"

"Sean Patrick McTeague." He spelled it. "Dee-oh-bee twelve seventeen fifty-eight, in Chicago. Two arrests in the city, if you've got access to that data base. Enough?"

Boyle bestirred himself, looking pained or perhaps only peeved. "Let me get a pencil or something," he said.

◆

There was a message on his machine at home: call Area Six. "We want you to look at some pictures," Reichardt told him over the phone.

Both detectives were there when Cooper arrived, Benitez dapper in a blue blazer and Reichardt looking like a funeral director in a very dark gray. "We got lucky with the fingerprints from the Manning apartment," he said. "The FBI's a bunch of pricks, but they're good with fingerprints." He opened a folder and fanned a poker hand of eight-by-eleven sheets across the desktop. Each sheet bore front-and-profile mug shots, prints and other data. "Recognize anybody here?" said Reichardt.

All the men were dark-complexioned and heavy-featured. Nonetheless, it took Cooper about three seconds to pick out the man he'd gotten a glass of water for at Regis Swanson's. "This guy," he said. "The one that looks like Ernest Borgnine."

"And we got a lucky winner," said Reichardt, deadpan. Benitez was smiling, leaning back in his swivel chair. Reichardt replaced the other four sheets in the folder. "You did it. You matched the prints to the man."

"Who is he?" said Cooper, looking into the eyes in the photo.

"Ricardo Soliz. Also known as Ricardo Fernandez, Ricardo Campos, Dick Campos. Colombian national, California resident since '79. People I talked to in L.A. tell me he's reputed to work for Oscar Cisneros, a big coke importer out there."

"Alleged. Alleged coke importer," said Benitez. He was smiling faintly.

"I'm sorry, *alleged* scumbag. This guy works for him. Has a bad reputation. They call him Ferocious Dick out there."

"The story is, in Medellín he was '*El Feroz,*'" said Benitez. "Ferocious. Here he's Ferocious Dick."

"That's a riot," said Cooper. "Any sign of the other guy?"

"We got prints off a glass but we're still waiting for the G to get back to us on those. From my pals in L.A. we think he might be a guy called Randy Shoop, known as Turk. Don't know much about him except he's been associated with Cisneros in the past. Did he look like a gigolo, the guy in L.A. asked. I said I'd pass the question along."

Cooper smiled. "Could be. I would have said show biz."

Reichardt nodded, a big jaded-looking man with too much work to do. "Sounds like we've got the right pair. You keeping an eye out for them?"

"Trying. Can I run a name past you?"

"Sure."

"Sean McTeague. Arrested for possession a few years ago. Connected to Regis Swanson because his mother claimed Swanson was his father, back in fifty-eight."

Reichardt put the folder in a drawer. "So?"

"I'm just collecting people who might have a grudge against Swanson."

"Sean McTeague?" said Benitez.

"That's right." Cooper spelled it. "He's on your computer. I'm just throwing it out there because somebody who had it in for the Swansons started this, and this is the only somebody I can find who had anything to do with drugs."

The detectives exchanged a look. "It's a thought, I suppose," said Reichardt.

"Something to follow up, maybe," said Benitez politely.

"Just in case you run out of things to do," said Cooper.

The cellular phone buzzed as Cooper was pushing west on Van Buren, El trains rumbling overhead. He handed the phone to Swanson in the back seat. Swanson answered, listened for a moment and handed it back. "It's for you," he said in a tone of wonderment.

Cooper drove one-handed with the phone to his ear. "You got a personal assistant now?" said Boyle.

"Sort of. What'd you get?"

"Grab a pencil."

"I'll remember. Just give it to me."

"As of last month Sean Patrick McTeague, date of birth as noted, Social Security number you don't give a damn I assume, was paying bills at 1718 West Winnemac. You want a phone number?"

"Seventeen-eighteen Winnemac?"

"You got it."

"OK. Give me the phone number, why not?"

Boyle gave it to him and Cooper muttered it a couple of times while jockeying closer to the rail for the homestretch. "Thanks, partner. What do I owe you?"

"That's it? You won't be needing any further services? I lend a commanding presence to interviews, you know."

"I don't think so. I don't even know what I'm going to do with this guy. If anything."

"Well, shit. This was worth maybe a couple of beers."

"I'll have my personal assistant bring over a case. Thanks, man."

When Cooper hung up the phone Swanson said, "Since when are you taking personal calls on this phone?"

"Exceptional circumstances," said Cooper. "I'm trying to find Rosie McTeague's boy. The one she tried to palm off on you."

After a moment Swanson said, "Why?" in a tone of deep suspicion.

"Just a hunch. Just a shot off the wall."

"What are you going to do when you find him?"

"Maybe nothing at all. Speaking of which. What was the name of the guy Rosie married? The Outfit guy?"

"Damned if I know. Don't tell me you're going to talk to her, too."

"Maybe. You want me to say hi for you?"

"I think not," said Swanson, after a moment's thought.

◆

1718 Winnemac was a storefront in the middle of nowhere, one of a file of shops on a quiet side street that had all closed and been converted to residences or just stayed empty. Across the street were bungalows; to the west the street ended at the embankment of the Northwestern railroad tracks.

Cooper sat in the car and looked at the place, thinking, so what? He had an address now to give the cops, the address of a storefront that looked empty. He got out of the car and crossed the street. The big front window had been made opaque with a dark vinyl sheet that was peeling down at the corners, but Cooper could see through the panes of glass in the door. The patch of floor he could see was empty of furniture but six or seven envelopes that looked like junk mail were lying just inside the door where they had been shoved through the mail slot. There was a doorbell and Cooper pressed it a couple of times, not expecting an answer.

Out of mere stubbornness he rang at the next storefront over.

There a woman answered after half a minute or so, a tall, thin, fever-
ish-looking woman with blond hair showing dark roots, dressed entirely in black. Behind her Cooper could see an easel and some
canvases stacked against a wall. "He moved," the woman said. "A
couple of weeks ago. The landlord's been showing the place."

"He wouldn't have mentioned where he was going, would he?"

She shook her head, starting to ease the door closed. "I barely
knew the guy. All I know is, he threw a bunch of stuff out in the alley, piled all his shit in his car and left."

Cooper thanked her and did the same.

◆

"Moreland."

"Finally. I've been trying to get you all afternoon."

"MacLeish. Hey, what's going on with your boss?"

"When I can talk, I'll talk to you. Right now I've got a quick favor
to ask."

"It better be quick. I got a world-shaker going on the computer
here and we're coming up on deadline."

"You got the sources for everything that's happened in Chicago
for the last fifty years, you said once."

"At least. I'm at the center of a vast network of information here.
My agents are everywhere."

"Terrific. This goes back about thirty. A woman named Rose
McTeague married an Outfit figure sometime in the sixties. I need to
know where she is now. Who was the guy, what was her married
name, how can I find her."

"Oh, that's all, huh? Somebody got married and you want me to
look it up. Why can't you go to City Hall and look it up yourself?
I'm busy here."

"You're a shortcut. And it's part of the story. Maybe."

"This has something to do with Regis Swanson's crack-up?"

"There's no crack-up. You've been listening to the rumormongers
again. Listen, I don't know if it does or not. It's a hunch. Just find out
for me, will you?"

"I'll see what I can do. Where are you?"

"In a car, running up the boss's phone bill. Let me give you the
number."

"I get the inside story on Swanson in return?"

"If there's a story. But there isn't one. Not yet."

◆

Ferocious Dick was on the couch, in a T-shirt and bare feet. He looked like a derelict hockey goalie in the nose guard and bandage, two big fat shiners staring on either side of the nose. The TV was on and there was an open bag of potato chips on the coffee table.

"Fat City, huh?" said Turk, closing the door. "The immigrant dream. While you've been laying here watching Oprah I've been working." Ferocious Dick grunted. "And we got our work cut out for us." Turk pulled a six-pack out of the brown paper bag he was carrying. "We can keep these in the freezer or something." He opened a second bag and pulled out two foil-wrapped burgers and two orders of fries. "Chow time. They wouldn't do a fried egg."

Ferocious Dick swung his legs to the floor, grunting softly. Turk went and took a long piss, shaking his head at the pink shower curtain and the little-girl knickknacks in the bathroom, then came back and popped open a beer. He took one look at Ferocious Dick, chewing slowly, painfully and with a good deal of noise, and daintily rescued his lunch from the litter on the table and went to sit in a chair by the window.

"He packed the girlfriend off out of town this morning." Turk unwrapped the burger and peered at it. "I'm sitting there, a block from his house and across the street, waiting for the guy to leave so I can go up and make the acquaintance of the lady. He and the lady come out with some luggage, he puts it in the trunk of a big old Mercury and they take off. I followed 'em out to the United terminal at O'Hare. Bye-bye girlfriend."

Fries spilled from Ferocious Dick's mouth as he made a low guttural noise.

"So what do we do now?" said Turk. He finally took a bite of the burger. After he swallowed he said, "Who's left? We're running out of time and running out of people to lean on. Looks like I'm gonna have to exercise some creativity here." He ate and looked out the window, watching near North Side traffic below. "Son of a bitch," he said after a moment. "I think we got everything we need right in there in the kitchen."

Ferocious Dick stopped chewing and looked at him.

"I had a feeling she might come in handy yet," said Turk. Ferocious Dick shook his head and resumed eating. "And," said Turk, "we can think about payback, too."

Ferocious Dick grunted.

"That's right. We may not get the million bucks out of him, but we'll sure as hell make him sorry he busted your nose."

◆

Swanson dropped heavily onto the back seat of the Marquis and slammed the door. Cooper waited for orders, ignoring indignant honks from behind. Swanson stared out the window, unfocused. Cooper wondered if the man had aged ten years in the last hour, or if it had happened gradually over the last two weeks and he just hadn't noticed till now. "Take me someplace . . ." Swanson left it hanging for a moment and Cooper eased away from the curb. "Take me someplace where I can sit in the sun and not be bothered for a while," Swanson said. "And drink something."

Cooper looked at the man huddled on the back seat and decided it was no time for remonstrations, not even gentle ones. "Anything in particular?"

"Something with a kick. I think I deserve a discreet binge today."

Cooper stopped at a liquor store in the South Loop and came out with a pint of bourbon in a paper bag. He fought his way east to the Drive, went south, and took Swanson out along the causeway to the Planetarium. The lake was a stunning aquamarine dappled with sunlight, the sky a deep and lucid blue that invited total neglect of earthly duties. White sails moved just perceptibly far out on the water. Tourists milled on the steps of the building; cars jockeyed for parking. "What the hell are we doing here?" said Swanson.

Cooper circumnavigated the Planetarium, found a parking spot on its north side, and led Swanson down the grassy slope to the terraced base of the promontory. The skyline of the Loop rose in geometric majesty a mile away, sharply defined in the limpid air. Cooper took a seat on a slab of concrete and handed the brown bag to Swanson. "You wanted a place to sit and drink," he said.

Swanson took a look around, incongruous in his six-hundred-dollar suit. The closest person to them was an old black man fishing a hundred feet away, in overalls and a sweatshirt and a battered Panama hat. Swanson swept the concrete with his palm and sat beside Cooper. He pulled the neck of the bottle out of the bag, plucked at the seal with a thumbnail, gave up and set the bottle on the ground between his feet. "I don't need to drink," he said.

They sat in silence, both looking at the skyline, for a long time. It was just a little chilly in the unflagging breeze. "I'm broke," Swanson said finally. Cooper nodded. After a moment Swanson went on. "Or maybe that's the wrong word for it. That old fellow over there wouldn't consider me broke, probably. I'm going to have enough left to live in moderate comfort while I look for a job, they tell me. Maybe even a trusting new partner. I guess that's not really broke."

"Lots of people doing worse," said Cooper.

"Sure. Tomorrow Buzz is putting me on a plane to Palm Springs, where I'm going to stay in a condo and relax. Until this whole thing is over and I decide what to do with myself, Buzz suggested. I'll be a very comfortable pauper for a while. I'll have some savings, all the personal possessions I can salvage from the house. I had to give up the house. Buzz tried his damnedest to save it but it had to go into the pot. I'll have to find a place to live. Buzz offered to let me stay with him but I think I'd prefer to stay at the club until I find something. At least they haven't kicked me out. Not yet, anyway."

Regis Swanson let out a long and eloquent sigh. He was leaning forward with his elbows on his knees, his hair ruffled by the breeze. He appeared to be looking at the distant skyline. "It might do me some good to travel light for a while. You tend to accumulate a lot of material possessions when you have money, without trying very hard. And when I get right down to it I realize they don't really mean all that much to me." He reached for the bottle again, either because he had reconsidered or because he needed something to concentrate on suddenly. This time he was successful in getting it open and he put it to his lips and drank, then scowled at the label. He held it out to Cooper.

"No thanks. I'm driving."

"Sure." Swanson replaced the bottle between his legs. "You know what really hurts?"

"What's that?"

"It's not the money. I know nobody would believe that, but it's not the money, not really. It's sitting here looking at that skyline and thinking I'm not going to be adding anything more to it. That was what I really liked." He stared at it for a while. "Putting up a good building, seeing it standing there, seeing people using it, looking at the way it fit into the city. I was even starting to learn a few things. I was starting to think about the sociology of it, making sure buildings had shops at street level to keep the block alive, that kind of thing. I had things I wanted to do for this city. I was just starting to understand the whole thing, what makes a city work. I had plans for that lot at Adams and State, you know where Montgomery Ward's used to be? If I could get my hands on the land I was going to put up a building that would show what a city could be. Shops, housing, office space, a performing arts center. Live, work and play in the heart of the Loop. It won't happen now. That's what hurts." He reached for the bottle again but set it down without drinking. He looked at Cooper and said, "I'm feeling sorry for myself. Consider it part of your job to listen."

Cooper looked into the haunted eyes and saw a man who had been sitting on his feelings for fifty years or so. Regis Swanson looked as if he were just hanging on. "Hey," said Cooper, "you just took a punch in the gut. Two or three. Go ahead and feel sorry."

"You'll get that bonus. I'll make sure you get it."

"I'm not worried about it."

Swanson looked north and east, into the wind, into the clean emptiness over the lake. "I'm sixty-two years old. I screwed up two marriages and one son. I've had everything a man could want except the love and affection of a family. Now I don't even have money." He shook his head. "What a waste of time." He looked sharply at Cooper. "I guess they're right. The rich-bashers, the wealth-haters. What's to like? I've been piling up money for forty years and look where it got me."

When it occurred to Cooper that he was expected to comment he said, "I don't know about your personal life, but I take a look around, and most of what I see was the result of somebody who had money and ideas. That's the way we do it in this society. We let people get filthy rich off their good ideas and other people's sweat. Most people seem to think now that's the best way to get things done, even the ones who do the sweating. You've had your share of good ideas. Whatever you can say about your life, it hasn't exactly been a waste of time."

Swanson nodded, his look going vacant. After a moment he smiled, bitterly. "You're really earning your pay today."

Cooper shrugged and they were silent again for a time. Swanson's head began to droop and then he was supporting it on his hands. "I want my boy back," he said quietly.

Cooper cast a look over his shoulder, just checking, waiting for the dam to break. There were a few other people around but nobody near enough for embarrassment. The old black man was reeling in his line with an air of patient futility. Cooper waited and sure enough Swanson's shoulders began to heave, silently at first and then with sobs, just loud enough to make the old man look.

"That's all I want," Swanson managed to get out in an inhuman voice. "Just give me back my boy and we'll start over."

Cooper stared across the water at the handsome city on one of the

finest days in the history of creation and listened to a grown man cry.
A hundred feet away the old black man packed up his gear and labored up the slope, and finally Regis Swanson was quiet. He sat up
wearily, pulled a handkerchief from a pocket, blew his nose and
wiped his eyes. He stowed the handkerchief, took a few deep
breaths, ran his fingers through his hair, and examined his nails, all
without looking at Cooper. "Well," he said. "That's not going to happen, is it?"

"No. But there's a lady in the hospital who might enjoy seeing you
when she's better."

After a long moment Swanson said, "Maybe." He cast a sharp
look at Cooper and said, "Run me back to Northpoint and then I
don't think I'll need you for the rest of the day. Tomorrow you can
get me out to the airport. I'll have the bonus for you and we can discuss severance pay and that sort of thing. I'm sorry it didn't work out
better." He reached for the whiskey bottle. "I don't want this," he
said, tightening the cap. He looked around, a little dazed.

"Here." Cooper took the bottle. "I've thrown quite of few of these
into the lake. Usually half-full." He stood up, wound up and slung
the bottle sidearm in a long glinting curve through the clear air. It hit
with a gentle splash and disappeared.

◆

The phone went off as Cooper was maneuvering out of the Northpoint garage into traffic. Cooper handled the phone with one hand
and the Mercury with the other, sliding east toward the lake.

"Still joyriding, huh?" said Moreland.

"Six-pack on the seat, pedal to the metal and catching up on my
phone calls to Australia. You get anything for me?"

"Yeah. I talked to an old hand with a long memory and a thick address book. He remembered Rosie McTeague. Mostly because of her
husband, Leo 'Three Finger' Pecci."

"Means nothing to me."

"He died in Leavenworth or someplace like that a few years ago.
He took a fall for some higher-ups, they say."

"Does your old hand know where she is now?"

"No, but he thinks she still goes by her husband's name. It would
have cachet in certain circles, you know?"

"So I'm looking for a Rose Pecci?"

"I guess so. What for?"

"Just a chat about old times," said Cooper.

◆

Cooper stopped at a gas station on Chicago Avenue and tanked up, then pulled the Mercury to the side of the lot and went into the office and asked to see the phone book. He looked in the book without high hopes; if the lady was still in the Chicago area at all there was no guarantee she was in the city. Try Cicero next, thought Cooper, thumbing through the pages.

And then there it was, in black and white: *Pecci Rose 1800 N. Lincoln.* Cooper stared at it, wondering if it could really be that easy. He noted the number, shoved the phone book back across the counter, and went to the pay phone at the corner of the lot. When he punched in the number he got a busy signal.

What the hell, thought Cooper, it's not that far.

The address was a residential hotel at the end of Lincoln Avenue, across from the park. Finding a place to stash the big Marquis was a problem and Cooper finally had to leave it in the park, near the south end of the zoo. The hotel had seen better days, like all residential hotels; there was a dusty, faded lobby with a speakerphone and a row of buttons with labels. Cooper found *Pecci* and pushed the button. He stood for what seemed like a long time looking out the big glass doors at the trees in the park across the way, and then a tinny voice came out of the speaker. "Yes?"

"Mrs. Pecci?"

"Speaking."

"I'm a friend of your son Sean's," said Cooper. "I have something for him."

There was a silence. Cooper stood with the shamefaced certainty of the unaccustomed liar that she had seen right through him. "What is it?" said the speaker.

"Can I come up and talk to you?" Cooper shouted into the phone.

He thought he'd lost her; seconds went by and then the speaker said, "Four-twenty-one," and the door buzzed. Cooper jumped for the handle.

The elevator rumbled and creaked but got him there. There was a long green carpet and a long file of closed doors on either side. Cooper found 421 and knocked. There was a peephole in the door and Cooper stood back a foot or two to give her a good view. Finally the door opened six inches and stopped as it reached the end of the chain.

Whatever color Rose McTeague's hair had once been, it was blond now, as blond as money could buy. She was thin, almost withered, but she had dark eyes that flashed in a face on which no effort had been spared: mascara, false lashes, rouge, lipstick of an alarming shade of red. Gold earrings peeked from under the blond hair. She was on the tall side and she wore white pants and a loose white knit top. "OK, buster, let's hear your story," she said with a bright smile.

It took Cooper a moment to find his voice. "I'm trying to get in touch with Sean. Your son?" He waited for some response, but she only blinked at him. "I'm hoping you can tell me where I might find him. I've been to his place on Winnemac and they tell me he's moved on."

"Not again." Now the long painted face was frowning at him. "The rascal."

"Um . . . I take it that means you can't help me."

"Honey, I never know where that boy is. He just floats in out of the blue sometimes."

Cooper nodded. "When was the last time you talked to him?"

She frowned at him a little longer and then suddenly the door shut in his face and re-opened, the chain released, and she was beckoning him into the apartment. He walked into a living room that had a closed door on the right and a narrow passage on the left that gave a glimpse of a bathroom at the end. There was just room enough to move in, furniture just solid enough and clean enough to sit on, and a view that just cleared the trees in the park to give a glimpse of the lake. A small color TV sat atop a buffet, a commercial in progress but the sound down. Rose McTeague closed and locked the door and came and pointed him to a heavy couch near the window that looked as if it might fold out into a bed.

"I saw Sean a week or so ago," she said, sitting on the very edge of an armchair opposite the couch. "He didn't say anything about moving."

"Must have been a spur of the moment thing," said Cooper. He opened his mouth but nothing came out; faced with the real live article, alert and expectant six feet from him, his invention was failing him. "I have something for him," he said again.

She looked him up and down. "I don't suppose you can tell me what it is," she said.

Cooper considered his audience. "I owe him some money."

Her face went through a couple of changes and she said, "I see."

"I've been away," said Cooper, hoping for the right note of vagueness. "I just got back in town. This is money I've owed him for some time. He may have given up on it by now. I want to make sure to get it to him."

She gave him a long shrewd look and said, "That's very good of you."

"He'd do the same for me," said Cooper.

Rose McTeague said nothing. "What's your name?" she said finally.

"Cooper," he said. "John Cooper."

"And you've been out of town, you say?"

"For a while. I was unavoidably detained."

Her smile was understanding. Cooper returned it, the sensation of ice cracking beneath his feet starting to fade. The smile vanished and she said, "Where was Sean living when you were last in touch?"

Cooper frowned, stalling, and decided just about anything would do. "Where was it? In a place on Montrose, not too far from Clark Street."

"I don't remember that one," she said.

"I don't think he was there for very long. There was some trouble with the landlord over a party he threw or something."

The smile came back. "You do know Sean, I see."

"We go back a ways. You wouldn't have a phone number for him, would you? He might have kept the same one."

"He didn't have a phone. I could never get in touch with him. Like I said, he just breezed in from time to time to say hello, take me out to lunch, things like that."

"And you saw him a week ago?"

"Yes. He seems to be doing well, I must say."

"Oh yeah?"

"Yes. He gave me these." She brushed the blond hair away from her right ear to reveal an earring. "Aren't they lovely?"

Cooper peered at them. "Very nice."

"I didn't get the impression Sean is in desperate need of your money right now."

Cooper stared at her. He watched the hair fall back over her ears. "Ah," he said.

"But if you want, I'd be happy to keep it for him."

Cooper nodded. "There's a thought."

"I'm sure he'll be in touch before too long. Sean's like a bad penny." She flashed a smile. "And I am, after all, his mother."

Cooper looked around the room, with its air of thinly disguised penury and solitude. "I'll think about that," he said. He looked back to see Rose McTeague watching him, intent. "Let me try a couple of other contacts first," he said.

She shrugged, the temperature visibly dropping. Cooper rose.

"Don't go yet," she said, raising a hand. "Let me give you something to drink."

"I've got places to go." On his feet he wavered, body language stammering as he looked around the place, trying to pin down what was probing at the perimeter of his awareness. "But I'll be in touch."

"Fine." She was heading for the door, having played her cards, concerned now only with speeding him on his way. He followed her to the door. She opened it and stood aside.

Cooper turned in the doorway. He looked down at her from a six-inch height advantage, looking for her ears under the sweep of blond hair. "Those really are nice earrings," he said.

She was startled, but her hand went to her hair again. She smiled and said, "Of course. They're real gold. I don't know where Sean found them."

The earrings were tiny feline figures, little solid gold cats dangling from her lobes. Cooper smiled at them and murmured something appropriate. The memory had crystallized; he knew where he had seen a figure like those before.

"I used to tell Sean he was like a cat, when he was little. He was so quiet and so clever."

Cooper took a deep breath. He needed to get out into the fresh air, into the bright clear afternoon. "Yeah," he said. "That's the kind of guy Sean is, all right."

◆

Inside the restaurant, in muted lighting falling on red flocked wallpaper, the evening rush was beginning, but there was no Charlene in sight. The hostess that approached Cooper was lissome, Asian and pretty. "I was hoping to leave a brief message for Charlene," he said.

"Charlene only works here Tuesday and Wednesday nights," said the hostess, setting him straight with firm courtesy. "You could leave a message if you want." She was already eyeing the paying customers behind him. Cooper thought for two seconds, thanked her and left. Back in the car he got Swanson on the phone at the apartment.

"We're kind of busy here," Swanson said.

"Charlene," Cooper said. "Nate's ex. I need her address. Phone number if you have it."

Two seconds went by. "What the hell for?"

"I think she can throw a lot of light on this."

"What have you been up to?"

"Stirring up the waters. I need to talk to her."

After a brief silence Swanson said, "Wait a minute." In less than that he was back, and he read her full name, a phone number and address into the phone. Cooper was prepared to commit her number to memory, but when he heard the address he decided not to bother; he could be there in ten minutes.

She lived in a big courtyard building on Irving Park. There was a sort of gatehouse with a locked gate. Cooper found her name on the panel by the speaker and pressed the button. No voice came out of the speaker but after about ten seconds the buzzer went off. Cooper went through the gate and down the long courtyard, looking up at the balconies. He thought he saw movement in a window.

Going through a door at the rear of the courtyard and up the stairs, he heard a door open above him. When he reached the third floor landing he saw her standing in an open doorway. Her hair was unbound, falling around her shoulders. This evening she was in jeans, tight jeans that hugged a shape to kill for and a corduroy vest over a chambray shirt. Tonight there was no gold at her throat but Cooper knew he had seen it there, the same small stylized cat figure. She was watching him with a faint frown, not welcoming.

"Yes, you've seen me before," he said, reaching the landing. She had one hand on the doorjamb, perhaps ready to duck back inside.

"Who are you?"

"I drove you around the block a week or so ago."

She recognized him and showed it by stiffening a little. "What does he want?" she said.

"He wants to know what happened to his son," said Cooper. "That's why I need to talk to you."

He was still at the top of the steps, not advancing, but she drew a little further inside. "I was on my way out. I have a performance tonight."

"It won't take long. At least I hope not."

"What do you want?"

"I want you to tell me all about Sean McTeague."

◆

McTeague was not the youngest person in the place—the waitresses had been selected for youth and stamina—but he was certainly the youngest customer. He made his way through the gloom of the cocktail lounge to the back, where Harold Berger sat alone in a booth, facing the front. A man in a tux and a gray shag rug was poking experimentally at the keys of a shiny grand piano, trying in vain to recapture a tune he had once known.

McTeague set the Marshall Field's shopping bag on the seat opposite Berger, shook hands across the table and sat down. In front of Berger was a glass that was empty except for a few melting ice cubes. Berger looked at the shopping bag and blinked several times, with feeling.

"Nice place," said McTeague.

"Used to be," said Berger. "Too many geriatric cases in here now."

"They need to touch up the paint, get in a new musical act, try to draw a younger crowd."

"Then where the hell would I go?" Berger laughed, a little messily, finishing with a cough.

A waitress appeared and McTeague pointed at Berger's glass and then ordered a Jim Beam straight up for himself. "I think I'm pretty much set," he said.

Berger nodded, intent, eyes large and a little wet behind the lenses. "No more trouble?"

"No more trouble. I've got a suit, an attaché case and a plane ticket to Miami and beyond."

Berger nodded. "That's right, don't tell me. Going away for good?"

"No. Just for however long it takes to open a few accounts here and there."

"Good. Did you call Manny Levenson?"

"We talked. We're meeting in Miami."

"Fine. Twenty years ago he was the best. Now I don't know, except he's stayed out of jail and he's got a house in Miami Beach. I figure that means he'll be able to help you. And with an intro from me, he'll treat you right."

"It'll be fine."

They fell silent until the waitress brought their drinks. When she had gone, McTeague reached into the shopping bag. He pulled out a tall cardboard box with a red ribbon around it and plunked it on the table next to Berger's glass. The old man looked at the box, which bore the label of his favorite scotch, and caressed it gently. "You didn't have to," he said.

"That's so you can put one down at home whenever you want, if she'll let you."

"Let me? I'll have to hide it from her if I want to get any." Berger's eyes were distinctly misty now. He raised them to McTeague's.

McTeague reached into the bag again and pulled out a manila envelope that bulged in the middle. He placed it reverently on the table next to the box. "You didn't want a check, you said."

"No." The old man laid his hand on the envelope, as if prepared to swear on it. "I don't want Uncle Sam crashing the party. Besides, I've had fun these past weeks. This'll give me a chance to get out and about on my own account again."

"Enjoy yourself." McTeague picked up his glass and tossed off the bourbon. He reached into his shirt pocket, fished out a bill and tossed it on the table. "That ought to cover things. Leave her a big tip."

Berger picked up the bill and handed it back to McTeague. "Forget it. I can afford a round of drinks. I think I can even afford to buy one for the young lady in the booth over there. She's been giving me that old come hither look, if I'm not mistaken."

McTeague looked and saw a woman who was a decade younger than Harold Berger at best and looked more interested in the smoke rings she was blowing than in any fellow drinkers. McTeague slid off the seat. "Best of luck," he said.

"My boy," said Berger, "you've taken ten years off my age, just like you promised."

McTeague looked back as he reached the door and saw Berger coughing, hanging onto the edge of the table for support.

18

"HE KIND OF came out of nowhere," said Charlene. Her head was turned away from Cooper, looking out the window at the shopfronts going by. "He showed up at a party Nate threw. I think it was a couple of years ago. We talked—I mean we like, flirted a little maybe, but nothing serious. I was with Nate and I wasn't looking for anything else. It was one of those things that happen at parties, you know. You have a good time. Nate was off flirting with somebody himself, probably. It was one of Nate's all-nighter deluxe affairs and there were a lot of people there. I just remember talking to him, and that was it."

"That was it? You talked to him once?"

"No. He was around a few times after that. Other parties, other people's houses, once or twice in a bar or something, I don't know. I wasn't keeping track. He was just one of those people I knew."

"Did Nate know him?"

"I guess so. I mean, I assume so. I never talked about him with Nate. See . . ." There was a pause. Cooper eased to a stop at a red light, watching traffic, waiting for her to go on. Finally he had to turn and look at her. She was staring gravely ahead. "Well, I could tell he was attracted. And there was one time he did kind of make a pass. I turned him down, but . . . maybe I made it kind of ambiguous. See, there was attraction there for me, too. But I was still trying to make it work with Nate. So I basically told him sorry but this place is taken. Maybe gave him the impression I would take a rain check. And I never mentioned him to Nate."

The light changed and Cooper put the car in gear. "Did he ever talk to you about Nate?"

"No. We hardly ever talked. Just an occasional hello, you know? Like I say, he was just an acquaintance."

Cooper nodded and made the turn onto Belmont, driving slowly to prolong the interview. "When did he show up again?"

"About two weeks ago. I hadn't seen him for a long time, more than a year. He just came over one day and said he'd heard I was un-attached. He brought me the necklace."

"About two weeks. Do you remember the day?"

"Yeah. It was the day Nate was killed, it turned out."

Cooper drove, frowning at taillights. "And since then you . . ." He searched for a delicate phrase.

"Since then . . . we've seen each other a few times," Charlene said with dignity.

Cooper nodded. "Has he said anything about Nate?"

"Nothing. When I told him about Nate being killed he didn't come around for a couple of days, and then when he came back we just never talked about it."

Cooper turned right on Clark Street, heading north. "That neck-lace cost an arm and a leg. Has he shown any other signs of being flush?"

Charlene had not answered by the time they got to the theater. Cooper pulled over and looked across the street. It was a little store-front space with the name of the theater painted on the front window and a banner above the door touting the name of the play. Cooper looked at Charlene. She was still staring out the windshield, but after a moment she turned her face to his. She looked calm. "Did he kill Nate?" she said.

Cooper shook his head. "No. But I think he set him up."

It was a lovely oval face, with large dark eyes and a sweet full mouth, but now it was very grave. "Why?"

Cooper pondered for a moment. "My guess is he thought what Nate had should have been his."

"What?"

"Long story. And it's just a guess."

She closed her eyes briefly, then rubbed at her temples with her fingertips. She took a deep breath and looked out the windshield again. "I knew it. There was something dangerous about him. Maybe that's why I was attracted."

Traffic went by. Cooper looked at his watch. "You're in plenty of time."

"Terrific. I have to give a performance in an hour and I'm a wreck."

"When are you supposed to see him next?"

She sighed. "I don't know. Maybe tonight, late. He said he was going to be out of town for a while and he'd come see me before he left."

"Where's he going?"

"I don't know. He was a bit mysterious about it. He wanted me to come with him, but I can't. I've got the show."

"Where does he live?"

"On a boat. He bought a boat he keeps in Montrose Harbor. That's where he's staying."

"What's the name of the boat?"

"Some woman's name. Wait a second. *Lucrezia,* that was it. As in Borgia." She looked at Cooper again. "What should I do?"

"Nothing. Don't say anything to him. I'm not even sure I've got it right."

"Oh, thanks. Thanks for destroying my evening on a whim."

"Whatever happens, just go on doing what you're doing."

"How am I supposed to do that?" She was opening the door, giving him a bitter look.

"I don't know. Enjoy the danger, I guess."

The door slammed and Cooper watched her trot across the street.

◆

Cooper drove home, thinking about whos and whys and hows, thinking about who wanted what, about who to call and when. Soon, he thought; maybe now.

There was a white paper McDonald's bag fixed to his mailbox with masking tape in the entranceway of his building, just below the name tags that said *MacLeish* and *Froelich*. On the bag somebody had written his name with a marker, just the surname, in big black capitals. Cooper peeled it off the mailbox; it felt light enough to be empty but something tapped on the sides of the bag when he shook it. He looked inside. There was a piece of paper with something written on it, folded in quarters, and something small and oblong wrapped in a square of toilet paper. Cooper looked at the note first; it said *Wait by the phone.* He looked at the small wrapped object at the bottom of the bag for a moment, wishing he could just turn around and leave everything and go back a few weeks and start over.

He dropped the note and reached in and fished out the object, feeling it through the tissue, queasy already. He dropped the bag and slowly pulled the tissue apart to reveal a human finger. It was somebody's little finger, judging from the size, and there was no blood, just a pale wrinkled finger sitting there on a square of toilet paper, with a neatly trimmed nail.

Cooper took a deep breath because he needed to control all kinds of physiological reactions that were coming on hard. He wrapped the finger up again, stooped to retrieve the bag and the note, put things back in the bag, and pulled out his keys, fumbling a little as he tried to get in the door.

Upstairs he put the bag on the dining room table and stared at it for a minute, thinking no, no, no: I saw her get on the plane. He wanted to look at the note again but was afraid to open the bag. He went to the phone. He realized his knees were shaking and he swore quietly and urgently.

He read Darcy's number from the pad by the phone and dialed it; the call went through quickly and there were four rings and then a female voice on an answering machine, giving nothing but the number he had reached and a polite request to leave a message.

"This is Cooper, calling for Diana. If you can hear me, please pick up the phone. If you're out, please call. Darcy, if Diana didn't get there, please call me." He read his number into the phone and hung up.

He stared at the bag on the table again and got control of himself. He went to the table and opened the bag. The note was written with the same marker, in the same block capitals. *Wait by the phone.* Cooper carefully laid the finger on the table on its square of tissue and bent over it. It had been chopped off close to the hand, and none too neatly; the bone was crushed. Cooper laid his own hand next to it and saw that it was smaller than his little finger. Is it hers? Cooper forced himself to ask. What am I supposed to do, take a fingerprint?

"You're a dead man," he said aloud, addressing the phone. When he had steadied a bit, he wrapped the finger up again, popped it in the bag and took it into the pantry to put it into the freezer, thinking the police were going to have to see it. He had left the note on the table and he looked at it again. "You're dead," he said, laying it back on the table.

When the phone rang ten minutes later, Cooper was standing at the window looking east into the darkness over the lake. He had been thinking and he was calm. Walking to the phone, he was hoping it was Diana but ready for anything. "Yeah," he said.

"Ready to talk?" The voice was masculine and familiar.

Cooper almost told him he was a dead man, but he had decided that would have to wait. "I don't have your fucking money," he said.

"Never said you did," said the man. "But you can get it."

"Listen to me. The man you want lives on a boat in Montrose Harbor. He stole your money, and he set it up to look like Nate Swanson did. Whatever money he hasn't spent is most likely right there on the boat with him. You've been killing the wrong people from the start, asshole."

"You've been busy, haven't you? You think this one up all by yourself?"

"Let's deal, OK? I'll give you the name of the man and the name of the boat when I see the person that finger came from step into an ambulance."

"Uh-uh. The deal is this. You bring me one million in cash tomorrow morning or another finger comes off. We've had enough dicking around. You know where to get it, go get it. Then we'll talk."

Cooper had to think about it, leaning on the wall and squeezing the receiver. He had thought enough to know that most likely the finger didn't belong to Diana, but it sure as hell belonged to someone, and having that someone's life hanging on his decisions was putting sweat on his brow. Finally he said, "Try this one. You put her in that ambulance, and you can have me. I'll meet you at Montrose Harbor and we'll find the son of a bitch together. We don't find him, you still got a hostage. If we do, you got what you want. You couldn't ask for a better deal. You don't have to wait until morning. We can wrap it up tonight."

This time the other man thought. After a very long few seconds he said, "Where the fuck is Montrose Harbor?"

"North Side. Get on Lake Shore Drive, get off at Montrose, go east toward the lake. You'll go through the viaduct under the Drive and over a rise where the bike path goes under the road and you're right there, you'll see the boats off to the right. I'll park on Montrose, just past the rise. I'm in a big old Mercury Marquis. You park ahead of me, let her out. There's a hospital a block west, right on Montrose just the other side of the Drive. When I see her come past me heading for the hospital, you can step back and talk to me. Until I see that, anybody tries to come near me, I'm out of there. Got it?"

Silence. After ten seconds Cooper had to ask if he was still there.

"I'm here. You got yourself a deal. Provided we can find you. I got to see you and I got to see nobody else. No cops, no suprises."

"That'll be easy. Where I'm going to park, there's wide open spaces all around. There may be a few other cars parked there, but it won't be too hard to check them. Just get under the viaduct into the park and start looking for me. What are you driving?"

"I think we'll just keep you guessing on that one, man. What time we talking?"

Cooper checked his watch. "How about ten o'clock?"

"Make it eleven. We're coming from a ways away."

"OK, eleven o'clock. Remember, I better see her walking."

"Hey," said the voice. "I'd be willing to bet you'll see her running."

◆

On the Drive the red taillights sailed in the dark ahead of Cooper. He was early, an hour early, but he had work to do. Cooper knew he was fallible, and he knew that he could be wrong about Sean McTeague. There was absolutely no proof McTeague had done what Cooper thought he had done, and if he hadn't then Cooper had just passed a death sentence on an innocent man. Cooper hoped he had enough time to find Sean McTeague and have a frank talk.

What he really wanted to do was keep on following the taillights, just keep driving until he was a long way from trouble. There were one thousand reasons not to show at Montrose Harbor and only one in favor, but it counted: that finger had come from somebody. Every rational thought he had told Cooper it couldn't be Diana's, but it didn't matter. Somebody was hurt and in danger of worse, and Cooper wasn't going to have worse on his conscience. Cooper's choices boiled down to playing it safe and wishing an unknown victim luck, or weighing in and giving it a shot.

There wasn't really any choice at all, he decided.

He eased down the off ramp at Montrose and went left at the light. He came out of the viaduct and went over the rise, and the park spread out before him: dark fields to the left, a thicket of masts on shimmering black water to the right and the nearly deserted road, wide and well lit, running ahead toward the lake. There were maybe a dozen cars parked on the two-hundred yard stretch ahead and he could see people moving under the lights along the harbor walk, off to the right. He pulled over as he came down the rise and parked. He switched off the lights and the ignition and looked in the mirror. There was nothing moving behind him.

He leaned over and took Regis Swanson's revolver out of the glove compartment. He broke out the cylinder, saw six rounds in place, snapped it back. He laid it on the seat beside him and wondered about the best way to conceal it, the best way to avoid using it. He pulled out his shirt tail and loosened his belt by one notch. He picked up the revolver, leaned forward and worked the gun into his waistband at the small of his back. Then he got out of the car.

He walked across the grass toward the water. The harbor was three hundred yards long and a hundred and fifty wide, enclosed by a spit of land that curled back on itself and left a narrow passage between two light towers at the south end. Boats were moored to the edge of the harbor wall and at stardocks floating out on the water. On the far side there were slips that extended out from the wall. The walk ran all the way around the harbor to a knoll with trees near the light towers. There was a railing at the edge of the concrete and there were lights at intervals. There were a few boats moving in the harbor despite the late hour and there were people on the walk, just strolling.

His plans were poor stuff as plans went, starting with how he was going to find McTeague; there were a couple of hundred boats in the harbor. He leaned over the rail to check the stern of a sailboat. Futile, he thought. He straightened up and scanned the walk ahead. It was time to use his head; there was a harbormaster's office up ahead somewhere; there would be a list. But it would be closed.

Think, Cooper told himself. If he lives on the boat, it's probably hooked up at one of those slips over there, where they have electric and water connections. If he's there, there'll be a light.

Cooper walked, along with a scattering of idlers, past a fenced-off area where small boats lay keel-up on storage racks, past a low brick building with darkened offices and the lighted windows of what looked like a yacht club bar, past a launching dock to where the walk began to curve around the closed end of the harbor. A few fishermen leaned on the rail, keeping late hours.

On the exposed side the breeze was brisk coming off the lake and the downtown skyline glittered far across the black water. Here the boats were larger, big cabin cruisers. There was a chicken-wire fence, head-high, blocking access to the water's edge. He reached the first line of slips; a long narrow platform extended out into the water with perpendicular branches that formed docks wide enough for two boats. The entrance to the platform was blocked by an inner fence that extended for ten or fifteen feet to either side of a locked gate.

Looking for lights in portholes was easier said than done; the boats were closely packed and it was next to impossible to see the boats at the far end of the line. He moved slowly along the fence. There was some activity on the slips; low murmurs and an occasional footfall came from no particular direction.

I don't know what the hell I'm doing, he thought.

The fear was there now. Find a way to get out onto the slips, he thought. He went all the way to the end of the fence, just shy of the point where the land curved inward before sweeping around toward the passage out to the open lake. He stopped beyond the fence and leaned on the rail. Where the fence ended there was nothing, absolutely nothing, to prevent a person from stepping around the end and walking up to the inner fence. Where the inner fence ended it would be a simple matter of nerve and firm handholds to slip through the rail and creep along the edge of the harbor wall to the ramp that led down to the slip. As security, it was a joke.

Cooper looked around. There were cars parked, as always, on the drive that ran along the crest of the breakwater, but they were a long holler distant and the occupants no doubt had their own concerns. The closest pedestrians were a hundred yards down the walk. He slipped through the rail.

Ten seconds later he stepped onto the ramp and looked down the dock. All the slips were occupied; there were perhaps twenty boats, ten on each side. He listened for a moment but heard nothing to discourage him from going on. Most of the boats were moored with the stern to the dock and it was a fairly simple matter to look at the names in the light from a line of lamps on posts.

Cooper's expectations were low; he was on a fool's errand with the clock ticking and no more bright ideas to replace this one. He was already wondering if he could strain his luck enough to sneak onto the next dock up the way when he found himself staring at the name *Lucrezia*.

It was a big cabin cruiser with a high canopied bridge, streamlined and gleaming in the faint light. It was moored to the perpendicular slip that jutted out from the central walkway. There was a ladder that led up to the bridge and beside it a sliding glass door that would lead to the interior. There were four portholes along the side but there was no light showing inside

Cooper stood and looked at the boat and thought about tactics. Urgency was contending with uncertainty, and if there had been any plausible excuse Cooper would have turned around and fled. Instead, he stepped carefully over the gunwale down onto the deck of the boat, causing it to rock gently.

"Freeze," said a soft voice. Cooper froze. The voice had come from above. Cooper looked up to see a man in the shadows under the canopy on the bridge. "Put your hands up, way up," the man said. "Now turn around and get the fuck off my boat. Take it slow."

Cooper turned; he had seen the glint of something metallic up there. Lowering his hands just enough to keep his balance, he stepped back on the gunwale and then on the dock. "McTeague?" he said, hearing somebody coming down a ladder.

"Lay down," the man said. "Face on the dock."

"You got it," said Cooper, obeying. He heard feet on the dock behind him. "You expecting me or you just like to sit in the dark?"

"Put your head down."

Cooper watched feet wearing black sneakers pad past his head. "I need to talk to you."

He felt hands on him, starting at the ankles and working up. "Nobody I don't know needs to talk to me."

"How about Charlene? Could you spare a moment for her?"

McTeague found the gun under Cooper's shirt and wrestled it out. "I don't see Charlene. Instead I see some fool with a gun."

"This fool's a friend of Charlene's. And I've got a gun because of what happened to her."

After a long frozen moment McTeague took a few steps away from Cooper. "Talk to me," he said.

"Well, you know all that money you stole?" Cooper waited, but McTeague said nothing. "The people you stole it from sent two guys to get it back."

"Don't fuck with me. What happened to Charlene?"

"They got her," said Cooper. "They'll let her go when they get their money back."

There was a long silence. McTeague said, "How'd they find her?"

"I don't know. But they got her. She called me on the phone, and she wasn't acting. She said find you, so I did."

"Who are you?"

"What the hell does it matter who I am? If you have to know, I'm the guy she ditched when you showed up. Now can I stand up and talk to you man to man?"

Cooper lay with his cheek to the boards for a very long moment, waiting for McTeague to sort out the lies, waiting for a gunshot. Finally McTeague said, "Move slow. There's a light switch just inside the cabin on your right."

◆

Turk had a nose for the type of neighborhood he wanted, and as he headed up Broadway past Irving Park he knew he had found it. Liquor stores, closed-up shops, bars with signs that said *Cerveza fria*. And women in doorways. He turned, circled the block, and came up toward Broadway again, slowing. He pulled to the curb at the corner and the woman in the black miniskirt stepped out of the shadows, making eye contact. Turk beckoned her with a wave of the hand and leaned over to open the door of the van.

She had long frizzed hair and bright red lips; she looked good enough to eat but Turk had other things on his mind. She was also a pro; she looked into the back of the van before she climbed all the way in and froze at the sight of Ferocious Dick back there in the gloom with his nose guard on. "Uh-uh," she said.

"Relax," said Turk. "He's harmless. Here's the easiest hundred bucks you ever made." He was holding the money in her face, five twenties fanned out like a poker hand. "Up front, for fifteen minutes' work. You don't even have to blow anybody."

She had seen weirdness before, but that was money right there six inches from her nose, and Turk knew she would at least listen, hanging onto the door frame. "What's the catch?" she said.

"The catch is, the Oscar committee won't be watching. What we need is an acting job. You want to hear the details?"

She looked at Ferocious Dick again, and Turk could see her making one of those decisions whores make every night, the kind of decision that leaves them old and tired and occasionally dead. He lowered the bills to his lap. "Honey, you got plenty of competition around here. Everybody wants to get into show business."

She hopped up onto the seat and slammed the door. "Up front, you said."

Turk raised the bills again, and she removed them from his hand with a swift practiced motion. He put the van in gear and slewed away from the curb. "That's what I like," said Turk. "A woman who can make up her mind."

◆

"If you don't want to give it up, we're going to have to scam them somehow," said Cooper. He was sitting on a large settee upholstered in maroon leather that curved with the side of the boat. McTeague sat opposite him across a small table, next to a wet bar and fridge. The roomy saloon of the boat was softly lit but there was enough light to see the silvered .357 magnum in McTeague's right hand, trained on Cooper's chest, and Swanson's revolver in his left, dangling between his legs.

McTeague had gray eyes, very calm, under dark hair going gray, cut short on top and long at the back of the neck. He had a strong unshaven jaw that peaked in a cleft chin. He was action-hero handsome, dressed in black from T-shirt to sneakers, and he was not pleased by what Cooper was telling him.

"You could be lying through your teeth," he said.

"I could. There's no reason in the world for you to believe me. Except I'm trying to do you a favor. I could have just told the opposition where you were."

McTeague kept on looking at him and the .357 didn't waver. Finally he said, "Tell me about the opposition, then."

"Two men. One Anglo, one Hispanic, I think, though he doesn't appear to speak any known human language."

"You talked to them?"

"Hell, I slugged one of them. That's why I picked up the piece. I don't think he'll be too happy to see me again."

Something like humor flickered for a moment in McTeague's face. "So what's the plan?"

Cooper had figured out two things about Sean McTeague, one a maybe and the other for sure. It was possible McTeague cared about the money a lot more than he cared about Charlene. And it was damn certain that the second McTeague saw the hostage, whoever she was, all bets were off. "It's pretty simple," Cooper said, "such as it is. I'm supposed to meet them over there at the park entrance at eleven o'clock. They're supposed to have Charlene and I'm supposed to have the money."

"Nice of you to set this up without telling me."

"I was flying by the seat of the pants, partner. What was I supposed to do, tell them to go ahead and shoot Charlene?"

Here's where we find out just how Charlene stacks up against a million dollars, Cooper thought. He watched McTeague watching him, tense and wary, and he could see calculation going on, hard questions being asked and answered. "Eleven o'clock," said McTeague.

Cooper nodded. "A little under an hour from now. And straight across the harbor."

McTeague was still looking at Cooper but he was looking right through him; he was looking at something a long way off but getting closer, something he didn't like at all. "I guess you're right," he said, coming back.

"About what?"

"We'll just have to scam them."

"It better be good. Because Charlene has to walk away from it one piece. That's my bottom line."

McTeague blinked. "OK. We're on the same page."

"Can I make a suggestion?"

"Sure."

"Try the old steal-back. I'll hand them the money and take Charlene, you jump 'em and take it back, as soon as Charlene's clear. I'll tell them I shot you or something, they won't be looking for you."

McTeague smiled, with what looked to Cooper like real amusement. "That one's as old as the hills, man."

"Simple but effective."

"It won't work this time."

"Why not?"

"Number one, there's not enough of the money left to buy her back."

"I was afraid of that. What's number two?"

"You think I'm going to let you out of my sight with what's left?"

Cooper shrugged. "I'm open to suggestions."

McTeague leaned back slowly. He raised the muzzle of the .357, then laid it gently on his thigh, no longer pointing at Cooper. He was looking through Cooper again, and this time his jaw muscles rippled, just perceptibly, under the skin. After a fairly long silence he said, "What it boils down to is, we're gonna have to take Charlene away from them."

"I'd say that's about right, if you don't have anything to give them."

McTeague smiled, less a movement of the face than a strange light in the eyes. "And if Charlene means anything to me."

Cooper's eyes flicked to the .357. "That thought had occurred to me."

"How did you know I wouldn't just shoot you and take off?"

"I didn't. That's another reason I brought the piece."

McTeague's smile reached the lips. "Well, I hope you're willing to do what's necessary."

After a moment Cooper said, "We're talking about something fairly drastic, I assume."

"Unless they scare easy."

"You give me the piece back, I'll use it, if that's what you're worried about."

"You'll get it back when I'm ready. Where are you meeting them, exactly?"

"I told them at the bottom of the slope, just past the bridge over the bike path."

"Not a lot of cover there."

"There'll be a few cars parked there, but they'll check them."

"Yeah." McTeague transferred the .357 to his left hand, slipping the index finger through the two trigger guards and letting the guns dangle. He rose and went to the open door. He stood looking out into the night for a moment, swaying just the slightest amount as the boat rocked very gently. "OK," he said. He turned, a gunslinger leaning in the doorway, nonchalant. "I have a feeling we probably ought to keep it simple."

"I'm glad to hear you say that."

"If you can get them onto the boat, get them inside here, nobody's going to hear a couple of shots. And that's a pretty deep lake out there."

Cooper was starting to get a fix on what kind of person he was dealing with, looking into the calm gray eyes. "What about Charlene?"

"We're not talking very long ranges in here. I won't miss. Just make sure you don't."

Cooper thought. "What if they won't come aboard? What if one of them stays behind? They won't leave Charlene alone."

"Then we'll take them one by one," McTeague said. "You just get one or both of them onto the boat. Tell them you found the boat but I wasn't here. Jump on board, knock, nobody home. Come in and wait. A nice little surprise for McTeague."

"They'll buy that? The boat being unlocked and all?"

"I went down the dock to borrow a cup of sugar from a neighbor. They'll buy it if you sell it right. That's your part."

"And once they're in here?"

"The first thing they'll do is start searching the boat. They'll look in there"— McTeague nodded toward the darkened forward compartment—"and that's where I'll be."

Cooper shook his head. "A lot could go wrong."

"A lot already has gone wrong. I can still cut and run."

Cooper looked at the guns in his hand. "OK. When do I get the piece back?"

"When you get back here. They could search you." McTeague walked slowly along the cabin to the forward end of the low table, away from the door. "It'll be waiting for you here." He leaned down the tapped the underside of the table with a knuckle. "I'll tape it here, handle toward the couch. Just sit within grabbing range and be ready. It'll come away pretty easy. If things go right, when I shoot the first one, the second one won't be paying any attention to you or Charlene. I might even get them both before you have to do anything."

Cooper looked again into the cool gray eyes. "You're not the nervous type, I take it?"

McTeague smiled. "Not when I make the rules," he said.

◆

If he can see us, thought Cooper, it could get tricky. From where he sat in the Marquis, at the foot of the gentle slope down into the park, Cooper could not make out McTeague's boat in the jumble of craft moored along the slip across the harbor. He was aware, however, that McTeague might well be able to see him. And if he saw a female figure running away, whether or not he could tell it was not Charlene, it was a good bet he would make for the high seas. Cooper felt outgunned, outnumbered and out on a limb.

Who wants what? Cooper asked himself again. He picked up the car phone and dialed a number from memory. "Area Six," said a voice.

"If you can get a message to Detective Reichardt or Detective Benitez, tell them to call MacLeish, that's M-A-C-L-E-I-S-H, at the following number." He read out the number of the cellular phone. "Tell them if they want the people who killed Nate Swanson, call that number and call it fast." He repeated the number and switched off the phone. He held it for a moment, then reached into his shirt pocket and fished out the slip of paper on which he'd written the DEA woman's pager number. He punched it in and then laid down the phone to wait.

She called first, within three minutes. After Cooper identified himself she said, "What's happening?"

"You want your million dollars?"

"What million dollars?"

"The million dollars you've been chasing from the start."

"Who's been chasing what?"

"Look, in about forty-five minutes the two guys that killed Nate Swanson are finally going to meet the man who has their money. That money could be yours. And there's a very nice boat you could probably seize in the bargain."

"Where are you?"

"The boat is named *Lucrezia* and it's docked at the westernmost slip on the south side of Montrose Harbor. You get onto that boat and you'll find the money and the man who stole it. But you better hurry, because right around eleven o'clock two guys are going to come and try and take it away."

"Whoa, hold on a second."

"Montrose Harbor, eleven o'clock, the last dock out near the end of the hook. Have fun with the money," Cooper switched off.

The second call came five minutes later, and it was Benitez. "What's going on?" he said, distant and perhaps sleepy.

"The two guys who killed Nate Swanson are going to be at Montrose Harbor around eleven o'clock. In half an hour or so. They're looking to get their money from a guy that lives on a boat moored at the last slip on the south side of the harbor. The boat is named *Lucrezia.* If you want to get them before all hell breaks loose you'd better get some people here. But please, please don't make it obvious with a lot of flashing lights and stuff, because then I'll get shot. See, I'm supposed to take them to the boat."

There were two seconds of silence, and then a brisk, "South side of the harbor?"

"The last row of slips at the west end. If they see cops, things get bad for me. If all else fails I'm just planning to go into the water. I'm driving a brown Mercury Marquis but I don't know if we'll be in my car or theirs. That's about all I can tell you."

"That's not a lot to go on. I can't work miracles."

"I don't need a miracle. Just maybe a cop or two in the right spot."

◆

Cooper waited; cars went by. Nobody slowed and he recognized nobody. A squad came by just before eleven and disappeared around the bend ahead, heading away from the harbor. There was no sign of the cavalry coming over the ridge.

As soon as he saw the van in the mirror, creeping over the rise, Cooper figured this was it. As it came by he looked up; there was nobody in the passenger seat and he couldn't get a fix on the driver. It pulled over just beyond him, and then it began to back toward him slowly. Suddenly all the thoughts Cooper had repressed were right there; he wasn't sure he could function if he saw Diana come out of that rear door.

The van halted a yard from his fender and the rear door came open. The woman stumbled as she jumped out, tottering on high heels, but she recovered, steadying herself on the hood of the Marquis. Her left hand was entirely wrapped in a white cloth, perhaps a towel, and she held it to her breast. She shot one look at Cooper; she was young and pretty and heavily made up, and she had the eyes of a woman who has looked into hell. She made it to the sidewalk and began to run, clumsily but urgently, long legs flashing under a black miniskirt. Replacing her in the doorway of the van was a round dark face crossed by the stark white X of a bandage under a protective mask. The man had a gun and he was pointing it at Cooper through the windshield.

Cooper took a look at the woman making tracks in the mirror and felt his relief at seeing a stranger contend with a cold, white rage. Cooper reached for the door handle. It wasn't personal now; now it was just battle again. There were wolves in the woods and Cooper was on the side of the sheep. He opened the door.

The man in the back of the van kept the gun trained on him and Cooper knew it wouldn't take much of an excuse for him to pull the trigger. Cooper walked up the side of the van to the driver's window, and there was the long handsome face with something a little hard about it, no hair this time, just a black baseball cap worn backward. "Satisfied?" he said. "I told you she'd be running." The back door of the van slammed and the dark man came around to stand at Cooper's right. He had a hand in the pocket of his jacket.

Cooper looked up at the tall man for four or five seconds, just getting a grip. "Let's go do this," he said finally. "I found the boat. I don't think the guy's there, 'cause everything's dark. I don't know how hard it is to break into a boat, but we can try. It looked to me like a crowbar would do it."

The tall man stared at him for a moment. "So why haven't you done it already?"

"I just found it, didn't have time."

The tall man looked at him without expression for a second or two. "Jump in."

Cooper went around the front of the van and got in on the passenger side. The small dark man got in the back and pulled the doors shut. "Where's the boat?" the tall man said. Cooper told him and he put the van in gear and went at an easy pace, following the road around the yacht club and out onto the breakwater. Cooper had his hand on the door handle, waiting for movement behind him, but he heard nothing.

When they reached the slips he pointed to them and the tall man pulled over and parked. Cooper got out and waited. The short man climbed out the back carrying a tire iron. Cooper watched him but said nothing. There were a few people along the harbor wall, a few cars on the road ahead. "Let's take a look at the lake," said Cooper.

"Nice night for it." In the backward cap and a flannel shirt hanging open over a black tee, the tall man looked like a Motörhead fan in line at the Aragon, two beers away from mayhem. The other man walked about ten feet behind them, holding the tire iron close to his side.

Cooper took them along the road to the circular loop around the knoll and then cut down to the water's edge. He was calm, all the old stress symptoms there but under control. Cooper had walked into firefights before, and he knew the only way to have a chance of walking out again was to keep the lid on.

At the bottom of the slope they leaned on the rail, with the slip where McTeague's boat was moored fifty feet to their right. "Anytime you're ready, we can go in," Cooper said. "That gate's not going to stop a six-year-old."

The tall man looked at the arrangement and said, "That's a fucking invitation." He turned, scanning the slope above. Cooper looked out over the water, waiting for the sound of car doors slamming, cops or federal agents sprinting down the slope. After a few seconds the tall man said, "OK, take us in."

Cooper walked slowly to the end of the fence. Again he went through the rail and crept along to the ramp. He let himself down with great care and looked back to see the two men standing there at the end of the fence, watching. Cooper walked quietly down the ramp, looking ahead along the length of the dock. He paused, listening, and then looked back and waved them on.

The tall man came first, shuffling along the rail, with the other man waiting at the end of the fence. A car came along the road above and everyone froze until it passed. Then the tall man stepped lightly onto the ramp and came to join Cooper. The other man had come along the fence to the gate and stood looking through it.

Cooper looked out along the double line of boats, listening. He heard only distant city noises and the faint breath of the lake somewhere behind him. *I have about a minute to live if things go wrong,* he thought. He looked at the tall man, who motioned him forward with his chin. There was no gun in evidence yet, but Cooper figured there would be soon. He started walking.

Cooper trusted McTeague to do what he had said he would about as much as he would trust a rusty fragmentation grenade. All he wanted was to get into the water. At least the boat was still there; riding high in the water, larger than its neighbors. Cooper checked the bridge this time and saw no one.

"There you go," he whispered, pointing to *Lucrezia*'s stern ten feet ahead.

There was light showing through the sliding glass door into the interior. The tall man stared at the boat, and now Cooper could see the gun in his hand. They stood still for a few seconds and then the tall man turned and waved once. Cooper looked back to see the second man moving away from the gate, along the fence.

They waited, and after a minute full of soft careful noises coming down the dock the second man was with them. The tall man put a hand on Cooper's arm and pushed gently. "You first," he breathed. "Friendly, like." Cooper stepped to the stern of the boat and stopped. There was a creak on the dock and he turned to see the little dark man circling behind him, holding the tire iron.

Adios, Cooper thought. There was just enough space between *Lucrezia* and her neighbor for a man to disappear into the black water. Cooper had played his role, made the introductions, and it was time to take his ball and go home. He had turned away, starting to lean, to brace for the cold of the water, when his head split in an extravaganza of light and pain, subsiding into blackness. When next he was conscious, he was being hauled away from the edge of the slip and dragged to his feet. Enough of him was there to make his legs work, at least until he was shoved over the gunwale and landed in a heap in the bottom of the boat. He was on his hands and knees and starting to make sense of a world full of pain when two more people dropped onto the boat, making it rock. Somebody grabbed him under the arms and pulled, and the door was torn open and then he was shoved through it into the lighted interior of the boat, where he fell against the low table.

Nothing happened, just long enough for him to focus and see that the saloon was empty, and then the shooting started. The shots were loud and inexplicably behind him, outside the boat. Cooper hugged the deck, hands over his head, and waited out the fusillade. Suddenly it was silent except for a deep growling moan that trailed off quickly, and he was sorting out impressions; six or seven shots, two or three guns, somebody hurt. Cooper stayed where he was, stone-still, dead-still.

Feet were pounding, somewhere, and then the boat rocked again and someone was at the cabin door. Cooper hoped he looked as bad as he felt and evidently he did, for the footsteps withdrew, went hurriedly up a ladder and thumped overhead. After a few seconds the floor began to vibrate as a powerful marine engine just beneath it came to life. It roared and then steadied at a deep rumbling idle, and the footsteps sounded on the ladder again and then on the dock. Cooper started wondering if he could swim with a broken head.

What sounded like a coil of line dropped into the stern of the boat, and the rapid steps went along the slip toward the bow. It was time for a look and Cooper raised himself on one elbow, pain shooting down the back of his head into his neck, and made out a figure slumped against the gunwale in the stern of the boat, a dark man with crooked white teeth fixed now in a permanent grimace below a white protective mask.

Cooper had pulled himself up to a sitting position, just inside the door, hoping he had it in him to get off the boat and then out of the water, when two figures came into sight on the dock, feet pounding as they braked after a long sprint. One was male and one was female, and the man was hollering over the noise of the engine. Cooper didn't fix on what he was saying, but he saw both of them with drawn pieces, aiming in perfect unison, arms stiffening as they pointed down the slip toward the bow of the boat. There was a long second of immobility and then the arms relaxed and the eyes widened; somewhere there was a splash. The woman started down the slip but the man grabbed her arm, spinning her around and almost putting her on the dock, saying something Cooper couldn't hear over the noise of the engine.

Cooper sagged away from the door, hurting. The boat rocked as two people jumped into the stern. "Come on. We got maybe five minutes," the man said.

"What do you mean? Aren't you going to call it in?"

"Sure. After we search it."

Just outside the door, she said, "They'll get a team over to search it. Why don't we see if we can keep this guy alive here first?"

"Fuck him." There was a chilled moment's silence and then the man was talking low and fast. "Toni, time to be a grown-up. This million bucks is off the map. We're the only ones who believe in it, and I'll be god-damned if I'm going to let the Suits have it. Now you've had the same training I've had. You know there are about five places on a boat like this where people hide things. Working together we have a chance to find it and get it out before the shit hits the fan."

No, thought Cooper. Why did I have to hear this?

"J.D.," said the woman, "call it in. Now."

"Or what?" he said, and stepped into the cabin, where the first thing he saw was Cooper, on his back between the settee and the table, eyes open and a hand on the edge of the table, head raised. "Mother fucker," said Jasper, quite calmly. He drew his piece from under his windbreaker and leveled it at Cooper.

Cooper just stared back. Toni was in the doorway behind Jasper. Cooper looked at her and said, "Are you going to let him shoot me?"

Toni squeezed in past Jasper. "He's not going to shoot you," she said. To Cooper she didn't sound convinced. Jasper was looking at Cooper with a look of great self-restraint under pressure. Cooper had no place to roll, duck or run and nothing to bargain with.

"You want to buy my silence?" he said. "I'll make it real, real simple. I go over the side into the water and I was never here." There was no change in the intent blue eyes or the steady hold on the piece. "I led those two to the boat and then jumped off the dock into the water and you never saw me again. All I want is a chance to swim."

Everything marked time for a moment. "J.D.," said Toni.

Jasper seemed to lose interest from one second to the next. He shoved the piece back into the holster at his hip and moved forward, past Cooper toward the bow. He went through a hatch into the forward compartment and Cooper could hear him tearing at things: drawers, cabinets, bedding. Slowly Cooper levered himself up to a sitting position. Pain was echoing from one side of his skull to the other and down his neck. With Toni's help he made it up to sit on the couch, head in his hands. Jasper was trashing the forward compartment. Cooper opened his eyes and looked at Toni standing over him. The look in the dark eyes said nothing he was able to read. "You better move," she said softly.

"Uh," said Cooper. He leaned forward, steadied himself with his hands on the table, and tried to rise before sinking back. "Give me a minute," he said.

"Try for thirty seconds," said Toni. "Take a life jacket if you have to, but you better lose yourself fast and stay lost."

In the forward compartment there was a heavy silence and then rapid movement; Jasper came through the hatch into the cabin, looked at Cooper and said, "You wanted to swim, swim."

"Like a fish," said Cooper. He rose, made it to the door, paused with his hands on the frame, and looked at the body lying in the stern. He turned in the doorway. "Where's the other guy?" he said.

"What?"

"Where's the other guy?"

Jasper said nothing for one full second. The boat rocked and there was a wet thrashing sound and somebody came up over the stern, arm extended. Cooper was backing out of the doorway and falling onto the settee before the image had quite registered. Jasper had time to get his piece halfway out before the man hanging onto the stern gunwale shot him. Jasper fell back through the hatch and more shots came, a fast wicked volley up the gut of the boat. Toni was staggering the length of the cabin, bouncing off the counter on the other side, hand on the butt of her automatic but not getting it out. Cooper pressed back against the wall as hard as he could press. When silence fell he saw Toni on her knees, head down, gun still in the holster, a hole in her blue T-shirt high on her right shoulder starting to well with blood. Jasper's legs were moving, in spasms. Aft, the man with the gun was clambering into the boat.

With an old infantryman's quick grasp of essentials, Cooper wondered if the volley had emptied the gun. Bad bet, he thought. Light, he thought next, still on essentials, and found the switch by the door. He flicked it, hoping, and the cabin went dark. The footsteps in the stern stopped and Cooper went for the far end of the settee. He sprawled headlong and twisted to feel for the gun under the table, hearing Jasper gasping and thumping on the deck, hearing movement in the stern again. He ran his hand over the smooth, bare underside of the table, two or three times, frantically, but found nothing there.

Cooper had time to get over the table and find Jasper's legs in the dark, but no time to find his gun before the light went on and the tall man was there, his left hand coming away from the switch, cap gone, dripping water and raising his piece. Coming out of his crouch, Cooper had an impression of a very big gun muzzle and wide eyes making a quick choice. The choice was him, and there was time only for hopeful thoughts of good trauma surgeons.

From the floor Toni squeezed off three quick shots, left-handed, each one higher than the last on the tall man's torso. They stood him up and knocked him back against the frame of the door, and though his gun kept pointing at Cooper he never pulled the trigger. He wheezed and slid slowly to an awkward leaning slump in the corner of the cabin, looking at Toni with amazement. "Agh," he said.

Everything was quiet and then Cooper came out of his freeze and went warily around the table. He kicked the automatic clear of a limp right hand. The tall man gawked at him and gurgled and coughed up something that choked him.

Toni was on her knees still, face screwed tight with pain, the gun in her hand. "Jesus God," she said. She looked at Jasper, who had stopped moving but was making noise, a hollow breathy moan. "J.D., Jesus."

"Fuckin' . . ." squeezed out Jasper. Cooper went and leaned over him. He could see one hole in him, in the center of the belly.

"There'll be cops all over the place in a minute," Cooper said. "His chances are pretty good."

Toni had made it to her feet, her right arm close to her side. She steadied herself with her good hand on the wall, looking down at him. "J.D. Stay with me now." She was pale and shaken but under control and Cooper knew it was now or never.

"Here they come." Cooper could hear sirens now, not far away. "The deal still goes?" he said. "I was never here?" He was backing down the cabin.

She looked around and managed to fix on him for two or three seconds. "Go."

Cooper passed the tall man slumped in the corner and saw bright eyes focused on him. He stopped, leaned close. "Him, he'll make it," he said. He put his index a foot from the long handsome face with something hard about it. "You, you're a dead man." The bright eyes were fading and now they looked scared, scared to death.

Cooper stepped out into the stern of the boat, looking right and left. There was nobody in sight on the dock and nobody could see him from shore because of the boats on either side. Cooper stepped over the legs of the small dark corpse to the gunwale. Without stopping to think about whether he could swim with a headache that was coming back hard as the adrenaline ebbed, he swung his legs over the side and let himself slip, a long way down, into the cool black water of the lake.

19

BY LATE JULY, Lake Michigan has finally lost its winter chill, and the water was just cool enough to put some zeal into Cooper's sloppy Australian crawl. It was a long swim, a long tiring haul in the dark with injury and fatigue making a hundred and fifty yards into the English Channel. Cooper did it in stages, from the end of the dock where *Lucrezia* was moored out to a stardock in the middle of the harbor where he rested hanging onto a drooping line, sheltered by the wooden hull of a sailboat, watching the blue flashing lights multiply on the breakwater above the mooring slips. Finally he pushed on to the long, low launching dock on the far side.

As he clung to the edge of the launching dock, panting, he watched for another quiet swimmer disturbing the black glassy surface, listened for soft plashes in the dark. When he was sure there was no one to see him, he hauled himself with great effort out of the water, lay motionless for a minute, and then crawled up to the walk, his head pounding. Across the harbor, an ambulance accelerated, siren rising to a wail. It came around the long sweep of the breakwater and passed Cooper, going full tilt, when he was halfway along the walk.

The Marquis was where he had left it. Cooper had some trouble getting his keys out of the pocket of his soaking trousers. As he stood at the door of the Marquis wrestling with wet khaki, a car parked a hundred feet behind his flicked on its lights and drifted down the slope toward him. Cooper watched it come, too tired even to worry.

Benitez braked and leaned over to unlock the passenger side door. "What happened over there?" he said as Cooper got in.

Cooper sagged on the seat. "I don't know. I took them to the boat and then went right in the water, like I said I would, took 'em by surprise. Just after that the shooting started. I hid out under the dock, hanging on to a piling. When the shooting was over I started swimming. Then there was a second round of shooting. I didn't stick around."

Benitez looked at him for a long moment, as blank as a wall of stone. "Want to tell me about the first part of the evening?"

"Sure. But first, there's one guy who got lost in the shuffle. He went in the water like I did, and I don't know where he got out. Of course, I don't know if you're interested in him."

"Try me."

"This guy McTeague I told you about."

Benitez stared and then, in the evil yellow light from the street-lamps, Cooper saw him smile. "McTeague? Oh, yeah. I could get interested."

Cooper stared back. "Good. 'Cause I think I can tell you where he's headed."

◆

The light in the massive gatehouse was out, creating an ideal venue for robbery and assault. From the car Benitez and Cooper watched the woman approach warily, keys out and head up, before venturing up the steps. "That her?" said Benitez.

"That's her."

"Shit, I can hardly see her under there." Benitez had procured a cup of coffee from the mini-mart at the corner and nursed it for twenty minutes. He raised the cup to his lips. "Looks like she's in. Keep your eyes open for him now."

Cooper was tired of sitting in damp clothes, just beginning now to shiver a little, perhaps from the chill, perhaps from the crack on the head. Fire shot down his neck with every movement. "You were saying."

"Yeah. See, normally the dick who gets the first one gets all the files, once somebody finds a connection with other cases. Should have been the people working on Dexter who got these. But we got 'em 'cause they got so much work out on the West Side. Like we don't. Anyway, once somebody talked to the DEA and decided that Nate Swanson getting popped had something to do with Dexter and company, we got stuck with all of them. And the other day we got one more."

"The guy you mentioned. In the park."

"Yeah. Rolando Brown. Turns out Dexter had a piece of paper in his pocket when he got shot, had a phone number on it with the initial *R.* by it. Somebody got around to finding out whose number it was, and up comes Rolando Brown. Well, the same somebody finds out Rolando Brown got himself shot a week or two back, sitting in a car out by the lake up at Foster or around in there. Bingo, we get his file too, 'cause now he's connected with Dexter. So the day after I talk to you, whenever that was, I take a look and what do I see? They got nowhere on Rolando, but a name kept coming up when they asked people who he hung out with."

"Sean McTeague."

"And nobody could find him." They were silent for a moment, watching. A car went by slowly, cruising for parking, and disappeared around a corner ahead. "Rolando got killed the same night Dexter apparently got ripped off. So I'm interested. I'm real interested in this guy." Benitez took a sip of coffee without taking his eyes off the street. "Except I got a feeling he ain't showing up."

"Maybe not. It was just a guess." Cooper closed his eyes, resisting the temptation to feel the lump on the back of his head again; it wasn't going anywhere.

"So we give it another fifteen minutes and then I'm afraid you gotta come out to Belmont and Western with us and go through it all again. We'll get you home by sunup, don't worry."

Cooper sat as still as possible. He wanted to be dry, he wanted to be asleep; he wanted to be somewhere far away. Vancouver, he thought. Fir-covered slopes. The sea.

He opened his eyes and stirred, wincing. "He's had plenty of time to make it here from the harbor, even on foot. Are we sure he didn't go in the back way?"

"Personally, I'm not sure of anything. But I think Fritz would have seen him if he'd tried the alley."

"If McTeague was fast, he could have been up there before your partner got here."

"Could be. You worried about it?"

"McTeague right now is going to be wondering how much and how willingly she told me. He knows I lied to him. And he's going to be pissed."

Benitez checked the mirrors, looked to the front again, raised the cup. He gave a slight shrug. "I got no reason to go up there."

"No." Cooper was watching the courtyard entrance which had swallowed Charlene, a hundred feet away and across the street. He was having a hard time sitting. "Can I stretch my legs a little?" he said.

Benitez looked away from the street to give him a long cop look, a reminder that for all the easy chat Cooper was still just another problem to be solved. "Don't blow it. And don't go far."

"No." Cooper left the car, looked back to the lights of the filling station and mini-mart at the corner, ahead along deserted sidewalks to the distant lights of the Drive. He walked slowly to a point opposite the gatehouse. He looked down the long courtyard and remembered walking along it to Charlene's entrance at the end. He could see the windows of what would be her apartment. They showed light, and as Cooper watched, someone moved across one uncurtained expanse. It was Charlene, and the way she moved did not look like somebody unwinding, somebody popping a beer or making for the TV set or heading for bed. She had moved with more decision, or tension perhaps, than that.

He watched, uneasy, until he saw the second figure cross the room. He sprinted back to the car and tore open the door. "There's two people up there," he said. "I think it's him."

Benitez said nothing, gave no sign of alarm. He merely reached for the switch and flashed his headlights once. Then he took the keys out of the ignition, opened the door, pitched the coffee cup with its dregs into the street, and got out. "You stay in the car," he said to Cooper, slamming the door. Cooper got in and watched through the windshield as Reichardt came up the opposite sidewalk to meet his partner. The two detectives talked for a few heartbeats at the foot of the steps and then Benitez jogged for the mouth of the alley, a second baseman taking the field, while the old defensive end disappeared into the gloom beneath the tiled roof of the gatehouse.

Cooper waited. Through the open windows of the car came the murmur of the city after midnight: distant cars, music somewhere close. Sean McTeague came out of the gatehouse. He was sleek and still damp, black T-shirt and jeans hugging the lean feral frame. He was carrying a black knapsack in his right hand, and he was walking briskly toward Broadway. Cooper watched him, frozen. McTeague walked like a man concerned about pursuit but so far a couple of steps ahead. Nobody came out of the gatehouse after him.

Cooper watched him draw even on the opposite sidewalk and then leaned over and gave him two quick beeps on the horn. McTeague snapped a look and Cooper scrambled over the hump to the driver's seat. "Hey," he said through the open window.

McTeague stopped dead and looked, shot a glance behind, stared for two more seconds, and came across the street under full steam. Cooper watched his hands and wondered what to do next. "Jump in," he said.

McTeague thought about it for maybe a second, looking at Cooper with intensity, then came around to the passenger's side. "Let's go," he said, landing heavily on the seat with the knapsack between his legs, slamming the door. "Fast."

Cooper looked at McTeague, lean and taut and very, very intent, and all he could think of was to keep him talking. "Just a minute."

"We don't have a minute. Move."

"I got one question first."

"Fuck. What?"

"Why Nate Swanson?"

McTeague looked as if he had hit a wall at a hundred miles an hour. From edge-of-the-seat nervous he had gone to frozen stare in half a second flat. He opened his mouth, closed it again, then settled, eyes narrowing. "Who the fuck are you?"

"I asked you a question."

McTeague's eyes flicked to the gatehouse and back. His head came down about fifteen degrees and in a showdown voice he said, "Start the car and I'll tell you all about it. Just move."

Cooper shoved his hand in the trouser pocket where he kept his keys. It wasn't much of a stall, and he tried another shot in the dark. "Swanson's not really your father, you know."

McTeague stared but quickly realized it was a luxury; his eyes flicked again. "The fuck he ain't. Now move, for Christ's sake."

Cooper had his keys out and at a leisurely pace he shook out the key to the Marquis and reached for the ignition. "You got the money there in the bag, right? And you had the bag on when the shooting started, so you could take it with you if things went wrong? That was smart." Cooper jabbed at the ignition, raised the bunch to the light, sorting, waiting for his next cue, waiting for somebody to come yank him offstage.

"OK, you want a cut," said McTeague. "Fine. I'll give you ten thousand." A zipper made a small tearing sound. Cooper looked at the hand sliding into the knapsack. "Shit, here they come," said McTeague, sticking his chin out toward the gatehouse.

Cooper almost went for it but remembered Rolando Brown in time. When McTeague brought the .357 out of the bag Cooper hit him hard, backhand across the face, snapping his head back but doing nothing to stop the slow-motion upward swing of the gun muzzle. With his left hand Cooper grabbed, knocking the muzzle up to the ceiling and getting a grip where it had a chance of saving his life, around the cylinder. McTeague rallied with strength, nearly knocking Cooper off the gun with a jab to the chin, but Cooper was focused on that cylinder; he could feel it straining to turn beneath his fingers. He put his right hand on McTeague's face, feeling for the eyes, distracting McTeague for a moment but then taking another shot to the face; he roared with pain and rage, bringing his right hand down on the gun as well. Now he had a grip nobody was going to break, left little finger behind the hammer and thumb wrapped around the front, right hand squeezing for good measure, head down and forward to hide from the blows.

Things were at that point when Benitez tore open the door and screamed "Freeze!" in a voice that broke like a fourteen-year-old's. Cooper felt things go slack by degrees, looked up to see Benitez's .38 jammed in McTeague's temple, and tightened his grip, unbelieving. "You, mister. Let go of the gun," said Benitez, voice and the situation very much under control.

McTeague let go suddenly, and Cooper was holding a .357 magnum with the muzzle pointing at his face. He dropped it to his lap, grip easing slowly, sagging against the door. "Out of the car," Benitez was saying. "On the ground. Move." McTeague climbed out like an old man with arthritis. Running footsteps sounded on the street behind Cooper, and Benitez said, "Get the gun from him," pointing into the car. Cooper looked to see Reichardt pulling up at the window, panting, piece drawn. Cooper held the gun out grip first and Reichardt took it and went around to join his partner on the sidewalk.

"Where'd he fuckin' come from?" said Benitez, aiming at McTeague on the pavement.

"He went off the balcony. What was I gonna do, jump after him?"

"Not at your age, I guess."

"Put him on the car. You, shithead, on the car."

Cooper had climbed out the driver's side door. He clung to the car for a moment, his legs dubious, nearly blind with the pain in his head. "She OK up there?" he said when he could talk.

"He slugged her," Reichardt said. "Big tough man hit a lady." He had put his gun away and given McTeague's to Benitez. He was patting McTeague down, carefully. Splayed on the trunk of the car, McTeague was looking at nobody, eyes fixed on a point somewhere out in the street.

Across the roof of the car Benitez said, "What happened out here?"

"We had a little talk about family," Cooper said. "He just wants what's coming to him."

McTeague's head snapped up and his eyes met Cooper's. Cooper made his way unsteadily around the front of the car to the sidewalk. Benitez watched him. "You OK?"

"I hope so." Cooper leaned on the roof of the car again, head down.

"If you're gonna puke, try and miss the car," Benitez said. Perhaps out of delicacy, he moved behind Reichardt to the rear of the car, holding both guns.

After a moment Cooper opened his eyes. When they focused he saw the black knapsack, unzipped, just at the edge of the sidewalk where it had fallen as McTeague had left the car. Inside it Cooper could see paper. He closed his eyes again. Reichardt was giving McTeague the Miranda blessing, in a soft monotone.

When Cooper opened his eyes again the knapsack was still there. Many thoughts went through his head, and he shoved it with his toe, just enough to make it fall between the curb and the side of the car. He straightened up. Reichardt had the cuffs on McTeague and was pulling him away from the car. The look on Sean McTeague's face reminded Cooper of looks he'd seen on the faces of men hit in firefights and on the way down, dead on their feet, dead with their eyes open.

◆

"It's all over," said Cooper.

"What's all over?" Swanson backed away from the door, looking at Cooper with alarm. He was nattily dressed and neatly groomed and except for the gauntness and the shadows under his eyes and the ten extra years he was the Regis Swanson of a month before. Behind him Hayden rose from the sofa by the spectacular window. Swanson's luggage sat in a pile on the carpet.

"Everything." Cooper made his way across the room and, remembering the finish on the expensive coffee table, dumped the knapsack on the sofa. "The men who shot your son are dead. The man who framed him is sitting in a lockup looking at life in jail. I don't know if that gives you any satisfaction, but if you'll look in the bag you'll see something that might help get you back on your feet again."

Swanson and Hayden just gawked at him for a while; they looked at each other once and then Hayden said, "Why don't you take it from the top?"

Cooper nodded. "You got any coffee made?"

"In the kitchen," said Swanson, reaching for the bag as if he were afraid it held some small but possibly dangerous beast.

"And aspirin. I could use some aspirin."

"Try the bathroom." Cooper went down the hall and found aspirin and downed it. He went into the kitchen and found a mug and filled it from the coffee maker. When he came back into the living room Hayden was taking manila envelopes out of the bag and putting them on the table. He peered inside one and gave Cooper a slightly stunned look.

"Where the hell did this come from?"

"I rescued it from a gutter about four this morning. Originally it came from a bunch of crackheads, probably. It's been washed and dried a few times. There's something less than the original million there but it's a good chunk of money. I'm not sure how traceable it is. Probably not very. And I don't think anybody's looking for it right now. That was put together by a very careful man."

Hayden reached into the bag again and pulled out Regis Swanson's .38. "What about this?"

"Oh yeah. That was in there too. It's been around the block a few times but it never got fired."

Hayden and Swanson exchanged a long look. "Sit down," said Hayden to Cooper.

When Cooper finished telling them about it, Swanson was on the sofa staring out the window at the sun climbing higher over the lake and Hayden was standing with his back to the window, hands in his pockets, watching Cooper.

"There's no way we can possibly risk keeping it," said Hayden.

"Fine," said Cooper. "I just took it because I figured the government has enough money already. And because they owe you."

Swanson leaned forward and poked at a stack of bonds spilling out of an envelope. "I don't know that I'd really want it," he said. "Given the associations."

There was silence for a moment and Cooper felt it stir, deep down. It was temptation, it was major, and Cooper knew things would never be the same if he listened to it. "Better you than me," he said.

He stood up and went to the window, drawn inexorably by the view of a high-flier's town stirring to life. "If you don't want it, there's probably an outfit somewhere that's doing something valiant but hopeless that could use an endowment. I'm going to leave the ethical dilemmas right in your lap, because I've done my job. Once I get you to the airport I resign." He sipped coffee and turned to look at Swanson.

Swanson nodded, very slowly. "I owe you a bonus," he said. "A big one. A thousand dollars won't come close."

Cooper took a deep breath. "Can I make a request?"

"Sure."

"Give me the Mercedes. I'm going to need a way to make a living when you're gone."

Swanson said nothing for a moment and then smiled, the ghost of an old self-assured Regis Swanson smile. "It's yours," he said.

◆

Cooper shoved money into the slot, plugged one ear with a finger and leaned close to the phone, trying to shut out the clamor of the long echoing concourse. Far, far away, a woman said "Hello."

"Let me talk to Diana." His head hurt too much for niceties.

"Just a minute."

When she came on the line Cooper's knees went suddenly weak, strangely infirm at the sound of her voice. "Cooper? Are you all right?"

Nothing but the sound of her voice, and he wasn't sure his legs could hold him. "I'm fine, baby, I'm fine."

"I was trying to call you all night long. What happened?" Puerto Rican staccato was back in her voice, anxiety leaching the usual smoothness out of her English.

"All kinds of strange things. Listen, I'm on my way. I'm at O'Hare now."

"You're coming?"

"Of course I'm coming. Can you get out to the airport and meet a flight at nine-thirty? United 595."

"Wait a minute, wait. Where's a pencil? Oh God, it's good to hear your voice."

Across eighteen hundred miles of telephone line Cooper could feel her, close enough to hold and too far away. Christ, he thought, astonished by the force of the reaction. "I need you," he said, growling.

She said his name, and he could barely hear her above the tumult of ten thousand people with ten thousand places to go. Only you, he thought, hearing her voice break, nobody else.